DEATH OF A GODDESS

By

William Dittoe

ISBN: 978-0692700730

For my Wife

DEATH OF A GODDESS

CHAPTER ONE
The Tattoo

Hot! she thought, *so unbearably hot!*

A small bead of perspiration collected from the several on her forehead and quickly ran past her brown-framed glasses. From there it dropped to the forest path as if eager to escape her growing apprehension. All her thoughts focused upon the oppressive heat. It sucked moisture from her pores as if attempting to drain her warm body of the very essence of life. The narrow path before her was becoming difficult to see, especially in the dim and eerie light of her guide's torch. Its dancing flicker wove mysterious patterns upon the leafy floor like invocations conjured up to frighten away the approaching spirits of darkness.

The forest trail twisted its way through massive trees, their upper limbs vanishing beyond the faint torchlight and their lower branches draped with thick, shadowy vines that resembled hideous serpents. Pamela hated snakes and with a shudder stepped involuntarily closer to her guide. She tugged self-consciously at the clinging, damp fabric of her white, cotton dress where heavy perspiration glued it to her warm body. The sun had long set and she had not seen Charles since early afternoon. Her Brazilian guide, an older, silent man from the local village, had come to escort her.

But to where?

When she left her dilapidated lodging tucked within the small village the sun's final light was fading into the dusky swelter of a tropic night. The few natives she had briefly met were a quiet people; most short of stature, dark-skinned and polite as was her guide. But she really didn't know them and without Charles, had growing misgivings about following a stranger deep into the rain forest. She began to berate herself for the rash impulse that had brought her into the depths of the Amazon.

They had been traveling for a considerable time now, and she felt hopelessly lost within the forest gloom. She followed timidly behind the man as he plunged deeper into the fertile undergrowth with each step increasing her uneasiness. After the sun had set, the foliage took on a menacing look and low branches seemed to accost her as she passed. The soaring forest trees reached high above blocking out any hope of light. She was certain that there must be the moon and stars somewhere above, but all their luminous efforts to penetrate the darkness were thwarted by the dense canopy of the great trees.

She also knew she was far from the artificial lights of any city, the only possible illumination coming from the flicker of her guide's torch. Pamela desperately wished to retreat. Tell them she changed her mind and hurry back to the village. From there she could quickly boat up river to San Paulo. She could then fly back home to her safe, familiar surroundings. There she would be safe from the dark forest and whatever mysteries it contained. She was now certain that her romantic notions of escape were ill-conceived, even childish. She wanted no part of the Amazon jungle. It was foreign to her, and perhaps deadly. The path they followed twisted slightly at times, but for the most part plunged relentlessly forward into the darkness. Now and then a small rise or fall in terrain, or the cry and scurry of an unseen animal, would break the monotony of her journey. Mostly though, the night was still and the tropical dampness hung heavily upon her. When she anxiously mentioned the idea of returning to the village, the guide only said, "No lady, you come ... you need to come!" His voice was passionate, even compelling, and she could not help but to follow.

She was startled by a tree root that caught her shoe and she felt a deep scuff tear into the brown leather. *Brown,* she thought abstractly, always brown, as was her hair. Not chestnut, not dark brown, not streaked with honey, just brown. It seemed as if her entire existence was brown ... plain ... vague ... neither one way nor another.

Why couldn't my shoes be red, just once?

Pamela had always wanted red shoes and the thought returned her to a time some thirty years ago. She was seven and remembered the thrill as the sun glinted off the store window, brightly lighting the shiny, red shoes as images of spotlights played upon the stage of her mind. She whirled and danced in the wondrous shoes as people looked on with admiration and envy. Her fertile mind held these images as treasures and she ran home to excitedly blurt out her young dreams to her mother. The quick response chilled her as her mother's cold glare was accompanied by sharp, biting words.

"That's absurd, child. Only hussies wear red shoes!" Pamela's little heart fell and she quietly ate her supper. Later that night, within the sanctuary of her bed, as tears blurred the tall, soot-covered ceiling of their old house, she secretly danced in the red shoes. Her young mind also wondered what a hussy was. Her mother's whining voice accompanied her throughout life.

"Be sensible, child ... foolishness will only lead to trouble. You'll end up in a situation!"

Anything mother feared or couldn't understand was a "situation". Now the drab brown shoes, the sensible shoes, carried her feet over the soft forest path deeper into the unknown. Faint echoes of mother's voice drifted slowly off into the night air, diminished but not entirely gone, adding to her tension. The brown leather contrasted sharply with her white dress. The heat of the tropics was unbearable to her and she wore the old, white cotton outfit hoping it would be both appropriate and cool. It was from the age when fashions were short and the abbreviated length always infuriated mother. It now clung to her body, damp with perspiration and its white snugness silhouetted her form against the forest darkness. Each step caused the dress to creep up upon her thigh now wet from the tropic heat.

Maybe mother was right ... maybe she was in a "situation".
Where am I?

And now, with a growing sense of urgency, *Where was Charles? What do I really know about Charles?*

He seemed polite enough but in many ways was as unknown to her as the encompassing forest. Feeling self-conscious and exposed, as if she were on display, Pamela was thankful mother could not see her and was glad the darkness covered the flush that tinged her cheek. She knew all forest eyes were upon her and could hear the trees themselves whispering, "hussy, hussy" as she passed by.

The forest trip seemed extraordinarily long. Not only had she no idea where she was being led, but her total unfamiliarity with the forest, with any forest actually, lent to her uneasiness. She was a girl of the plains, small towns and expansive cornfields.

She now wished she had asked more questions when the old man showed up and announced he would lead her to the meeting spot. But her entire life was passive. She was always reluctant to voice any concern or opposition. She was especially hesitant to speak with strangers and now followed the quiet man with head down and in dumb obedience.

The relentless tropical heat made her groggy and her mind wandered. Images of her past life rose from the dark forest floor and entered her mind like a possessing spirit. Her uneventful life now seemed like a series of blunders … events placed before her more as a series of obstacles rather than the natural ebb and flow of a normal life. Memories of her childhood shaped by the inhibiting presence of her mother pressed upon her.

She remembered her college days, an uneventful four years that, with passing but undistinguished grades, gave her a teaching diploma. Then her disastrous marriage to Stan … all these memories came back in a continuous and unstoppable stream rising out of the tropical night.

The face of Tom, her first date ever, floated past her. Mother never let her date when she lived at home and she now was well into her eighteenth year. She was a freshman in college and thankfully away from mother's endless control. Tom was polite and to her inexperienced mind as thrilling as her first impression of the coveted red shoes. The evening was perfect – a dinner, movie and now they sat in Tom's car. He drew closer to her and, after talking, kissed her. At first, her body responded and unexpected emotions caused her to press close to him. However, years of deep repression suddenly overwhelmed her and her body stiffened involuntarily. Slowly she started to cry and her weeping gradually grew to uncontrollable sobbing. Tom expected a return of passion or perhaps even a rebuff, but her crying was unexpected and confusing. His only recourse was to sit in his car as she ran to her dorm, his hands raised in puzzlement and supplication. She now wished she could laugh at the confused expression on Tom's face … find some relief in amusement. Only, the experience was so hurtful and humiliating that his image turned into a mocking specter, causing her to wince and look around the forest darkness in profound embarrassment. She now could see why she was so emotionally warped … why Tom never called again … why her marriage or any close relationship never could last.

More objects floated out of the tropic's stifling air. Her childhood playground experiences where she and Stan remained alone, standing on the side watching others in sandlot games. They were the leftovers, selected last, if at all. Sometimes they were chosen together, usually by some older child that felt sorry for them. Both were awkward and without athletic skill. Pam and Stan … two of a kind. Hurtful rhymes were made up with typical childhood insensitivity, cutting deep into Pamela's mind. Pam and Stan … the leftovers. Perhaps this is why, when she returned from four years of teacher's college, Stan was available, delivering bread to supermarkets, bowling and passing life still on the sidelines. Perhaps this was also why they were married a year later … Pam and Stan. It was just expected that they would wind up together. Now they were divorced. That also was probably to be expected.

Her jaws tightened as she thought of him. She really didn't dislike him. In fact, her anger toward him was only because he didn't have anything to dislike. He just existed, stumbling through life with monotonous steps of his unchanging daily routine. He was brown, plain brown … like her.

The Amazon heat struck her full force as she started up a small rise in the forest floor and she impatiently brushed damp hair from her eyes. She wished to pull her dress away from her body to allow some air, hot and wet as it was, to pass over her skin. Anything to relieve the clinging material that now rubbed over her with each step. She restrained the urge, fearful that the guide would turn and see her.

Her thoughts returned to her memories and she tried to think of some event in her marriage that had any real significance. Their life together was bland at best … consisting mostly of work and dull evenings at home. She would read, correct papers and retire promptly at eleven o'clock. Stan's evening schedule would start after work in mid-afternoon and revolved around the TV Guide and dinner. She remembered one of the rare times they were invited out socially. It was a disaster for her, although Stan remained unaware of her feelings. There was nothing particularly unusual about that, she thought while watching the passing tree trunks. He perceived any sensitive issue dimly, if at all.

The Fosters, Susan being a teacher in her school and Mike her husband, invited them to a cookout. Jim and Nancy, friends of the Fosters, were also there and the early evening was spent in pleasant chatting, women about children and work and the men about sports. Stan seemed comfortable enough and could recite line-ups and sporting stats with the best of them. Pamela enjoyed the talk about work, but was more uncomfortable when the conversation turned to children.

The disaster came after dinner, when they moved inside. All except Pamela had drunk several beers. She, being raised properly, limited herself to one. The talk gradually drifted from the commonplace as small hints of sexual innuendoes entered the conversations. Jim told a joke, extremely off-color, Pamela thought, and then Susan, much to Pamela's discomfort, did not allow the women to be outdone. All were in hysterics when Susan, normally quiet and pleasant, came to the punch line. Her sweet, innocent smile combined with explicit words, brought a bright flush to Pamela's face. She awkwardly excused herself and went to the bathroom. When she returned, the group had assembled downstairs in a paneled room facing an oversized TV. Mike and Susan were sitting together on the carpeted floors leaning against the sofa and the Fosters were squeezed into a large overstuffed chair. Someone had turned the lights down and had lit candles.

Stan was on the couch and as Pamela sat down on one end, Nancy explained in a giggle that she was now presenting Jim with a belated birthday present. As she pushed the play button, the large screen was immediately filled with images that stunned Pamela.

Male and female bodies were pounded into her mind. She looked over at her hosts who were now smiling and exchanging whispers. Jim was obviously delighted and they sank down even further together into the chair.

Pamela reached over, "Stan," she whispered in a panic, "we must leave." The images began to push past her inhibitions, overwhelming her carefully prepared "fortress". Stan only sat quietly staring at the large screen with a detached gaze as if he were still outside patiently waiting for mustard.

That evening had shaken Pamela in a fundamental way. Feelings of shame and embarrassment were mixed with anger and confusion. She couldn't understand grown people behaving as she had witnessed but her real dismay was caused by Stan. His lack of any emotion disgusted her. She also knew, however, that much of her anger was directed towards herself and her own reluctance to voice her opinion. She had once again remained passive and her anger actually rose from not being able to express passion about anything. Finally she buried her confusion by simply stating to herself that she was a sixth-grade teacher, nothing more. The next day she rose as usual and went to school. All was stable once again. Her world was well-ordered with her classroom neat and under control. However, she could not look at Susan anymore and avoided her as much as possible.

The Amazon heat was making her drowsy. She focused on the steady back of her guide to keep her on the small trail but her mind continued to wander.

I'm leaving now, Stan.

She remembered these words as if she had just spoken them. She sighed at the thought of the final days of her marriage. It stopped as it had begun, almost without notice by anyone. Pamela knew that she didn't contribute much to the relationship. Cooking and cleaning were done without any special effort. After all, this was expected of the wife in all marriages in her rural town. Other than that, their lives were of two people living separate existences. Pamela never thought of herself as particularly bright and struggled to think of ways to participate in conversations. Everyone assumed she was just quiet, she considered herself to be dull. Physically she detested herself. Knowing she would never be beautiful didn't bother her. Knowing she was average infuriated her. She would far prefer to be tall and ungainly thin or short and plump. Being plain and nondescript was intolerable.

They were well matched, she thought, Stan was as dull as she. His attempts at conversation were juvenile and repetitive. He would come home from a day of stocking grocery stores with baked goods and announce, "Well, I delivered the bread so I can bring home the bread."

Pamela dutifully laughed at his cleverness, at least for a few weeks. Stan never seemed to notice she eventually stopped responding. His one attempt at spontaneous creativity came when he returned home from a state fair with a license plate that read "Stan and Pam". She winced when she saw it. He never noticed that either.

Parting was inevitable. Their relationship was empty at the beginning, without any real communication and empty when it ended. Even their physical relationship was void of any real feelings. No passion … nothing she would relate to as romance … it just occurred at infrequent times. Sometimes afterward, as Stan slept, she would lie awake with no real thought or emotion, just a vague emptiness that wished for something … anything. An unknown or unthought-of experience … just something more. She would then shrug and go to sleep.

The darkness of the forest felt heavy as if its weight could actually fall upon her.

"It must have been my wild side," she hissed out loud.

The guide looked quickly back at her and then continued. The self-incrimination and vehemence of her emotional outburst startled her and she continued on through the forest in unthinking silence, fearful of the memories of events that occurred years ago and thousands of miles away.

Their trek through the night seemed endless and Pamela was becoming thirsty and fatigued. The relentless heat was causing her to walk in plodding steps and she followed the steady torch as if it were a powerful instrument of mesmerization. Her memories continued but took on a less threatening tone and with this she became dimly aware of another subtle difference; the forest path had changed somehow. Perhaps she was becoming more aware, better accustomed to its nuances. Through the dim torchlight she now noticed more of the leaf patterns; the tree trunks were larger, straighter. It was still night but the area was somewhat less dense now. Also the memories that she had suppressed for years and in their recall had released upon the forest path seemed lighter, less burdening. With this, she once again allowed the memories to flow.

Her father stood before her, young and handsome, as her seven-year-old mind had known him. He was a quiet man, medium height, slightly built and exceptionally polite. Pamela always, even at her young age, wondered how her mother and father came together. Their personalities and outlook on life were so vastly different. She was critical and opinionated; he was of a kindly nature and possessed a spirit quick to celebrate the common events of a hard life. Their family always kept together and lived an uneventful existence in their small town in Iowa. The only observable difficulty, except of course for mother's moods, was the coolness some of the neighbors showed toward father. She came later to know it was because of the darkness of his skin. Mother never spoke of it and as far as Pamela was concerned his outdoor work just kept him deeply tanned. She and her father never found much time together, mainly because of the long hours required by his work with the highway department. The most precious moments came in the evenings when he found her in her room and inquired about how things were, asking short questions about school or friends. Sometimes he would sit on her bed and make up fantastic stories about strange lands, deep forests and ferocious beasts. They always had a happy ending though, and he then would kiss her goodnight ending her day with warmth and security. Now the dark trees and forest chatter along the path she traveled brought this memory to life and she wondered if her father actually had visited dense, forbidding woods such as these. Her memories of her father were the most precious, for he brought the only bit of needed stability to her young life. She often wondered what might have been if she had known him longer.

A shrill animal sound erupted from the brush close-by causing her to start and cry out. Her guide did not turn this time, only continued his brisk pace through the darkness. Her mind gradually drifted back to her reveries and she found herself with her father once again.

This time it was the carnival ... a place of bright, multicolored lights, whirling machines and young unkempt men all but accosting people as they passed by their games of chance. All these images blended into a smear of temptations to her young and impressionable senses. Father allowed her to indulge in everything. Nothing was forbidden this day. Rides and games, and especially the food, all were attacked by Pamela with an unaccustomed vigor. Quite unlike her later reserved behavior. She enjoyed herself immensely and they laughed together until the sun began to sneak behind the shantytown that bound the carnival's edge. Late towards evening the beginning of unidentifiable concern entered Pamela when she was eating one of many hotdogs. She glanced over and noticed her father staring intently at her as if he were trying to record her every feature. Her heart sank momentarily but she quickly dismissed the uneasiness. Purposefully burying it under mountains of sugar-coated elephant ears and enormous handfuls of pink, fluffy cotton candy.

As the light of day faded, her father lifted her to his arms and said they would now visit a place in which memories were made. She wondered about this as they left the fringes of the carnival and approached a small back street lined with assorted shops. Father entered a tiny alley and stopped at a window lit with a dim yellow-orange glow, its small, hazy glass covered with ornate drawings. An old, brown woman quietly muttered a greeting to them as they entered the semi-dark shop. Pamela was immediately overwhelmed with a clutter of fantastic shapes and objects. The old woman watched her with interest as she turned in small circles eager to see each item. Her father began conversing with the woman and Pamela turned to wonder just who would live in such a wonderful place. Not since the red shoes had any windows or stores of goods brought such a fever of excitement. Pamela returned the woman's gaze.

She must be a gypsy!

Although she had never seen a gypsy, the woman surely must be one. She looked old ... very old to Pamela, and frail, almost withered by age. She moved with effort and breathed heavily when she spoke. At one time she must have been large, for now great layers of skin hung in folds over her shriveled body. Her clothes were of rough cloth and brightly colored and woven with strange patterns of large leafs and stylized animal shapes. With all of this she had a kindly presence and remained still as Pamela inspected her intriguing display.

The room held many objects Pamela could not identify or understand. Most seemed to be items carved in old, rough wood, perhaps branches or tree roots. There were numerous bottles, some in strange, even grotesque shapes and often covered with green moss or brightly colored feathers. The most fascinating were the smaller bottles on a low circular table against the back wall. These were shaped to resemble animals and their carved stoppers added a strange life to the containers. There was a large forest cat, its head and paws appearing to claw its way to freedom, struggling to emerge completely and escape. A slightly larger container was a bird with large, open wings attempting to take flight. She approached with curiosity to discover a long, sensuous, black glass bottle whose upper portion twisted into a hideous serpent, coiled, deadly and ready to strike. Pamela immediately shrunk back from the image. Her terror of snakes forced her to retreat to her father for protection.

All this the woman watched with keen interest. She then shuffled over to Pamela and without a word took her small hand and led her into an even darker back room separated from the storefront by a tattered, food-stained drape. The heavy cloth also had bizarre animal images woven into its ancient fabric.

The rear room was even more fascinating than the front shop, and while the items in the front were obviously for sale or trade, this cluttered place seemed more hallowed … almost sacred. Its main source of illumination came from dozens of lit candles placed throughout the small room. Shelves covered the rear wall, except for a narrow half-hidden passage that disappeared into somewhere dark and forbidding. Large, heavy tubs with pieces of fabric, feathers and beads that were obviously the stock for her trade occupied the floor and lower shelves. Bottles with multicolored liquids, perhaps also potions of her craft filled the remaining shelves to the ceiling.

Unlike the other room, this space was much lower, almost cave-like and the wavering candlelight struck the upper surface producing bizarre shapes accenting the strange surroundings. The whole place spoke of mystery and brought a startling freshness to her small mind. Within all this newness lay a familiarity that gripped and held her with a passion that brought vertigo to her simple world.

As fascinating as this was, Pamela's young eyes were drawn to a sidewall. It was lit with tall wall sconces holding dripping candles. The sconces were wood and each carved into an animal, its mouth bearing the flame. This wall contained countless drawings hung at random and completely filling every available space. Some overlapped others … some obviously hung in haste and canted from the rest. She beheld fantastic images, knives and swords struck at hearts with names artfully scrolled over them. There were numerous animal shapes … eagles with soaring wings, leopards crouched to attack, along with scores of geometric shapes with a selection of colors that rivaled the carnival lights beyond … all strange, yet wonderful. Her father smiled warmly as if he was accustomed to the bizarre images that filled the cramped space.

The woman had seated herself at a small table against one of the image-filled walls and carefully watched Pamela as she slowly turned, enthralled by the countless designs that flooded her young, impressionable mind. Somehow, her father gently explained how one of these artful images could be hers forever, how the woman could place it on her body … hers to keep with her at all times.

This, she thought, *was a wonderful idea. Finally ... something of my own ... a possession that would be completely mine!*

She immediately searched for red shoes. Finding none, she studied the animals, shuddering as she noticed several snakes, coiled and deadly as the bottle heads. Then after a few moments of serious study, her eye was drawn to a small image half-hidden beneath another paper. She walked to the wall and carefully pushed aside the larger drawing to reveal a round, glowing shape surrounded by a beautiful, lacy scroll. Rays sprung from the silver globe and touched a multitude of smaller shapes that were mysterious and inviting. She didn't understand what they were, but the overall impression called to her and touched a responsive chord within her young soul.

"This one," she said to her father. He looked at her with a sudden seriousness and bent down close.

"Are you sure, my dear?" he said quietly.

The old women leaned close over the table and the flickering candles lighted the worn creases in her old face forming complex patterns of light and dark upon her ancient skin.

"This one," she repeated with conviction.

Pamela tried to be brave as the needles washed the image into her smooth skin. They had agreed that her left upper thigh would be the most private and discrete. The image was small and intricate and the women worked her craft with skill and gentleness. She hummed a strange lilting melody as she worked and at various times went to the shelves to acquire small amounts of liquid from her bottles. Pamela could not see which one she used but thought one to be with the stopper shaped like a large cat.

"Please, not the snake, ma'am," she entreated softly.

The woman stopped momentarily and smiled, causing the candlelit crevices of her face to give way. For a brief moment she looked young and beautiful as if recalling a past life.

"All will be well, my child," was all she said and then once more became old and brittle and with the return of ancient creases, continued her art.

The flicker of the shop candles in her memories blurred and reassembled into the wavering torch of her guide refocusing her again on the trail. She wondered why that shop was so important to her life, although as she grew older she seldom thought about it. That evening was the last time she ever saw her father and she knew the image she carried with her was more than a memory, it was her treasured connection with him. Even now, in the sweltering heat of the Amazon, it remained a small but cherished memory of his importance in her young life.

Her mother grew older and increasingly bitter after this and when she finally discovered the tattoo she flew into a rage, yelling obscenities no doubt aimed at her husband. Pamela however was the only one available to receive her cruel outburst and became increasingly the object of her mother's biting temper. Pamela was now the wild one, the inheritor of her father's wild streak. Mother gradually turned from hurtful rage to self-pity and withdrew even more into herself.

Wild side? Pamela thought, *Was this what drew her to this forbidding forest, supposedly to some unidentified event promised by Charles? She was told it was to be an unforgettable evening.*

She shivered in spite of the hot tropic air. Grave doubts rose once again as to why she was following a complete stranger in a mysterious land. However, even with her growing concern, she noticed something strange. It was a small thing but unusual. This was the first time in her life that the memories of her father didn't totally devastate her. It was almost as though the strangeness of the forest was able to listen, receive the pain of her memories and, in an unbiased way, absorb them into its vastness. At this moment even her relationship with Stan did not seem such an embarrassment to her.

"I'm leaving now, Stan."

Her voice seemed to rise from the darkness once again. This time the ballgame flickered in front of the couch and she thought she heard him say, "Oh yeah … ok … see ya."

She picked up her suitcase and quietly closed the front door leaving behind Stan and the blare of the ballgame. She then walked the three blocks to mother's house to resume her old life.

Three months later, another door closed … both to the courthouse and on any form of companionship, as incomplete as it was. That night, she lay once again staring at the soot-covered plaster ceiling in the room of her childhood. There were no images of dancing red shoes, no cheerful wooden whistle of her beloved grandfather, no cotton candy, all had been crushed from her soul. Her hand reached down to her thigh and she softly touched the place that held the only permanent thing in her life, the image of a silver moon and its mysterious symbols.

"Something must change," she sobbed quietly, "please, God, something must change."

She was unaccustomed to praying but fervently hoped that this plea would rise through the darkness and be heard by someone who cared.

That winter, deep snow fell. Ice built up on roofs and walks. Sleet often covered the road surfaces and all the while Pamela's heart mirrored nature's wintry efforts.

Spring found her with an ice-encrusted heart that would assure her of solace and peace. She was becoming her mother. In April, a thaw came to Iowa but her heart remained entombed in the beginnings of bitter resentment.

At least bitterness is an emotion, she sometimes thought, although mostly she was unaware of the change that was occurring. She even occasionally snapped back at mother, which was unheard of previously. Of course, she immediately begged forgiveness and naturally, it never came.

April also brought the book and supply salesmen with their new stocks of textbooks. History books seemed more colorful this year and she was on the committee to select those needed for next fall.

As she paged through a geography book she found its pages about South America intriguing. It also looked warm. Her eyes traveled from sunny Mexico and through the restricted neck of Costa Rica. Venezuela always fascinated her. Then suddenly she angrily snapped closed the book upon the mysterious winding Amazon as it flowed sensuously through tropical Brazil. As she slammed the book upon her desk, pent up bitterness overflowed and her sixth-grade room violently closed upon her. Her once secure environment, the only place of refuge from her dull world, turned against her. Its map-covered walls shoved towards her. She felt the ceiling upon which she lavishly painted the constellations dropping. Objects of art used for instruction became mocking specters that hurled handfuls of color upon her. The entire sixth-grade world she had carefully prepared crumbled as she collapsed in uncontrollable sobbing. Slumped on the floor against her desk, she tried to pull everything into her cold heart to still the unbearable hurt … to smother and encase it in her protective ice.

"Pamela?" Her name drifted by trying to penetrate the ice. "Pamela?" Again a soft voice called, bringing her back to the room that had just violently assaulted her. The voice again called and a face formed close to hers. The man who was on his knees in front of her carefully wiped her tear-wet brown hair away from her face.

"May I help?"

Genuine concern seemed to come from the face. Slowly it registered … the book salesman! A wave of embarrassment turned to anger and she shook her head.

"Please go!" was all she could bring herself to choke out through a tear-swollen face.

A week later he returned and once again she found defensive remarks rising at his innocent questions. After a brief inquiry of concern, he proceeded to discuss the textbooks, giving advice, answering questions and using his best professional demeanor. This made Pamela feel more at ease and she tried to put aside the awful preceding week. Another week passed and Charles was speaking to her as if he knew she was in need of anything that would get her away from the stifling routine of her life.

"It's a unique promotional offer. Quite limited and offered to only a select few," he explained quietly. "Think of how much more your group projects on South America will be enhanced by personal experience. And this will occur from the enrichment through actual interaction with natives living within their natural environment."

All the words sounded perfect and well-thought-out. She had asked around and indeed offers were periodically made to promote certain books and supplies. None this lavish but still, certain perks were available. She discussed it with Hank Parnell the principal and received his expected curt dismissal. "It's your spring vacation, just be back by start of class."

"Why in heaven's name am I considering this?" she asked the ceiling that night. The trip would be foolish and need to be supplemented with a good part of her small savings.

She had never been bold or adventurous. Yet here she was, thousands of miles from her home. She took a deep breath of warm tropical air, partly from growing exhaustion, mostly attempting to rid herself of her self-incriminating memories.

The moist air startled her as it eagerly entered her lungs. Some of its natural sweetness became noticeable to her as if a small veil had been partially drawn, allowing her to glimpse a hidden secret. She wondered about this and then dismissed it as foolishness. The forest was dark and forbidding and the bobbing torchlight was eerie at best. Still though, she perceived that the air was becoming somehow different, more peaceful yet strangely demanding.

She shrugged again and her next step was filled with pain. An unseen branch, low and protruding into the path caught her thigh. Its sharpness tore through her dress and penetrated her skin just above her childhood tattoo. Small trickles of blood rose from the wound and began to cover her tattoo. It momentarily blended the entwined images into a new shape, one that became infused with strange and ancient symbols.

Pamela's blood trickled past the image and was absorbed by her cotton dress. The torch halted and the guide whirled sharply around when she cried out. He seemed concerned as he knelt to inspect her wound. Then, with great care and gentleness, pulled out a small cloth and cleaned the blood from her leg. She trembled at his touch but stood obediently still. After a moment the old man rose from his knee and glanced into her eyes.

~ 17 ~

"It is small, not a concern," he said.

As he turned to proceed, Pamela heard the old man add softly to himself, "Yet, it is everything." They then continued their arduous journey. A small animal hidden beneath the low plants, observed all this with interest. After it watched the torch pass by it disappeared deep into the darkness.

Mother died suddenly in early March. The house was now hers and she could see no great benefit from the madness she was considering. Still, some deeply buried inner word spoke to her.

Go!

As she pondered her decision, she reached down again and without thought rubbed over the moon-shaped symbol upon her thigh.

A plane had carried her to Miami. During the flight she still fretted over what may be a frivolous use of her small funds and wondered if she could be back in time to start class. She also didn't know how far she needed to travel by boat.

Now these things were no longer of importance for she was deep within Brazil. Pamela shook her head in dumb amazement at her foolhardy commitment. A book salesman named Charles was to show her the intrigue of the Amazon, that she might take this knowledge back to a sixth-grade class in Iowa. The folly of this now amazed her and both anger and fear flared within her.

Feeling vulnerable and helpless she glared at the age-wrinkled brown back that led her farther into the forest. As the huge trees looked down upon her, Pamela began to wipe away tears. She was now carrying her repressed fears and hurtful memories along the dark path. Her mind held the trials and intimidations of her life before her as if she were in a procession towards a sacred place. It was as if she was seeking an altar of an all-wise entity on which to place these cruel injuries, hopeful to find some form of acceptance and desperately needed healing for her wounded soul.

CHAPTER TWO
Andrew

Glassware tumbled to the hard surface of the pristine laboratory floor bursting into tiny sharp shards, its contents coating the adjacent white cabinets with a thick, greenish film. A curse of exasperation and fear came from the tall, young technician. He stared at the deep gash in his hand where he had unsuccessfully grabbed for the flask. His shoes and pants glistened with the slick substance as it oozed over his lower body.

He turned with hands up to plead his case as he faced the charge of a squat, heavy man who, upon regaining his composure from the exploding flask, waded through the slime to confront him. The youth towered over the older man but still flinched at the shouted obscenities, which berated him in front of the entire laboratory for his eternal clumsiness. Finally, wiping heavy sweat from his reddened, puffy face, the older man stammered to a halt unable to think of anything that would reassemble the valuable potion without days of work. Another person stood quietly at the rear of the laboratory, his soft eyes carefully appraising the scene.

"Samuel, is it all lost?" he asked quietly but with a dangerous edge to his voice.

The squat man turned, his bluster gone and in a low nervous voice said, "Yes Charles, all of it."

His hands flexed as if trying to speak in place of his faltering voice.

"Steve was injured … a large cut," was all he could think to say.

The hand of the technician was now wrapped with a bloody cloth where he had tried to stop the falling glassware. The quiet man, his face seeming in shadows even in the well-lit lab, only shrugged. "That is observable; however, the question remains precisely what was lost?"

"Well," wheezed Samuel, sweat running down his round face, "the base formula is intact. We still have the original transgenic material. However, we will now need to reconstitute the altered potion. We will need time!"

His hands again moved in desperate pleading. His voice trailed off with his fingers still twitching to finish his appeal. The man walked slowly towards Samuel still seemly shrouded in shadows and, staring through Samuel, said absently but in a voice full of command, "We have four days and she will be there."

It was all that was necessary. The heavy man visibly trembled and immediately turned and shouted orders. As Charles watched people jump, his order obeyed, he turned to observe a small nook in the corner of the lab. He then spoke to the person within it.

"Cyprian, it is imperative that I speak with you at this time."

The youth, busy at a computer and seemingly oblivious to the event that had just occurred, shrugged and turned slowly to wander to the rear of the lab. Charles watched the undersized boy walk with shoulders slumped and with an impatient scowl from being disturbed.

Cyprian's attitude and inflated sense of self-worth was difficult for other team members to tolerate. But Charles let a brief smile appear. He remembered how insufferable people thought he was at the age of eighteen. And he, like Cyprian, had also just completed a master's degree and was beginning his doctorate. The difference was in study nuances. Cyprian was more interested in biology, specifically biochemistry with research focused upon nucleic acid chemistry and structure.

A great addition to my cause, Charles thought.

When they had retreated to a more private part of the lab Charles said, "Cyprian, I will be gone for a few days. Therefore, we need to discuss your future actions that will occur upon my return. I will bring back some samples, perhaps a living one, which will need your specific talent. I promise your research will go directions that you have not yet considered possible. New frontiers are certain to be explored my young friend."

With that … he left.

It was noon of the same day when a man entered a small bakery in downtown Atlanta. He was casually dressed and, although his face seemed slightly distorted by grayness, smiled charmingly at the young woman behind the counter. He looked over the wide selection of goods and ordered six rolls, a sweet mixture of imported Brazilian flour, nuts and tropical fruits. Paying, he again smiled, lifted his bag and walked to the front of the shop. As he opened the door to leave, he gracefully stepped aside to allow a graying, stocky man to enter. Once again he demonstrated his disarming smile and with a small bow, more an elegant nod of his shadow covered head, left the small shop.

"Good morning, Andrew. It's a slow day so far. I'm sorry again about your father."

The young woman looked tired and a little bored, but her eyes expressed a tender concern for her employer. Andrew smiled, went around the counter and after fastening a large, white baking apron to his waist sighed and gently touched her arm with appreciation.

"Thanks, Marie. He had a long good life. I hope you and I can keep the shop as well-stocked with our specialties as dad did."

Marie just smiled and nodded. She knew who the master baker really was.

"Oh, the man that just left. He left his card, said he would call back. Something about your family home."

She slipped on her coat and called over her shoulder, "See you tomorrow."

Andrew looked quizzically at the card. It said only:

South American Bio-Research, Inc.
201 Rich Street, Atlanta, GA.

The forest path had perceptibly changed, or was it the forest itself? Or perhaps it was her. Pamela thought that the subtle change must be occurring within her, for she had never been able to recall such memories without overwhelming self-incrimination, or at least inordinate sadness. Perhaps the remoteness of Brazil helped distance her from past pains and disappointments. Whatever the reason, she felt as if there was a slight freshness to the humid air.

The heat was still oppressive but not as overpowering as when they first left the village. The dense undergrowth at the trailside had thinned somewhat and they now walked through a more lofty part of the forest. The incredible trees now seemed of greater girth and spread farther apart, their thick trunks growing limbless high above her. They no doubt stretched upward for hundreds of feet to vault into the protective canopy of tangled branches and leaves. The darkness hid most of this though, as the small torch struggled insignificantly within the tropic vastness.

With the undergrowth being sparser, the dirt path had transformed into a soft carpet of moss and a slight sweetness to the night air hinted of potent loams blended with the fragrance of tropical blossoms. From somewhere nearby, but hidden by the night, came perfumes of gardenia, orchids and other exotic scents. All this was a welcomed change to the monotony of what seemed hours on the trail. Most relieving though was the noticeable brightness just ahead. Perhaps they had finally arrived at the place of which Charles had vaguely spoken.

Her guide did not hesitate but proceeded directly towards the light with Pamela still following close behind. She was now committed, perhaps even trapped and once again fear twisted at her stomach. Then the silent old man abruptly stopped. He stood before a group of several large trees that formed a colonnade and pointed towards the partly obscured light beyond.

"Please, you go now," was all he said in his strange broken English and walked past Pamela towards the deep woods.

Pamela was stunned and stared blankly at his retreating back as it blended into the darkness. He had left her! Her heartbeat rapidly with fear and the fear quickly changed to terror. He had actually left her alone! She frantically glanced about wondering if she could remember her way back. Her instincts urged her to flee, turn and run until safe. But to where? She would be lost within seconds. In fact she was already lost. And then she would fall prey to the unseen dangers of the wilderness. Some large beast would fall upon her, strike her to the ground and devour her.

No, she thought, *it would be a snake!*

Of all the things that she detested most, it was snakes. Perhaps one was already silently approaching, coiling to strike. Her mind hurled grotesque images of terror at her; visions of sharp fangs, slashing claws and poisonous creatures sprang at her out of the darkness. She took a desperate step backwards. Then she heard a low nearby growl of a hunting panther. She panicked and with a scream turned and plunged forward between the huge tree trunks, which stood as resolute as sentinels and into the heart of a lighted clearing.

With trembling body Pamela collapsed to her knees and prepared for her doom. She waited in despair for a long while. All was silent however and she slowly raised her head to stare in stunned amazement. She had stumbled into a place of enchantment.

The sentinel trees through which she had just entered were an enclosing circle that created a majestic, almost sacred place. Its size and shape reminded her of a small, round church.

No, she thought, *more a temple with the trees.*

Its columns rising with tapering grace to culminate high above in a vaulted, leafy ceiling. The space had a sinuous elegance as if it had been sculpted by a master builder from living plants. To her left and towards the rear stood a small pool of water, its surface a deep black and very still. It seemed to be built into the side of a rock outcropping and three of its sides were bordered with low, flowering plants. The water facing Pamela was retained by a low stone wall. Stone steps parted the foliage and these flat rocks lead down into the pool.

Small, neatly arranged earthen vases with long ladles were set near the stone wall. On top of this wall was a thick, black form, its length covering at least twenty feet of the pool and trailing down into the still water. Here lay the quiet form of a huge snake. Its blackness seemed a reflection of the pool and its silent presence brought immediate paralysis to Pamela. Her eyes widened and she placed her hand over her mouth to keep from screaming. She remained frozen waiting for it to see her.

After a long time, she began to back slowly away from the pool going towards the far end of the temple. She continued to glance back towards the still, black form to assure herself it had not silently come for her. Then she began to notice that the space was far lighter than she would imagine. It was then that she saw the torches. They were much larger than the single brand of her guide and they were supported by ornate wood standards, each carved in the shape of a forest beast. These were lashed with leather straps to each tree and the dancing and flickering light of the flames caused moving patterns to play upon every surface emphasizing the majesty of the temple.

She shivered as she looked upon images of large cats, odd hawkish birds, snakes and other bizarre creatures she didn't recognize but were no doubt native to the Brazilian forest. The torchlight also fell upon great profusions of lush, tropical plants that grew in the fertile soil. The place was extraordinarily fruitful. Bountiful, vibrant, luxuriant plant growth all blossomed with the life of youthful exuberance. They were the source of the sweet, earthly fragrances that filled the temple with seductive scents. Hints of potent loam blended with the multitude of blooms - gardenia, jasmine, uncountable orchids and many other blossoms she didn't know, all blended into a heavy perfume that filled her with familiar yet unrecognized feelings.

Pamela felt herself tremble with fear, but also with a grave apprehension. She continually glanced warily at the black shape to assure that it had not moved.

Then she noticed the most significant part of the forest temple standing immediately before her … directly in the center of the temple stood six delicate columns. Like all other objects within the temple, they were placed in a circle as if to mirror the elegance of the sentinel trees. These, like the pool, were stone and were covered with loam and vines as if thrust from the earth by an unseen power. These straight, strong pillars ended a few feet above her head and supported a wood trellis that was covered with a canopy of leaves.

In the open center and raised a few steps up was a flat, circular area that glowed with a strange and eerie light. Its surface was covered with deep, soft moss, which sparkled with a silver-green life as it was touched by moonlight that fell through an opening in the upper temple canopy. This elfin light was filtered by lacy vines creating subtle patterns that danced upon the inviting surface. There could be no doubt that this was the focus of the temple. It was its altar.

She was intrigued, beguiled. And, in a captivating way, it called to her. Her mind urged her to run far away from the subtle power that was reaching out for her. She turned to escape, to somehow flee this growing nightmare but then she beheld the final revelation of the temple; people surrounded her! They stood quietly in a circle against the sentinel trees as if they had been quietly formed out of the very earth-power that enchanted the place.

Was she so entranced by the other wonders that she had not noticed them, or had they just arrived unseen, called forth by the same strange power that was subtly calling to her? Perhaps they were so silent that the shadows hid them until now. It was curious that they were all women, no children, but of all other ages.

They stood quietly looking at Pamela. Torchlight revealed their skin to be a deep brown in contrast to her paleness and they were dressed in short skirts woven from native multicolored fabrics. She could see their patterns echoing images of the same forest beasts that hung over her.

The women wore no tops but instead were covered with the tropical blossoms. They looked remarkably cool. She glanced down at her damp dress and felt it itch in the oppressive heat.

They stood in a semicircle facing the center and patiently watched Pamela. To the other side and just to the left of where she had entered the temple space stood a group of large drums. Other women stood behind these and they also were silent. All present seemed to watch and wait.

She realized all the native eyes were on her. They were not threatening eyes, but held a look of expectation. Pamela felt self-conscious and wished that someone would come forth, greet her, and explain what was to occur. She looked quickly around for Charles, desperately seeking a familiar face.

The heat remained unbearable and her sweat-soaked dress became an irritation that increased her apprehension and brought her to the verge of tears. She tugged at it hoping for some bit of relief from the heat.

"What do you want!" she finally screamed out at them.

One of the women, seeming to sense Pamela's raising hysteria, smiled slightly and walked to the pool. There she drew forth a ladle full of the black liquid and walked slowly towards Pamela holding the ladle with both hands before her in solemn procession.

With a slight bow she extended it as if an offering to the gods of the forest temple. As thirsty as she was, Pamela did not wish to take anything from a place such as this. She shook her head and bit her lip.

The woman looked puzzled then slightly turned and said one short word over her shoulder to the others. Four women responded by going to the pool and filling the small buckets with the liquid. They then passed it to the other women who drank deeply and passed it on to their companions. Pamela now became slowly aware that the women had been quietly playing a simple rhythm on the drums ... a slow, soft beat that signaled the commencing of something.

Upon drinking, the women started swaying to the drums while continuing to stare at her. The liquid looked refreshingly cool, even delicious as the women consumed it. Her journey had been long and Pamela's thirst became unbearable. The older woman once again offered the ladle to Pamela. Still she resisted, fearful of all she had seen. The woman smiled once again and lifted the ladle to her own lips and drank as if to assure her guest that the liquid was harmless. She once again filled it and extended it to her.

She bit her lip and trembling, Pamela reached out her hands and took it, staring at it as if it were venom. For all she knew, it was. After all, wasn't that a hideous snake by the pool? Perhaps these people were servants of the serpent waiting to poison her and complete some unspeakable ritual using her as the object of sacrifice. All of this Pamela thought as she raised the long-handled cup and, as always in her life, obediently drank.

Hands still trembling, she could not believe what she had done. After a brief sip, her thirst overcame her and she consumed several large swallows all while staring into the woman's large, brown eyes.

Strange, she thought abstractly. *Her eyes too were brown, plain brown.*

The liquid was not dark when in the ladle, but clear and tasting slightly fruity. It was water but undoubtedly had other ingredients which added a rich, spicy flavor. Pamela stood quiet for a moment and allowed the liquid's coolness to spread with welcome into her inner being. She then once again lifted the cup and drained the remaining contents.

When she began to return the ladle to the woman, she noticed she had returned to the women and like the others was moving to the drums. The tempo had increased somewhat and the women were holding hands, their feet tracing small, intricate patterns on the forest floor in the beginning of a tribal dance.

The drums were now almost hypnotic, their rhythms calling forth strange, deeply seated emotions, finding and exploring carefully hidden places she had buried years past. Pamela did not want to listen and tried to hold her hands over her ears but her arms were heavy and she felt drowsy as if a soft cloud had descended and, lifting her, carried her suspended into the sky. She was being embraced and seduced by the primitive music, the exotic fragrances and the hypnotic swaying motion of the women.

Pamela then realized that the women had removed their flowered halters and their bare breasts were moving to the soft rhythms of the drums. She knew she should be embarrassed by their brazen display, but somehow, deep within the security of the forest, it seemed natural, the way of the Amazon. It also seemed astonishingly free and inviting, for this must be how their tribes lived. And cool … an escape from the oppressive heat.

Even in her floating condition, Pamela knew she was blushing and again felt the urge to run. But she could only stare at their movement and found her own feet wanting to follow, to be free in response to the hypnotic influence of the drums.

The tom-toms were louder now and resonated deep within her chest. Her mind was foggy and her upper body began to mimic the soft sway of the natives. Suddenly the white dress with its damp roughness seemed impossibly confining. It was unbearably hot and prevented her freedom to move, to join the invitation to dance.

She watched all this from a protective cloud, and was astonished as she saw her dress slip down over her own breasts, past her thighs and fall still to the ground below. She noticed from afar her feet move unsteadily to the dance as she stepped over the white fabric and moved closer to the center of the forest temple. The women stepped forward to gently support her. Pamela's heavy arms reached out to keep from toppling, to slowly float down to the forest floor.

She was tired, disoriented and greatly fatigued by her travels and the long forest journey. The moss-covered altar was overwhelmingly inviting and she struggled, with the women's help, towards the lush beckoning of its softness. She knelt upon it feeling it yield to her. Her hands sunk deep into the soft, living carpet as she pulled herself towards the center. Turning she allowed herself to fall slowly backwards letting the luxurious mossy surface catch her and embrace her. She looked up and saw the fullness of the bright moon and allowed its silver light to wash over her body feeling both cool and paradoxically, deliciously warm.

Her body flexed and stretched as if it were being embraced by a lover's touch. Parts of her mind cried out to her to run, to cover herself and flee. But the liquid that ran through her body stilled these urges, calming her fears. She fought dimly with conflicting emotions, but the soft, mossy bed captivated her and commanded her body to revel in this newfound delight.

As she stared at the moon, she became slowly aware of a tingling sensation in both arms. She slowly looked away from the moon and down to her arms to be mildly surprised to see two young females kneeling beside her. Their brown skin contrasting her moon-washed paleness. Both had black and red markings on their face, upper arms and chest as if they were painted with the mysterious animal images of the temple. Pamela noticed her arms were being gently anointed with fragrant oils that the youth were pouring in generous amounts from small vials. The first was carved with foreign symbols and capped with a beast head in the image of a forest cat.

It felt soothing as they rubbed it into her, softly covering all her skin. They worked in unison and upon completion of her arms began pouring oil on her torso and chest again massaging it deep into her body.

Upon completion of her breasts, shoulders and neck, one of the young girls impulsively leaned over and brushed Pamela's cheek with a soft kiss. They then began with another group of vials, these with different but equally strange markings. They began anointing her thighs and legs with their same methodical thoroughness, rubbing and soothing all areas of her lower body. Even her feet were covered with the invigorating oil by their young, strong hands.

Pamela had no idea why she was allowing these strangers to touch her body so intimately. Perhaps it was because she had never protested anything as her way of surviving, but somehow this was different. It was almost as if they demanded that they be allowed to prepare her body for a long-awaited event unknown to anyone, save perhaps the moon itself, as it watched from its lofty place in the tropical sky.

Then the young women both stood and studied their handiwork for a moment, the one who brushed her with a gentle kiss shyly smiling, the other solemn as if chosen to perform a sacred rite. They both bowed slightly and departed.

Pamela remained still, allowing the scented oils to penetrate her pores, feeling its strangeness tingle and work deep into her. Again, parts of her mind and body resisted, warning her of grave consequences ... of a disastrous end from permitting herself to be used so brazenly.

Is this my wild side?

Had this wildness pinned her to the moss as a butterfly to a specimen board, immobilizing her and preventing her from protesting the foreign hands that anointed her body?

Once again, the soothing liquid coursed through her blood and restored her to a calm, almost tranquil state. She remained still for a long while. Then the moon became partly hidden. She blinked to focus more clearly and found that she looked into the face of the woman who had first given her the drink. Pamela knew that she should consider this woman as dangerous, for she must have drugged her, but her rising protests were smoothed away by the woman's gentle smile and soothing hand on her forehead.

The older woman brushed Pamela's hair back and taking out another small vial, presented it to the moonlight above, as if seeking a blessing. She then unstopped it and began to softly anoint her head and face with the fragrant oil. This liquid had a sharper, more pungent odor, still pleasant but more demanding in its presence. This bottle was elegantly slender and ended in a sensuous black-coiled neck. Pamela felt the gentle touch to her eyes and ears. The woman placed oil on her nose and small drops in her nose and ears.

Pamela felt a creeping warmness enter her, its tingle working its own mysterious purpose deep within her senses. Then with a smile the woman also placed a gentle kiss upon her forehead and rose to leave.

Through the silver light Pamela thought she noticed a small tear glistening on the woman's cheek as she turned and returned to her place among the others.

Pamela lay still on the moss, feeling warm and strangely at peace … even at home. She knew now that the first drink had potent herbs that no doubt contributed to her sense of well-being, but she also was aware that an unidentified but profound change had begun within her body. The tranquil state possessed her, embraced her and then seemed to lift her into the dense foliage above.

Her consciousness rose into the air to be greeted by a large, silent form perched upon a branch. Intense eyes pierced hers with unimaginable wildness. An immense bird acknowledged her presence by slowly spreading its majestic wings. She looked above to the moon and accepted the warmth of its silvery touch. She then slowly floated back to her place on the altar.

As she lay upon the moss, she felt another presence by her side. She reached out expecting to be touched by yet another, but instead felt a new texture, not smooth skin, but a warm softness. Her hand ran through coarse, thick fur feeling strong muscles beneath.

Still enveloped within her protective cloud, Pamela slowly turned her head and stared directly into the deep, golden eyes of a forest cat. It was curled up at her side, its large head softly resting close to the childhood tattoo etched upon her thigh.

The moonlight fell from above and gently touched the mysterious image from her youth. The circle glowed and seemed to take on a shimmering new existence which enlivened the ancient markings, compressing them and melding them into new symbols of mysterious origin. As the circle tightened, the strange figures seemed to move. Suddenly they sent out a radiating pulse of fire that quickly spread a new wildness into her muscles, bones and sinew. Ligaments tightened, her nerve endings tingled and her blood seemed a conduit for the wild flame that coursed through her body. The heat was pumped from her stimulated heart to her brain where it enlivened neurons and synaptic connections. The figures near the cat's golden fur then glowed fiery red, sending additional energy flowing quickly into her body, its short but vibrant power touching responsive nerves and stimulating dormant cells.

Through all this she remained unconcerned, held peacefully by her tranquil dream state.

As the process continued, she became dimly aware that the cat had given a low warning snarl and quickly left her side. Then, total confusion struck the temple. An explosion of startled feathers came from above her. She heard, more than saw, the bird lift into the air with an angry cry and felt the heavy pounding of feet running in frantic haste.

Shouts of fear and screams of the women echoed through the temple trees as the torches silhouetted movement and conflict. She smelled fear as struggling shapes crashed to the ground. An unbidden reaction began in her muscles. Her face contorted into a snarl. Thigh and calf muscles tensed and then flexed into motion.

She rose from the moss as the large, ebony body of the snake glided past her. Instinctively, she leapt from the bed still half-dazed, and found herself in flight. She had exploded into action and within an instant hurled herself past the great sentinel trees in a frantic dash.

Crashing ahead into the deep forest, she obeyed a survival instinct that commanded her to flee. She ran unaware of direction, winding her way through the undergrowth as branches slapped at her bare skin. Her tender feet felt the pain of hard earth, small stones and twigs as she leapt over fallen logs to propel her body through the dark forest.

Her heart pounded as she ran, frantic to escape the conflict that had fallen upon the natives. The turmoil was quickly left behind and she now traveled through the silent tropic night, the only sounds being her feet striking earth, brush snapping back, and the rasp of her own ragged breath. The darkness confused her and she ran guided only by a new and strange instinct.

Suddenly, she found herself at the edge of a small hill. The momentum of her quick, large strides would not allow her to stop and she felt the soft earth at the ridge give way and her body pitch forward, hurling her over the brink of the bank.

She began to topple down the hillside towards the rocky stream below. Planting one foot into the bank, she pushed off using the crumbling earth to spring herself towards the small valley below. She frantically clawed at the air, fingers splayed, grabbing and lifting as her leg muscles coiled. As she was propelled forward, her arms beat instinctively attempting to lift her across the wide space.

Impossible, a small part of her mind repeated over and over as she glided awkwardly towards the opposite side of the stream. *Impossible!* And yet within a newer part of her mind, this seemed commonplace, natural. Then her legs came forward and her feet felt the sudden impact of dirt and small rocks. She tumbled, unaccustomed to falling from great heights.

Regaining her footing, she scrambled up the bank on the opposite side and once again the trees blurred past as she continued to flee. Finally, a long distance later, she broke into a small clearing and stumbled to her knees, heart pounding with fear and exhaustion. Her naked body, covered with soil and stained by forest plants mixed with her own sweat, slowly collapsed to the soft earth. With lungs straining for air and muscles twitching from exhaustion, she rolled over to face the sky above.

As she allowed the moon, the only sign of anything familiar, to wash over her bruised, soil-covered body, the shock of what had just happened overwhelmed her. She stared at the round, silver disk far above desperately wanting its light to somehow protect her, for she knew she was hopelessly lost in a strange and savage land. With exhaustion and dismay she placed her trembling hands over her face and wept.

CHAPTER THREE
The Woman

Mother should be calling her soon. She stretched, slowly turned over and waited.

But for what?

Sixth grade at Evansdale Elementary was becoming boring. True, except it was her only place of refuge from mother, especially now that she was living with her again. But her everyday existence was becoming so routine that it was almost an irritant. She shuddered when she thought of the day when her classroom had collapsed upon her and how she had later cried out for something, anything to happen.

How foolish! Oh well ... anything to have some time away from mother.

She stretched again and felt a sharp twinge of pain. She shifted in her bed and found that her legs ached and her shoulder seemed sore. Opening her eyes to look at the familiar, old ceiling of her room she blinked at the soft veil of white. She blinked again trying to focus the blur before her. The blur slowly became netting.

"Insect netting," she said. "The forest!" She sat up abruptly. Her legs, arms and chest felt as if she had run all night.

"Good Lord," she whispered to no one. "My mother's dead!" as if trying to comprehend what was real. And if that was so, and it was, then she must still be held within her nightmare. Drums, torches, the seduction and the hands, hands all over me! Then she remembered the shouts of panic.

"Dear God, what did they do to me?" She looked down. Her dress was still on ... she was clothed. She wiped heavy perspiration from her face and forced her body to the side of the small bed. She tried to calm herself and sat on her trembling hands to still them. Then she slowly dropped her legs to the floor. She took a moment to still her pounding heart and then pulled herself erect to warily make her way to the small bathroom. Perhaps some water to rinse her face would help. As she poured water from a crude clay jug, she looked up into an age-clouded mirror. A slightly different face seemed to stare back at her. She focused more intently with a look of puzzlement.

"Is this my wild side?" she whispered to the mirror.

No, don't be stupid! It was a dream, all a dream!

She wiped the sweat from her face with a dampened cloth. She continued to reassure herself.

"Just the effects of the horrible dream," she said to the strange face in the mirror. It must still be afternoon. Charles would be here soon to escort her as promised. There was no guide, no forest encounter. As she assured herself of this she stared at the water in the bowl. It was muddy. She looked more closely at her hands, at her fingernails. She bent and examined her feet. They were filthy with more dirt embedded beneath her toenails as if … as if she really had run somewhere. She looked again into the mirror with horror and fascination and hesitatingly touched her twisted, sweat-matted hair. Then, fearfully and with trembling hands, she began to inspect herself more closely.

She removed her clothes to find her legs covered with abrasions and scratches. After washing off her feet, she noticed numerous small cuts and found a large bruise forming on her left shoulder.

But her hair stunned her the most. Besides the sweat and oil build-up, she pulled tiny fragments of soft, gray-green moss from the stiff strands. Then a small, soft downy feather was dislodged and floated gently downwards to rest by her feet. She picked it up remembering the fierce, black eyes of the silent bird.

She found she could no longer stand and after struggling back to the small room, collapsed on the bed. She covered her mouth, trying not to move, not to think, lest she break into hysterics.

She remained still for a considerable time attempting to hold onto her sanity. Then, with great effort, she tried to focus on anything that might allow her to plan a way out of the village, out of Brazil. Finally, she could think of nothing more but to pack. Her hands shook as she took a pair of old beige slacks from her small case. She also withdrew a faded, ivory shirt. Staring at both she could not believe she had brought long pants and sleeves to the tropics.

A small curse left her lips as she fumbled for her manicure scissors. Cutting off the legs and shortening the sleeves didn't relieve any of the tension, and after pulling on the cutoffs and slipping on the altered shirt, she quickly stuffed the remaining clutter into her case. Then a small but demanding urge twisted her already tight stomach. This strange impulse forced her to go to the tiny window and peer out.

She looked down to the narrow dirt street and saw three men pointing toward her room. Her hair, matted as it was, raised on her neck and she turned and ran to the small bathroom. Outside, feet pounded on the wooden stairs and heavy bodies slammed against the door. Without thinking, she climbed to the table holding the washbasin and opened the small high window above. Her body ached as she crawled through the tiny opening trying to compress and bend to get through. She almost screamed, as she faced head down towards the dirt below. Then she fell with her arms frantically waving and clawing at the air to slow her descent. Her legs came forward instinctively allowing them to once again absorb the shock of a fall. Then she scrambled, half-running and half-stumbling through the twisting, narrow paths between unkempt village shacks.

The village was small and the men, whoever they were, would find her quickly, almost without effort. She now trotted while desperately looking for a place to hide and escape whoever was after her. As she wove her way behind the rear of some tiny huts, she tried to remain unnoticed. It must now be midmorning judging by the length of the shadows, and the tropic heat began to press upon her.

The clearing in which the village was built seemed to be hacked roughly out of the heart of the great forest. The opening allowed the full sun to fall upon the primitive structures baking them to unbearable temperatures.

As she worked her way cautiously among the small dwellings, she heard the muffled sounds of talking a short distance away. Her pursuers must be asking the villagers if they had seen her. It wouldn't be long until they discovered her. *And then … then what,* she wondered? Whatever, it would obviously not be good to be caught. She was almost through the village and the tall trees at the forest edge stood dark and beckoning to her. She could not bear to enter it. Her first horrifying experience had almost killed her. She would never go among the trees again.

Better to face those that sought after her, perhaps, she thought, *they even wished to help* – though her heart told her otherwise. The final shack stood before her, acting as a lone barrier to the wilderness that presented itself to her as a sanctuary. Then the door of the hut swung open and, in an unexpected motion, she was grabbed and pulled inside.

Her eyes struggled to adjust to the dim haze within. The bright sunlight outside contrasted violently with the small candles that attempted to light the crude space. Walls of rough, half-sawn boards let little shafts of muted light through cracks and un-chinked joints. They fell in soft ripples over small pieces of furnishings. The low ceiling was of undetermined material and dark. A dirt floor muffled her footsteps as she hesitatingly shuffled into the cramped dwelling. Standing to one side next to a small table was an older, somehow familiar woman. Pamela stared at her for a moment, watching how her held candle reflected its light from her native features.

They held each other's gaze and then Pamela blurted out, "You're brown." The woman frowned in puzzlement and then smiled.

"Yes, I suppose I am," she responded quietly and taking Pamela's hand quickly led her to a small cot and motioned her to sit. She then covered her with an old rough cloth and whispered, "You must remain quite still." Pamela was about to object when a heavy knock was upon the door.

"Dear Lord, they are here!" she started to say but the woman's hand was quickly over her mouth and she obediently fell silent. The old fabric was heavy and its musty weight distorted the discussion at the door. Voices in an unknown language became heated after a moment. She feared they would overpower the woman and search the small place. After a moment, though, it was once again quiet and then the rough shroud was taken from her face. The air, warm and moist, was welcomed and cooled the sweat as it drained from her face.

"Who are they," Pamela asked?

The woman thought for a moment while placing her candle down upon a small, rough-hewn table. "Those who follow an evil person," was the response.

Pamela shook her head.

"I don't understand. Why are they after me? Why do they wish to kill me?"

The woman's face held knowledge that frightened Pamela. "They wish not to kill you, my dear. This would be preferred. They seek you to take to their master. If he finds you, you will be subjected to unspeakable horrors."

The absurdity of this mystified her, yet she heard truth in the woman's words.

"Please," Pamela entreated suddenly, "can you find Charles? Please take me to him. Perhaps he can get me away from here. Somehow help me to get home."

The woman placed her hand to her mouth and paused. Finally, she quietly said, "Charles is not all he seems." Turning to gaze into the candle, seemingly for strength, she softly added, "And ... to our dismay, much more than we could have imagined."

Pamela looked around the small hut, her eyes now adjusted to the dim light.

"Who is he, and please, who are you?"

The woman sighed and sat on the cot near Pamela. Her presence was in a way reassuring, almost comforting.

"Charles is of our tribe. His purpose was to bring you to our native land and deep into the forest to a forbidden place ... a place that has brought shame and death to our people. We found out about your presence among us and simply asked one of our elders to meet you first, to bring you to us instead of Charles." She shrugged, "A simple plan. It worked for a time, but then we were discovered. The ones who seek you are separated from us, as is Charles."

Pamela didn't understand and was about to speak when the woman continued, "As for who we are, we are just simple people. This forest is our home, our heritage."

Her English was accented with a strange cadence that spoke of nature and the power of the earth.

"At one time we were a united tribe … we were content. We had small powers, powers that gave us support and assistance in our difficult life. These powers allowed us to live in harmony with nature and use it to benefit and enrich our simple life. We could understand the fellow animals that shared our forest, allowing us to live in harmony and tranquility. Life was still hard, but peaceful. Long ago someone, our memory no longer records just who … someone wanted more power. Perhaps the original intent was pure, but somehow it became distorted and dark. As their power grew, they became not masters but mastered. A great evil of purpose evolved and gradually factions grew and our people's heritage was fractured. Those who sought the increase of power achieved their goal, and thus were lost to their own lusts. Our entire people are now greatly reduced in number and few of us remain who still desire to be whole … somehow restored. But suspicion and violence are now our heritage."

The woman stopped abruptly and stared into the dark shadows of the hut as if watching the last fragments of her culture disappear. With a shrug of resignation, she turned back to Pamela and concluded with awkwardness, "For a while those with the new power thrived while we, who held the old ways, were diminished." She added faintly, "So we are now … diminished."

As she spoke, Pamela wondered about the previous night, the gathering of the women and whatever was done to her with their oils and potions. She stretched out her hand and stared intently as if to peer deep into the veins and small capillaries that carried the blood of energy and life to tissue, nerves and special cells. Flexing it she carefully turned and inspected what still looked like her hand of thirty-seven years. She saw no signs that hinted at any unusual events that may be occurring deep within her. However, something hinting of great power seemed to be calling to her. Fertile images were aroused in Pamela ... visions evoked by the woman's tale. She could imagine the forest's vibrant, green growth springing forth to bring life as it gave substance to the people. She also saw a balance between the tribe and the great forest, a relationship not of conflict, but a mutually supportive harmony. The woman's words and their accompanying images were making her drowsy and her body recalled the weariness and aches lingering from her long and brutal ordeal of what seemed only moments ago.

She wanted no more but to rest, curl up in the secure comfort of the candlelight and sleep until her nightmare had passed. But the story being told in the modest hut held her; the woman's words rang true and fascinated her, presenting precious glimpses into an ancient people and their honorable history. Her own brief encounter with the forest, as terrifying as it had been, gave a small insight into the story being placed before her. The small flames of the candles moved upon the woman's features and recalled a much older woman of a time far past who had gently placed Pamela's tattoo upon her thigh. The mystery and seriousness of her tale had come alive in its simple, quiet telling.

All this was now becoming too much to absorb and exhaustion from her ordeals caused her many questions to evaporate into the dim light. She stretched, unaware of a new grace in her motion, an almost feline elegance. The woman noticed however, but with a nod and a faint smile remained silent. Pamela then slept ... seeking some relief for her worn body and shattered emotions. The woman looked down at her and reaching out gently pulled Pamela's matted hair from her face.

"Sleep my child, rest well for your trials have only begun."

After a long while Pamela woke and found herself cradled in the soft, secure bosom of the woman. She shuddered as she instinctually knew what would be said to her. The village was now dangerous. She must return to the forest for safety. It was the only place, as treacherous as it would be, that could provide a haven from Charles and those that were still searching for her.

But she couldn't face that. She had no knowledge that would allow her to survive in such a hostile place.

Choices? She could think of none. *Stay or go. One was as deadly as another.*

Still something within the woman spoke to her. Not in words but found within the compelling tale she told. She was unable to say good-bye; her tears prevented her from even looking at the kind face that had given her a brief insight into a proud but decimated people. With a softly muttered "Thank you," she picked up the small cloth sack the woman had prepared for her and tentatively walked out of the hut to the forest's edge.

When she looked back at the modest dwelling where she had left the only person she now really knew and felt she could trust, an overwhelming sense of loss and foreboding came upon her.

Was this to be another person to be taken from her, especially now in her need? And at this moment when she was so vulnerable?

She looked at the forest beyond the village clearing, knowing she must once again enter. Return to the terrifying place that had so radically changed her only a few hours ago. She tried to walk with confidence and resolution, but had none. The forest stood before her as forbidding and impenetrable as yesterday. Knowing she could hesitate no longer, Pamela lowered her head and with a shudder, plunged into the brush. The towering forest trees immediately swallowed her and all the sun's light and with it … all hope.

CHAPTER FOUR
Andrew Kidnapped

The satellite crossing high above the equator was quickly moving beyond range. Once again, static broke into the conversation. A profusely sweating, fat man strained to hear the words as they faded and blurred with distortion ... *must quickly arrange for the second subject to arrive ... previous attempt unsuccessful.*

Again crackles of hissing noise interrupted Charles' sentence. He stared disdainfully at his small phone and began again, "Samuel, you know what is expected and have been given quite expensive and comprehensive resources. I require you to be successful!"

The force of his voice, though neither raised nor showing emotion, was sufficient to carry its command without need of technology. Samuel's hand shook as he replaced his phone.

You pig, someday I will get even for all of this!

Then he quickly arranged for two men to meet him at a downtown bakery.

Andrew's legs were cramping. The sudden blow to his head had left him groggy and had opened a large gash above his right ear. Still, the pain of cramping bothered him the most. He was stunned that someone would actually kidnap him. It made no sense. He had no wealth, no valued information. If he could only move his legs perhaps the circulation would resume, but they were bent awkwardly beneath him when he was dumped into a large trunk.

Not very imaginative.

He tried to rub the back of his neck, but could not raise his arm high enough. The confined air was not only sweltering but lacked oxygen. He banged his fist on the side of the trunk both in frustration and in hope that it would attract someone. His strategy worked. The trunk lid was jerked open and strong hands roughly held him.

The rudely applied hypo caused him to sleep for a considerable time. After many hours of darkness he struggled back to consciousness. He dimly began to wonder where he might be and who would wish to do this to him. His legs were now quite numb, even the tingling feelings were gone. He needed air and once again banged against the trunk side as best he could. Once again the angry reaction and the sedating needle.

Much later he heard sounds of metallic scraping through his drugged haze. Rough jolts of the trunk being moved further awakened him and suddenly the trunk lid swung open letting the shock of bright, hot sun overwhelm his eyes.

He squinted and his eyes streamed with tears as he was roughly pulled from his confinement. The air was untypically hot and humid even for Atlanta but still welcomed after the swelter of cramped captivity. Andrew was yanked to his feet but his legs immediately collapsed beneath him causing him to fall to a rough, oil-stained wood deck of an old boat. He peered beneath the small handrail and saw that they chugged past lush, green foliage bordering a river. Expansive trees rose high over him. It was a wilderness of luxuriant growth like nothing he had ever seen.

Still blinking from the blinding sun he tried to speak. All his raw and parched throat could bring was a cough. Finally he croaked, "Where am I?"

A fat, squat man sat in a worn lawn chair wiping sweat from his bright, pink face and looked up at Andrew. His only response was a maniacal grin.

CHAPTER FIVE
Lost in the Forest

Pamela stumbled back among the trees and was immediately overwhelmed by the forest's gloom. This seemed a place of perpetual twilight, no dawn, no sunset. Nor were there shadows to lengthen as the day grew old. The only standard found was the constant grayness of muted halftones.

After allowing a moment for her eyes to adjust to the dimness, she set off alone, lost and with the chilling realization that she was now hunted. She thought that she would stay close to the forest's edge, wait until night and perhaps chance that the men would be gone. She hesitated for a moment filled with trepidation and then started to push through the brush. After several minutes of wandering, she turned to see where she had been. To her horror it looked identical to what lie ahead. As she turned slowly in a complete circle, it became obvious that she had quickly become completely lost. The village might be only a slight distance away and remain entirely hidden within the forest's vastness. She could see no more than a few yards in any direction and the sun was hopelessly obscured by the tangle of leaves high above.

As she absently slapped at an annoying insect, the realization that the deep woods would be filled with animals flashed through her mind. She had been so overwhelmed by her return to the forest that she had forgotten about the animals. Terrifying images of wild beasts, insects and the relentless heat and humidity all pressed upon her.

She continued walking if only to do something. The heat was rapidly forcing moisture from her body and her shorts and cutoff shirt were drenched. Pulling at her matted hair, she wished that she had had time to wash better though this thought suddenly became absurd to her. She was lost within the Amazon forest and was concerned with dirty hair?

She knew she would die soon; this fact was inevitable, yet she continued. Each step was spent in wiping away sweat and watching warily for animals, though the thought of preparing for an attack was ludicrous. Whatever would she do if a forest cat would drop upon her? Her mind fought back images of snakes. As she again wiped sweat from her face she felt her hands tremble.

How long would it be … how long before I'll die?

Direction was meaningless, where north or south lie was of no importance. As she walked, she knew only that she had left one place, traveled for a distance, and was now at another place. Anything more was beyond her comprehension and in reality, meaningless. It would not help her to know where she was, she may die hundreds of miles from anything that might save her. She also might die while only a few feet from a hidden road or logging camp. She wondered if such things were in this forest. But knowledge of this didn't matter to her. Nothing mattered, for the end would be the same. All she could bring herself to do was wander through the endless twilight and this depressed her as much as her inevitable death. She would now end life as she had lived it, unable to determine her own path, to decide her own fate, to matter even a small amount.

Total darkness began to come upon her, not from the approach of night, but from the blackness that comes from deep despair. She was surprised to hear her mother's voice accompany her through the forest. Later she realized to her horror that it was the pitiful sound of her own low sobs.

She thought of returning to the village if only she could find it. Perhaps if she could avoid discovery, she could find a way to get back up river to the airport, back to Iowa. She longed for home, for her safe classroom. This now seemed to be where she must be, the only place she could regain her quickly eroding sanity, to save her life. She didn't want to die, but her survival in the forest was unthinkable. She had no skills or training that would help. Pamela also realized she was in no physical condition to withstand the rigor of a life in the wilderness. What did the woman expect her to do? In desperation, her mind thought of Charles.

Not all he seems, more than we could have imagined.

This strange statement left her with no one to turn to. She looked around at the vast amount of lush growth and towering trees. Once again, the solitude of the forest and the immensity of its presence dismayed her.

Most of the day was spent in nothing more than walking and stumbling through the jungle. No attention to direction, not looking for landmarks, she was unaware of anything. Nothing seemed to have meaning. After a while a dull vagueness set in; her steps were plodding, even keeping a wary eye for danger became less important. Often she thought to just lie down and let the forest take her, end the ordeal quickly. Yet even this would require a commitment and her blackness, the years of carefully constructed bitterness and resentment that she always carried with her, kept her from doing even this simple act.

After several hours she seemed to drag her left foot more often than lifting it. Her profuse sweat was lessening and a tight twisting was gripping her gut. She hobbled to a fallen log and allowed her body to slump to the earth, the first rest in hours.

As she held her head in shaking hands, a small inner portion of her mind realized she was dehydrated and had not eaten for a considerable time. She stared dumbly at the bag she had been faithfully carrying with her and with considerable effort struggled to undo the tight knot in its rough fabric. Finally it fell loose and the opened cloth allowed its contents to tumble to the earth.

She stared at the objects in a daze and then realized that she was watching precious liquid drain away from a tipped container. With effort her weary hands fumbled to pick up a hollow gourd and stem the flow. Quickly, without thought, she lifted the small gourd to her mouth and emptied the water. It was warm and tasted of gourd rind, but her body quickly absorbed it and pleaded for more. As she mourned the spilled water, now no more than a damp stain showing dark against the earth, her attention shifted to the remaining scattered contents.

Pamela wondered if it was the last of the woman's food, for all her existence seemed without any material goods. She picked up a yellow-green fruit the size of a small orange. It was tough-skinned but yielded under pressure indicating softness inside. Lying next to her leg was a wrinkled, brown paper covering a square lump, which she unwrapped to find what resembled bread. It was heavy and limp, almost sticky from the humidity. She broke off a portion, almost needing to pry it from the main loaf. A slightly nutty flavor was barely detectable; mostly it was dull and even after much chewing, still difficult to swallow. She cursed herself for not saving a bit of the water.

After a few more bites of the small loaf she discovered some dried berries. These also were chewy but went down without effort. They had sweetness to them and she mixed a bit of doughy bread with a few berries to make it more palatable.

Finally, it came to her that there may be some moisture within the fruit. Her hands seemed to lack the strength to tear into the rind so she worked a small hole with her teeth. This was just enough to allow her fingers to continue tearing at the opening and be able to bite into the core. Juice sprayed over her and the pulp yielded a slightly bitter liquid. It was wet and welcomed.

With a juice-stained face and blouse and sticky hands, she attempted to carefully rewrap the remaining food, tying the cloth back over it and fixing a knot similar to the woman's handiwork. Pamela wondered if the woman would be in trouble for helping her. She was grateful for her protection and kindness. A sudden sadness came upon her and she muttered half-aloud, "I never asked her name."

Once she struggled again to her feet, she continued her aimless wandering, now even less aware of the forest's great presence. Her senses were blunted by her overwhelmed emotions. Imminent death treaded directly behind her, following step by step ready to take her when she finally fell. Exotic smells drifted by her, subtle colors and intriguing patterns went unnoticed, all meaningless, without importance. Her initial fear and near hysteria were now replaced with absolute despondency. Her despair was complete and her continued plodding steps were only automatic responses by her body.

At some point, she must have stopped to eat again, perhaps more than once, for her meager supplies were now gone and someone, possibly herself, had folded the cloth into a small square which she still faithfully carried. Periodically, the haze that clouded her mind would briefly lift permitting memories of her recent experiences to brutally overwhelm her. For the most part, though, she just placed one weary foot before the other. A small part of her would now and then notice some passing object or event and then let it pass into the surrounding foliage. The shrill cry of a hawk seemed to be one sound that frequertly attempted to call her from her despair but she dismissed it and continued her aimless journey.

Pamela's entire body was being devastated. Her skin was scratched in numerous places and purple splotches of growing bruises were forming on legs and arms. There were more small tears in her cutoff shorts and blouse and the upper part of her left sleeve was now totally gone, lost in one of the frequent falls caused by her fatigue. Her right leg quivered when she placed weight on it and all her muscles ached and were cramped from exhaustion and dehydration, yet she continued.

Finally, totally spent, she fell forward with not enough strength to place her arms out to absorb her fall. Her face struck the soft earth that became mud as it mixed with the sweat of her head. Several moments passed, lost in some misty state of semiconsciousness, as the cry of a hawk tried to break through the fog of her mind.

She rose slowly to brace herself with one arm. With difficulty she rolled over to face the expansive green shroud of leaves above. She stared upward for a long while in stunned exhaustion when a numb awareness told her it was becoming dark. Evidently she had made it through the day. She was still alive. But now she moaned with the realization that it would soon be dark and then she would surely fall prey to the night creatures. Too tired to panic or really care, even to weep to lament her death, she rose to her knees and then with a deep breath staggered to her feet.

After a few more weary and unsteady steps, she found herself muttering to the forest, "Please take me quickly."

This became her mantra as she lurched forward. A few moments later she found herself attempting to prepare for the night by looking for some form of shelter. Her plea to the great woods continued as she searched for protection.

"Please let it be over soon."

She sought a raised area to get her away from the ground but found none.

"I beg you, don't let it be violent."

Her weary pleas to the vast wilderness were now mixed with tears. In a halfhearted attempt, she tried to weave large leaves together for a rough mat but after several futile attempts abandoned the effort as weariness and lack of skill frustrated her.

Then suddenly and completely night was upon her. Even the moon could not penetrate the high shroud of leaves and the resulting darkness was profound. She now had to find her way by feel. This was not only unproductive but also dangerous. After a while, her eyes seemed to gradually adjust slightly to the blackness and though dimly, she could distinguish between large and small objects. She could also tell if there was a clearing or large amounts of brush, but beyond that anything more was hopeless.

After haltingly moving for several minutes, she was about to give up again and once more give herself over to the forest, to accept her doom, when she perceived a huge presence before her. A few more steps, one into a depression that caused her to stumble to her knees, she dimly saw a monumental tree hurling itself straight up through the darkness. Its mammoth trunk pierced the forest floor with spreading knees to stabilize its enormous weight. She stared blankly at the faint image looming a few feet before her, seeing only dark gray against deep black. It was so huge that she actually could sense the force of its immense presence. Perhaps this great tree would be the shelter she had sought, a place to find rest and some protection for the night. Staring forward, she stumbled into a small bush, dwarfed by the huge tree and unseen. She felt her way around the leafy shrub and cautiously covered the remaining few feet with hands outstretched until at last she touched the rough bark of its supporting knees.

"Now what do I do?" she wondered half-aloud. Her body was spent, but she knew she must somehow pull herself off the ground.

Her foot slipped several agonizing times, but she finally acquired a foothold and with a groan, heaved herself into the crouch between two large roots and collapsed. She rested for a long while and then tried to make herself as secure and comfortable as possible, to prepare for the long wait before her. She knew this night would seem an eternity. Sleep was out of the question. Not only was her position, wedged between two stout protruding roots, cramped and uncomfortable, but the forest stillness was now being broken by the sound of the night creatures.

Movements of brush and the small crunches and cracks of unseen inhabitants with the periodic cries of hunter and hunted, all began to unravel the small amount of her remaining sanity. She wondered if she would die in total madness, unaware of anything but her dark dementia. With all the night sounds surrounding her and pressing upon her, the most horrifying were the unseen and unheard images. These brought the soft, quiet cough of the jaguar and a slow but relentless approach of the snake. Her mind clearly saw them. She was certain that they were almost upon her, silently closing through the darkness to take her. Her teeth clenched to keep from screaming and her heart fluttered against her chest. The complete blackness was as total as the dark closet that was her place of punishment when a child. The darkness transported her back to that cramped place. Even now she was tormented by her past.

"Please mother," she entreated through her tears, "please, let me out. I'm sorry that I am evil. I promise I'll be good." With that, exhaustion claimed her and she slept.

CHAPTER SIX

The Detective

"You say he has been gone for more than forty-eight hours?" inquired the young detective.

The deeply concerned look upon Marie's face showed the extent of her distress. "He has never done this before. He is, was, always prompt and would call if delayed."

"Does he have family? Perhaps there is someone we can call to begin our efforts," the man asked.

Marie just shook her head. "His father died a few weeks ago and now there is no one. I believe he said there were relatives in South America somewhere. Andrew didn't speak of them often but if he did, it was with both fondness and humor. He said he must go to look up his family tribe some time. I never knew what he meant."

The detective looked thoughtful and scribbled notes onto his pad.

"Was he from South America?"

"No," Marie said, "though his father was."

The young man crossed over to one wall of the bakery and stared at a large photograph. "What's this?" he asked.

Marie crossed over to him and pointed to a small group of numbers on the bottom of the frame.

"These are GSI coordinates. It is a satellite photo that Andrew found. He was always curious about South America. Even took several night courses at the local community college."

The man stared at the image with a puzzled look. "I don't get it. It's just a fuzzy, green mass."

Marie looked deeply into the photo seeing an endless sea of lush green growth with tiny, twisting blue threads sensuously winding through it. After a long moment, she said thoughtfully, "It's the Amazon rain forest. Perhaps it's his father's home."

It was dawn. At least it was brighter. Awareness that she had made it through the night slowly came upon her. That she had somehow survived stunned her. She struggled to awake. Rubbing her tired muscles, she attempted to massage the soreness and fatigue from them. The sun, still beyond the tangle of foliage above must be up, for the blackness was becoming a gray that allowed some recognition of shapes around her. She began to realize this must be the pattern of dawn in the forest. No real sunrise, just a gradual brightening, a dispelling of the complete darkness of night into the gloom of day.

She was alive! This amazed her. The exposed tree roots, the knees that had provided her a place of refuge, were now cramping her body. The ground, only a few feet below, seemed a huge drop. Stiffly, she tried to rise to lower herself down, but the residual exhaustion built up from the previous two days had been too much for her body and she slipped from her perch tumbling ungracefully to the earth. Pamela lay still for a moment allowing the ache in her muscles to subside and then stiffly rose to look around.

"I'm alive," she said in dismay to the vastness of the forest.

A twinge of pride hesitatingly pushed past her amazement. She had actually survived for more than a few hours. This was now the second day. She stretched and felt the soreness of her body ease slightly. As she turned to see where she had spent the night, her eyes followed the great tree trunk as it rose upward to disappear into the high, dark green tangle above, its limbs providing layer upon layer of massive outstretched perches and avenues for the communities of forest creatures that called it home.

Her amazement and pride in survival quickly vanished. As she was confronted by the mighty power of a single tree, she realized the entire forest stood before her, vast and uncaring. She was nothing to its immense being. She also knew that another day lay before her. The truth of this brought an abrupt return of yesterday's depression that had worked its way into her soul.

Sitting down upon one of the lower roots, she tried to assess her situation. Suddenly overwhelmed, she put her face in her hands and cried. A bitter, half-laugh choked out and she knew mother was right. She always had been right. She was truly in a "situation". Her wild side had won, had seduced her. Surviving for a single day was not an accomplishment; it was foolish to believe so. It just prolonged the inevitable.

She looked down and realized she was not only alone, but had nothing. She never even had time to put on shoes when she ran in panic from the village. Her shirt and cutoffs, after only one day in the forest, were torn and grimy with dirt and sweat stains. As she cradled her head in her hands, she was shocked to realize another thing. Her glasses were gone. She could not even remember when it had happened; the seductive ceremony, the flights through the woods and village, her day of wandering … all blurred together. She blinked and looked around. Strangely the normal blur without her glasses was missing, or at least lessened. She shrugged at this and stared at the dreary woods before her.

Finally she struggled to her feet and knowing not what else to do, continued her trek deeper into the forest. Her body was still sore and her leg muscles ached. Her journey, a repeat of yesterday's trek, became a mocking mirror of her life. This time, though, she stopped more often to rest … an uneasy rest filled with a vigilant look for danger, especially for prowling animals. Suddenly it dawned upon her.

Where are the animals?

With the exception of insect's constant buzz and the restless chatter of birds, she had seen no animals. This puzzled her and occupied her thoughts as she wandered towards nowhere. Surely there should be an abundance of life within the forest.

The other thing she could not avoid was the fact that she was starving and without water. She was in a world of vegetation and hadn't the slightest idea whether anything was edible. Looking around she hoped to find some type of fruit tree, perhaps one with fruit like the woman had placed in the cloth.

The cloth! … Where is it?

She must have dropped it, or maybe left it near the tree where she had spent the night. Then this idle thought also passed and her wandering steps became more erratic.

Every so often a small, bright spot would appear on the ground before her to bring a momentary point of cheer and briefly interrupt the constant gloom. She would glance up to find its source but it would be quickly gone or perhaps would shift to highlight a branch, and then move to fall upon some higher foliage to bring a new freshness to its normally muted colors. When it would leap to a branch, the bark would take on a lively play of yellow-brown with the deep crevices showing dark sienna.

She longed for the sunlight to be constant, not displaying the trickery that teased with life and then rudely pulled it back. Still, she tried to be thankful for the brief amounts of light caused by a wind moving some high leaves or perhaps by a small bit of the canopy not complete enough to totally obscure the brilliant, hot sun that intensely burned above the forest. But these tantalizing plays of light were not often enough to really dispel the muted darkness that was her constant companion. After a while, Pamela felt that the forest was playing a cruel game. She was being shown light, the source of energy and salvation, only to watch it gleefully ripped away, leaving her to contemplate the remaining darkness and her own frail mortality.

As she trudged on, she fixated on her fate; how she would die, what time it was, and whether this part of Brazil was in the same time zone as home? All important questions she felt, and actually with no meaning. Her life was everything and yet meaningless. Who would take over her sixth-grade class and did she really care? Her thoughts were scattered and distorted, even watching for animals seemed less important.

Then she was abruptly brought out of her reveries, for ahead and to all sides laid a dense tangle of high brush that filled the forest before her with a barrier of twisted branches. She continued forward winding her way between and around the ever-thickening grooves. Soon it became an encompassing sea of twisting and interwoven small branches and she found herself engulfed within an impenetrable living mass of overgrown shrubs. She couldn't go back, for by now she had no idea where back was and in a short time the struggle just to advance a few feet quickly exhausted her.

She was trapped within the overgrown brush and desperately fought to work her way through the oddly shaped plants. They extended only a few feet above her head and were no more than large bushes, yet their twisted limbs formed a barrier to her every move. The small, deformed branches were odd, of a dark wood that seemed to be slick, as if polished, rather than bark-covered. The leaves were tiny and thin and the tips curled as if afflicted by drought. Their edges were sharp and if struck from the side could inflict small cuts. Sometimes the brush was so thick that she went branch to branch not touching the ground for a considerable distance. She fought with dense twigs and the distorted leaves as she attempted to push her way forward. Small snags tore at her tangled hair and ripped more openings in her shirt and shorts. Her feet slipped as she tried to step carefully across the branches and blisters began to form.

It was during this arduous struggle that she finally saw the first of forest creatures. Small, rodent-like balls of fur resembling groundhogs wandered across the forest floor, small enough to pass beneath the tangle without being hindered. They paid no attention to Pamela, but continued upon whatever important mission prompted their scurrying journey. Somehow they made her passage more bearable as if they were telling her survival was possible, but she also knew they were creatures of the deep woods and she was soft, foreign and ill-equipped for any hardship.

She was even less prepared for her next encounter. As she twisted her body to squeeze between the tangled limbs, she found a small but tough vine growing throughout the warped branches. It further complicated her passage as it wrapped itself throughout any small openings that she found. Parts of the growth became so thick that she needed to pull back the vines, ripping them away from the strong, deformed limbs to secure only the smallest opening to wiggle between. She pulled herself forward, sometimes almost sideways, and still several feet from the ground just to inch through and advance a scant few feet. Her strength was almost totally spent and after a few more minutes of struggle, she slipped and fell. The entangled web of vines caught her and held her suspended, thoroughly exhausted and trapped within the binding restraints of the forest's luxuriant growth. She twisted frantically, thrashing to free herself, but this only increased the secure grip of the vines. Finally she collapsed allowing herself to be caught within a hammock of twisted virulent bindings. Her body ached and the many small cuts burned. Trapped, exhausted and despondent, she slipped into unconsciousness.

As Pamela lay suspended within a cocoon of lush green, the small rodents stopped momentarily to watch her sleep. Some drew close and rising up on short legs sniffed and gently nosed her cut and bruised body. A few curled up nearby and lay still as if required to be in attendance as she slept.

Through midmorning and into the early afternoon, Pamela was cradled by the forest growth while her body gained a small amount of much-needed rest. From within her deep slumber, she faintly became aware of a soft, high-pitched buzzing sound. It came and then quickly vanished. Moments later came a crescendo of more buzzes until the air was filled with a loud scurry of humming.

Her eyes slowly opened but saw only the dense branches above her. She tried to rise but was still bound by the vines. After several unsuccessful attempts, she reached overhead and grasped one of the more stout branches and by pulling and twisting finally worked herself free of the binding tangle that had held her.

Her sleep left her slightly more rested but she still desperately needed food and water. Perhaps the forest, in a caring way, had provided the means of rest for her. The thought dismayed her. The forest was known to her as brutal and deadly. At best it was only a vast, uncaring wilderness that simply tolerated her presence because of her insignificance.

She began to once again struggle through the growth noticing that the vines in this region were in bloom. As she inched forward, small scarlet blossoms became more profuse and their heavy, sweet fragrance hung suspended throughout the brush. Their scent seemed thick and powerful enough to support her without the tangled limbs.

She felt a breeze brush by her head and sensed darting presences that quickly passed. Then another soft humming and again a slight breeze cooled her face. It was then that she encountered the source of the buzzing as she saw a great abundance of brilliant iridescent birds. These tiny creatures, whose motion was more sound than sight, were feasting upon the sweet nectar within the bright blossoms. Starting, stopping, suspended upon a blur of small beating wings, she found the air filled with minute hummingbirds. Some paused only a hand away from her searching for the delectable syrup held within the red, trumpet-shaped flowers.

She traveled through a living sea of the small creatures happy for their companionship and thankful that they seemed to not be afraid of her presence. The time seemed to pass quickly among the small birds and then she was suddenly free of the tangled growth. It had stopped as it had begun, without notice or drama.

She continued on through less dense undergrowth, still not finding anything resembling a path, but thankfully without the twisted brush that had absorbed much of her day. She ached from the struggle, and nourishment and water were now becoming critical for survival. Her sweat had long ago stopped and she knew by her weakness and periodic chills that she was becoming dehydrated. With this, her black mood entirely possessed her and she struggled not to just collapse and sleep. She was unsure of the time of day. All her actions, whether plodding steps or the several stops to stare numbly at the growth surrounding her, were purely automatic responses. Her body was devastated, but the real damage was being done to her mind for she could no longer discern between actual darkness of the woods and the bleakness that ravaged her soul.

"Mother," she whispered to the woods. "Mother, I understand now. I see your despair. I feel your great hopelessness."

Later, by chance, she found a smaller tree standing alone among the undergrowth. She continued, almost wandering past it, but a distant cry seemed to call her momentarily from her blackness. She slumped to the earth and stared numbly around trying to focus. She noticed the obvious difference in this one tree. It was much shorter than the giant trees that grew hundreds of feet upward to provide the expansive canopy above. This one must have been a seed dropped by a passing animal.

She wearily dragged herself up to look closer and found it had a few small fruit upon its branches. Most though, seemed to be far above her and hopelessly out of reach. One smaller fruit was suspended from a lower limb and she tried jumping to snag it. Her lack of strength made her attempts futile. It remained several feet above her best effort, so she attempted to climb desperately wishing she had some childhood experience that would propel her upward through the small branches. She finally secured a foothold half a step up the rough trunk and pushing forward caught hold of the lower limb. Leaning out to grasp the small bit of food seemed beyond her depleted strength, but she desperately needed nourishment. With fingers outstretched, she almost reached it when her precarious footing failed and she tumbled to earth landing hard on her side and shoulder. Her ordeal had already left her body in constant pain and the fall dazed her leaving her doubled up and gasping to regain her breath. When she recovered her wind she tried to raise but a stabbing twinge in her shoulder caused her to cry out. She got up slowly and holding her limp arm and shoulder tried to walk only to stagger back and fall against the tree trunk. A pop and another cry of anguish left her sitting on the forest floor exhausted and in complete despair. She looked up at the limb and saw the fruit still hanging above her. It seemed to mock her hunger.

"You have won," she said to the forest and collapsed into blackness.

CHAPTER SEVEN
The Eagle and the Jaguar

Pamela lay face down on the earth gently cradled by the stillness of the great forest. Her body held her in slumber attempting to recover some small amount of the strength that had been continually drained from her. As she slept, a silent form glided on dark wings from the lofty trees above. A large bird quietly settled upon a branch directly over her, its intense dark eyes appraising her fallen form. After several moments, it spread its great wings and hopped to the fruit, the small branch sagging under its weight. With a single snip of its sharp beak, the fruit was freed and fell near Pamela. The bird then went to a higher limb and again dislodged another fruit allowing it to join the first. It stared down assessing its work. It snipped off a third fruit and looked again. Apparently satisfied, it lifted into the air and vanished into the high foliage above.

From the nearby brush another pair of eyes watched as a small rodent approached her. Then the forest stillness was broken by the sound of a deep, growling cough. This was warning enough and the rodent quickly turned and hurried to the safety of the undergrowth. The yellow-gold eyes then continued their vigil as she slept.

Several hours later she began to move, though the foggy remnants of unconsciousness still clouded her thoughts. Slowly and carefully she tried to rise up and the pain in her shoulder returned. She felt it, touching gently to assess the damage. *A broken bone would be fatal*, she thought. The irony of this came as close to amusement as she had had in days. She laughed ruefully at this silly thought. Unable to face the expanse of the forest, she lowered her head and moaned, "How much more? How much more must I endure?"

She didn't know whether she felt better or foolish by speaking to the forest as if it understood or would care the slightest if it did, but she was surprised that the pain in her shoulder was not as severe; in fact, it was only a deep soreness. She carefully felt it once again and realized that her fall against the tree must have relocated something. That her shoulder must have popped out when she fell from the tree and the second fall had corrected it.

Dumb luck!

As she rose slowly to her knees, she stared at three objects nearby. The fallen fruit lay only a few feet away. Puzzled, she looked up to the tree and then crawled to the nearest one. It appeared to be similar to the one placed in her small package by the woman. How could she tell though, perhaps these were poisonous? She smelled it. It had the familiar bittersweet odor but this gave her no real indication of whether it was edible or not. Then she turned it in her hand and stared at it and it seemed right. She could sense no harm; in fact, it seemed she could sense goodness in it. She shook her head at the thought that it *seemed to be right* and tore into the tough rind and began to open it.

Yes! It is the same!

And even with her tiredness, she eagerly ate the soft flesh inside. The fruit still tasted slightly bitter as did the other, but its juice refreshed her parched throat. She quickly finished the first fruit and was half through the second when she thought of perhaps saving a small bit for later. But this would be absurd. She desperately needed food and drink now. If she couldn't find more in a short time, this small bit would mean nothing. Even more of this fruit would only prolong the inevitable. She finished the second and half of the third and felt better.

She would eventually die from lack of proper nourishment or perhaps even of lack of water. It was not quite the rainy season and this month seemed abnormally dry. *How ironic this would be*, she thought, *to die of thirst in the heart of a rain forest.*

Her hands were slightly stained and sticky from the fruit. She wiped them on some large leaves the best she could and got up, admitting to herself that she actually felt somewhat refreshed. With that she again started to walk.

The day seemed endless and the monotony of her surroundings soon became a bland grayness that seeped like dampness into her soul. Gradually it grew towards dusk. The initial lift from the fruit had long ago worn off and the forest had once again become denser.

Thankfully not as binding as the impenetrable thickets of earlier, but still sufficiently overgrown to prevent easy passage.

She was hopelessly lost and the reality of her predicament began to be slowly comprehended. Her black mood increased and tried to once again envelop her soul, though mercifully not as intense as the despair of yesterday. It was now late into her second day of wandering and she had learned nothing, the forest was still totally foreign to her, a place of absolute terror. Most of the woods were now filled with dense undergrowth and she could seldom find anything resembling a path. Her constant fear was that she would stumble upon a dangerous animal, especially a snake. Thoughts of monstrous, black serpents constantly assailed her as she walked.

Snags tore at her tangling hair and placed additional small tears in her fragile clothing. Her feet were intensely sore and covered with cuts and small blisters. At times she thought she would actually welcome death, but most chilling was her fear of the mental darkness that could take her at any moment. Her ordeal was totally incomprehensible to her, one out of storybooks and now incredibly, her real life. She was lost, alone and miles from anything resembling a civilized outpost. She tried to force her mind back from this path as it began to crumble into hysteria. Better to be killed by the forest or its creatures than to be hurled into despair with her fragile mind retreating into absolute darkness ... to become her mother. With this thought, she acquired more determination and compelled her exhausted body forward through the tangled snares of the brush. Again, more sinuous vines, strong willowy branches and sharp-edged leaves lay before her all woven into a web designed to thwart movement. She frantically beat at them struggling to gain precious steps until she finally broke free into a clearing and fell to her knees, her chest heaving to catch precious air.

After a long moment, as she allowed her breathing to become more regular, she stared incredulously at the forest floor where she had fallen. Not far from her were indications that someone else had passed recently and in great haste. Soil had been dug up by the impact of long strides leading away from her through the overgrowth. She had no knowledge of tracking, but these impressions would be obvious to anyone.

Struggling wearily to her feet, she began to follow the evidence of someone's hasty passage. The prints showed bare feet that had struck the forest soil with great force. Obviously the person was running as the marks were spaced widely apart. They led, twisting through the great trees. Someone had expertly woven through this area with no discernible path, skillfully missing the large trunks, leaping over fallen obstacles and dodging tangles of underbrush. Pamela followed them as best she could and after a short while came to the edge of a small hill. Here the earth fell away sharply, running down a steep incline filled with protruding roots, rocks and low plants. Below lay a small stream that flowed through a natural gully. Its water ran shallow and since it was not yet the rainy season, the streambed showed several patches of dark, gritty earth. The opposite bank some twenty feet across the stream seemed flatter and gradually started upward, though not as steep and then once again disappeared into the forest. Her foot slipped as it caught loose soil at the top of the bank and she desperately grabbed a nearby branch to prevent herself from tumbling down the hillside to the stream below.

The other side showed a deep impression gouged into the soft soil as if something had been dropped into it. Suddenly she turned and stared with disbelief. She looked back towards the tracks through the forest. Images of the temple attack that had sent her in panicked flight through the darkness had all seemed a dream. Now the loose soil, a hillside and stream, could this be the spot where she flew across?

"Fly?" she said out loud. "God help me, I can't fly."

But the soil of the bank showed impressions of a slide. Then deep gouges indicated where she had coiled her legs and pushed out over the water. She remembered both the hysteria and the exhilaration as her body lifted her over the stream. Her heart now pounded in sympathy to the power of this strange memory.

"Good Lord!" she whispered to the trees. She stood over the small valley and stared at the other side some twenty feet away.

Suddenly she collapsed and sat down grasping the branch for support. She wondered what had been done to her body. And was it temporary or did she still posses these strange and frightening powers? It was obvious that she never flew but it was an impossible leap, not only for her but anyone.

She sat motionless, mesmerized by the hillside and creek far below. Water, much needed, lie directly below, but she couldn't motivate her body, as thirsty and desperate as she was, to move for she was awed by the expanse of the gully before her. It was wide enough to be humanly impossible to cross without falling into the creek, especially without suffering serious injury. Looking at her battered body, she saw no outward signs of change or any physical manifestation that could possibly show how she could have spanned the water, especially surviving the landing, and then immediately continuing her flight.

"Impossible!" she said, and through her mind's hazy recollection felt herself echo her reaction as she flew across the expanse. What had they done to her? A sharp cry rang through the forest. She raised her eyes to a branch above her to what seemed to be a large, dark hawk. It was fiercely beautiful.

"Who are you?" she asked with a trembling voice. Then she wrapped her arms tightly across her chest as if to contain her last vestige of sanity and redirected her question with eyes wide with disbelief.

"And now ... who am I?"

Time passed as she sat in stunned silence. Finding neither answers nor solace, she started down the steep bank. This time the descent went slowly and was filled with stumbles and slides until she reached the bottom. Part of the water ran through small openings between scattered rocks and she drank from the areas that had movement. It wasn't cool, but was the most incredibly delicious and refreshing water ever. She told herself not to drink too quickly or too much but her thirst overcame her and her body raced ahead of her mind's caution.

Finally, after satisfying her great thirst, she splashed the water over her head and then over her entire body becoming exhilarated by the simple act of being wet with something other than her own sweat. After a long while, she crossed to the far bank and lowered her worn body to the soft earth. She leaned back against the hillside and blanked all thoughts from her mind. Within moments, she was asleep.

Pamela saw or heard nothing for the rest of the evening and far into the night. Her total exhaustion held her as completely as the darkness that enveloped the gully. She slept as the night creatures began their quests for sustenance. She remained in deep sleep, unaware of the silent, padded feet that approached her through the blackness. A sleek form of a forest cat quietly approached her and after making a wide circle as if inspecting the area curled up against her resting body and began an attentive vigil.

Thirsty creatures sensed the large cat's presence and for that night went elsewhere for their drink. Periodically she shifted her position, but after her exhausting ordeal of two days her body demanded rest. It was beginning to become light when she began to stir. Groggy from her first full night's rest in days, she slowly sat up and with a large stretch bumped something warm and soft by her side. She felt it sleepily and wondered if the woman had found her and placed a warm comforter about her. In the next moment, a shrill scream bounced against the gully walls causing a startled cat to growl and spring across the water to the opposite side.

Pamela backed against the clay bank and stared into the beast's golden eyes. It sat quietly, a dozen feet before her, calmly appraising her. It then slowly wrapped its long tail over its front paws and remained still, the only sign of annoyance being a slight twitching at the end of its thick tail.

Pamela fought not to panic, but pure terror was beginning to rip away at her forced stillness. She shook uncontrollably and was certain she now faced her death. The long, feared moment had come at last. She dug her hands into the earth trying not to wail, to scream and claw at the bank behind her … anything to escape what she now faced. Then with a strange casualness, the large beast yawned hugely and rising, stretched its long, feline body. With that it turned and with two great leaps sprung up the bank without looking back. Then it was gone.

She stared at the empty bank before her and shook her head with a stunned laugh. Tears of shocked relief were mixed with puzzlement.

A yawn? Do I even bore the animals?

She felt giddy both from amazement that she remained alive and in dismay that anything so unbelievable could occur. She had heard of wild animals not hunting unless hungry, but why was it curled up by her side? After a long while staring towards where the cat had vanished into the trees, she rose and drank once again, still looking wearily up the hill.

Hours later the shock of her experience faded and she focused upon the fact that she was still lost. Her idea to follow the footsteps from her frantic dash from the forest temple only led her through more of the same terrain as she had traveled the previous days. Thinking that perhaps she could find the temple was absurd but it was still a chance. She had hoped that a village would be nearby or perhaps the woman would find her. These desperate hopes quickly faded as she struggled again through overgrown brush. All the while her mind carried images of the refreshing water she had left behind. With no container, no way of carrying even a small amount with her, she drank as much as possible, and then ruefully left the small stream to begin the journey back. Only she had no idea if she was actually going back.

After another hour of wandering, she decided finding the temple or any person was hopeless. She found a less dense portion of the forest and wearily sat down. After a moment, she decided that she would stay put and try to deal with reality. It was now her third day and incredibly she was not dead. Now food and water were the crucial items necessary for her continued survival. So far the menace of wild creatures didn't present the problem she had originally imagined. In fact, the puzzling behavior of the large cat was her only significant encounter with an animal. Therefore, food and water were her main concern. While thinking about this, she avoided the question as to why any of this should matter. That it was still only a matter of time for her.

She forced back this thought and decided to actually look for food. But where to start? She got up and started her quest by looking more closely at the foliage as she walked. Leaves obviously were not good. She questioned herself as to what she really knew about plants. Could she, she wondered, actually identify vegetables or fruits? She was no farmer but she was not entirely ignorant about everything. She had also heard of people eating insects, perhaps grubs, though hungry as she was the thought of this revolted her.

After a while, she found a group of small plants growing beneath a clump of shrubs. She tried to pull up some of the more leafy stalks to see if they had large roots or perhaps might be tubers but they were either stubborn and broke off or yielded shallow, thin roots. She then crawled a few more feet and tried another group of plants. These had broad, dark green leaves, some with a delicate red vane. *Strange,* she thought as she tugged at the tough roots trying to dislodge them. She had come to believe all was gray in the forest. These colors were muted but still distinct. She worked one loose and a long, whitish root broke free. She brushed off the remaining loose soil and thought of wiping it clean on her clothes but they were so dirty and sweat-stained that she finally resorted to using one of the broad leafs. She then broke off a small portion and cautiously smelled it. Her stomach ached from emptiness and she found her mouth watering as a slightly pungent odor came from the broken root. Small beads of moisture oozed from the vegetable. At least she fervently hoped it was a vegetable, or at least edible.

Then a strange feeling came upon her. The smell and texture before her seemed right. Again the sensation of being able to sense a natural goodness rose within her. She dismissed this notion as nonsense and bit slowly into the root. It was slightly bitter, but palatable and she chewed the small piece and swallowed. Perhaps she had just poisoned herself. Yet her odd feeling told her that she had not, that the root was not only edible but could sustain her for a while. She then ate more eagerly and found herself pulling up more plants. Some broke off at the ground, but most actually tore free.

She kept eating, trying to spit out the loose soil that clung to the root's small crevices and continued to devour as many as she could pull up. Her stomach began to ache and she again thought that perhaps she had stumbled upon something toxic, but she rationalized that her stomach had been completely empty and the ache was from the shock of actually eating after a long while.

After consuming several of the carrot-shaped roots she sat down and quietly looked around at the forest. This was the first time she had actually looked at the woods. Until this moment her time was spent fearfully awaiting her death. Now she noticed that there seemed to be more color around her than she previously thought. There was a subtlety of delicate hues and variations of textures and shadings that her despondency had hidden. Still though, the fact remained that she was lost and even with the discovery of two edible plants, her hopes of anything more than a prolonged death were absurd.

She rose and continued her wandering, though at a more leisurely pace, while looking for other edible roots and in the hope that she would find other trees with small fruit. They contained more moisture than the roots and she thought constantly about the flowing stream of water she left early in the morning.

An hour later she discovered another type of fruit-bearing tree, these like small, red bananas. Most appeared not yet ripe but a few were soft and sweet. A few minutes later her stomach was as full as it had been in days. Water, however, was now the item of most importance. As she continued to travel she searched for some small streams, a pond, anything that might hold water. Even with the food she had found, her lips were dry and her throat was becoming rough and scratchy. Then as if someone from above had realized her plight, a deep roll of thunder descended through the high trees echoing as it traveled throughout the forest. A short time later she heard the first patter of rain beginning in the upper canopy. A few moments afterward, an intense shower had worked its way to the lower regions of the forest. Rain patterns beneath the trees were erratic with some areas receiving a full deluge while some areas seemed to avoid the drops and remain relatively dry. She watched with fascination as small rivulets ran down branches gathering force and streamed into the air to land farther down. These streams continued to gain momentum as they fell and bounced through the leaves or branches. She seemed to be beneath a large, multi-streamed shower created for giants.

Then she suddenly realized she was watching precious moisture drop to the ground and disappear into the dry soil. She frantically ran around looking for some way to contain a large stream of water gushing past her to the earth. She thought of removing her shirt and soaking it up, but the notion of drinking water mingled with her own sweat repelled her. Finally in desperation, she found a large leaf and bent it to form a crude cup. It filled quickly but presented a problem in drinking as it twisted in her hand. However, her persistence led to the first full drink since early morning.

With her thirst satisfied, she stripped off her shirt and shorts and stood under the strong stream allowing the water to pour over her head and body. She let the spray dance upon her worn muscles, reveling in the newness of an old experience. Arms and head raised, she let out a joyous cry. It was delightful. A shower at the most elegant resort could not have provided the easing of her cramps and lifting of her spirit as this small stream of rainwater that had worked its way down countless leaves and limbs to provide her with cool refreshment.

After a while she used the remaining dwindling stream to roughly wash out her tattered clothes. She rung them out as best she could by hand trying not to tear them further and then put them back on. Their wetness felt cool and immensely more pleasant than their previous dirt and sweat-drenched condition. Then with a full stomach, a good drink and semi-clean clothes she resumed her journey.

Time to her was still meaningless. She thought it must be midafternoon by now but this was only a guess. Her mind was becoming occupied with something that had nagged her constantly, and now that food was temporarily solved became one of increasing concern.

Her thoughts kept returning to the ceremony in the temple, her frantic flight through the woods and the impossible leap over the stream. Something had obviously been done to her, but her memory was still clouded, perhaps from a lingering effect of the drugged water. The change that had been made in her was of such magnitude that she didn't know how to even think of it, let alone understand it.

As she walked she continued to keep a vigilant eye out for danger knowing that she remained as lost and hopeless as ever. Her travels were now more evenly paced, more deliberate, but this was unconscious, brought about by a growing awareness of the land. Yet whenever she would stop to rest or search for more fruit or roots, she found herself staring intently at her hands and inspecting her legs as if expecting to find some physical manifestation that would explain how she could have accomplished what had happened.

What were those potions that were used in anointing my body? How might they be altering me in unknown ways?

These were the mystifying questions that she carried with her as she walked.

She continued on deeper into the woods now trying to identify any familiar landmark. Even with the recent good fortune, the forest remained strange and forbidding. Pamela glanced around at pockets of darkness. Menace still exuded from each one and she could feel her chronic despondency once again seep into her soul and start to close upon her. At times her mind refused to accept her plight; she closed her eyes tightly and knew she must still be asleep in Iowa. Yet another part of her mind, a newly awaking area of her brain was focusing upon the forest and its powerful presence.

As she fought to not only comprehend her plight, but also bring some sense as to why her continued struggle for survival was so necessary, an unseen metamorphosis was occurring. Changes unaware to her, for unseen and minute alterations were occurring deep within her cells. Unnoticed to her was how her body now reacted to her new environment; her steps were becoming controlled, sure and silent. She unconsciously stepped over small hidden rocks, carefully avoiding twigs and small, broken branches. Each movement hinted at a new awareness and contained a subtle feline grace. Her heart still beat fearfully and her eyes darted about searching for danger, but her vision was becoming acutely farsighted and steady and her gaze focused with a hawkish intensity. However, even as these deeply hidden changes continued to occur within her body, her mind still remained ready to vault into the darkness that had consumed her grandmother and then her mother.

She spent the rest of the day speculating about her body, while desperately fighting off the urge to flee into the false security of her personal darkness.

Towards the late afternoon she caught herself totally absorbed not only in the search for food but cataloging in her mind the vast array of plant life. Later, another fact came to her attention while digging up a root. The soil in most places of the forest was poor. It showed none of the richness that she remembered being present in the temple. Eventually her efforts to discover more edible plants were rewarded as she had found at least two additional ones. Now her attention was directed towards a different looking fruit found hanging from a low bush. It was more like a large, darkish berry and she turned it over carefully inspecting it. Something seemed not quite right about it. At least it did not seem to have the same goodness she had sensed within the others. She bit cautiously into the skin just breaking it open and taking a small amount on her tongue. She quickly spit it out as her sense of taste made her shudder and a deep instinct rose to tell her of the small fruit's dangers. Not only was it bitter, it was wrong! Even without the taste she knew it was harmful.

But how?

She left the bush with a confused shake of her head and continued deeper into the forest.

The end of her third day was fast approaching and her fatigue, though not as overwhelming as yesterday, was causing a return of cramping to her legs. Even with the food, some now carried with her, she knew she was still trapped in a foreign land. With the fatigue came the return of her personal darkness. A darkness that recalled a short story read during her freshman English course.

Maybe Hemmingway was right. This place was nada.

She longed for a simple, clean place, one brightly lit, to drive out the gloom that was seeping into her being. She remembered a few months ago when, in her room, she had desperately prayed, at least she thought it might have been a prayer. She had cried out a forlorn plea for a new place, one to help dispel the chronic darkness of her own personal twilight. And now she was immerged into the perpetual twilight of the rainforest.

"Nada!" she whispered to the trees. The place was nothing! She had left her own dreary nada and was now in the vast nada of the forest.

She wasn't strong enough for this. She never had the will or strength to fight for any cause. Her life was one of avoiding conflict, of running from confrontation. How could she continue to struggle with odds so vastly in favor of the great forest that held her captive?

Yet she found herself once again searching for another resting place to spend the fast approaching night. She had passed several large trees earlier in the day but now the growth was less imposing and she could find nothing suitable to her. Finally, as the last light was absorbed by the dense foliage above, she slumped down by a fallen tree and waited to accept the darkness.

CHAPTER EIGHT
Andrew's Welcome

Andrew struggled to his feet and tried to brush dirt from his clothes. His bound hands prevented him from having much effect and then he was pushed forward again, forced to maintain a relentless pace through a wilderness he had never seen or even imagined possible.

He had learned not to speak for his initial questions were met with silence or if he persisted, a cruel blow. So he trudged obediently behind his captors, head down in an effort to stay unobtrusive. He was not sure how long he had been traveling; the drugged state of initial confinement may have been for several days and he knew they stopped and slept twice within the deep forest.

By the feel of the growth of his beard, this was at least the fourth, perhaps the fifth day since he was taken from Atlanta. As he was thinking of this, the natives leading the group broke into a small clearing cut from the towering trees. It was obviously at one time a village. Now it was a depressing collection of decaying huts, empty and forlorn. The entire area was encased within a damp grayness that seemed chilled even within the tropic heat. Two large metal folding tables had been set up in the center of the bare earth clearing. They contained various testing equipment, glassware, and electronics, all compact and expensive looking. Andrew was half-dragged to an old lawn chair and dumped into it. The fat man, still wheezing from the long hike, had two of the natives strap him down and tear open his shirtsleeve.

Andrew struggled and received another blow. A rubber tube was tied to his upper arm and his forearm veins were wiped with alcohol. His struggle continued as the blood was taken and stored into various vials. The fat, sweaty man roughly tore the tube from his arm as a tall man materialized and seemed to drift through the mist towards them. "Samuel, we have no reason to be rude to our guest. Please be civil."

Samuel looked up from the vials of fresh drawn blood with a smug glare, but said nothing. The gray mist seemed to be spreading throughout the village but was more intense around the man that had spoken. His gray robe blended with the mist and seemed totally out of keeping with the heat of the forest. He walked forward to stand over Andrew and with a charming smile said softly,

"Welcome, Andrew. Thank you for coming."

Pamela woke in the middle of the night. It was still totally dark and she had no idea of how long she had been asleep. It had seemed like hours before she had dozed off for the sounds of the forest night were both fascinating and frightening. This time she sensed the warm fur curled up against her thigh. The cat was back. It had obviously returned sometime during the night. But why, she wondered? She desperately wished to scream but was too tired and too terrified to move, so she just waited trying to keep her breath regular and her body still. The night passed and she must have again dozed off, for the large creature was gone when she woke.

"This can't be happening!" she muttered to the forest as if it was a presence capable of understanding. Only she knew in reality that though the great woods seemed to be an entity with a life and destiny of its own, she was totally insignificant to it. Whether she lived or died was of no concern to it, for the forest's measure of time and existence was eonian.

She rose and stretched, still stiff and sore, but with a vague feeling that her muscles were somewhat less fatigued than yesterday. Certainly better than her first days in the forest. She paused to think.

This was day four.

She was certain of that, but what day of the week was it? Friday noon? *Yes*, that was the day she had left America. But how many days had she traveled? Perhaps three, then two more, and then four? This made no sense to her and she finally gave it up as now quite unimportant.

She was hungry! Not the desperate need for nourishment that had been the life or death mission of a few days ago, but a genuine craving for food. Finding it came more quickly this time and she began to rely upon her instinct to locate various roots and small fruit. She also found numerous small pockets of water standing in low areas probably accumulated from rain showers during the night. After she had eaten, she tried to place some normalcy into the day by considering her morning forage as breakfast. Then she began her customary travel through the woods.

After a few moments she stopped and abruptly sat down on the forest floor.

To continue to wander is stupid ... and totally unproductive!

Perhaps she might better find her way through the woods if she would stop and actually look around. At least this would be better than her previous attempts to, she then realized she had no idea what she was attempting to do. Survive? Yes ... that was her driving purpose. But somehow she had survived for four days and, as miraculous as that was, she still now wished for more order in her life. After all, all those years in a single classroom were the essence of order. Pamela quieted her mind and wondered if class had started yet. Of course it had. She knew life would continue without her. The quick scramble for a substitute and then the world would turn again. She would be missed for the moment of a blink, no more. Her classroom would be someone else's and the students would learn and grow and soon forget Mrs. Pamela Somers. The gloom in her heart increased as she realized that there was no one back home that would miss her.

She stretched and looked around at the forest. The high trees still prevented direct sunlight from reaching the lower levels but after observing the plants before her more closely, she began to notice subtle patterns within the leafy structures. To her astonishment, there seemed to be an abundance of color. It was just more muted than in the surfaces that received full sunlight.

For the next several hours she sat and quietly studied the small patch of forest around her. The terrain was relatively flat though towards her left was a small rise that disappeared into the underbrush. To her right were two larger trees, each about three arm's length across and they no doubt reached into the bright sky with their upper limbs.

Smells were something she had never thought of as demanding awareness. However, when she stilled herself and closed her eyes, she could recognize the decay of fallen leaves, branches and other organic matter. It was not the unpleasant odor of rotting but the musty smell of transformation, one source of life to another. She also detected the subtle perfumes of blossoms that light breezes carried to her from nearby parts of the forest. Other scents were abundant but unrecognized. She wondered if this was a greater awareness using her natural abilities or came from enhancement of her senses by whatever physical changes had begun within her. She was now totally convinced that something far beyond her understanding had happened to her.

For a long while she took simple pleasure in observing the textures of tree barks, the great variety of plants and the incredible nuances in color before her. She was sure that they had always been there but her despair had hidden them in the gloom of her mind. That was a few days ago. Was she still that person? If not, then who was she? For this, she had no answer.

As she sat, another unexpected thing occurred. She noticed animals. Small, furry creatures wandered at the edge of the undergrowth, unhurried and seemingly unaware of her presence, though at times she noticed a quick glance at her as if they wished to assure themselves that she was not harmful.

All this fascinated her but the most intriguing of all were the insects. She had vaguely been aware that she should have suffered many bites, but in reality had none. Now she watched as insects of all sizes and shapes scurried about her, but never touching her. This seemed unnatural and she was wondering how to determine any truth about these strange matters when she noticed an opportunity approach. Did she have the nerve, she wondered? A large, dark spider had crawled from under some nearby leaves. Pamela clenched her jaw and remained still, forcing herself to not move. The creature, only a bit smaller than her fist, crawled towards her. It seemed to be coming directly for her and she dug her fingers into the dirt and held her breath. The hairy body approached to within a few inches of her leg and suddenly stopped. It raised its front two legs and waved them about seeming to assess its location. Then it quickly turned, and without further hesitation, detoured completely around her. It then proceeded back to its original course, continuing its journey on the other side of her. This gave her no real information and she could only shake her head in bewilderment.

After a while of further rest and observation, she got up and stretched. She hesitatingly admitted to herself that she felt a bit better, at least for one lost in a forest. She also knew within her heart that her survival was probably more chance than skill. With that, she took a deep breath and set off again.

Later in the day she discovered another stream, near in size to the previous one. This one, however, was not lying within a deep gully but flowed in a small depression winding through the forest between the large trees and overgrown shrubs. She wondered if it was the same stream and if she should follow it, but decided she didn't know which way it ran and this would be of no use. After drinking as much as possible, she washed as well as she could and continued into the forest.

She was growing quite tired and was thankful that she was becoming more aware of her surroundings. Pockets of dark undergrowth, though still requiring caution, didn't appear quite as ominous, but now a new nagging concern was rising within her. It rose from a growing uneasiness, a vague feeling of illness that seemed to be focused within the pit of her stomach. Could she have eaten something, she wondered, or perhaps the stream's water was tainted? But this feeling was more fear than sickness and its source lie just out of reach of identification.

Eventually she reached a clear portion of the woods, still canopy-covered, but with little undergrowth except a single small tree. Knowing that it held her favorite fruit, she ran swiftly and giving into a sudden impulse to leap, bound over a fallen log.

Never in all her life had she run and jumped as she just did. However even being able to have this newfound burst of energy she could not imagine vaulting a stream as she had a few nights ago. She turned and stared at the distance she had just quickly covered and the log that was effortlessly crossed and didn't know whether to be exhilarated or terrified. She inspected her hands and legs discerning no outward manifestation of change.

"Well, no claws yet," she muttered softly to herself. She did feel stronger though and had noticeably better muscle tone in spite of her ordeal. She knew that diet and rigorous workouts could produce this effect, but also was certain that most was from an unnatural physiological event begun by whatever strange biological occurrence had resulted from being anointed with animal potions.

Her college chemistry and biology were insufficient to allow any familiarity with biomechanics but no doubt something greatly beyond her understanding of nature was occurring within her. She knew also that she should be hysterical with fear, but instead found an unexplainable calmness trying to evolve within her. An acceptance that now gave her the beginning of a peace, even an acceptance of purpose, though she had no idea what that purpose may be.

Pamela looked around at the forest and then above her as she sensed another presence. A large bird was sitting on a limb looking down at her. She assumed it was a hawk by its size and the sharp talons and curve of its beak. She returned its steady gaze thinking that the great bird appeared to be watchful, as if it was concerned about her.

"Foolish," she whispered to herself, and proceeded to the fruit tree. This time the yellow-green fruit was within reach and after gathering several, she found a comfortable place to eat. She sat resting on her haunches with the fruit held in both hands and easily stripped away the tough rind. Biting into its yellow flesh sprayed pulp and juice over her. It was sweet and seemed cool in the tropic heat. *Funny*, she thought, that the heat that overwhelmed her the first few days seemed more bearable now.

Drops of juice fell to her legs and she watched the liquid run over her soil-covered skin etching small paths in the dirt. Images of caged jungle animals tearing into thrown food came to mind. Was she now as wild as that? But the thought was quickly dismissed as she stared around in awe at the grandeur of the forest. She paused for a moment and then holding the fruit slightly aloft gave thanks for its gift of sweetness and nourishment. Most food during her life had either been a chore or a necessity. This now was a blessing.

She rested there, almost content, looking at the forest with a freshness unthinkable only a few days ago. Her first experience of the land had proven it to be a place of hostility and violence, but now she was being shown a different, almost serene side. She knew now the forest was dangerous, but not cruel. It had its own laws and its beauty and majesty were balanced with the inevitable cycle of life and death. This she could accept, for it was so different from the darkness that had claimed her grandmother then mother, and still hovered over her. This death was clean and natural, the other tormented and everlasting. She was still in the forest's semidarkness but her gloom was no longer the primary ingredient in her evaluation of the land. Alone, covered with sweat and dirt and with ragged and stained clothes, she found it astonishing that she was almost at peace. Maybe she felt comfortable with the forest precisely because of its perpetual twilight, for had she not spent her entire life living in shadows. She had always thought of her life as brown, but indefinite shades of gray more aptly described her existence. Now she could intimately relate to what she first thought of as perpetual gloom, for she now realized it was actually vivid life that was unnoticed only because of its subtlety.

This life required one to become more sensitive to nuances, to be more observant of delicate shades that others more accustom to things brightly lit would never see ... and might never consider to exist.

Could it be Hemmingway saw things darkly precisely because of well-lit places?

She was not a philosopher and shrugged off the complexity of this thought.

Now, unexpectedly, she found herself in the very heart of subtle beauty and in reality knew nothing about it. Her only knowledge of rain forests and the Amazon came from sixth-grade youngsters doing projects. She knew little of the climate, the land, and especially its people and their customs. Just as in many respects she knew precious little about her own heritage.

Pamela thought of the woman in the village and wished she could know more about her and the tribes that lived somewhere within the wilderness about her.

Where are the native villages?

She had traveled for a great distance by now and had encountered nothing.

Who was it that had walked over this very spot? Where were the women, the children and especially the hunters that would support the people with their skills? How large were the tribes, and most of all, where did they originally come from? I know nothing!

She then promised that she would learn about the land and its people. Of this she was sincere, but she also realized that her being alive was only due to plain luck and it was only a matter of time before it would end. A wave of profound regret twisted in her gut and tears welled up. She didn't want to die.

Not now! Not after so much!

And the questions, so many now. Not only about the people, but also about herself, about whatever was happening to her. Questions about what she was becoming. She sat down abruptly and held her head in her shaking hands.

The cat … why? Why would a wild animal curl up and sleep by me? So much, so much!

It was a long while before she could bear to get up. It was now becoming dark again.

Another day … I guess I've made it through another day.

She cared about this, but the knowledge of the perils of the night brought increased despondency. Pamela tried to recall what day it was, four she guessed. But it made little matter. With that, she curled up on the ground and went to sleep.

CHAPTER NINE
The Beast

A small, silent troop of monkeys peered down from the high limbs overhanging a misty forest opening, curious about the heated disagreement raging below. Three men were standing near a large pit by the base of a gigantic tree. From the charred gash in the earth there rose a gray, misty substance, too viscous for fog, but light enough to float through an abandoned village, enveloping it with its hideous touch, appalling as a shroud. Samuel and two technicians were engaged in a spirited debate that appeared destined to break into violence at each word. The older man's chubby face was swollen, exaggerated by a deep crimson flush. His khaki apparel looked comically out of place, as if he had thought old jungle movies to be the fashion for the Amazon. One technician, younger than Samuel, but almost as heavy, slammed his pudgy hand hard upon an equipment-laden table and jutted out his large jaw in defiance.

"It HAS to affect the main strands of the DNA! And this must be the key to the cell changes observed to date, even though we can't yet detect the subtlety of the distortions. If we can just return to the Atlanta lab where our equipment is infinitely more sophisticated we can isolate the trigger substance within days."

"You dolt!" screamed Samuel, his face contorted with fury.

"Your opinion is of no importance! We don't have the luxury to return. We have been directed to perfect the serum here and now, by trial and error if necessary. We have learned much from the animals. If we proceed intelligently and use the human subject this time, carefully monitoring him as we go, we may gain sufficient data to please him. Otherwise ..." His voice grew quiet and fear mingled with disdain clouded his puffy eyes.

Andrew observed the conflict from his bound position. He strained to catch glimpses of the quarrel through the elaborate scientific equipment that covered two folding tables set within the center of the dilapidated village. The cleared center area of the camp allowed a diminutive amount of tropic sun to pass by the great limbs of the forest trees high above, but the mist captured it and diffused its light rendering it ineffective. Charles had left early in the morning leaving simple, curt instructions to the men. He departed saying that he needed to find and bring back, if still alive, a lost lamb. Samuel and the others were directed to complete a particular process involving a thick, greenish substance. Once finished, they were to gather special plants somewhere and then gather at "our opponent's magical pool". This he said with a contemptuous smile and slipped silently into the grayness.

After a few hours of intense work, the men carefully packed a portion of the equipment into protective containers and dragged the tables into an old, decaying hut. They then jerked Andrew to his feet and set off into the forest, laden with various metallic packs, weapons and struggling to pull a large, canvas-draped cage. The wheels bounced and jostled the heavy container as it passed over the rough soil of the village floor. Andrew froze as a low guttural howl as chilling as the gray mist rose from beneath the enclosing canvas.

The sleep of depression held her until the middle of the night. This time she woke when she sensed it quietly approaching her. She lay very still and allowed the cat to come to her. A strange mixture of terror and fascination held her captive waiting to see what it would do. Perhaps it would give her some insight into what was happening to her.

The silent pads approached and seemed to circle the area. There was practically no light so she was puzzled as to how she could so clearly sense its presence, following it step by step as it moved towards her. Suddenly it moved quickly and stood over her. Pamela felt its hot breath fall upon her face and she began to panic, biting upon her tongue not to scream. Then, just as quickly, she felt its warm body drop down next to hers and let out a huge breath as it settled against her legs.

The entire experience was beyond belief by now and she remained still, waiting for something to happen. After a long while, she realized that the cat was asleep, its breath long and regular. The other forest sounds, silent when the large cat was moving, resumed and she could again hear the night birds and the soft sounds of foraging in the high limbs above. *Why*, she thought? Of all that had happened, as unbelievable as this dark and haunting experience had been, this mystified her the most. She hesitated and then slowly and carefully reached her trembling hand towards the animal. She had almost touched it when a cry of anguish came from the trees above. A night hunter had found its prey. She started and remained still for a long while, quieting her pounding heart. She then again extended her hand and gently touched the warm fur beside her. A growling rumble immediately started within the cat and she jerked her hand away letting out a muffled gasp. Now she was dead! She was sure of it. "Stupid!" she shouted to herself. "Stupid!"

She waited but nothing happened. The cat remained by her side, the low growl continued as warning to let well enough alone. Pamela took a deep breath and resolved to remain still until it left. It had left the previous nights and she desperately hoped it would remain consistent to its pattern. Yet something nagged at her. Something was not right. Was the cat sick? Perhaps seeking comfort as disease ravaged its body? No, she could sense health within the animal. It was something else like … a befuddled smile came to her and she put her hand back on the cat's huge chest.

"Good Lord," she said softly. "You're purring!"

Pamela stretched and yawned. The sun must have been up for a long while. The forest seemed alive with energy and life. Small creatures, one looking like a strange armadillo, went about their business and the small bits of actual sunlight that had worked its way past layers of leaves highlighted their activities. She arched her back and gracefully rose, stretching once more. She actually felt good. The cat had left early as its custom and she still grinned in puzzled incredulity.

Breakfast came easily and her walk was close to a leisurely stroll as she inspected the forest. Her thoughts were of the people once more and she tried to reconstruct their presence among her as she traveled. Foraging women carefully watching over playing children as they scampered among the tall trees and lean hunters were the inhabitants that her mind created. Only she had no idea of reality and no way of judging between truth and fabrication. All the while there remained a slight uneasiness lying within her. It seemed to be the same nagging sensation that had made her slightly ill yesterday. But today it strengthened as she walked as if she might be approaching its unknown source.

Towards midday the feeling was ever-present and uneasiness had turned to dread. The forest character had changed somewhat during the last hour and she was moving up what seemed like a series of small plateaus. They were still enveloped within the tall forest trees but remained perceptible. The persistent unrest slowly intensified and she found the feeling similar to her awareness of wrongness when she sought food. But this was different. This seemed to be an unnatural illness, unlike a berry that would, as part of its nature, be poisonous. The berry was simply inedible. This increasing dread seemed to rise from something that, even with her heightened senses, she could not identify. This came from something that simply should not exist.

Pamela continued on, dreading that she might stumble upon the source of the unnaturalness, but unable to decide upon any other course. Animals became fewer and she glanced upward often as a large bird called down to the earth below. The queasy feeling increased until there was unbearable tension within her entire being.

She traveled for an hour more, her progress greatly slowed by the wrongness that seemed to rise from the earth itself. Finally she saw a small clearing a few yards before her. Quietly and cautiously she approached the opening and tried to see what was ahead. She had come upon a village for there were numerous crude huts in a semicircle within the clearing. Large trees hung over the small space, allowing some light to fall in the central clearing, but they still were mighty enough to prevent full sunlight from reaching the dirt floor.

Pamela crept fearfully forward only to find the village abandoned. The dilapidated huts, some built upon log stilts, seemed to be decaying, their thatch roofs and woven branch walls half-down. Only one structure appeared to be intact and it stood to the rear of the circular court and beneath an immense tree, its broad trunk rising high into the forest green above. She stared at it in disbelief, for several feet from its base sprung a tangle of broken and twisted limbs writhing as if deformed by some agonizing event totally foreign to the great forest. Pamela was stunned. The mammoth tree had been stripped bare of all bark, as if its flesh had been torn away by an unspeakable act of unrestrained violence. Lower portions of its wood looked charred as if a sinister power had touched its heart and blackened it with corruption.

Beneath the burnt trunk stood a large slab of stone, its shape and ponderous weight like that of a sacrificial altar. It was stained with heavy, black drippings that ran from the top surface down the sides to the earth. At one corner, nearer to the pit, was a large stone vat that seemed to be placed to gather whatever substance ran from the altar. The sight of this sent a chill into Pamela's heart.

The entire village reeked of illness. Fire pits were in disarray and the earth seemed barren and desolate. The lone hut standing closest to the violated tree had a dark opening that spoke of a forbidden peril. She felt as pained and abused as the village as she walked through its center to stop before the hut.

She hesitated and then peered into the darkness. The lack of light distorted the interior but she could make out silhouetted forms of what appeared to be tables with heavy blocks covering them. They made no sense to her and their presence seemed contrary to the naturalness of the forest. Ruts gouged into the earth showed where they had been dragged from near the tree and into the recesses of the hut.

Pamela's stomach churned and the overwhelming wrongness of the village appalled her. She hesitatingly crept closer to the great tree and noticed an odd blackness at its base. A pale, gray mist slowly rose from the dark hole and she knew this was undoubtedly the source of the ill. An evil that would bend and warp all it touched.

To her great horror, it called to her. An indefinable urge gripped her and she found herself being drawn to the darkness. It pulled her closer with a horrid fascination until she stood within the cold mist watching it swirl seductively about her, caressing her tender skin with its dark invitation.

As she peered over the edge to see into its depths, the blackness recognized her and spoke to her years of torment and depression. It promised fulfillment and peace if she would surrender to its call. She knew she would finally be free of the endless wandering and hardships of the forest and her own personal despondency if she would only topple into the blackness … give herself to the gray mist that summoned her soul. Pamela began to tremble uncontrollably and fell to her knees. She crawled closer to the precipice unable to resist the seduction to find peace, as black as it would be. When she peered over the jagged edge and stared into the deep pit a decaying vileness rose up, carried upon the mist to surround her in its embrace. Its powerful stench was filled with unspeakable ill, of the natural goodness of the forest being somehow violently assaulted and its life cruelly twisted into tormented depravity. She crawled forward and teetered at the edge on the verge of toppling into the blackness. She could hear her name being called. It was her mother's voice that invited her to find peace within the dark void.

"No mother! No!" She rose and staggered back gagging. After a few feet her legs gave way forcing her to crawl from the dank mist retching for clean air. Even in her darkest moments she could not conceive of such hideousness as contained within the pit. Its bottom was obscured by an impenetrable blackness beyond human understanding, but within gaps in the dark mist she saw descending stone stairs littered with pieces of once living creatures distorted beyond recognition. It was a charnel pit of unwanted brutality. It dismayed her. It was horrifying to think that she was so easily drawn to it, heard its call to hurl herself into its depths. But most heart-wrenching was the realization that the great wrong she had just beheld, full of rotting flesh and warped carcasses, had allowed her a glimpse into her mother's tormented soul. She had just witnessed the final state of self-destructive bitterness. Pamela placed her hands over her face and shook uncontrollably, for she also saw her own fate, the seduction of darkness, had she not been given the healing gift of deliverance by the forest and its people.

The fundamental evil of the charnel pit and whatever it represented revolted her. She crawled to the center of the decaying village and with her head buried in her hands, wept bitterly. She wept for her mother, allowing her years of frustration, resentment and rejection to be carried by the mist to empty into the pit, releasing it forever to the depths where it belonged. After a considerable time, she finally stood and without looking back, returned to the solitude of the forest. She fervently wished for her mother's final rest to be filled with peace.

In all his life, Andrew could not imagine that anything so horrible could actually exist. Only a brief glimpse had shown him that whatever it was, it was spawned out of the blackest of hatred.

Charles had somehow found them in the forest, and after calmly saying that he was in need of a "more direct approach", had the men loosen the cage allowing a warped and misshapen form to rush howling into the deep brush. It half-ran, half-loped as it disappeared giving the appearance of a deformed man that had been bent from his natural shape into something that was more animal in its being.

The men were obviously terrified and intensely relieved after the thing had quickly vanished. Charles watched the forest long after it had disappeared as if he could follow its progress as it ran to complete whatever sinister mission it had been sent upon. He finally turned and extended both hands towards Andrew. "My friend," he said with a wide smile. "Have you been well-treated?"

With that he once again vanished into the forest.

Their trek continued, the men still pulling the cage, now considerably lighter with the beast gone. Their mood seemed to lighten also, and the two younger ones bantered back and forth, mostly in crude humor. Samuel also picked up the pace, but his perpetual scowl silently showed his contempt for the youth, as brilliant as they were.

Andrew wondered why they had left the village. Not that he was sorry, for it had contained a depressing gloom that seemed to prevent the sun from reaching even a small portion of the village clearing. He felt certain that it was more than the heavy foliage above that had cast such a pall over the decaying shacks.

From what he could pick up from his captives talk, they were traveling to a different part of the forest, apparently one that contained a pool of water necessary for continuation of their experimentations. His blood had proven "adequate but not pure", whatever that meant. Samuel was still menacing, but somewhat more reserved whenever Charles was present. It was becoming clear however that Samuel despised Charles and seemed to be growing tired of his overbearing manner.

During the time in the village, Charles had formally introduced himself to Andrew. He was charming and debonair, conducting himself with wit and the best of social graces. He elegantly presented his story in a quiet and confident voice. A voice, Andrew noticed, that seemed to possess the qualities of a snake charmer. He knew that behind the soft, almost mesmerizing smile was a person with deadly power.

As the tale unfolded, it became clear that Andrew's father was the key as stories of forest tribes and old powers were hinted at without being fully explained. Then Charles had placed his hand lightly but firmly upon Andrew's shoulder and said, "Patience, my friend, a small detour for a few special plants and then you will have the opportunity to contribute to our important endeavors."

Andrew's heart fell, for he knew he was totally without hope.

CHAPTER TEN
Too Many Questions

Evening in the forest was a time of transition. Pamela sat on a small log watching the activities of day animals gradually give way to the nocturnal creatures that claimed the night as their own.

After leaving the horror of the abandoned village she experienced conflicting emotions mingled with unfamiliar moods. It took the remainder of the afternoon as she attempted to identify and sort them, eventually to abandon any hope of comprehension.

The village experience had left her both drained and curiously refreshed. The images of torn and grossly abused forest creatures that had littered the dark, rocky slopes of the pit continued to haunt her. Yet her mood was lighter, no doubt due to her being able to release at least part of her tormented past to the care of the forest. It, she rationalized, was much larger and therefore more able to deal with them. *Strange,* she thought, she almost felt that the great expanse of the woods was more caring, more benevolent than she had originally believed. Time would tell about that, but she remained alive somehow and now knew that the forest and its creatures were involved in ways that she could not understand but could no longer deny.

After she put some distance between herself and the village the feeling of dread had gradually diminished and later faded into almost nothing. But for the last hour it had returned in a form that while subtler, was yet still unmistakable. The same nagging unrest that had slowly intensified before brought a return of the fear and conviction that it was born of malice and despair.

Pamela had grown accustomed to the multitude of forest odors, most wonderfully rich and exotically pleasant, occasionally though, some odor would remind her that the harsher side of the forest brought death and decay. This was a normal part of the life cycle of the woods. The dread however that hung over her was not that of natural deterioration, but more as if the forces of the grave were gleefully inflicting a great, ulcerated wound upon nature itself.

The night sounds slowly intensified as the setting tropic sun withdrew the final light of day. Most of the clamor in the trees fell silent; monkeys above were nesting themselves and the small chatter of nocturnal birds wove into an evening song. All of this she watched from her place on the log. *How different*, she thought, than the first night that she had been led to the temple. It seemed months, not days ago and that night had started something still beyond her comprehension. She was now waiting, not with the terror of the first night lost within the forest, but with anticipation. Her weariness had long ago turned to exhaustion but she still sat patiently, waiting for the night to come.

Finally, after darkness had encompassed the forest for an hour, she heard and then saw it approach. She slipped down from the log and curled up on the soft, mossy ground letting the cat snuggle up against her. Pamela then placed her head on its large chest. With that she slept.

Images of grotesque creatures clawed their way out of the misty pit and with a shriek hurled themselves at her. She awoke with a cry and sat up shaking and gasping for breath. A great foreboding hung over the forest and the vague uneasiness of yesterday was now almost palatable. She rose immediately and fearfully glanced about as if expecting her nightmares to materialize and fall upon her. The cat had left and she was again alone.

The woods looked dreary as a low morning fog clung to the underbrush allowing shadowy pockets of gloom to provide shelter for her nightmares. The sun had not been up long and she was thankful for her improved night vision.

The day's inhabitants had begun to forage or hunt and in the forest they were no doubt also being hunted. Pamela thought they looked different somehow. They appeared to glance around uneasily, as if they shared her apprehension. She tried to shrug off the tension and convince herself that it was the residue of her dream. Breakfast, she decided would help. Finding fruit now came without effort. Glancing around usually allowed her to find a small tree or shrub that would yield something edible. She could now identify several plants that if pulled up had nourishing roots and water. While not plentiful, they could be found in vines and small pockets beneath the larger trees. Mostly though, she relied upon her sense of "right" to direct and protect her.

Soon she had several pieces in hand and sat down to eat. As she tore open a grapefruit-size fruit, two curious things came to her attention. The first was the realization of how effortless it now was to open its tough skin. Thinking back only a few days, she remembered the struggle with securing even the smallest opening. Now a slight twist and the first tear allowed her to use her growing nails to quickly strip away the skin. It was little challenge and she bit into the juicy flesh thankful for it.

She flexed her fingers and stared at them.

Dirty and sticky!

But she wished she could see past their grimy surface to detect something unusual, anything to give some hint as to what was occurring deep within her body. She then clicked her nails against each other hearing a loud, tough snap, but close inspection showed only her nails with half-gone polish and a somewhat increased length. Pamela shrugged at this. She was beginning to accept strangeness as the norm.

The other thing of interest came from the deep stains on her thumb and forefinger. This darkness had remained after she had found some berries that she discarded after finding them inedible. The markings they left reminded her of the black lines drawn on the faces and bodies of the native women at the temple ceremony. Her thoughts turned again to the forest people.

"How little I know about you." She said this as if expecting them to materialize from the morning dew that covered the low plants like a soft, protective veil.

After she had her morning meal she came upon a lofty part of the woods. She appreciated the grandeur of the large, high-limbed trees that soared upward to provide a cathedral like space similar to that which she had encountered a few days ago. She walked more leisurely now, resting and trying to regain some composure after her brutal dream. The feeling of dread persisted but thankfully was not increasing. Her mind now brought forth images from the soft fog. The journey to the temple had been filled with haunting from her difficult past. These encounters were misty forms of the ancient people that once inhabited the land. Soft apparitions that filled her with wonder, mystery and intrigue surrounded her.

How many had passed this way before me? Who were the people of the forest and were those in the temple their descendants? They were certainly not the savages of the storybooks, but must have been people like me. Thinking and feeling and loving, different in culture, but deeply caught up in the same daily joys and struggles that make up any person's day.

For some reason the shy young girl, perhaps no more than an early teen, who anointed her with oil, came to mind. She had smiled and softly brushed her cheek with a kiss. Who was she and how did she survive in such a wilderness, with the lack of all the things Pamela once thought essential? They had no supermarkets, television, cell phones or minivans, any of the essentials of modern life. She felt a deep respect for the people who lived in harmony with the great land that provided their home, nourished them and no doubt embraced them as they returned to the soil upon their death.

She stopped abruptly.

Charles! Where does he fit in all this? Had he looked for me? Perhaps there are search parties even now scouring the deep woods. Too much to think about!

Too many questions that she had no possible way to answer.

After that, the day seemed endless and she felt both the residue of the earlier dread that left her nerves raw with anxiety and a slight reoccurrence of her chronic depression.

By mid-afternoon her steps had become plodding and she wished for nightfall to come. She realized then that she was lonely. For days now she had just existed, surviving with little thought or much effort. But now she longed to see someone, to speak, carry on even the briefest of conversations. Now she looked forward to the night, hoping for the return of the only companion she knew.

She lifted her head suddenly and drew in a sweet fragrance that was carried through the trees by a slight breeze.

How can I sense this? I had a tough time smelling cooking onions back home.

Again she tried to look inward at her body, imagine what her blood and sinew might be doing. She realized her body had somehow changed, and no doubt was continuing to change. Even her mind must be going through a transformation. If not she would surely be insane by now, wandering in a tormented state, oblivious to all around her. Yet she was being healed, even with periodic desires to slip back into despair, she was being healed.

Perhaps it had actually started on the forest path to the temple, the night that had begun her trails. But most of all, even though she did not fully understand it, Pamela knew that the discovery of the wondrous manner in which the forest can nourish life was key to her survival. People could, if done correctly, form a true partnership with the land and the animal life, all supported by the immense complexity of the plant life. Now, could she actually find a place within all of this? Too many questions.

The woman ... she must have the answers that I need. But how to find her?

She continued through the forest attempting to clear her mind and trying to appreciate all she encountered, but images of the pit and her growing loneliness pressed upon her. The feeling of dread was still hanging faintly in the air and continued to make her slightly queasy, like the dull ache of a tooth. She was thankful though that it had lessened since the early morning and was so far manageable.

It was in this frame of mind that she wandered into a clear portion of the woods. Since entering the forest she had only glimpses of actual sunlight; now, directly before her fell a light of such intensity that she had to squint and blink to adjust to its brilliance. High trees with great, expansive limbs formed a verdant wall directly before her with the light working its way down through the dark, green veils and curtains that formed the upper canopy. *The first brightness in days*, she thought, the sight touched her, warming her heart. Then she halted, completely stunned by the shimmering myriad of colors cascading from the great trees.

Thousands of colorful shapes danced and swayed upon a gentle forest breeze. Somehow the colors were brilliant yet subtly delicate. Vibrant points of earthy, golden yellows, mellow greens accented by deep browns, rich burgundy and brilliant white were woven into an extravagant tapestry that began in the upper most branches and tumbled from limb to limb until stopping head height off the forest floor.

Pamela slowly approached in amazement, eager to discover what could bring such enchantment to the constant twilight that she had experienced until now. She walked for several paces until she stood directly beneath a living fabric composed of thousands of miniature orchids. The soft breeze working its way through the forest tangle caressed the blooms and set them into a stately dance of constantly changing patterns. Delicate moss and feathery ferns provided the background to the living embroidery bringing warmth and delight to her tired and worn existence.

Pamela spent the next few hours quietly sitting in the presence of the flowers, enchanted by their rich colors and soothing fragrances. Then, after a long while luxuriating in the simple beauty of the woods, she was compelled to leave her idyllic spot, for an overwhelming sadness came upon her, so much that tears clouded her vision of the loveliness before her. Pamela desperately wished for someone with whom she could share her incredible experience.

"Look!" she wanted to cry out. "See what the great forest has done!"

But she was hopelessly alone and would remain so, no doubt forever. With this realization, she rose to return to the twilight of the deep woods, longing for the return of the forest cat and at least for the night, comfort for her growing loneliness.

CHAPTER ELEVEN
Transgenics / The Beast Attacks

Charles had left Samuel with brief but apparently precise directives and then had evaporated into the brush, quickly and silently. The rest of the band, with an additional four natives accompanying them, continued to obtain plants and then proceeded on to the "pool" whatever that meant. Andrew had attempted to start a conversation with Samuel a few times but had been rebuffed with either a glare or a blow and warning.

"Not changed a lot, have you, you jerk!" he muttered to himself.

Later, as they hurried through the heavy growth, one of the technicians eased alongside of Andrew and grinning broadly said, "He's not so bad when he's not under so much pressure. Except, of course, for some of his stranger habits. Charles has always made him nervous."

He chuckled casually, as if he was strolling through a meadow, oblivious to the tangled, overgrown vegetation that encompassed them. Andrew tried to gesture with his bound hands and asked, "Why … why am I here? It makes no sense to bring someone all the way from Atlanta?"

Again the slight laugh, "Hey man, we need your blood, it's as simple as that. I'd think that by now, after giving so many samples you would put that together."

They walked in silence for a while, Andrew in puzzled thought and the other whistling softly as if headed to a summer picnic.

Finally he asked Andrew, "Know anything about genetics?"

When Andrew remained silent, he shrugged and continued, "Transgenics is the process of implanting genes from one species into the DNA of another. We are simply using this wonderfully prolific laboratory," he gestured to the forest, "for a source of materials."

"You can't change me into a wolf or whatever, so why don't you just let me go?"

Andrew tried to reason that this reply made sense, but it rang hollow and he knew that fear came through in his voice.

The technician stopped and looked earnestly into his face, "You would be better off a wolf when it is over." With that his smile vanished and he walked on in silence.

Another typical day had begun for her.
Could being lost and forgotten ever be considered typical?
She pondered this as she munched on berries and some fresh roots. Yet this morning was different. She could feel it and kept glancing around with an uneasy tightness in her stomach.

Then a sudden chill touched the nape of Pamela's neck and she jerked around as if the gray mist had rushed from the pit through the forest to seek her destruction. She felt the intensity of the dread quickly increase and knew instinctively that some terrible blackness was aimed directly at her heart.

She started to walk but each tormented step caused her to flinch at every shadow and start at the slightest of sounds. Her fear intensified and she glanced about expecting the horror of her nightmares to fall upon her. The forest chatter grew silent and a chilling vapor seemed to rise from the earth as if she was standing upon corruption itself. Then, without warning, violence erupted from the nearby brush. Horrifying sounds of a brutal struggle filled with angry snarls and a low, eerie howl ravaged the silence of the forest. It was quickly over and Pamela stood alone staring at the dark brush to face whatever horror was hidden there. Slowly, she became aware of a low, black shape that made its way through the underbrush. It kept itself always partly hidden, working closer to her. For a moment she thought that it may be the forest cat, but as it drew nearer the feeling of dread overcame her and caused her to suddenly retch from unbearable terror.

The thing drew closer, seeming to savor the fear that it instilled within her, feeding upon her horror. Finally, a monstrous and deformed creature slowly emerged from the brush and entered the clearing. It was hideous, larger than her cat yet not upon all fours, but bent over and grossly malformed, looking as if at one time it had been upright but its body had somehow been warped. The creature had small patches of red-orange hair, but was mostly covered with a black mottled skin, slick with large splotches of soreness. Its twisted body seemed to quiver with pain and it stood silently appraising her with an evil stare.

She remained motionless, unable to breathe. Death by the animals of the forest had been expected, but this was unbearable. Then it started slowly towards her, head low and jutted forward with stiff-legged purpose. The beast emitted a rank odor and its foulness overwhelmed the natural sweetness of the forest air. It was unimaginable that such a creature could exist. It approached with a calculated deliberateness as if it found her terror delectable. Its breath seemed to steam even in the tropic heat and its lips were pulled back in a distorted snarl exposing long, yellow-stained incisors.

Most disturbing though were its eyes. They were large and misshapen, blood-red and spoke of a cruelty and malice that seemed impossible. They stared at her … transfixing animal eyes, yet with something more within their glare; for deep within the gravely hurt beast laid an unimaginable injury that had somehow altered its natural state, changing it into a monstrosity. It seemed that it was this perversion that caused the creature's overwhelming misery. The great injury shone bitterly within its eyes as if it were dismayed by its own damaged soul.

She tried to back away but was frozen, impaled to the spot with fright. The creature approached yet closer, its dark skin wet and oozing illness. She knew that the beast would rip her apart, not for food, but to gleefully destroy a living being out of sheer hatred.

She must run. She knew she now had the ability to run, but her legs were rigid with terror. It paused in its approach for a moment and its malevolent eyes seemed to look inward as if assessing the state of its own torment. The creature's twisted form seemed to cause it insufferable anguish. Then its eyes quickly refocused upon Pamela and with a roar sprang at her with blinding swiftness, hurling itself at her throat.

Her eyes widened with panic as the final seconds of her life approached. Her heart beat franticly pushing blood, enriched with adrenalin, through her body. Without thought, her new instinct for survival demanded that she duck low. Again, without thought, she gracefully shifted her body to the side. The charging, black shape passed over her and tumbled to the earth unable to twist its grotesque body to strike her.

Without hesitation, Pamela sprinted with the same energy as she had the night of the temple attack. After a few long strides she found a large, fallen branch wedged in the side of a huge tree. She leapt forward striking the branch with her left foot, launching herself to a high limb. From there she frantically pulled herself to a point some twenty feet above the forest floor. Looking back she saw the beast pacing beneath her, glaring up and emitting a low, guttural howl. It circled, fixing its eyes upon its prey with intense malice. The impact of what had just happened was beyond comprehension and the unbidden reaction of her body dismayed her.

I can't do this! I'm not capable of such things!

She held on to the limb wrapping both arms tightly around the branch and tried to bury her face into its rough bark for protection.

God help me, who am I? What have I become?

She then experienced the quick return of her indecisiveness, her inability to act in the face of conflict. She cringed and held tight to the tree. Then she looked down upon the maddened beast and was horrified to see it suddenly leap towards her trying to dig its claws into the wood to reach her. It slowly pulled itself towards her inching closer to her. Its eyes fixed directly upon her as it climbed bit by bit by sinking claws deep into the bark. But halfway up, its disfigured body shuttered with pain and it fell to the earth with a convulsive thud. After two additional attempts it abandoned its efforts and paced restlessly as if the natural life above it mocked its existence. Its vile odor drifted up to her, revolting in its hideous illness. With her eyes tightly closed, Pamela tightened her grip and fervently wished she could pray.

CHAPTER TWELVE
Alone Again

The woman sat with her hand supporting her weary brow. Most of the candles from the evening had extinguished themselves in a final sputter of wax, leaving the cramped hut dark and forlorn.

She wondered what more she could have done for the pale women that they had lead to their desperate ceremony a few days ago. She didn't believe she was dead but had no way of knowing, relying only upon small rumors of Charles's group still looking for someone.

Tales were also about another foreigner brought to the woods, no doubt to further the delving into her people's ancient secrets, and this news had brought despair and additional fear to the village.

All their hope seemed to be placed in one woman, one that seemed naive and unaware of her strengths and heritage. Would she survive or die, or perhaps wander the forest forever?

Then the women's doubts and guilt turned upon her with great incrimination. She had to do it, she argued with herself. There was no choice but to send her fleeing to the safety of the great woods, besides, it would take time for their oils to be absorbed. But the forest was harsh enough for the forest people, even with their experience and natural awareness. How could this one survive? She seemed so lost, so fragile. The woman took a deep breath.

"I must not despair," she admonished herself, "she is our only hope."

Pamela was unsure of how long she had been in the tree. She still clung to its rough bark being conscious only of her fear, the sweat that ran heavy upon her and her ragged breath. The stench of the beast continued to hang in the moist air, but had lessened somewhat. She wanted to open her eyes but was terrified that she would panic and fall. As she tried to calm herself and still her pounding heart, a voice broke the forest stillness.

"Pamela?"

Startled, she cried out, almost losing her precarious grip.

Was the beast gone?

The call came again. "Pamela, how did you come to be up there?"

The voice was soft and seemed filled with concern. She opened one eye to peer down. Charles stood at the base of the tree several feet below staring up at her. His expression was a caring one, reminding her of the unsettling time when her dark emotions caused her classroom to become a place of dread. He seemed as gentle and sincere as on that day. Yet there was a fleeting indication of another expression lying subtly beneath his smile.

Amusement?

"There ... there was an animal," she said.

How stupid that sounded!

"I was terrified." She heard her words but they sounded hollow and insignificant in comparison to what had happened.

"Well, as you can see everything is well now. The creature must have been frightened away. Perhaps some larger animal came by and it left."

The way he said it, it all seemed so plausible. Why did everything Charles say seem so well-considered and believable? The beast was surely not afraid of anything. To the contrary it seemed capable of reeking incredible violence upon whatever it encountered. Surely the forest itself would fall if it were given ample opportunity.

Charles continued to look up at her. His pensive gaze seemed slightly clouded, as if the sun, if it could ever reach down through the high leaves, would never quite brighten his countenance. He appeared thoughtful for a moment and then said quite simply, "I was worried about you, Pamela."

She had been lost for days and expected the first sight of another person to be more dramatic somehow. For some reason she recalled the attack upon the temple ceremony and the horror of her days in the forest but said nothing. She was too weary to be deceptive; her non-responsiveness only followed her typical path in life, one of least resistance. She heard him talk from a cloud, her thoughts blurred and unfocused. Someone had actually found her, she was thinking. She should be exultant with joy. Her horrible ordeal was over and she would not die. Now she would actually get back to Iowa. But all this was obscured by the veil that he seemed to evoke. Charles continued in his soft almost enchanting voice, "Well, we will be able to converse much better once you are down."

He extended his hand as if expecting her to leap gracefully to the forest floor. She shook her head and muttered through clenched teeth, "I can't get down, I'm afraid."

Charles again looked thoughtfully for moment and then without a word gracefully climbed to assist her. After much gentle coaxing and reassurance along with his supporting hand guiding her, she awkwardly descended.

As they negotiated the descent, she needed to rely upon his outreached hand. At first his touch caused her body to shrink violently away. As they progressed the touch seemed more bearable and as they neared the ground it was as if he had exuded a seductive narcotic which made his strong grasp not only a necessity but also desirable.

Finally, she reached the safety of the ground and with an effort, pulled her hand away. She shuddered, emotionally flinching from this disturbing feeling, and clenched her fists tightly while folding her arms to her body as if wishing to ward off the strange and compelling emotion. Charles had stepped back and was quietly waiting for her to recover from her ordeal.

With being safely on the ground, she now looked more closely at him and stared at his odd appearance. The business suits that he had always worn in America were gone. He stood before her dressed in a comfortable robe, gray if anything, but in reality with no real color or pattern discernible within the diminished forest light. *Strange*, she thought, he appeared to be wrapped more in shadow than an actual garment. He was smiling slightly and she struggled for something to say. Again the feeling of hope and salvation tried to surface and many questions stirred within her but confusion overcame them. A shrill cry caused her to again try to clear the fog that seemed to enshroud the forest. All she could think of was, "Thank you."

Charles seemed to sense her confusion and began to lead her on a slow walk through the forest, softly talking as he went.

"We were quite concerned about you Pamela. Very fearful that you had met with some harm. The forest can be most forbidding and dangerous. I'm thankful that we have finally found you."

He glanced at her and smiled, a strange glance with many possible meanings, and then continued with his monologue. As he talked the words became both soothing and confusing as if she was being charmed by the melodic tone of his voice but without understanding the actual words. His speech and demeanor were calming and reassuring and she followed him, trying to comprehend, but feeling as though she was being led by the hand as a small child. She shook her head slightly to clear it, and again heard a distant, sharp cry through her mental fog. But his voice drew her back and she continued to follow obediently. Once before, she had trekked behind a person in these dark woods and had been changed forever. She wondered where she was now being led and to what purpose?

Charles spoke of many things, Pamela catching only partial phrases. The forest and its wilderness, foreigners, ancient people, chemicals and plants all blended together into an indecipherable mass of words. He then slowly began to speak of her and her life, talking about her past and almost reminiscing about her family.

The gray blandness of his robe seemed to dissolve his words and reform them into a tranquil cadence that soothed her ... reassured her. Yet, all the apparent safety that was now being offered by his presence would not completely cover an uneasy feeling arising from some deep instinct.

The distant cry heard moments ago grew somewhat clearer but was again pushed back by the calm voice that lead her deeper into the woods. Pamela looked around desperately, seeking anything that might help her discern the truth or at least ward off the feeling of complete tranquility he seemed to bring.

Not all he seems, more than we could have imagined.

Memories of the woman's voice tried to alert her and the cry high above became more insistent but the voice, with its softness and now with an intimacy that embraced hidden parts of her being, soothed her apprehension. Why did she feel so powerless in Charles' presence? Was he what he seemed? Or was this a false peace … an illusion that would lead her to her final destruction?

He walked slightly ahead of her as if leading her to an important occurrence, but the words, they spoke of her inhabitations and fears. The words told intimate details of her life, unfolding her bland existence before her as if holding out the promise of healing and salvation. He seemed to possess an uncanny knowledge of her difficult past, her hidden and repressed torment and offer a balm of solace.

"You are most unique, Pamela. Of all of those who dwell in these great woods, perhaps in the entire world really, you are without doubt ever so special."

His words seemed to flow from the grayness of his garment, indistinct and soulless. She could only understand a few words for they blended into a fog that distorted her vision and twisted her senses.

"It is the blood, Pamela … your blood to be more precise. I realize you do not comprehend the significance of your importance to us. But now that the lost sheep is to be returned to the fold …" He stopped and turning looked directly at her. "You have no idea, do you? Ah well, you will still be remembered for all times for your contribution in restoring the Tlaltecuhtli. After all, the birth of an empire requires the death of a Goddess."

She shivered in spite of the tropic heat as if a frozen shard had been plunged into her heart. What was he doing to her?

"Charles," she wanted to say. "Who are you?" Her instincts told her to flee, but her mind had been captivated by his calming words, binding her tight and holding her helpless. She was in his power and unable to resist, for part of her mind told her to surrender, that he had come for her … for her healing.

Yes! That was it! Charles was the healer.

It was he that had been with her in her trails. Not the forest, that impression was false. She had been seduced by its hardships, but now, now Charles had found her and would free her. She must run to him, throw her arms around him for protection.

Perhaps … perhaps, he even loves me! Yes, he would save me, maybe even give me the love I've never had. The woman … she poisoned me, more than drugs, they filled my body with hideous poisons! The woman was the false one and had tried to keep me from Charles, sending me to my death in the forest.

She then remembered the touch of his hand as they descended the tree. It was deliciously warm and inviting. Pamela stood before him and prepared to yield to him. He would surely do whatever was best for her.

Charles stood near with a bemused smile and held out his hand, "Come Pamela, the wonders of the old people await us. It is a new era."

Her mind was now totally wrapped in the same gray mist that covered him as seductively as a shadow. He gently grasped her hand and she found delight in it. His touch spoke the language of the black pit and extended to her its dark offering of peace.

They walked together through the forest, he softly talking, and Pamela head down and mute. After a short distance farther Charles glanced back once again at her. A curious look crossed his face causing him to draw close to her. He stared in puzzlement at her thigh and suddenly his face distorted in anger.

"They dare!"

His exclamation was more of an explosive hiss. He grew close and stooped down close to her thigh. She stood in confused submission as his fingers traced over her moon-shaped companion. Pamela trembled at his touch; it was violent and seductive. It was inviting and revolting. He rose up and grabbing her wrist glared into her face.

"Who … who dares to interfere with my destiny?"

She stared blankly at his rage, her mouth open yet speechless. He yanked her forward and continued at a madly increased pace pulling her in the wake of his swift strides. They had traveled for a short distance more when the cry above became angry and urgent.

Charles suddenly turned and raised his arm over his head while uttering a curse and a startled shout of pain. Large, dark wings beat about his head causing him to drop her hand as he attempted to ward off the sharp talons of the forest bird.

She shook her head and saw a horrifying expression of intense hatred and unbound cruelty cloud Charles' once placid face. Pamela backed away dismayed as he fought the attacking bird, and then turned and plunged into the deep woods as terrified as if the beast was once again in pursuit.

An hour later she was fairly certain that she had lost him, but now her depression returned for, despite the seductive darkness of his company, Charles was the first human seen in days. Her struggles would now continue and, most distressing of all, she was once again alone.

CHAPTER THIRTEEN
Vespers of the Tropics

Even in the dimness of twilight, the vista before her was extraordinary. She had for some reason assumed that Brazil was flat or gently rolling at best. How could she know otherwise? For the trees had always prevented her from seeing more than a stone's throw in any direction. Now she was looking down upon the subtle variation of colors lying hundreds of feet below. It was breathtaking. It was all green. But the variety of green was astonishing. Deep emeralds muted by the evening dusk laced with brighter olives and limes lay directly below. Farther out soft, feathery mounds contained earthy, dark jades mingled with smoky, gray tones that recalled the silver-greens of willow bark in the fall.

Here and there small patches of fog drifted through the upper foliage, carving light and dark patterns that brought texture and variegation to their billowy forms. She stood atop an immense ecosystem. The soft crown of the leafy canopy was silent, but she knew within it lay an incredible richness of organic life. The activities of millions of creatures hidden beneath the protective trees were now obvious to her.

Pamela was stunned and humbled to think that she had traversed the forest, somehow survived it. During the last week she knew that day changed to night, but within the forest the transition was gradual and always muted. Now she stared in quiet fascination as the sun spread its final glorious touch of warmth and disappeared, leaving behind a rich, reddish glow as if the treetops had been anointed with an evening blessing. She had just witnessed the vespers of the tropics.

As she continued to stare at the expansive valley, now dark and the domain of the night creatures, she rested her hand upon the wounded cat's chest to again check its respiration. *It's too shallow,* she thought, though she had little experience to guide her. Its eyes, once bright and wild, were dull with pain and only half-open. They had been that way for hours. She could not comprehend how it had guided her to the rocky shelter after enduring such grievous gashes in his shoulders and neck. Pamela felt helpless, she wanted to cleanse them, somehow tend to them, but she had no knowledge of how to proceed. The wounds themselves, though vicious-looking, were not as concerning as the infection that had quickly set in, leaving dark, oozing spots of festering illness.

She glanced up again at the valley to find it not only now dark but also blurred by her tears. The cat twitched suddenly and struggled to lift its head. It held it slightly up for a painful moment and then collapsed and began to pant heavily. She shook her head helplessly and stared at its prostrate body.

How did you find me? Was it your last effort to protect me, and why?

After her confused encounter with Charles and escaping whatever he had planned, she was convinced now that it was filled with darkness. She had become more despondent than ever. Then somehow, the cat had come. She remembered the heart-wrenching sight as it slowly limped towards her, stopping for a time to allow its severe pain to ease. Its once sleek form had been savagely ripped and its hind legs quivered with exhaustion. How long had it searched for her, especially in such anguish?

Their journey to its lair was not long in distance, but had consumed much of the remaining day. Sometimes the cat would stop momentarily, with its head held low and muscles twitching, it seemed to be looking around for water. She patiently waited for it, all the while filled with loathing, for she knew that it was the beast that had gleefully ripped into it. The brief but violent clash that she had heard was obviously the cat's valiant efforts to protect her. The fight had been short, for no forest creature could possibly stand before the hatred that drove the beast's warped nature.

Twice during the arduous journey the cat stopped and sat down, tongue hanging out and its chest struggling for air. It was during these pauses that she noticed a large bird silently watching. She could only wonder if it was the one that, with some innate forest wisdom, had protected her. She stared at it and knowing nothing else to do, nodded in acknowledgement.

Finally she was led to a rocky outcropping with a small opening that formed a shallow cave. It was from here that she had glimpsed her first view of the Amazon from above. Her arrival flight over the land had been at night and the long boat trip showed nothing but muddy water engulfed by overgrown vegetation. From here though, she saw the land drop sharply away and she had stared in fascination at the soft expanse of billowing green before her.

Far out, winding sensuously through the fertile land was a deep brown line, obviously a great river. *The Amazon*, she wondered? In reality she had no idea where in Brazil she actually was. Why did she trust so easily? She had chided herself.

She stood where she had watched the sun set, but now it was far into the night and the cat was near death. She had felt helpless when she had wandered through the land, but now she felt both hopelessness and rage. The grossly damaged animal lying before her had given its all for her, even to the point of death and she was powerless to do anything but watch.

Its respiration had become shallow again and its festering wounds were beginning to give off a fetid odor. Now and then its muscles quivered briefly but it mostly lay still. She knew the end was near. Suddenly she sat down by its side and with a cry, struck the earth violently with her fist. She stared intently at the suffering cat and then rising ran into the darkness. Perhaps she could find something to place upon its wounds, something to absorb the poison, somehow staunch its deadly advance.

After several yards into the forest she realized how foolish her impulse was. Even with her improved night vision she would not know what to look for. Still, she had to try, attempt to provide some relief to the cat's suffering. Tears streamed down her face as she glanced helplessly around. She found, partially by feel, a few broadleaf plants and quickly tore off a few leaves. Perhaps they would work. She turned to start back and heard the forest's night sounds. It was at this time that the cat would come to her, coming to curl up by her side. She choked back her tears and listened thoughtfully to the woods.

After a few moments an unexpected calmness came upon her. She remained still, quiet for one of the few times since she had been in the forest, tranquil in her feelings and just listening ... allowing her new instincts to emerge. Her mind, with its recently created synaptic connections and enriched blood, was waiting to assist her, lying dormant until brought forth for service.

Head down, she remained still for a long moment. Finally, she went forth again into the darkness and not knowing why or how, gathered a small flower. She smelled it and gathered three more. Then she searched for a few minutes until a certain low plant yielded a large, fibrous root. These items she carefully wrapped into the larger leaves and hurried back to the rocky lair.

Upon returning to the cat she laid out the plants before her and found a smooth, flat rock. She then scraped the dirt off the root and smashed it into a stringy lump. It gave up some liquid and allowed her to mix in the blossoms, crushing them with a smaller rock.

Pamela stared at the mixture for a moment and then rose quickly and dashed again into the forest. A short time later she returned with a handful of small berries and added three to the concoction.

This is stupid! I have no idea what I'm doing!

But her calmness prevailed and she carefully placed the mushy substance upon the wounds. The cat either knew she was trying to help or was too ill to resist. Either way it remained still as she placed the final protective broadleaf to cover her messy preparation. Then she sat by the still form realizing how bone-tired she was. She looked out over the valley and saw the stars in the clear night sky; they were indistinct as her grief and tears obscured their beauty. Not knowing what else to do, Pamela curled up by the cat's side and slept.

CHAPTER FOURTEEN
Blood and Power

The confusion, if it were not for the screams of anguish and terror, would have been comical. Startled men ran about, some searching for weapons, some for hiding places, a few grabbing long-handled cattle prods. The beast had suddenly returned, crashing through the brush and into the camp, glaring, lips back and crouching low as if wanting to ravish the entire group. Then it came at them, seizing the nearest man and savagely ripping his chest and thigh. Most scattered.

Samuel and two others, after regaining their composure, forced the creature back into its cage by repeated use of the cattle prods and finely subduing its rage with a tranquilizing dart. The native that had suffered the violent attack was writhing on the ground gravely wounded by the beast's claws and teeth, but his torment seemed to come mostly from the yellow froth that quickly began to seep from his torn flesh. The technicians tried to hold him still and were beginning to treat him when Samuel pushed them roughly away. He then calmly drew a revolver and without a word, shot the native twice.

Andrew jumped as the loud reports pealed though the forest. "Damn, Samuel! You killed him!"

The technician that had confronted him earlier raised his fists and screamed, "Why? We could have helped him!"

"He would be dead in minutes. I did him a favor."

Samuel turned away, ignoring the outraged man and walked to the caged beast. The warped animal was unmoving except for a slight twitch in its jaws and its heavy breathing. Its eyes were half-open, set with a malevolent glare in its drugged state.

Andrew stared at the scene, horrified at the unexpected violence. The creature had been highly agitated when it returned to the camp, looking as if its thirst for blood and carnage had been stimulated without finding fulfillment.

Samuel remained at the cage for a long while with his hands thoughtfully rubbing the back of his thick neck. He seemed to be saying something to the creature, but his voice was too low to be understood.

It took several hours for the horror of the sudden attack to pass. The quick killing was still a shock to Andrew who watched Samuel with contempt, though careful to avoid eye contact. The beast had gradually wakened and sat morosely in the back corner of its confinement as if it were sulking. Its eyes however remained filled with intense hatred. Most of the men gave it a wide berth glancing warily at it as they attempted to bring order back to their small camp. Two of the natives had dragged the body into the woods and returned a short time later, silent and with heads down.

Later, Andrew awoke and saw Charles sitting on a log that had been rolled close to him. He seemed absorbed in whatever was contained within a palm-held computer that he compared with notes in a black, leather binder. Samuel was leaning over his shoulder and commenting upon various items that seemed important to their task. Without looking up Charles unexpectedly said, "Well Andrew, I hope we did not rudely rouse you from your slumbers." His tone was even more sarcastic than his normally irritating manner. Andrew remained silent. He must have dozed off and had not heard Charles return. After a few more minutes of quiet but intense discussion, Charles stood up and walked closer to stand over him. His face had large, red welts and a wrapping that only partially hid deep parallel slashes from his forehead to his lower cheek. His mood reflected the angry cuts and the grayness of his appearance seemed to seep into Andrew's being causing a chilled shudder. Andrew stared at the wound for a moment and could not resist commenting.

"Pretty vicious sheep around here."

His remark caught Charles off guard for a moment and anger flared in his dark eyes, then his focus regained its inner arrogance and he gave a slight smile. "Ah my friend, the forest is full of mystery. I just encountered a slight one that I must ponder. Only a fleeting trifle."

Andrew became disgusted at his overbearing and condescending manner.

"I'm not your friend and you're an arrogant jerk!"

Samuel's head rose up at this with a slight smile crossing his lips.

Charles looked amused and drew closer to Samuel holding his hand to cover his stage whisper. "Careful, Samuel, he might snap his bindings and turn upon us any moment."

Andrew glared impotently at the two and then just lowered his head, thinking the blackest of thoughts.

After a few more calculations with his computer, the last ones added by hooking it to a small satellite dish to apparently access some stateside data, Charles sat down again and looked serious.

"You are quite costly my ..." he stopped and smiled briefly, "Andrew, I should say in deference to your boldly stated preference. Yes, very costly for that short communication link was several thousand dollars. However it, and with this you should be very pleased, showed quite definitely that your blood is acceptable. You will receive your first treatment immediately. Samuel will first require you drinking a small amount of the plant mixture we have procured at this encampment. I am told that it is not very pleasant, but it is necessary."

A technician approached with a small beaker of heavy, green liquid and held it towards Andrew.

"Go to hell!" was all that he could think of, and clamped tight his jaws.

The young tech leaned close and whispered almost with sympathy, "He will force it down your throat and probably choke you while it's going down. Believe me, it's much easier this way, and it's not poison."

Andrew shook his large frame defiantly and was immediately grabbed and held. The slimy potion was poured into his mouth and he gagged. After a few moments of misery, they had forced the entire amount into him and his mouth tasted as if something had died in it.

Charles had watched with amusement and then reached into his pocket for something. He tossed a small object towards Andrew letting it fall in the dirt by his bound feet.

"I am not totally without compassion. This may make up for a small amount of your discomfort." With that he turned and walked towards the other side of the camp and conversed with the natives that had been nervously guarding the caged creature.

Andrew looked down to see a small candy mint lying just out of reach.

Several hours had passed since he had been forced to drink the "gunk" as he called it. Andrew had expected to experience some ill effects but outside of some minor cramping of his stomach he felt ok. He had not eaten well since his captivity, so it was hard to tell just how he felt to any accurate degree.

Charles seemed intent on having the group complete last minute refinements of some plant-derived potion and get them moving to another location. During the last hour of their packing he seemed to enjoy annoying Andrew with reminiscing on his achievements while dropping oblique hints about his purpose. It mostly seemed the fantastic ravings of a madman and Andrew soon grew weary of his smug banter. Finally, a word was repeated often enough that he grew curious and asked, "What is all this babble about old blood?"

Charles perked up at this and looked please that perhaps a true conversation might occur. "Ah my ..." he stopped and began again, "Andrew, I meant to say. Andrew, you have blood within your veins that, by way of your father, is descendent of our ancient people. He was, by way of his father, half-blooded. Your mother, while no doubt a wonderful person, was unfortunately of common stock. Thus you are satisfactory but not perfect. We need at least half old blood in the veins. Therefore your role in our quest for reinstating our great heritage will be one of experimentation. Be certain that it is assuredly important, although due to your mother's unfortunate genes, less than we had hoped for. There is another however, that, when we relocate her, will also contribute to our great quest for restoration. Her blood is exceptional in its purity as her father was the actual last of the old ones. Both his mother and father were pure."

Andrew looked blankly at him, convinced more than ever that he was a lunatic.

"You seem puzzled, Andrew," Charles continued, "but it is all a matter of heritage and genetics. Our blood carries much of this genetic code that by way of our lineage, makes us who we are and in this case, more importantly, who we may become. The one that I will assuredly find once again is quite special, for unlike you, and unfortunately also unlike myself, has a much higher degree of pure old blood. But of this, you need not to be concerned. It is doubtful that you will meet her. Your contribution will have been completed by then. In fact once we gather at a very special pool your involvement will flash by quickly ... a brief, but never-the-less glorious moment!"

With that Charles turned and left as Andrew's horrified expression distorted his face with helplessness. He could no longer restrain himself and shouted in desperation at Charles' retreating gray robe, "You're honest to God nuts!"

The gray form stopped and turned. Charles slowly walked back with a bemused grin.

"Perhaps you don't understand, you have no choice in the matter so you might as well accept your fate. But in fairness, I will try to explain what you will become. We are altering your DNA by adjusting certain areas of the strands to be more receptive to blending with animal proteins. Most experiments have been dismal failures, but other scientists have not understood the one crucial key to success ... I do." He said this quite casually, but with unbearable arrogance.

"That key is the necessity of a trigger substance. It's really quite simple. A catalyst must be introduced to make compatible links within the centromere. This is done, not with other animal proteins, as others believe necessary, but with plants. It is at once simple and complicated. We are wonderfully evolved. Our blood is close to seawater as most know. Most, therefore, believe we have evolved primarily as animal life. Yet we have a remarkable symbiotic relationship with vegetable life. But the exact connection, found in minute cell processes, is more difficult to determine. You see, my equipment has extended our range of informatics by ten to the sixth power, which greatly aids our research. It is this preciseness that allows us to fundamentally adjust the messenger RNA. This I am sure you realize is the key, Andrew. We will actually be able to change the conserved sequences. And this," he gestured to the forest, "is obviously, even to you I would think, a wealth of materials for our needs. It's the plants Andrew. We are all linked to plant life in ways others cannot imagine."

Charles paused for a moment as if questioning how much to reveal to Andrew. He then continued as if uttering a profound truth. "The potion that is now within you is adjusting your blood chemistry so that the next dose of animal serums will be accepted … thus beginning the transformation. The complete process should take several days, possibly a week at most. You will receive a second plant serum prior to the animal serum. Perhaps tomorrow."

Andrew looked in disbelief at Charles and then his eyes quickly crossed the camp and stared in dismay at the chained beast.

"That's what you're doing? Was that once a man?"

"No, no; that was only a forest creature. Most interesting, don't you think? Imported actually … one of our best efforts to date, though we expect more dramatic advances soon. And just think Andrew, your contribution will provide the breakthrough. Does this not make you proud? You are to be our first human!" He paused again and placed his fingers together as if about to say something of great importance.

"Unfortunately the other subject has temporarily eluded us, which is a shame for as I said her blood is far richer. However here you are and we will make do. 'Tis not deep as the ocean, nor as wide … '" Another infuriating smile and he continued, "I see you are fascinated by our creature, no doubt wondering what you will become. The intriguing part is … I don't know. Our computer models, I mentioned that you were quite expensive, project many fascinating possibilities, but in reality it is still a great mystery. You will remain human … well, we think mostly so. But there will be some aspects that may be very disagreeable to you. I hope you find it all as captivating as I."

Charles stood over Andrew with his wide smile, teeth white and perfect, a most charming smile. It terrified Andrew.

"As for being nuts, I believe the cliché is, 'Good Lord man, you're insane!' and then you must add, with great passion of course, 'You will never get away with this!'"

He drew closer to Andrew's face and in an almost whisper said, "I'm not insane, Andrew. And, most unfortunate for you, I will indeed get away with it. Perhaps if we were back in Atlanta ... but here ..." He looked about at the vastness of the forest and gestured with arms wide spread, "Well, who will stop me? There is no law ... in fact, here, I am the law. And if the truth be known, I am about to control the so-called laws of nature."

Andrew looked at him in disbelief, "It's not nature's laws and surely not your laws. You're screwing around with God's laws!"

At this Charles looked suddenly serious and most deadly. His flippant demeanor vanished abruptly and with a very quiet but chilling voice said, "Perhaps your God ... not mine. My gods are ancient and when one understands them, most powerful! Some of my ancestors, not all, but the bold ones knew the source of their power. It is the blood. Most of them incorrectly believed that the gods desired appeasement by offerings of blood. This was only partially true, for the letting was intended to bring change. Regrettably the changes were incomplete and therefore my people were forced into decline. We were chased from kingdom to kingdom, to finally arrive here, displaced and with history and knowledge in fragments."

With this Charles drew even closer to Andrew and hissed, "I stand at the threshold of reviving the ancient secrets of life and death, Andrew. Pray to your God for mercy, for my gods will shortly demand your life!"

CHAPTER FIFTEEN
Changing

Astonishingly, the cat's fever had broken. Its respiration was still shallow but mercifully now regular and unlabored. Had her concoction actually worked? She had slept fittingly the rest of the night — both from her deep concern for the suffering animal and also from the nagging questions that incessantly grew from her bizarre experiences.

She stared at the jaguar lying quietly at her side. She could now begin to see its returning health as the rising sun placed the lair in a soft haze. *Impossible,* she was in the heart of the Amazon, inches away from a forest creature that should have either silently avoided her, or simply killed her. Yet it had shadowed her — protected her. And she had somehow devised a concoction of plants that evidently had stemmed the poison and now seemed to be supporting the return of its strength. Pamela placed her hand upon its chest and thought she saw an eye slit open. Only a few short hours ago it was near death. She shook her head in disbelief and tears welled up, but she was smiling as a warm joy worked its way into her soul.

"Please live," she said softly, "please stay with me. I have no one now."

She looked out over the green pillows of forest treetops and knew what she must do. She must find the woman. She must have answers, for how had she known what plants to pick ... and how much to use? Just a few hours ago, she had run in panic ... stumbling franticly and blindly through a strange, dark forest. Yet somehow, she had gotten it right!

How? she wondered, *What in heaven's name had been done to me? I must have answers!*

Pamela blinked back the tears and stretched out her hand as she had done so many times before. "Why can't I see you change? I know you are changing I can feel it now!" she whispered to her body.

The woman ... she knew! But how do I find her?

She took a deep breath, remembering last night … how she had forced herself to stillness … made herself listen. Pamela quieted herself and waited.

Staring above into the greenness of the leaves she waited. She waited in earnest silence for a long while, yet nothing came. Finally, she patted the cat gently and gathering some water in a large cupped leaf left it by its side. Giving it one more hug she said, "Please wait, I'll be back as soon as I can." Feeling foolish, as if it would understand her. She then set off, not knowing where, but in need of finding the village, the woman … and hopefully, with her help, desperately needed answers.

It was midmorning before she found anything familiar, no real landmarks were obvious to her for all the trees were high and of great girth. All was verdant, all directions looked similar.

How did the natives find their way around?

She was used to streets with houses and signs and numbers. And at least if she did get lost there would always be someone to ask for help, or she could even use her cell phone.

Suddenly the sorrow of leaving the cat along with a feeling of growing desperation brought the return of her blackness. It was impossible! She knew she would never find the village or the woman or now even her way back to her cat. *My cat*, she thought. Yes, it had come to that. Her only source of friendship … her tenuous link to sanity. *And now*, she thought, *even that was probably gone*. She sat down glumly, feeling like finally abandoning her struggles.

How long had it been now, how many days lost? Even Charles would be welcome at this moment.

That thought immediately brought an unbidden chill to her. As she sat holding her forehead with depression and weariness working their way back into her spirit, a quiet chirping sounded from above, a sound that was now familiar. She knew that the large bird was somewhere above.

Go away! How much more can the forest give to me?

Pamela thought of the cat, her cat and its persistence, and reluctantly looked up. The dark bird sat a few feet above staring at her with the same intense eyes as she had seen in the forest temple. "Do you also want to help? The cat almost died you know. Go away!"

They continued to stare intently at each other. In a moment the hawk spread its broad wings and gracefully lifted into the air. It swiftly dodged limbs and wove its way for several yards ahead of her. Then, as silent as a gentle breeze, it returned to her and continued its penetrating gaze. Another moment passed and the bird repeated its swing through the forest and returned. Pamela glared at it.

"Forget it, I know what you want. I'm not going."

The hawk again flew its route this time with a piercing cry.

"Please, I'm so weary," was all she could mutter as she slowly rose and obediently began to follow the bird. She had followed the old man into the darkness unquestioningly. She walked into the unknown forest at the unspoken bidding of the woman. She had allowed her body to be anointed with mysterious oils and she dumbly followed a forest cat farther into the deep woods.

"Good Lord," she mumbled, "I even would have followed Charles to who knows where. I'm repeating my life back home. I can't even make one decision of my own!"

Yet she continued to follow the bird. Though anger with her indecisiveness made her clench her hands into small impotent fists, something else came to her attention. She thought she knew where she was! The forest was becoming lighter, not in brightness, but the air was somehow more alive, fresher. *The Temple,* she thought. *It must be near,* for the fragrance of flowers and potent loam was increasing.

All the memories of that dark night, the pounding sounds of the drums, the cool liquid that soothed and seduced her … all came upon her. Images of the attack and her frantic, impossible dash through the dark woods … her panic as she stared up in shock at the moon, lying lost and hopeless in the forest. She had been led to the very place that began her plight several days ago. Now, in the light of day, as muted as the lower forest was, brilliance shone from between the majestic, sentinel trees that ringed the sacred space with their towering and resolute protection. She could see small glimpses of brightness that indicated a richness that she had not yet seen in her days of journey. She was drawn to this light, compelled to go forward. The hawk flew directly between the guardian trees and she watched it soar up and out of sight commanding her to follow.

CHAPTER SIXTEEN
Avocado Green

"Avocado Green."

Marie glanced up for a moment with a perplexed expression and then continued to complete her transaction. An elderly lady, slightly bent and supporting herself with a polished oak cane, carefully placed the bread into her oversized purse. Marie had gently wrapped it in white waxed paper, reversed it and wrapped it once again. She then put it into the store's paper shopping bag. The woman smiled, nodded and moved with surprising swiftness through the door. Andrew, Marie remembered had always insisted upon carrying on his father's old ways, even to double wrapping all baked goods and then enclosing them in the store's old-fashioned bags.

"Plastic is plastic … cheap!" he would say.

Marie glanced over to Michael, who still gazed at the satellite photo of the lush Amazon. She smiled thinking this was the fourth time he had "just dropped by".

"Sorry Mike, I needed to take care of Mrs. Shay. She's really sweet. What's up about avocados?"

Marie was a full head shorter and tilted her head back to look up at the young man.

Was she standing a little closer this time? he wondered.

"Oh, just a silly thought," he said. "My grandmother had green, shag carpet. They called it Avocado Green. Don't know why I thought about it, guess it's the photo."

He turned towards her again and she expected the customary, "Sorry, nothing new about Mr. Guanetu." This time however he said, "We have a little more about that guy you said was here before he disappeared. Tracked the information down from the card. You know, the Biotech thing."

She continued to stare up at him now with even more interest. Perhaps there was some hope. Marie missed Andrew … missed his kindness and his slightly offbeat humor; she especially missed the gentle fatherly conversations they had when the store was slow.

Andrew had been showing her how to make some of the goods and she had been determined to keep the shop open and stocked as best she could. She grabbed a small sign and placed it in the window officially closing the shop for lunch.

"Is it allowable to buy a detective a sandwich? I've got to hear every detail. Let's go over to Bernie's. "

He followed her out the door, having to hurry to keep up. Did he dare hold her arm as they crossed the street? He hesitated and then decided not to.

The small cafe was not crowded and they were seated at a quiet table by the back wall. They had just pulled in their chairs when Marie could wait no longer.

"Please Mike, tell me what you have found." Her voice became sharp and urgent and Mike felt he needed to be very pointed in his response.

"I'm sorry Marie, I'm not trying to get your hopes up. This may not have anything to do with Andrew's ..." he caught himself, "Mr. Guanetu's disappearance. I'm not sure what to make of it really. The card is from an organization that has many arms, mostly dealing with biomedical supplies. It is owned by a Charles Smith. Interesting fellow, apparently originally from Brazil, though I'm not sure if there is a connection here."

They both remembered the satellite picture.

"He came here some years ago, a graduate of the ... uh, Universidade de Brasilia." He stumbled slightly on the words. "Pardon, I don't know foreign languages very well. From there he came to the States and went to Georgia Tech. Got a Masters in Biomechanics, whatever that is. At the same time he also got a degree in Anthropology. Apparently he's some sort of expert in ancient South American cultures. Then the guy gets a Ph.D. in some kind of 'plant stuff'." Mike shook his head slightly as if he found this amount of intelligence both impressive and slightly distrustful.

"Anyway, about three years ago he started this Biotech business. No one is sure just what they do and they don't seem to have many customers. I guess the guy has wads of money, apparently from numerous biomedical patents he developed while in grad school.

Out of curiosity, I found one of the old faculty members that remembered him. 'Damn brilliant, but irritatingly arrogant,' was all I could get out of him."

He looked across the table and saw her face filled with disappointment. Mike fidgeted for a moment looking for something to say.

"I don't know if all this really ties in ... if at all. Sorry Marie, I know it's not what you hoped for."

There was a long silence, both absorbed in their private thoughts. Finally Marie nodded her head morosely and stared into her cup for a moment more. He held his silence allowing her to struggle with her frustration. After a while she looked up and smiled slightly. "Thanks Mike, I really appreciate the effort. I know that you have gone far beyond what is required. I'm really afraid ..." She hesitated for a moment, "Mike, I'm afraid this is not going to turn out well."

His hand moved forward awkwardly, wishing to take her hand ... to offer some sort of support. "I'll hang with this as long as I can Marie, you're worth ..." he caught himself again, "the effort's worth it."

She rested her elbows upon the table and lifted her teacup before her. After a small sip she lowered it slightly and peered over the brim. There were small tears in her eyes but her smile towards Mike was very warm.

CHAPTER SEVENTEEN
The Temple

They must be centuries old! she thought as she stepped between the massive trees for the second time. They formed the outer confines of the temple and each were several arm spans in breadth. Her eyes followed the swift path of the soaring hawk as it skimmed the gray trunks that ran limbless far above her before branching elegantly into a vast array of delicate branches wrapped with lush foliage.

She remembered several days ago when she fled past them as panic from being abandoned in the tropic darkness overwhelmed her. Then, they had appeared as formidable as unyielding guards securing a Bastille.

She remembered her terror as she first stumbled between the trees and fell to her knees, certain her life was about to end. Now the interior of this great place was filled with a solemn serenity, as if some hallowed occurrence had just brought peace and blessing to the forest. Each massive trunk still held the large, carved candleholders with leather bindings firmly attached at head height, their spent brands now only trails of dripped wax. These were the sconces that created the eerie light that had heightened the seductive atmosphere of the strange nocturnal ceremony. The hours of darkness that had left her forever changed. And changed in bewildering ways that she neither understood nor desired. She turned and stared upward, studying the towering space. It was all different. A week ago it was a place of dread.

Now, saturated with health and vibrancy by the intense sunlight, the temple was stunning!

Yes, she thought, *this was most surely a temple ... elegant in its immense majesty but inexplicable as to its existence. Why ... why was this place to be found in the heart of a vast uncharted wilderness ... secluded secretly within a forest with few people and nothing that anyone would think of as civilization?*

Bright light poured down from its open center. Cerulean sky, the first seen directly overhead, was warm and beneficial. It not only brightened the space but also soothed her aching spirit. She walked farther into the temple reveling in its luxuriance, head held in a solemn tilt as if expecting the intonation of celestial music or the utterance of a divine pronouncement.

As Pamela moved silently across the soft forest carpet, a serene sense of the familiar came upon her. An accord stemming from a sensation of rightness … of a flourishing healthiness, suggesting the way the world was meant to be. A natural harmony of earth and vegetation and all inhabitants of the immense forest lay concentrated within the boundary of the guardian trees.

A kindred spirit stirred within her, a quickening of recollections, not from her altering experience of several nights ago but rising from some previously dormant memories, somehow instilled deep within her. This place was foreign to her, still forbidding and strange, yet there was a haunting familiarity that she could not identify, one that hung like wispy fragments of a dream, indistinct and disembodied.

Memories of her first encounter in the temple flooded back; the pool was to her left, its surface tranquil and reflective. Ahead were the sturdy pillars enclosing the mossy altar, their surfaces glistening within tropic radiance. And fragrances … the bouquet from multitudes of blossoms, the pungent scents of forest plants and odors of potent soils enriched the air, rushing into her lungs like a seductive embrace. She saw that most of the flowers were encircling the pool. They filled a large portion of the back edge, growing from the rocky outcropping that formed the boundary of the water.

The trees in this area had sent their gnarled knees to the water's edge and firmly gripped the rocks as if giant fists had reached out from above to lift the stony formations skyward. The poolside trunks had delicate lichen splotching the smooth bark with gray-green veins of feathery growth.

Dark emerald plants with slender swords for leaves gracefully hung suspended over the water poised to refresh themselves with its cool moisture.

Then the low, tan stones that fashioned the front edge of the pool drew her attention. Her stomach instinctively tightened and she drew in a sharp breath as she remembered the black body of the immense snake that had silently draped the top ledge of the wall. Thankfully it was nowhere in sight, though she found a slight tremble beginning in her legs.

But it was the stones themselves that held her attention. In the darkness they were no more than a lair for the serpent. Now, brightened by the sun that fell upon the soft stone, subtle shapes and intricate patterns became visible. Carvings within the rock's face allowed forms and shadows to recall a language of ancient times. The patterns were foreign yet familiar ... glyphic that she knew must be symbols portraying the history of a great people. It was all too much ... too much to absorb.

She backed away feeling bewildered and overwhelmed by all that had happened to her. She couldn't bear anymore. Her hands covered her mouth to keep from screaming for someone to help her, but knowing that none would come. The magnificent trees formed a great boundary and she was sure her screams would be sheathed and then absorbed by their primal power.

Pamela looked at them with renewed awe. They rose straight upward expanding into a great, leafy vastness more intricate than the complex stone tracery of soaring gothic cathedrals. She stared upward in wonder as the sun worked its path over the myriad of supporting limbs and branches to touch the delicate leaves. The light then tumbled through to finally reach the forest floor covering it with subtle patterns infinitely more inspirational than any stained glass of human temples. She listened carefully as if seeking a message of salvation proclaimed in the creaks of branches and slight rustle of the leaves as the upper wind currents played upon them.

Was she, she wondered, in paradise or would she find it an illusion and be forced to retreat again with her questions unanswered to the darkness of the forest. To wander once more with no reason to be ... to continue perpetually confounded by the mystifying transformations she had experienced.

A soft cry from the hawk interrupted her reveries and she watched it silently glide from the temple heights to gently alight atop the encompassing pillars of the altar. Pamela saw then that she was not alone. There, before the soft, mossy circle … the place where her body had been anointed with potent ointments and exotic oils stood the woman. It was she that had sent her fleeing to the safety of the forest. She stood silently staring at Pamela for a moment and then, sitting down on the altar's risers, she smiled.

CHAPTER EIGHTEEN
A Friendly Conversation

Odd! Andrew thought, staring at the markedly different man sprawled casually on the ground in front of him. He was stretched out comfortably, almost lounging and chatting in an amenable manner as if with an old school chum that had been a friend for ages.

He wasn't sure which Charles he preferred. The Charles that had taunted and tormented him with insufferable arrogance and condescending remarks or this new and seemingly incongruous image of a straightforward and agreeable companion. He was relating to Andrew information regarding his condition and what was to be expected. The discussion was serious but this new side of Charles had adopted a casualness that conveyed an almost soothing demeanor, as though all would eventually be well despite the compulsory unpleasantness. Of course, it would be Andrew that would bear the main effects of this necessary procedure, but nevertheless it was presented to him as being an honor.

Andrew could see now, how this person could persuade people, bend them and lead them in whatever direction best fit his personal vision of purpose. Gone was the overbearing attitude of self-aggrandizing. Instead, the new side of Charles presented a quiet confidence and almost gentle manner, that wished for nothing more than understanding of the essential appropriateness of what must transpire.

He was carefully told that his DNA would first be altered and then reconstructed. This was being done for reasons that would eventually better the fundamental direction of nature and correct the inherent folly that was now ingrained within mankind. Charles was the close friend that was explaining the rationale of this as he calmly unfolded the sequence of events ... the expected changes that would develop as the process ran its course within Andrew's body. It was not a long story and its brevity reflected the fact that this was also true of his life.

Andrew felt as if he were sitting in front of a wise and kindly old doctor who had been charged with relating the details of an illness to him. He heard words of caring concern and facts that indicated the course of his ailment and details of his condition. The words were technical and of no meaning to him. Changes brought forth within minute cells and molecular structures were discussed but of no significance to him. Derivatives of plants and potions extracted from animal proteins were gently and sincerely explained and their expected reactions summarized for him. The final outcome, still uncertain and experimental, was presented in a voice filled with compassion.

The conversation then drew to an end with Charles smiling and gently patting Andrew upon his knee to rise and slowly walk away to the center of the village where he would oversee the administration of another stage of his treatment. Then they would proceed to take the three-hour hike to a forest pool that he had heard mentioned several times previously. Whatever was expected to occur there was unclear. The only sure thing to Andrew was the certainty of his condition. It was assuredly terminal.

CHAPTER NINETEEN
Cinta

Pamela stared incredulously at the woman. It had been at her urging that she had been thrown into an experience so bizarre that all questions, especially those that had driven her to this spot had now vanished. Her mind was overwhelmed and could not sort through the vast urgency that had been her companion as she wandered through the forest, compelling her to try to bring comprehension to her situation. Now a clutter of subconscious and shapeless utterances tried to organize themselves into the urgent questions that seemed so vital only moments ago.

Before her was only the second human face that she had seen for days and now she desperately tried to sort out a flood of fundamental issues that she had carried endlessly through the woods. Her head reeled and her mind could not focus upon any of the myriad of possibilities. All were now trying to surface at once, clamoring for attention.

She stared blankly at the woman, her mind whirling with a blur of uncorrelated thoughts.

How, how is it that I am still alive? The cat ... the cat came to me, mostly at night ... though now it's my companion. It almost died! Why? Why has this all happened ... happened to me? My body's changing! What did you do to me? What am I now! Why!

The temple swirled and everything before her blurred. Her respiration grew rapid and darkness enclosed upon her as she collapsed unconscious to the soft earth.

Slowly the cool water brought the green of the tall canopy back into Pamela's focus. The woman gently cradled her head in her lap and was wiping a damp cloth upon her forehead. She stared into her brown eyes, slightly set in a strangely similar fashion of an Asian indigenous or native cast. Her skin was medium brown and she had a pleasant, round face. Small, white beads of various sizes comprised a short necklace and were like the earrings that fell from each ear. Her thick hair was dark and cropped short as if cut with a crude, dull instrument. Remnants of black face markings with hints of red showed upon her forehead and upper cheeks.

Pamela thought how strange it was to be held gently in the arms of a savage. This woman was native to the deep forest, perhaps a descendent of headhunters. Perhaps her tribe even now, Pamela's eyes widened and she struggled to get up.

"Shush dear," the woman said softly while pushing her gently back. "You have had undoubtedly great difficulties. Rest and be quiet for a while."

Once again she heard the strange, lilting cadence in her voice. Pamela obeyed and sank back trying to figure out how she should respond. Struggling with her emotions she finally asked, "How did you know to come here?"

She was puzzled as how the woman had known to arrive at this place and at this very time. Was she waiting here all this while for her … here, at this spot all of the time she was struggling desperately through the forest? The woman smiled and glanced up at the bird resting placidly above.

"And how is it that you came here?" she asked in return.

Pamela was puzzled and then she followed the woman's eyes to the hawk. "Why, the bird led me … how did …" She shook her head, confused and with growing aggravation.

"Please," she suddenly blurted out, "I have so many questions. How is it that I'm still alive? That bird follows me. I think it even protects me. It's impossible! Too much has happened! I'm changing …"

Her head spun and she couldn't hold another thought.

"For God's sake what have you done to me?"

Her voice shook with pent-up frustration. "My whole body is doing strange things … there's even a cat!"

Again the woman smiled gently but a new look of deep concern surfaced and she softly said, "Yes, questions … there are many questions. I will answer as well as I can. But you must know that I am quite limited in what I do know. I am one of the few in our tribe with some schooling but my background and education in these matters is far too little to understand. And there is much old knowledge that has been lost."

Her voice trailed off and broke slightly as if recalling a fragment of a forlorn tale that was only partly known. There was an earnest tone in her voice and Pamela felt whatever the words would be they would be truthful. She looked around at the temple trying to draw strength from its tranquility. Knowing that she must have answers, she struggled up and sat next to the woman.

"What happened that night? Why did you take me into the forest and do those things to me?"

Pamela looked the woman directly and saw her bite her lip as if seeking the proper way to speak of something unspeakable. After a small pause the woman stiffened slightly and began. "You were brought to us partly by years of design and that night, by good fortune. We didn't know where you were for many years but some of us never gave up hope that you would come."

Pamela's brow knotted and she felt the vertigo close around her again. This was nonsense.

Return to us?

Her anxiety increased and she felt more helpless than within the adversity of the forest. She grasped the woman's arm and struggled to pull herself up from the mossy steps.

"This makes no sense. Please get me out of here!"

Her voice was now becoming shrill and ringing with desperation, "I want to go home! Please, please get me home!"

Tears welled up and she struggled to keep from hysterics. "Where is Charles? He got me into all of this, let him get me home. It's not fair!"

The woman looked distressed and a great sadness darkened her face. She gently placed her arm around Pamela to comfort her and said, "Yes, it isn't fair. You have been subjected to more than anyone could ask, and without anyone to speak with or bring you understanding. Forgive us."

She chewed on her lower lip again and stared up at the high foliage as if entreating the temple's gods for courage.

"Charles," she said, "yes, I suppose it all does start with Charles. He was always different, strange and gifted with a way of leading those about him. He was taller, smarter and quicker to understand, even when just a youth. He was also quick to challenge, even the elders … even the Shaman. He would form little bands of the other youth to explore the land. After a while he was more content to go off by himself. Some say he found the hidden village of the old ones, but of this he was silent. Our Shaman was certain that he found out the message within the stones. It was after this that he grew more distant from us. Finally he disappeared from our village. He was still young, maybe fourteen years or so. We found out later that he walked all the way to the logging camps and from there went to the large cities to enter school. After this we knew no more." She stopped at this, as if to continue without some respite would be unbearable.

Pamela was caught up into the story. She remembered the same woman weaving a tale within the candlelight gloom of her hut and the elegance that flowed with its simple telling.

After a pause and a half-smile directed at Pamela that seemed more intended to shore up her own courage she continued, "It was many years until we saw him again. He had grown and changed much, but his arrogance remained. As did his leadership, for he divided our people, deceiving many to believe that his talk about the old ones and future glory was the truth. Many though did not believe him and our Shaman challenged him. It was at this time that our Shaman grew sick and quickly died. I am the only one left that has some understanding of the forest and the plants and animals, though I'm not a Shaman."

Again a pause and Pamela could see the strain that the story was bringing. She held her forehead and kneaded it gently for a moment as if trying to gain strength. Then she continued, "You have heard me speak of the old ones. This you need to know … this you must understand. Many, many years ago … many of our generations ago, a remarkable people came into our forest and lived among us. They looked somewhat as we do but were like gods to our ancestors. Their wisdom far surpassed even our elders and Shaman. They were driven from their land and had wandered from place to place and after a while were once again driven even farther, finally coming to our forest. They were wise above all, yet they had a great burden that they carried with them and with it, a great sadness."

At this the woman hung her head slightly and in an almost whisper said, "They also had a great stench of blood upon them. It was not the kind that offended the nose but one that came from their heart. Yet with all their knowledge, they were a sad and weary people. It is said that they came to us wanting only to find peace and a resting place. They stayed with our people and gradually their minds seemed to diminish and as they died out, so did their wisdom. Our people always believed they kept most of it within their hearts as if sharing it would call for too much, even require us to give up our own blood. Some of them married into our tribes, most of them kept to themselves to keep their blood pure. Yet in all this, they remained a sad people. After many generations the last of the old ones died. As much as they tried to keep their heritage alive, they seemed to tire and the immense weariness of some great trials finally extinguished them. It was told that they came long ago from a vast city that was beautiful and contained imposing marvels. But something happened that made all their knowledge distorted and dark. They developed a thirst for blood and it became deadly. Powerful foreigners came and conquered them, killing many and driving some of them away to seek other lands. We were the final resting place for a desperate few of them."

Pamela found that she had huddled closer to the woman and was now intently listening as if this dark tale somehow involved her. Perhaps there was something that might explain the changes within her.

After another deep breath to steady herself the woman continued. As she spoke the sun worked its course above and streams of intense light fell through the center of the stone columns to drench the mossy altar with a radiance that demanded attention to her words. "Over the many years a few of the old ones built a village as their home. It was unlike any other my people had ever seen. Somehow they were able to dig the earth and form stones.

Some of these were carved with symbols whose meaning was unknown to us. They erected an immense place that rose in a series of long raises that had a great stepped building on top. This was eventually abandoned and reclaimed by the forest. It was said that the top of the structure was open and led down to their secret place beneath the village. There, some continued their bloody ways. Most of this is now only tales from long ago. The children of the old ones also lost most of their knowledge. Only one thing remained from them."

At this the woman's voice grew quiet and in an almost sacred tone whispered, "Among the stones with the writing ...," She pointed to the rock wall by the pool. "... there were bottles of strange potions and mixtures that we could blend with certain plants. These, the old people carefully used to strengthen their blood. We never understood this and assumed that it was brought from their old cities. The old ones were said to be one with the great forest. My people live within our land and our Shaman knew many things, but it was said that the old ones were in balance with the forest and could understand through their heart," she placed her hand reverently over her breast and with an intense look continued in a hushed manner, "... through the blood that drove their hearts, what the plants and earth said. They also seemed at peace with the animals, being neither hunter or hunted. They never ate the flesh of the animals but sustained themselves upon plants. They greatly surpassed even our wisest Shaman. They seemed one with the forest."

Pamela stared at her, the tale had struck a frightening cord deep within her, but the cause was still indistinct, as if she was hearing something of vital importance to her, but in a haze that distorted the true meaning. She was pondering these words as the woman's tale continued.

"When you came to us that night we took the last of our precious, old oils and anointed you."

Pamela stared numbly at her as the significance of this final statement began to penetrate. They had used some ancient and powerful potions from a culture of blood worshipers upon her. Her body was subjected to a primitive ritual from the bloody past of some savages. She stared at her body in dismay.

"Dear God, what have you done to me? Why?" Pamela sank down to the ground hopelessly repeating the word. "Why? Why?" She looked up to the woman expecting some answer but only saw a horrified and wounded expression as if the forest lady's world had just collapsed.

"Forgive us," she said so softly that it sounded more like a mournful breeze. "We had no idea what the potions would do to you. We could only hope that your old blood would sustain you, adjust and help revive our diminished tribes. We still don't know what it will eventually do. Forgive us." She said this so quietly that it was hardly a movement of her mouth.

"We could only pray to our ancestors and whatever creator there is that you would be protected ... that somehow you would survive. If Charles had taken you as he planned you would now be warped beyond belief. We have seen his works. They are hideously evil!"

Her tone and mood was quiet and desperate as if there was an urgency driving her. After taking a swift breath she continued, "I told you that Charles was always strange ... detached from us as a people. He is also brilliant. Our people are not unintelligent but we are inexperienced in many ways, especially of things beyond our forest home. After Charles found out the darker part of the old people, he left for many years. This I have already said. He studied about the plants and what deep mysteries lay within them. Even our Shaman could not understand all of this. All we knew was that his return would end our simple life and distort the goodness that lies within our forest. He will pervert us and twist our minds and bodies in an attempt to use our natural skills and the powers of the old ones for his own purpose."

Pamela's dismay and rage began to fade as she listened to the woman. She remembered the depraved look of Charles as the hawk furiously tried to ward him away from her.

With a weary sigh the woman continued, "Our people have lost most of our ways and peace now anyway. As I said we are now greatly diminished. Years ago people came into our forest and cut our trees and tore into the land with machines. They also killed many of us who tried to fight with them. Even the ones who came to help us brought sickness and death to us. This has left any expectation for our future generations greatly reduced in strength and numbers. You were our last desperate hope."

She took Pamela's hand into hers. The years of hardship and uncertainty were in her eyes and her voice now grew tired and aged. She stood up and led Pamela towards the pool.

"Please come", she said wearily. "This too is part of the story, the part that eludes us but still is the mystifying strength that will revive our people."

She led her to the stone wall that enclosed the front of the tranquil water. There the woman pointed out the carvings within the rock's face. "The old ones told us many tales, some written in the stones. This one tells of a goddess that had many children. Some of them wished to kill her but an unborn child within her protected her. The other stones tell of a poor and sick god who becomes a great sun. They said that their Empire would have a glorious rebirth, but that it would first require the death of a goddess."

Pamela stared at the inscriptions. They were strange, yet familiar to her. She somehow knew these markings but could not interpret them. It was more a sense of being here before, of having the stone's meaning buried somewhere deep within her, however somehow inaccessible. Pamela sat wearily down upon the pool's edge and shook her head. Perhaps she could make the woman understand … make her help her.

"I still don't understand you," she finally said, "I'm just someone who has made a tragic mistake. I don't belong here. I need to get home. Don't you understand? I was here trying to get experience for teaching, and I suppose even some adventure for once in my life. But I'm not supposed to be here involved with your problems. I'm sorry for them but I desperately need to get home. You took me to your ceremony and my emotions overwhelmed me. Your drums, your drugged water, it was all too much for me!"

Pamela's voice was now filled with desperation. Then she hesitated and lowered her eyes, "I even took off all my clothes!"

The woman looked up at this and smiled. After a moment she broke into a little chuckle.

"My dear, our world is much different. We do not need your fashions here." Still smiling she placed a comforting arm around Pamela. "Perhaps you were just returning to the old ways. We are all brothers and sisters here and there is no shame."

Pamela tried to return with an embarrassed smile but it was halfhearted and ended up to be just a distortion upon her face. She sat down and tried again to be understood, "I still don't know why you took me! Why not one of your own people, get one of your own tribe?"

The woman looked bewildered for a moment and then stared intently at Pamela. "Of course! You really don't know do you? Charles never told you. Now I understand your confusion!" She looked solemn and said simply, "My dear, you *are* of our tribe."

Pamela stared in disbelief. The woman was surely mad.

"Your father's father was Krekon. His mother was called Apoena. They were both descendants of the last of the old ones. Their blood was pure. People from outside our forest, they called themselves missionaries, came to help us, though we were content. They brought sickness to us and many of us died. Your father's parents were among them. When they died, your father, still a child, was also sick and the foreigners took him to be cured. They never came back and we found out later that he was taken to America to live with the missionaries. You were born of your father's seed and now are the only one who carries the blood of the old ones. There are stories that perhaps other tribes may have had some of the old people but of this we have no word, though we did understand that Charles might have brought another to the forest. This is still unclear to us."

Pamela was stunned. This was nonsense. She was an American, a melting pot American. Now she was to accept that part of her heritage was rooted within the dark forests of Brazil? That her father was a savage, a throwback from Stone Age savages?

Impossible! Mother was English and my father was ... She grew uneasy and bit her lip remembering. Her father was an orphan. He

... she stared at the trees above ... he was the adopted son of a missionary couple that died when he was a teenager.

She stared anew at the woman. There was no savage here. There was gentleness and wisdom within her face, a curious mixture of brown skin highlighted with faint, indigenous features. These people only wished to remain within their home, to live a simple and contented life in harmony with the forest. To the world they were ignorant and without sophistication, but in reality they had a profound understanding of the truths of nature. If anything, Pamela thought, she was the savage. Those from outside these great woods were the violent intruders that had brought death and destruction to the forest and its people. The woman stood quietly before her as if expecting no answer.

Yes, Pamela thought, *I am the savage here!*

But now a new awareness began to surface. If this was really true then she was also a native. Impossible! The dark wings of vertigo again overtook her and she collapsed to her knees and grasped handfuls of the soft earth. She was a native? This was her tribe? She stared at the dark, fertile soil as it spilled through her fingers. This was her land? But why was she changing? Why was her body capable of such incomprehensible feats?

She looked up at the stone wall before her and at the strange symbols carved within their face. They were still unintelligible to her, but one she did recognize. A moon with strange surrounding runes lay in the center of the low wall. It was curved and sinuous and in the shape of her tattoo, set before her like a word of either deliverance or damnation. Could this be what would allow her to finally understand the strange occurrences?

"Why?" she asked, looking up with hope. "Why is this symbol here and why have I carried it with me all these years?"

At this the woman looked relieved as if she had been expecting Pamela to hurl her years of pent-up frustrations and anger at her, berating her for her suffering. She shook her head slightly as if to clear these trepidations and said, "When we found out that your father was in America and had just had a child we were in great upheaval. Our people were dying from the diseases and were fighting to keep our land. But we were driven back farther into the forest as the great trees were cut. In desperation we sent one of our women to find your father and see if you could be brought back. She took part of our potions with her. She, as we, believed that the old ones' ways might be brought back to reverse our grave plight. The tattoo was the way of getting the potions within you, to mature as you grew. We were startled when you chose the temple's symbol. This was not planned but came from your heart."

She paused to see if there was some understanding of the desperation that drove them to such costly extremes.

"You still have this precious blood within you and we believe it is now enriched in ways we cannot understand. As the tattoo allowed the potions to mingle with your blood over the years your body was being prepared for our final anointing. We lost track of you for a long while but Charles unwittingly brought you to our village. We simply sent Toma to bring you to us before he sent his men. It worked long enough to allow us to have the ceremony. When we were attacked you fled into the forest. We would have never found you if not for your guardian bird. Pamela, we have no idea what the potions will do to you ... what to expect. We are praying for you to finally restore us ... keep us from going into extinction. But we still do not know what to expect."

She then sat down uneasily on the stone wall and stared directly into Pamela's eyes, brown eyes fixed upon brown eyes.

"God forgive us, we are desperate."

With this heartfelt utterance the great strain of the small tribe's ordeals overcame her and she began to softly weep. Pamela was bewildered by all these words but her heart went out to the great sufferings that this woman and her people must be enduring. This time it was she that offered comfort as she instinctively held the sobbing woman. As she tried to soothe her she wished that she had been able to just once hold her mother ... to embrace her as she was this stranger. It was a long while before either broke the silence; each contented to let the past hour be held at rest by the tranquility of the temple.

Finally, it was the woman who rose and said, "We must go. Charles is still looking for you and they will soon notice that I have gone from the village. Trust in yourself and what your instincts tell you. I know it is hard but you have unseen friends watching over you. You will be well if you trust your heart."

Pamela grabbed the woman's arm, "Wait, I can't accept all this and then just wander back into to forest! I'm not made for this life. I'm still just a small town girl from Iowa. And my body is changing. I understand things, but don't know how or why. How can I believe all this?"

The woman simply said, "Your gifts will sustain you. Depend upon them and depend upon your guardians. We must go now."

The woman turned to leave and once more Pamela again grasped her arm. "Wait, at least tell me your name and how I can find you."

With this a peaceful smile lightened the woman's face.

"I'm sorry for my rudeness, I am called Cinta. Trust your new friend my dear."

With this the hawk swooped low and glided through the sentinel tees and into the forest.

"And the cat," Pamela said earnestly. "Why does it follow me?" It was sitting quietly by the outer trees. For how long she didn't know, but it had apparently sensed that it was time to arrive. It looked as if its health had returned and Pamela's heart was surprisingly glad.

"So many things I don't understand," she continued, "why do I have a tame cat? Aren't you afraid?"

The woman stared at the sleek animal and grinned.

"This also is your gift. The hawk and the serpent along with the magnificent creature sitting before us all came the night of the ceremony. We were at first startled but realized that your blood was indeed powerful. It called to them. They are as wild as any within the forest. They came to you, not us. Go now Pamela, and seek peace as you grow."

Cinta stepped forward and gently kissed Pamela's cheek. Then turning quickly, she disappeared into the dark woods.

Pamela was alone again except for the comfort of the cat ... her cat. She stared at the tranquil water. It looked clean and cool.

But the snake! she thought, recalling its large form draped sinisterly over the stones. As inviting and refreshing as the pool looked she sighed and walked toward the waiting cat. It rose as she approached and rubbed against one of the barrier trees. She gently touched it upon its shoulder and with that the two walked between the trees, returning to the forest. Returning to the place she was told was her heritage.

Andrew was yanked rudely to his feet and pushed forward.

Good old Samuel, he thought, *always to be counted on for being ...*

He went through countless insulting names trying to find the most appropriate for him. Andrew decided that they were all fitting and rattled off a series of vile expletives towards the boorish, squat man ... under his breath of course. They were on the way to the pool ... the infamous pool.

He was tired of hearing of these exotic places that were unknown to him, especially since it probably would be his last stopping place. He longed for the comfort and warmth of his small bakery and wondered about Marie. She was like a daughter to him. He loved her company, especially since he seemed to always be too busy for marriage and children of his own. In fact he never had much interest in women in general, finding most of them either shallow or too aggressive. Also he knew that his idea of romance and the mystique that he believed to be the very heart of romance was considered out of touch with the real world. The woman that would captivate him, intrigue him would need to be the embodiment of mystery. A modern Circe, hopefully however less inclined to change him into livestock.

His stomach gurgled a bit and he wondered if some strange things were starting to happen in him? He didn't feel much different though after the last dose of gunk before they left and wondered when to expect changes to begin, and wondered with great trepidation what they would be. He needed something to distract him from whatever lay ahead. Andrew admitted to himself that he was frightened; in fact it all terrified him. He was again jerked forward and let out a curse towards Samuel, this time out loud. Samuel glanced back at him and only smirked.

CHAPTER TWENTY
The Serpent

Was the forest brighter?

She couldn't tell as she walked on in stunned silence. The cat stayed close to her side as if sensing that she desperately needed some form of companionship. The trees seemed more majestic. Was this really her forest? Was she truly a part of the Brazilian landscape with these people as her tribe?

Tribe? she thought, *A strange word to apply to any family relationship.* This was only for primitive people, surely not her. She looked with new interest at her body.

Old blood? What kind of people would the old ones have been, to be so respected, and at the same time, so feared by the tribes? She looked intently at her arms and flexed her hands.

Suddenly she turned and stared with open mouth at the Jaguar. "Good Lord!" she backed away a step. "You are a wild animal!" Yet she really had no fear. The cat sat down and patiently waited for her to make up her mind. She turned again to inspect her body. Her legs and arms were stronger; she could feel more power in them. But this would happen with hard exercise at home.

"Dirty!" she said. She looked at the buildup of mud and sweat from the days struggling through the forest. Suddenly the pool and its cool water became overwhelmingly inviting. She needed to feel clean again. Even if it wouldn't last she desperately needed to feel some relief from the constant forest grime she carried. Perhaps she could think more clearly with a quick rinse. She remembered the woman's warning that she was hunted.

"I promise I'll hurry," she said and turned back towards the sentinel trees and the pool within the temple. Pamela passed again between the ring of trees and was once more within the serene temple. *Strange,* she thought, *how much this place first had made her tremble so.* Now it was like returning to a place of rest. Perhaps a rapid wash would refresh her, prepare her for however long her next stay in the forest would be. She approached the tranquil pool, its surface still as glass reflected the rocky boundary at the back.

Sweet fragrances drifted across the water from the hundreds of blossoms that lie at the base of the trees.

But the snake! she considered, as she peered into the depths of the pool. It was pristine and as clear as the bright sunlight. She could see all the way to the rear of the pool and saw nothing. Besides my cat is here, she assured herself as she slipped from her tattered clothing. The water closed around her as she glided into its luxuriant coolness. Shimmering ripples bounced across the surface and distorted the foliage's reflections as if caught in an impressionistic watercolor. The water seemed to caress her with both sweetness and a seductive embrace. Her tiredness melted and floated away with the accumulation of soil and sweat. She drew energy and a new vitality from the liquid as it enveloped her within its nourishing essence. Pamela lay still, allowing days of soreness and tension to soak away. Her cat peered over the rocky edge and then settled down as if a sign of approval, yet with head held high and ears up and alert. She sighed and reveled within the pool's embrace and enjoyed the serenity of the temple.

Time passed and she abstractly reminded herself not to dawdle, to be aware of any danger, but the delight of being clean pushed back any fear. After a long, luxurious soak she began to wash out her clothes. They were beyond torn now and much of the plant stains were now permanent.

As she rinsed them within the clear water a sudden chill rose across her back and was then gone. She looked around but saw nothing. The temple remained as tranquil as before. She slipped into the wet garments and prepared to climb out of the pool, then sighed and sunk back into the water.

"Just a minute more," she whispered to the cat and let herself float blissfully once again within the beneficial liquid. Time seemed to be suspended and the water's touch healed her body and soul. She was at peace … all was well.

Suddenly she sensed a great wrong! Something of immense brutality was approaching from just beyond the guardian trees. With a short growl the cat slipped out of the temple and she began to rise in panic. Someone … something was coming! She tried to bolt out of the pool but before she could react she felt a sudden pressure beneath her. With that she silently disappeared beneath the water. She struggled for a brief moment but her clipped scream was ended as she was pulled to the bottom of the pool and then dragged towards the back rocks.

Eyes closed and hands frantically flaying at the strong, black coils that enveloped her, her lungs began to grow desperate for air. Her mind screamed in terror as she was towed across the sandy bottom. Then just as quickly she was released.

Her face broke the water with a cough and she took in quick gulps of air. She could just stand with feet on a sandy bottom and head barely above the surface. But all was dark. She twisted her head around to see that she was somewhere without sunlight ... and she assuredly was there with the serpent! Pamela fought back panic and desperately searched for an escape. Then she saw a slim sliver of light slightly to her right. She crept slowly forward and saw that she had been dragged to the pool's rear and under its rocky outcropping. Inching a little farther allowed her to peer over the fading, small ripples that marked her disappearance.

From this position she could see that a group of men had entered the temple. Only legs were visible to her and she counted several people pacing around the edge of the pool. Some were dipping containers into the water and then, rising up, disappeared from view. Several appeared to be native legs but she could not be sure of this. If she had not been grasped and pulled to the spot beneath the rocks they would have surely captured her. Then who knows what they would do with her. *But the snake!* Was it still somewhere close by, perhaps directly beneath her?

Panic began to overcome her again and she moved her feet with chills that made her tremble. Then she saw another pair of legs, these were shackled and stumbling as if being jerked forward. The legs staggered and then collapsed showing a large man striking the ground and disappearing behind the front wall. He was quickly dragged upright and it seemed as if another man had struck him as he was pulled forward.

Then, before she could adjust her position closer to see what had happened, other legs came into view. Pamela froze, for these she knew. They were thick, strong, black leathery stubs that stood over the pool. Slowly a massive head bent low and hovered just above the water's surface. Two red eyes glared across the water staring directly at the spot that hid her from sight. They glared with brutal menace as they fixed upon her.

The beast was with them! Could it see her? Had it discovered her and was it now pointing at her? She froze and tried not to retch as its foul and gangrenous smell drifted across the water to fill the tiny enclosure that hid her. Her heart pounded against her ribs and she began to shake uncontrollably. Then the beast lowered its head to the water and began to drink. It took two laps and screamed with pain, shaking its misshapen head and howling as if scalded. The creature backed away and rolled trying to rub its fanged mouth in the dirt. Men pulled on its chains and tried to upright the writhing beast while laughing and with some speaking in native dialects. Then as if this had been a sign, they gathered up more water in glass containers and were gone.

Pamela remained hidden, safe for a moment. *Were they really gone?* She didn't have the courage to go out to see. Then she remembered the snake. She held her breath as if this would keep the lurking serpent away and peered carefully out across the water. With an uncontrollable shudder she carefully glided out from beneath the rock and looked about.

The temple seemed empty. She waded across to the front wall trying to move silently while half-expecting the snake to strike her. She frantically ran the last few feet and quickly pulled herself out of the water turning to stare at the pool. Nothing was there except quieting ripples where the last vestige of her presence faded from the surface. Pamela continued to stare at the pool, now still and menacing. She shuddered to think that a short time ago it had been so inviting and tranquil. It had cooled her, soothed her. How could something that contained a presence so deadly be so seductive?

As she continued to reflect upon this, she gradually became aware that the water was slightly stirred and a black form was slowly emerging from the pool. The darkness then materialized to become the large head of the serpent. It gradually pulled its thick body several feet out of the water to stand directly before her. Its long tongue flicked towards her twice and then it remained motionless.

They stared at one another for a brief moment, Pamela transfixed and paralyzed with fear. Then as unhurried as its appearance, it sank down into the pool and was gone. There was not one ripple to mark its being there. She cautiously backed towards the trees with eyes fixed upon the water. A low cough behind her told her the cat had returned. She finally turned to greet it and then proceeded to the forest.

At the edge of the great trees she stopped and hesitated. Pamela turned back to the pool to again face it. Its surface was still and shiny, now as calm as glass. She stared in astonishment for a moment and then stepped forward a few paces.

"Thank you," she said quietly. And then touching her cat she disappeared into the forest.

CHAPTER TWENTY ONE
A Place of Darkness

Why? Andrew wondered, *Why would we travel all that way to the pool and then abruptly turn around to trudge back to the village?*

The men glanced about now looking nervous and any small talk had vanished after they left the pool. The confident swagger of the younger technicians was gone and they whispered together as if something disastrously important had showed up, or perhaps failed to show up.

The beast, now kept sedated and chained, periodically growled and shook its head as they journeyed, as if the water still burnt it. He was thankful that something had postponed whatever treatment they had planned for him at the pool. The temple he mused, with its pool of enigmatic clear yet dark water. When the small troop had first entered between the towering trees that enclosed the serene leaf-vaulted space he had been awestruck. The place was alive, bathed with brilliant sunlight that had worked its way through the domed canopy and touched the earth with an extravagance that had warmed his heart. For the first time since he had been taken and forced to dwell within the gloom of the forest, his spirit was buoyant and a serene joy had touched his soul. Within this space, his mind had heard the blissful sounds of the forest gods calling for celebration. *So much for opera!* he chided himself. He had always loved the escapism found within the great operas. Their ability to transport him to idyllic and mysterious worlds helped ease his normally mundane life. Of course that routine existence had been abruptly interrupted and he now shook his head, reminding himself of the reality of his situation. He was a prisoner and his life was in great peril.

No hope here of a happy ending, he reminded himself. At least, he mused, the tragic operas had a redeeming value to their heartrending endings. There would be nothing noble about his approaching death.

Then a most curious thing had happened. As they approached the pool and while the others became busy with assembling and testing of the equipment, he had noticed movement from the corner of his eye, a very brief and disquieting shift in the water that indicated that they were not alone. The tranquil pool directly ahead of him had contained a dark form that was quickly disappearing into the shadows of the rear of the pool. It happened so fast that he believed it to be a trick of light, but with one exception … the water still contained faint ripples that indicated a passing presence. He had almost pointed and called to the others but held back. He had found through recent experience that the less said, the better. Besides, the mood of the technicians and especially Samuel had become exceedingly agitated as they performed some chemical tests on the water.

Whatever had disturbed the pool's stillness was soon gone and the small surface undulations had quickly vanished. No one else seemed to notice and Andrew quietly permitted a smile to accompany him on the return trip. It was nice to have something hidden of his own for a change … a small secret, even if it was also a mystery to him.

He also took pleasure in Samuel's discomfort. Since Charles had not accompanied them Andrew assumed that Samuel was in charge and was returning with some sort of bad news. He hoped that Charles would hand Samuel his head, except the transaction and any resulting unpleasantness might also involve him. *Oh well,* he thought, he had long ago stopped trying to anticipate events, besides, his legs were growing weary and he would be glad to get somewhere to be allowed to sit for a while.

The peace of the forest pool still lingered within his memory as they walked and he longed to return to the sunlight and the majesty that he had experienced there. He had no idea that the forest could have such a pleasant side. *Tristan und Isolde,* he wondered, *perhaps Pelleas et Melisande? Or maybe Dvorák? Perhaps Rusalka could be within the pool! Ah Andrew,* he scolded himself, *how long will you be such a romantic fool?* Would he soon begin to actually see nymphs? Yet for some reason, his heart hung on to the possibility that it was a water nymph that had stirred the pool. But unfortunately he knew that they were returning to the abandoned village, and it, unlike the bright forest temple, was a place of darkness, one reeking of death and soon ... his death.

CHAPTER TWENTY TWO
Lost Teacher From Iowa

Pamela loved Elm trees. They alone, of all the trees that she knew, were a form that represented a stately elegance, their refined shape resembling a gradually opening flower, perhaps an Easter Lilly. This was probably why Elms were planted along the main street of her hometown. The trees stretched out towards each other and embraced at the middle of the road to create an arch of soft shade, their leafy enclosure providing welcomed shelter from the summer heat to both walker and auto. They were not as imposing as the great trees of the forest, but they were familiar and friendly, companions of her childhood. In her youth she would walk down the street, sometimes kicking small stones that had become dislodged from the deformed sidewalks, whose concrete surfaces were chipped with age and raised and canted by the tree roots that pushed up to the surface seeking the summer water.

Her house was on this street, set back at a respectable distance, an indication of its earlier importance in the community. It was a stately house, erected on an important street lined with the stately trees and perhaps, through no coincidence, named State Street. But all that was from a previous time. All the large houses were now past their prime, plagued with constant problems from lack of upkeep, with paint chipping from the siding, sagging gutters and tall, old windows that made heating and cooling of the former mansions impossible.

If she would continue to walk south down her street and past her house, she would go through the brief downtown to arrive a short time later in the country. Little had changed since its earlier more prosperous days, mostly in the twenties, and like many other small towns having little industry, it saw businesses closing or limping along at best.

Once out of the brief business district and past the last few houses, the great vastness of grain fields would abruptly begin. The countryside seemed infinite, especially in the winter. On a snowy, gray day the fields of once high, summer-green corn would become indistinct and desolate, an expanse where the horizon was lost, and earth and sky blended seamlessly.

For thirty-seven years this had been her life and though it was as plain as the vast, gray fields in winter, it was still her life, life with a certain comfortable predictability. Yes it was dull, but it had a purposeful security in its blandness. It was also her past.

She looked up at the trees that she now walked among with renewed interest, trees that were such an integral part of the Brazilian landscape. They were huge, impossibly tall and though the trunks were constantly darkened by lack of direct sunlight, they remained imposing, even intimidating. *Was this now home?* she wondered? Could she truly be a child of such an exotic place? If this was true and if her father had stayed in the forest, then she would be as the woman, a daughter of the rain forest.

The impossible tale of the woman still rang in her mind. She had been walking for over an hour now. Much of the time just wondering if her mind could possibly absorb anything else before true madness would claim her. Again the dark fear arose of being absorbed into the shadowy mental illness of her mother and grandmother, the destructive pit of self-pity and bitterness. But *her* madness would be different. Her insanity would come from her mind being unable to accept such an overwhelming story.

After her days in the deep wilderness, the forest was no longer a place of gloom and dread; it was becoming a place of great majesty and power. But it was assuredly not *her* forest. It could *not* be her forest. This she argued with herself as she traveled among the great trees and pushed through the low tangles of brush. This was *not* hers! She fervidly repeated this to herself to hold on to what she knew as her life, as her past. This could not be her heritage! Yet a small shudder of realization ran through her as she tried to vehemently deny the woman's tale. A shudder that made her pause and gently finger her tattoo. She looked up into the vast green of the leafy shelter, and then touching a trembling hand to her mouth, knew that somehow there was no other explanation.

She whispered, "Impossible!" to the forest, or maybe to the cat, perhaps to no one.

She stopped and realized that she had been talking softly to herself as she aimlessly walked towards nowhere.

"I'm from Iowa!" she suddenly exclaimed to the cat. She looked again high into the lofty trees and screamed, "Lord help me! I'm just a lost teacher from Iowa!"

Tears welled up and flowed as the foliage greedily absorbed her outburst leaving only the constant forest chatter to remain, reinforcing her utter desperation and loneliness. In all this she knew that her mind now also came to realize a truth that she had unconsciously shunned, one that directly contradicted her words. She was not alone. There was now another in the woods, one that Charles had obviously arranged to be here. And more astonishingly, she also knew that she must confess that she was not lost. Pamela suddenly turned towards the direction from where she came and stared.

Days ago, when she had first encountered the overpowering might of the woods, she had been shocked by how quickly she had been confused by the dense growth and had become hopelessly lost. The forest had enclosed her in an endless tangle of brush, trunks, limbs and leaves, all dark and brooding and designed to bring her death. But now, she *knew* the forest. Somehow she knew! She saw the subtle differences in the character of the trees, their height, shape and texture. She saw how the brush was thicker in places and realized how smells and light changed as she traveled, and more than that … she knew exactly where she was! As incomprehensible as this was, she could no longer deny it.

Pointing an unsteady finger over the cat's shoulder she exclaimed, "That's the way to the temple, an hour and a half."

She glanced over her own shoulder to the left. "That's how we get to your lair."

The cat tilted its head at her curiously as she sat down close and spoke directly to it. "We go past the stream and travel up a slope. I know it is a slope now, about two hours from here."

She twisted around. "And I can get back to the woman's village if I return to the temple and go right for an hour. That way … it's that way. I can make it in half the time if I run."

She jerked around and nodded her head with clenched fists, "That way is the pit."

Darkness seemed to tumble out of the high trees at the thought of the place that had called her to yield to destruction … to hurl herself into the gray mist to end it all. Bile rose in her throat as she recalled the vileness of the discarded body parts that littered the stone stairway as it disappeared into the gloom.

"I will never go there again." This she declared with a shudder and great resolution. "It's impossible to even think of it."

With that she rose and continued her unwilling trek towards the direction of the dark, abandoned village.

Ow! Why on earth are they tying me up? Andrew wondered. The rope didn't cut into his wrists but was snug enough to be not only hopelessly binding but also extremely uncomfortable.

"Just where do you think I will go if I'm not tied?" he asked the native that had lead him to a small tree at the edge of the camp. There Andrew was pushed to the ground and bound. The man didn't speak. Perhaps he didn't understand English. Whatever the reason he simply completed his task and walked back to join a small group of fellow natives.

Andrew knew that his question was not entirely honest for given the opportunity he would definitely run for it. But to where he wondered? Surely he would never get back to anywhere he would recognize. And the most frightening of all was the assurance that the creature would undoubtedly be loosed to hunt him down. The picture of this was unthinkable to him. Yet, with the right opportunity he would rather face the forest and hope to somehow elude the beast rather than face the future filled with altering drugs, assured agony and most likely a very hideous death.

Yes, he thought, tugging on his bindings, *loosen these just a bit and I'm out of here!* He gave the rope another small test jerk and uttered a dark oath at the native's competent craftsmanship. He might work the fastening loose in a day or two, but by that time he probably would be dead.

With this he slumped against the small tree in total despair, desperately searching his inner being for some way to find even a small bit of hope. After a while he found to his surprise that he was softly crying. Andrew took a deep breath to steady himself and knowing nothing else to do, began to quietly hum.

CHAPTER TWENTY THREE
Andrew's Rescue

The cat sat down abruptly and stared at Pamela. He had been acting strange for the last hour, a restless mood that sometimes had him lagging behind, sometimes pacing and seeming as if he was nervous about something. Its head was up with ears alert as if he was anxiously expecting an attack and was preparing to bolt to safety. *Strange*, Pamela thought, *such a large and powerful beast yet obviously growing more distressed with each step.* She finally sighed and turned to sit down by it. *So odd*, she thought again as she placed her arm around its neck to comfort it, *this is the one that at first horrified me and now always brings me comfort.*

"What's wrong?" she quietly asked as she tried to ease its obvious agitation.

Yet she knew precisely what was wrong. They were now near the abandoned village. Close to the source of the great ill that had been filling the forest with trepidation for the last hour of their travels. The beast that had so severely ripped into the cat was obviously near. Pamela could feel it and was sure this was what the cat also felt. Its monstrous wrong was evident to her senses. Why had she come this far when she knew that the village both terrified her and called seductively to her?

It was growing dark; night was quickly approaching. She was now only a stone's throw from the perimeter of the village and the decaying and deserted place containing the horrors of the gray pit filled the air with a vile stench. *Did the ill-begotten beast make this its lair? That seems fitting*, she thought.

A slight tremble began within her legs as she recalled the depravity found within the village lying before her. Panic suddenly gripped her and she stood up to heed the cat's sense of self-preservation.

Run! She told herself. *Get out of here!*

Her mind rebelled at the thought of the decaying village. She had been again drawn to it, somehow seduced, as if something had dragged her against her will. She had once again succumbed to being completely unable to determine her own will. *Run!* she told herself again. She turned and tapped the cat upon the shoulder.

"You're right," she whispered, "we've got to get out of here!" The cat sensed her fear and quickly rose, also eager to dart from the place. Yet as she began her retreat, her ears caught a strange, out-of-place sound. She stopped to listen, intrigued by the unfamiliar resonance that drifted tenderly through the woods. Looking back to the direction of the village, she found it to be the source of the soft refrains.

Yes, Pamela was sure of it now. The sounds formed into a quiet tune that caught a gentle wind and drifted through the forest. It called to her. It was a mournful melody, beautiful and rich, full of passion yet tinged with despair. Its loveliness beckoned to her, overshadowing the ill of the pit. She hesitated and then slowly crept forward towards the refrain's source, drawn by its ardent call. The cat froze and lay back with ears flat to its head and tail twitching, as if confused by her stubborn refusal to flee from the menace lying just ahead.

This is impossible! Pamela thought, yet she knew in her heart that it must involve the man she had seen shackled at the pool. Possibly the one the woman referred to as brought to the forest by Charles. She shuddered and inched forward to see better. She crept along half-crawling, half-crouched over. The tension from being so close to the horror of the village masked the ease in which she moved. Her body glided gracefully over the earth but her rising panic hid it. Soft murmurs drifted from the camp but her ears focused only upon the mournful melody. She glanced back to see her cat pacing at a distance. But through all of this it was the call of the grave reaching out its seductive, gray tentacle that terrified her the most. The depraved vapor that oozed from the pit filled the air. It reached her and entered her lungs to tenderly coat and entwine her capillaries as if attempting to possess her soul. She felt like swooning but a gagging rose instead from her stomach. Pamela swallowed hard and forced herself to move forward. Directly ahead of her she saw a dark shape slumped at the base of a small tree. Another few feet and she would be directly behind it. Then she stopped. Something was wrong. The humming had stopped suddenly and all was still for a long while. Pamela stared at the dim figure of the man directly before her. His head was bowed and his large shoulders drooped with despair. Then a soft, muffled sound replaced the melody. His large frame hunched forward and quietly shook. Pamela placed her hand to her mouth in sympathy as he began to softly weep.

"Charles, you bastard! What have you done to him?" she uttered to herself.

Her anger pulled her forward to stop directly behind the tree. From there she began to struggle with the bindings that held him. Her hands trembled and she found the knots were beyond her skill. Suddenly he became aware of her and stiffened. With his head erect he listened intently. He remained still for a moment and then tried to twist and glance behind him.

"Shush!" Pamela whispered, struggling with the stiff rope. He said nothing but nodded his head. More time passed and she continued to be baffled by the strength of the rope and the complexity of the knots. Her heart pounded as she tried to find some flaw in the bindings.

"I wish I could help you but I'm tied up at the moment," the man whispered.

Pamela stopped and gaped at him. *How incredibly stupid!* she thought. *We are both in danger and he thinks it's funny.*

"Idiot," she mumbled resuming her battle with the ropes.

"Pardon me?" he said softly.

Strange, she thought, he didn't seem panicked. *Why not? I'm practically hysterical and he just thinks it's funny.*

Pamela shook her head and glanced fearfully about as frustration mounted. Then she tried to jerk at the bindings. He tensed and let out a muffled "Ouch!" She desperately tugged again and rubbed at the rope with her nails looking for a weakness. With this her longer nails sliced into the tough rope. She stared in the semidarkness at the small rip and then attacked the rope again with her hardened nails. They slowly yielded and the tear widened.

"Uh, whoever you are, I don't mean to hurry you but I believe they may be back over here soon." His voice seemed calm but tension made it shake slightly. She knew she was quickly running out of time.

"I'm trying! Ok!" she said impatiently. "I don't want to break a nail!" She fought at the cords again.

"Well, I'll make you a deal," he whispered. "Get me out of here and I'll get you to the nearest manicurist."

A few more slices and the bindings fell loose.

"Great, make it in Rio," she said self-consciously. "Now please be quiet and let's go."

Pamela watched him struggle to his knees. He seemed stiff and awkward, probably from being tied for such a long while. She retreated and tried to urge him on, glancing back and nodding at him to hurry. *Too much noise!* she thought.

"Shush!" she whispered. He stumbled forward trying to keep his balance.

After a few yards she thought, *Rio? Why did I say such a stupid thing?* She glanced back and saw him struggling to keep up.

It will be dark soon! she thought. *We will never make it.* She ran the few paces back and grabbed at his arm.

"Please! You've got to hurry!" She gave another frantic tug at his arm. "They will send the beast!" She saw the quick recognition of the truth and fear rise in his eyes.

"Don't I know it," he muttered and tried to hurry forward. They had traveled a short distance more when she saw that she was again leaving him behind. She gave another wave over her shoulder for him to hurry. The darkness was almost upon them now. Soon they would be caught within the total blackness of the forest night. She heard him fighting for breath. *We won't make it,* she thought again. He lagged back and then stopped, hands on knees, gasping for breath. Pamela dashed back and stood before him, her hands flexing in desperation.

"Wait," he gasped. "Just a minute, please."

He struggled for air and then looked up at her with a quizzical look. "Who are you?"

He stared at her for a long moment, squinting at her in the semidarkness. Then he smiled and exclaimed, "Or should that be, *WHAT* are you?"

He chuckled at this as she blinked with incomprehension. Then again with a nervous motion she grabbed his arm and pulled him forward.

"Just someone passing through from Iowa," she said desperately. "Now for God's sake, hurry!"

At that moment the terrifying howl of the beast echoed through the forest. Terror froze them both for a moment. Then they plunged ahead into the dark forest, knowing that now they were hunted.

CHAPTER TWENTY FOUR
Eternal Journey

Before time, a voice of unlimited power smiled and spoke a word of love into the darkness, calling forth a burst of brilliant light that filled the void as immeasurable particles of matter were brought into existence. These first elementary bits of nature, spinning randomly, would later combine into light atoms. One of these, a solitary oxygen atom, was created and expelled as were unimaginable others from that compressed core of energy that was that first cosmic discharge, the prelude of all life. This lonely atom hurled silently through space for billions of years until a slight but relentless gravitational pull drew it, along with innumerable others into a cooling and congealing accumulation that finally spun itself into a mass of planetary size. The atom drifted in the high upper atmosphere, tumbling through the thick, dark clouds, circling for eons in the midst of violent electrical storms and swift winds that launched it into a continuous loop high above the forming mass of solid land below. Eventually, at a time unknown to it, the oxygen atom met with two hydrogen atoms at precisely the correct moment to form a molecule of water. This mite of water, now within clouds of similar companions, whirled about for uncounted revolutions of the slowly cooling mass beneath to form a dense vapor that condensed into droplets of the liquid of life.

These precious drops of life-giving fluid, periodically struck by violent winds and chilled to below zero degrees centigrade continued their unhurried journey. At these times, the water molecule and its companions were changed to elegant crystal lattices that would reflect and refract the light into a myriad of colors. Then finally warming slightly, it reformed into a liquid and now heavy enough, dropped to the ocean far below. The tiny drop combined with trillions like it, helpless individually, to become a vast army of fluid that shaped and moved continents, their combined might slowly sculpting and shifting enormous masses of land over the age of planet making. The water circulated through the land, often in vast torrents that carved away mountains and formed rivers and lakes. These violent currents cut their way into large caverns that fell deep into the heart of the earth, moving swiftly past limestone crevices, swirling out small pockets that shifted and tumbled as fierce earthquakes and unrelenting volcanoes expanded their handiwork.

Its journey momentarily halted, the water drop found itself again sucked upward by steamy clouds and returned to the sky to resume its endless voyage. It then was returned in a brutal thunderstorm to rest placidly for years within a peaceful lagoon. Later, recycling continued as it circulated through the gills of large fish. Then darkness enveloped the fish as a lurking primitive crocodile swallowed it whole. The water molecule combined with other chemicals to become stomach acid until the creature pulled its tired and ancient body to the shore and fell victim to the nemesis of all life, age. It died with the unrelenting sun beating upon it. Finally, in the normal course of nature, it gave up its moisture to the clouds freeing the small drop to be once again lifted aloft. Years later it returned to the ocean, to be moved by slow currents that covered the globe, to brood in the semidarkness of the sea for countless ages. Then it was lifted to the sky to yet again fall to a high mountain stream over South America. The water collected into a river to flow and disappear into the ground fissures and into a large subterranean cavern, revisiting for the third time, to float blissfully with its companions. It was then scooped up into a metal container abruptly halting this particular journey. From there it tumbled into a mouth to disappear into the darkness of another creature, to once more continue its eternal journey.

Charles finished the drink of cool water gathered from the underground stream and stared at the cup as he pondered the ancient stone carvings before him. He was staring with anger and astonishment. He had missed something! All these years of thorough planning and he had not seen the most elementary and simple of signs.

The water! Somehow he had not taken into account the small but distinct image of a pouring cup on one of the stone carvings within his rocky subterranean lair. Charles stared at the remaining drops of liquid in the bottom of the cup with disbelief. He was stunned.

"They tainted the water," he said softly. He now understood. He had missed the simplest of things.

"They simply tainted the water," he whispered again into the darkness. His voice seemed calm but his words were tinted with ominous shadows. Then the cavern rang with shouts from above and the howl of the beast. He hurled the cup into the stream and made his way up the rough stone stairs, savagely kicking torn and decaying pieces of flesh from his way. Samuel was waiting in the middle of the camp. He ducked his head at Charles' approach and hid his trembling hands behind his back.

"He's gone, Charles!" he muttered. "Somehow he's gone!"

CHAPTER TWENTY FIVE
Eluding Capture

Andrew stumbled forward and desperately urged his body to pick up the pace. Sweat poured down his brow and stung his eyes. He ached and felt like throwing up. His heart raced and his breath came in short, frantic gasps. Finally he tripped and went down. Pamela was immediately at his side trying to pull him up.

"Come on ... it will be dark soon!" She sensed the quickly approaching darkness and thought of the first nighttime in the forest. How the blackness had rapidly engulfed her, immediate and complete. Now her strange, heightened acuity allowed her a degree of night vision. She could go on but was sure that she couldn't lead this man for even a short distance. Five minutes, maybe less and then they would be upon them. She shivered at the thought of the beast!

"Come on!" she snapped urging him on. She gave another desperate tug at his arm. It felt limp. He was exhausted after only a few hundred yards.

"Hopeless!" she muttered. "Hopeless!"

"I can't make it ... just can't." Andrew's chest heaved and he struggled to calm himself, "Sorry." He shook his head and sweat fell to the ground, "Please go, at least I'm out of there. Maybe ... maybe they won't find me."

Pamela sensed the desperation in his voice. He knew that he would be dead before light. She looked around frantically to see if there might be a place to hide. She pulled at him and whispered, "Down ... get down flat."

They could now hear distant sounds ... voices. Periodic stabs from flashlights swept through the forest. They were growing near. Andrew looked blankly at her for a minute and fell to the ground. He shivered into the tropic heat and then lowered his head and pressed his face to the ground.

"Keep very still. I'll be back," she said as softly as possible. Then she vanished into the darkness. He felt the sweat on his face begin to make a muddy paste on his cheek. Bile rose in his belly and he tried to swallow back his fear. He knew he was trembling. *Better here,* he thought. *Better here than at the village. Dead was dead but better here among the trees. Here in the forest.*

He thought of the woman. *Who is she?* he wondered. *Out of nowhere and here in the middle of the Amazon … Impossible!*

Then without a sound she was back. He started at her touch. She was rubbing some sort of material on him, covering his exposed skin.

"Who are …" he began.

"Shush. This is a moss. It will cover your scent." She then lay down next to him.

"Please, no sounds. They are almost here." Her voice was filled with conflict … part doubt, part command. Then a close-by howl froze them.

The next minute was filled with confusion and terror. Men were trampling throughout the forest shouting at one another. Strong beams of light passed through the brush and illuminated the lower trees. Some of them came within a few feet of them. Then it came. The gangrenous odor of the beast filled their lungs as its heavy feet crashed through the undergrowth. It sucked in great gulps of air attempting to get their scent. Andrew lay still and bit his lip.

Who are you? he wondered, trying to mask his fear by thinking of the woman next to him. He tried to recall her as she stood before him in the twilight. She was truly non-descript. He simply couldn't call to mind any identifying feature. Most obvious were her badly torn clothes.

Then a crash and something brushed his leg and let out a snarl. He tensed and bit his lip trying not to scream. Another poke at his ankle and it was gone. *Don't throw up!* he pleaded with himself. Then as quickly as they had come, the voices and flashlights faded and it was silent.

Pamela stared at his back. *Who are you?* she thought. *You must be the one at the pool … the one they had tied up.*

Andrew had his face turned away from her. He seemed to be a large man.

Long pants and shirt in this heat? He must be dumber than I am! she thought.

After a few minutes she moved a bit closer and whispered in his ear. "We should stay here. They will think we have moved on and won't come back ... at least for a while." She saw his head nod. "Can you get some sleep?"

He remained quiet. Finally he turned his head and tried to look at her in the darkness. He remained silent for a long moment ignoring her question.

"Thanks!" he said softly. He put his hand out and gently touched her shoulder. Then he put his head back down and was quiet. A moment later he rose again and lifted himself on an elbow and looked intently at her.

"You don't have a pillow do you?"

She blinked at him and shook her head.

"Oh, well ... thanks anyway."

Was he actually grinning? Again, a weird offbeat remark in the middle of danger. Did she detect a slight brightness in his eyes? With that he turned over and was silent. In a short while she could hear his heavy breathing. He was asleep.

Somewhere in the middle of the night Andrew was awakened. A soft whisper close to his ear said, "We need to move now. Get farther away from the village."

He nodded but turned back over. Pamela shook him and he struggled up. They walked far into the night as she led him through the blackness. Finally, she seemed satisfied and he collapsed once again to the earth. Then the dreams came.

The sun had been up for hours before Andrew stirred again. He groaned and tried to sit up. She wasn't there. Had she given up on him, he wondered? Finally realized that he wasn't survival material? *Wouldn't blame her*, he thought. He wasn't in top shape. In fact his doctor had chided him frequently for his high cholesterol and expanded girth. He groaned again as he tried to stretch. The interesting thing was that he was definitely in better shape than when he was rudely taken from Atlanta. He looked down at his waist.

"Probably twenty pounds less," he muttered. *Not quite slim yet,* he thought.

Then he remembered the dreams, especially the dream of the beast that had shaken him so during the night. It was intensely black at that moment. A complete lack of any light. The only senses available were his hearing and smell. He had dug his fingers into the stiff soil in panic. Absolute blackness! Then he had heard it. A soft sound, a voice somewhere a few yards away. It was very melodic … soothing and conversational. Then it was quiet again. Suddenly he sensed her standing over him.

"Shhh. Just lie down somewhere," she had whispered into the darkness, "he's ok."

Who was she talking to? he wondered.

She then curled up a short distance away. He must have fallen asleep again puzzling about what had happened. Now it was morning and he shuddered at his dream of the beast. The other one was of Dr. Bentley. Perhaps his out-of-shape body was tormenting him not only with a multitude of pains while awake but also in his sleep. He recalled his last visit to the doctor.

"Too much weight Andrew, you really need to do something. Perhaps walk more." *Well that he had, and recently,* he thought, considering his ordeal. He remembered the doctor's last words as he smiled and gently pointed to his belly. "Perhaps think of selling the bakery." Andrew grinned at this memory and tried again to stretch out the kinks.

"Hi."

He started at the soft voice that was directly behind him. He turned to see her standing a short distance away. How did she come and go so silently?

"Morning," he said. "Or is it? I guess I slept late."

She nodded her head slightly and then stared down at the ground. "Um, I …" she started awkwardly and then remained still.

Andrew stared at her. *Shy? After all she had done?* He groaned and struggled to his feet. "Oww!" His shoulder was bruised and stiff.

Pamela shuffled her feet a bit, unable to think of what to say. Finally it was Andrew who broke the uneasy silence. "Thanks again. They were doing ... well, very nasty things to me."

She just nodded stiffly and then gave a little shrug. Andrew stared at her, appraising her for the first time in the light of day. She stood before him, eyes down and fidgeting nervously with her fingers. *Medium build*, he thought, *not tall, not short. She wasn't slender but certainly wasn't heavy. Her skin wasn't really tan. It wasn't pale either. Hair an indistinguishable brown and somewhere between short and medium length.*

The only noticeable features were the stains and tears in her clothes. Then she glanced up. *Ah yes,* he thought, *her eyes!* They were large and a deep brown, but much more. They seemed filled with conflict and struggle. They were frightened and confused. Yet within all of the obvious inner turmoil there was an underlying strength. It was as if there was another person, someone quite unlike the one who was standing meekly before him, deep within her and wishing to be released. He held her eyes for a moment longer and then she grew uncomfortable and quickly looked away. *Yes,* he thought, *there is definitely something more here.* He stepped forward, and gently taking her chin, raised her head to him. Her eyes darted immediately to the ground. *They were worried and perplexed,* he thought, *and yet strong. Yes, all of that. But most of all — they were wild.* After a moment he sensed her uneasiness. He stepped back and said, "Well, can we go now?"

She seemed confused by this.

"Go?" she replied.

Andrew wondered if she was in some sort of shock, perhaps dazed by the ordeal of last night.

"Yeah, you know, back to civilization."

Her brow furrowed and her face clouded with a vague look as if what he just said was incomprehensible to her.

"This can't be your home. You said you were from ..." he thought for a moment, "Oh yeah, from Iowa. You know, good old U. S. of A."

She said nothing and took a few steps back. After a moment she said, "I really don't think that I should ... or can ..." her voice drifted off, indistinct and in obvious confusion.

Andrew thought for a moment and then eased himself to the ground. He sighed. "I just assumed that you had a plan," he said despondently. Then after a long moment he shrugged off his dejection and pulled himself up. He attempted to brush off his soiled clothes and ran his fingers through his matted, graying hair. He then tried to straighten his shirt and run a finger down a non-existent crease in his grubby pants.

"Well, where are my manners anyway? All this time together and no introductions. Gee," he grinned, "we even spent the night together." *Did she just blush?* he thought.

"My name is Andrew." He extended his hand to her. Pamela hesitated and then stepped forward and gave it a brief, awkward clasp.

"I'm Pamela," she said softly and quickly looked down again and waited. Waited for a remark, any disparaging remark like those that had come all of her life.

"Hello Pamela." He held her hand for a moment. "Thanks for saving my life. Whether it's for thirty more minutes or thirty more years ... thank you."

Andrew's heartfelt and gentle tone startled her. She looked up at him, stunned by the unexpected sincerity in his voice. She pulled her hand away and looked at him more closely. He was a mess. Sweat-stained clothes and smudges of dirt all over. The deep bruises on his face showed the cruelness of his captivity. Large circles under his eyes vividly told of his need for sleep. He was obviously not in condition but looked like he was fit at one time. Perhaps six feet tall and while not portly he was not a small person. His eyes were a strange green but in the dim light of the forest seemed gray. She was unsure of his age but thought it might be around forty and, she noticed, graying.

"Now what?" he said, interrupting her scrutiny.

She felt her face grow warm when she realized how intently she had been staring. She glanced away and thought for a moment. She then shrugged and shook her head.

"Well, I guess we can walk for a bit," she said.

How trite that must sound? she thought.

In reality she had no idea of what to do, or for that matter, even what to say. She had never been a very good conversationalist and now the thought of being with someone after such a long time alone was welcomed but unsettling. For the most part she was comfortable letting Andrew carry the conversation. She found it interesting that he didn't talk about himself or ask many questions about her. For the most part he seemed taken by the vastness of the forest, exhibiting an almost childlike quality of enthusiasm. Respect and awe was evident in all his words. He spoke of the incredible height of the trees. He seemed enthralled with the light that worked through the foliage to paint the forest floor with subtle and changing patterns.

These things he described mostly in terms of impressionism and often his examples went to musical terms or sometimes specific pieces of music. Some Pamela knew, most were strange to her. She had heard of Debussy but Ravel was unknown. He most often talked of someone named Villa Lobos. Once in a while she glanced at him, but mostly she walked patiently beside him, trying to see just what he saw. She could now understand his admiration, his absorption with the majesty of the forest. A few days ago, or had it now been weeks, she had been overwhelmed with the vastness of the deep woods and especially with its oppressive darkness. Now she realized that most of this came from her own interior gloom, the warped nature from her past that she had carried continually within her.

They stopped and she began to find fruit and small roots. She was now completely comfortable with finding nourishment, for it had become entirely instinctive.

Andrew found he was hungry and sought out a fallen log. After sagging down by it he watched her with great interest. *Ranger?* he wondered, *Military?* He shook his head. *No, not really the type,* he thought. Though in fact he had no idea what "type" that might be.

She disappeared for a brief time and then returned with hands full of various roots and berries. He watched as she rubbed soil and small leaves from them trying to make them acceptable. They ate in silence for a long time while now and then spitting out the inedible portions of their breakfast.

Finally he said, "Pamela?"

She looked up.

"They're still looking for us you know."

She simply nodded her head.

"Charles isn't likely to just give it up."

Again the nod and she busied herself with the small bits of food. He frowned and wondered if she actually knew about Charles. Then he tried again, "Pamela, do you have any idea at all where we are?"

This brought her head up again but she didn't look directly at him. *How can I tell him,* she thought. *How can I tell him I know exactly where we are? If I did,* she considered, *then I would need to tell him even more.* She shuddered. *And then tell him that I'm now changed into what, a mutant, a freak?* Her mouth drew into a sharp line and her hands trembled slightly at this thought but she hid it by fussing again with the berries. She knew he deserved a better response. She forced herself to turn and face him.

"I ..." she started but then put her head down, "uh, I think the village where they held you is back that way." She glanced up briefly and pointed over his shoulder. "Uh, we need to stay away from there." She glanced at his face. *How stupid I sound. He's not buying this,* she thought.

Andrew smiled slightly and rubbed at the gray growth on his face. "Ok, good ... good thinking." He glanced around, peering into the trees. "Now which way would be Rio?" His smile was now broad and infectious. "After all, when we do get out of here I recall owing you a manicure."

She frowned as she remembered what she had blurted out last night. She had felt foolish for saying it then and even more so now. Stress, dumb stress.

"That was dumb," she said, "I was nervous."

He then looked directly at her and his gaze demanded that she hold his eyes. "No," he said softly. "You were magnificent. I owe you my life and I will never forget it."

She thought of his words as they continued to walk. About how he looked at her when he told her he would never forget her help. "Magnificent," he had said. She had never had anyone treat her with such deference, such approval. Andrew actually seemed to respect her, even consider her as an adult, maybe as an equal. The only ones to really think of her with anything close to, perhaps friendship, were her father and grandfather. And she was very young then. She turned this in her mind for quite a while and was startled when he suddenly took her hand and pulled her to a stop. He kindly turned her towards him to assure that she would pay attention.

"Look Pamela, it's been at least half a day and we are still wandering through this forest."

His expression was no longer one of cheerfulness or serenity but one of intense gravity.

"I don't have the slightest idea where we are and even less idea of what to do now." His voice wasn't raised and his tone was still gentle but there was a growing urgency underlying his words.

"We simply have to sit down and figure out just what we are going to do to get away from here and especially from that mad man."

His words twisted her gut for she knew she had been delaying the inevitable. She also knew that telling the truth would leave her alone again, abandoned to return to her personal darkness. And this she could not bear. She fought back tears and turned and picked up the pace. After a few yards she heard him call after her in a soft voice, "Are you leaving me here?"

Dear Lord, she thought, *how can I do this? He will think I'm such a freak.*

She looked up into the vast green of the canopy. *And now I am!* she thought. *Now that's just what I am!*

She turned and let him see the tears run down her face … and was stunned by his expression. It wasn't the expected look of judgment or anger or even pity but one of tender concern. They stared in silence at each other for a long while and then sat down together, backs to a large tree, absorbed in their private thoughts. Finally enough time passed for him to smile and say, "Perhaps it's time to tell each other our stories."

CHAPTER TWENTY SIX
Retribution for Escape

Charles looked down at the twisted body of the native. Fortunately for Samuel he was still valuable, but someone needed to pay for the blunder of Andrew's escape. And the fact that this bungling group of fools could not yet find him was even more galling. He had considered feeding the native to the beast. Make all observe as an example of what incompetence brings. But his seething anger was too much to restrain. His normally calm exterior had given way to brief rage. He had taken pleasure as he swiftly pulled his knife from his robe and plunged its blade into the man's heart.

Perhaps he should have dragged him to the altar but that would have defiled the sacred stone. Blood was required he reasoned. But it should be the proper blood. The old ones knew that. They had built their glorious society upon it. Yes, blood was everything. And he was now without the very blood he needed. Charles clenched his teeth at the thought. Andrew had the required blood, imperfect as it was. And Pamela, the lost sheep, well hers was the old blood that was really of value. It was, except for the imperfection of her mother, the last of pure old blood. But now, thanks to his meddling adversaries it was tainted. He uttered a curse and shoved the native's body to the side.

"Clean up this mess, Samuel!" He then turned and stepped over the body to return to his subterranean lair. He must think of a way to find them both and quickly. He had tracked her one time, with the help of the beast. He would somehow do it again. *How could he have escaped?* he wondered. *He surely must have had help.* Then an incongruous thought came … *No!* he brooded. *She could not! She assuredly wasn't capable of such an achievement.*

CHAPTER TWENTY SEVEN
A Friend

Surprisingly it was Pamela that started the conversation. She was nervous and her bare foot fiddled with the dried twigs and fallen leaves before her. Her voice was low, almost a whisper and obviously unaccustomed to storytelling. She chose and assembled words carefully and without embellishment as if she was giving directives to her sixth-grade class. She was also self-effacing, placing blame upon herself for her predicament. Her "situation" she called it.

Her story was very condensed and, without revealing any personal reasons, related Charles' invitation to explore the Amazon for benefit of her class. She winced internally as she knew just how stupid she made it all seem. How could she say it was a hopeless attempt to escape the stifling reality of her repressed life? Now she was lost in the rainforest and should have been dead days ago. *And that night,* she thought. *How to explain that she was, what she thought, anointed? Yes, anointed in some strange, dark ceremony.* None of that could she mention. She held her forehead for a moment and thought, *What else? What else can I say that will make sense? Pardon me Andrew, but I'm now a freak. My altered body does strange, inexplicable things. That would be a great statement,* she thought. Her head began to throb and she felt the tears again in her eyes. *Freak! Dear God! I'm a turning into a mutant!* She wanted to shout at him, somehow make him understand that she just couldn't tell him. She … she wanted his company, wanted his polite friendship. She never had a friend.

"Pamela?" His gentle voice jerked her back from her reverie. He reached over and gently wiped her small tears away. "Pamela, what about Charles? Apparently you also know him. Somehow he obviously has an interest in both of us. With our being here, that is. You said he was the one who offered to bring you here. But why? What is he after?"

"Blood," she whispered. "My blood!" Andrew's mouth opened slightly but he just shook his head. They sat together in silence for a long time. Andrew had many questions but so little information from her. There were so many holes and gaps in her tale. How did she survive on her own for so many days? She really seemed to not be able to tell how many days she had wandered. Was she a seasoned hiker, perhaps an expert in survival techniques? She had dramatically saved his skin but now seemed somehow bewildered. Nothing fit.

He asked her small questions but her answers were vague, wisps of insubstantial vapor at best. He held his chin in his hand and stared at her. Stared at the quiet contradiction before him. Seemingly capable, yet weak, and possessing an inner strength that was in conflict with the uncertainty found in her words. Finally he shook his head and tried to let it go. Yet the woman before him was beginning to be more than baffling. She was intrigue wrapped in mystery.

He shrugged and thought that he had better continue the conversation or she would again slide into silent mode and these seemed to last for hours.

"Charles wasn't very creative with me." He sighed and smiled ruefully. "Just had his thugs bop me on the head and toss me in a trunk. Customs checks must have been lax as a few days later I found myself in a forlorn camp … the one where you rescued me. Bless you for that."

She shook her head slightly at this. *I'm not a hero!* she thought glumly, *I'm a freak!*

"They dragged me around from here to there a few times. Once to a lovely pool. It was the most beautiful place that I've ever seen. They were going to do a final treatment and …" he realized that he was rambling and getting ahead of himself. "They were giving me treatments Pamela." He grimaced and turned to look at her. "They were making me drink unspeakable potions and injecting me with … with stuff. I'm not sure what they want to turn me into. They are somehow messing with my DNA." He kicked in frustration at a clump of mossy dirt. "That beast … well he's one of their experiments." He grew very serious and stared into the dirt. "I don't think I'm dangerous. I hope to God I'm not." He clenched his fists and suddenly looked up and said, "I'd never hurt you."

She saw fear in his eyes and believed him. For some reason she didn't think this man would ever be unkind to anyone.

CHAPTER TWENTY EIGHT
Samuel

Samuel knew from an early age that he was different. He was twelve when his worried parents took him to a psychologist. Anti-social, conduct disorder, sadistic personality, this was a terrifying diagnosis to his parents. But he thought of it as just a way to describe to the world what he was. And what he enjoyed being. Yet he was intrigued by the person before him and, as terrifying as he himself was to others, Charles truly was the most horrifying person that could ever exist.

He remembered the moment yesterday when Charles plunged the knife into the heart of the native. Perhaps there had been anger that had motivated the sudden slaying. But to all observers Charles had seemed as cold as ever. Yes, he had struck quickly and then gave brisk orders. But through it all he seemed to be oddly detached from the actual event. There was a haunting, impassionate coolness that moved quickly past the act, dismissing it as something trivial. *Was he envious?* Samuel wondered. *No,* he didn't believe so. After all, Charles moved so quickly beyond the death that he couldn't have enjoyed it much. He, on the other hand, would have savored it.

Charles was a puzzle to him. All of the wealth didn't seem to matter to him. Just his precious theory about bringing back some nonsense by the way of ancient strains of blood. Samuel glared at Charles' back. *I've had a great deal of genetic education also,* he thought, *and I think you're just a crackpot … old blood nonsense! All your costly efforts are worthless! Well … except for my lovely pet.* He stared at Charles' back as he hunched over a bench filled with stone tablets. *How easy it would be,* he thought, *no crude knives, just two shots up close. Yet the time will come,* he mused, *time for an even better finale!* He glared at the bent over Charles again and savored the approaching time. *My pet will gleefully tear out your throat … and that opportunity will assuredly come!*

Samuel shook his head as he continued to watch Charles study the stones. How this place had come to be within the deep forest of

Brazil was puzzling to archeologists, or would be if they knew about it. How had stone temples, small versions of the pyramids seen within the Mayan and Aztec civilizations, come to this place? The writing upon these stones was truly amazing. It recorded the hidden knowledge of these great civilizations ... passed on their secrets. And Charles was slowly deciphering these mysteries. True, every year or so the South American forests gave up additional locations of these forgotten ruins. Just last year extensive new sites were found in Peru. But here among such primitive people, how could this be? Charles had obviously known the locations. He was one of the primitives. This brought a low chuckle to Samuel. *Yes Charles,* he thought, *you are a savage. Just another one of the dispensable savages!*

His thoughts were interrupted by the appearance of Eddie. That wasn't the native's actual name but as close as Samuel cared to come to the gibberish these pathetic people spoke. He was the only native left. The rest had quietly slipped away after Charles killed the man who "failed". Charles had also sent the technicians back to Atlanta two days ago with instructions to begin to prepare for his arrival, "shortly" he said.

There were now only three of them. Eddie had given the expected report. The two escapees were nowhere to be found. Samuel just waited. He knew it was just a matter of time before he could seek them with his pet. Perhaps even tomorrow. They were still here in the forest and soon would be great entertainment. He thought back to his childhood psychologist and his parents. He knew they would all be proud.

CHAPTER TWENTY NINE
Hunted

They had been walking most of the afternoon. Conversation between them would start up, become strained and then stall. Sometimes it was because Pamela would quickly run out of words. Mostly though it was from her not wanting to talk about anything that would allow Andrew to explore how she came to be within the forest, and especially whatever she was becoming. Now and then he would attempt to bring up home life by asking about her family or friends. It was mostly in vain. He did find out a bit about her school and her sixth-grade class. She even offered some small information about her hometown in Iowa. Yet when it came to anything personal, especially about family she became guarded, even agitated. Then they would walk on in silence until Andrew would begin another small inquiry and most of this would be met with vague shrugs.

Sometimes the high leaves above would let in a small shaft of sunlight that played upon the ground or highlight their faces. It was like a breath of fresh air to Andrew. Pamela seemed to never notice. Finally the forest light faded and then was gone. She led him to a small clearing in the vegetation and they settled down for another night. He tried to talk into the darkness and she shared a bit more, though with reluctance. Her mother was not well. She didn't know her father very well as he died when she was young. All just brief snippets without embellishment. Finally the darkness was complete and it became obvious that she would speak no more. Andrew wished her a cordial goodnight and tried to make his weary body forget about the rough ground. It didn't take too long and he was fast asleep.

Later that night a silver sliver of a moonbeam worked its way down to the lower part of the forest. Andrew woke up and started to turn over wishing for a sheet or blanket. Not that it was cool but just the thought of a blanket related so much to home. How he missed the routine of running his bakery. And there was his one vice ... dining out. *Well that,* he thought, *and the art gallery, and*

perhaps the concerts. Then the last trip to New Orleans was pretty special.
The jazz in the small outdoor parks always lightened his spirits.

He sighed and began to turn back over when he heard the strange, soft voice that he thought he had heard the first night. He quietly rose up on one arm and looked around. There in the heart of the silver shaft of moonlight was a strange ethereal vision. It appeared to be a woman kneeling on the ground in front of a large animal. They were in silhouette with the moon casting an eerie half-light over them. The woman softly touched the head of the sleek form sitting quietly in front of her. She then seemed to be whispering to it. Andrew shook his head at the apparition. And then the moonlight was suddenly gone leaving all in total darkness. He waited a long while but nothing else appeared. He lay back down puzzled and trying to again sleep, his thoughts no longer of home but now of mysterious shapes and intriguing figures. He finally fell asleep as fragments of a long forgotten poem floating by as wispy as a fairy's soft kiss.

As usual, she was up before him. Andrew tried to convince himself that he felt better, but in reality, he was still sore from his ordeal. He sat up to see Pamela waiting patiently with a variety of food stuff placed on large leaves by her side.

"Well, you will spoil me with the excellent room service." He didn't sound very cheery, and when he considered it, he had awakened quite annoyed. He put his hand on his chin and stared at her. She began to grow uncomfortable as she always seemed to do if he attempted to become too inquisitive. Still, this dodging had to stop. He ate slowly and thoughtfully while trying to plan some way of getting through to her. He tossed the small handful of berries aside and looked directly at her.

"Pamela, we are quite lost. Isn't that right?"

She looked up at him and then nodded. He waited for some response but nothing came. He continued.

"We have no one but each other. Would you agree with that?"

She bit her lip and tried to look away but his voice made her look up at him. Again the little nod. He tried to be firm but his heart went out to her. Somehow he sensed that there was some injury within her that was deep and afflicted with great cost to her soul. He crossed over to her and knelt before her having her sit down.

"Pamela, you need to understand that you can depend upon me. I will give my life for you just as you risked all for me. We are still being hunted. I know that it's just a matter of time before Charles and his thugs come after us. They might be close at this moment. Before that happens I want to know much more about the woman here before me. You are now part of my life whether you wish that or not. We are the only ones we have now."

He looked into her eyes and saw her retreat to a vague distance, as if she wanted to hide somewhere ... or from something. But he continued, "Won't you please share a bit more with me?"

She remained very still for a long moment considering his soft, gentle voice. Finally she looked directly at him and saw the utter sincerity in his face.

I just want a friend, she thought. Then she said in a whisper, "Yes, as much as I'm able."

The talk didn't flow immediately after that but she did try to say a bit more. Andrew saw the effort in all of this for her. *Perhaps*, he thought, *if I tell her some parts of my life it might help.*

After they had walked well into the afternoon he sat down abruptly and leaned back against the trunk of a large tree. He patted the ground by him and said, "Come on, I won't bite. You say your dad died when you were young?"

She just nodded but did sit down, however, not by him but a few feet away. He waited and continued, "My dad just died a few weeks ago. Just two weeks before these idiots captured me. He was quite a guy. My hero actually."

He watched her for a moment. She seemed to be struggling with something, some inner conflict or perhaps a memory that was part of whatever hurt she carried with her. After a long while she looked at him and said with a sadness, "Andrew, please ... please tell me about your father."

She looked so lost and forlorn that his heart went out to her but he tried to keep his response light. Both for her sake and also so his own heart wouldn't break.

He smiled at the thought of his dad, "Well … I really can't talk about him without also talking about my mom. They were so integrally connected. First of all, look around you." He gestured towards the great expanse of the forest.   "Hear the forest sounds?" They listened quietly for a moment. The movement of breezes through the foliage provided a beautiful counterpoint to the murmur of birds, monkeys, insects and other forest dwellers. It was rich and melodious.

"When I was young, dad told me of this wonderful sound. I never thought I would experience it myself. He was always intrigued by sounds. He would say that music is the only human endeavor that allows something greater to be transformed from the original parts. A symphony becomes something much more than the composer, the conductor and the orchestra. It's transformed into something significantly superior to the individual parts. He believed that we could hear the very voice of God in the experience. He was from a tribe …"

That word again! thought Pamela,

"… from around this area. I'm not exactly sure just where. Anyway he became aware when he was just a teen that his native music was insufficient. He left the tribe and worked his way to larger settlements and finally to Rio. And there he saw my mother."

Andrew smiled at this and stretched a bit on the ground. He waited to see just how she would react.

After a while she asked, "Well, then what?"

Ok, he thought, *a start of communication?*

"You need to understand Pamela, that my dad was extremely unsophisticated. He had literally walked out of the forest, away from a very primitive society and into a large and complex world. My mother was part of the Rio that was chaotic and bewildering to my father. When he saw her it was as if he had seen a vision. She was entirely different than dad. He was pure native, she tall, dark-haired and incredibly beautiful. She was an unusual combination of African and Spanish. Dad would look dreamy whenever he talked about her, even when he was much older and she was gone. Dad would say that he was the incurable romantic and that she was the wild one."

Pamela's head jerked up at this but she said nothing. Again he paused to see how she would react. After a longer while she repeated, almost impatiently, "Well, then what?"

Andrew smiled at that and continued, "They probably shouldn't have met. They were from such different worlds. Dad was working as an apprentice baker, mostly cleaning up things. When he would leave late at night he would walk by a certain dance hall. Wonderful music would pour from the open windows and he would sit on the walk beneath them for hours enthralled by the sounds, mostly the captivating rhythms. Then after a few weeks of waiting, and after the last notes faded into the dark Rio streets, a vision of such beauty walked from the entry door that dad was never the same. He told me of this only once and that was through tears that he couldn't contain in the telling. He was smitten he said. After that, he would go there directly after work and listen to the music. He found out later that the dance was mostly the tango. Mom was a teacher there and she would be one of the last to leave. He finally got up the courage to follow her one night just to see where she lived. It was obvious that she was from a poor area and he began to save his money. It was with the dream that perhaps he could buy at least one dance."

Andrew chuckled at this and looked at her.

"Pamela, he didn't have the slightest idea how to dance. Well, finally he got up the nerve to actually go into the dance hall to at least watch. He paid a few small coins and just sat quietly in a corner."

Pamela saw his mother in her mind. An elegant, young woman, refined and completely at ease with herself. Confident and with a smoldering energy, she would be dressed in a stunning, red dress, slit up the side to allow her to move to the seductive rhythms of the Tango. She knew how a man would be fascinated by the first sight of a woman like this. Then she looked down at her ragged and dirty clothes and winced at remembering how she appeared when she had first met Andrew. She put her head down in embarrassment.

"He did this for a couple of weeks ..." he continued, "... and then was stunned one night when mom came over and sat by him."

He chuckled again and said, "Scared him to death! She asked him if he wanted to dance and he just shook his head no. The following night the same thing happened and he told her that he didn't know how to dance. When she asked why he was there he simply said, 'To see you'. Somehow, and for a reason known only to her, she ended up teaching him how to dance after the others had left."

Andrew grew silent for a long time and Pamela sensed that he needed a moment before continuing. Finally he said softly, "How they loved each other ..." Then he got up and walked into the quiet of the forest.

They walked together for a while and it was Pamela that unexpectedly stopped and said, "My father left me, Andrew. My mother said it was because he hated me and that I was evil." Her eyes welled up at this and she wiped at the wetness with the back of her hand.

"I realize now that this wasn't true, but he still left when I was just seven. I always told people that he was gone on a long business trip, but in reality I never knew what happened. He was just there one day and then gone the next."

She was quiet for a long while after that. Finally she said, "I'm very happy for you. To have such a wonderful memory of two loving people is ..." She just shrugged and looked over at him. The first time she had actually fully looked at him, he noticed.

"Please Andrew, tell me more about them."

He nodded considering how vulnerable she sounded. How fragile despite her saving him from a dangerous situation.

"It's getting a bit dark now. Let's find a spot and stop for the night. I keep looking over my shoulder expecting Charles and his nutty henchman to show up."

"I don't ... sense them now," she said.

He let this puzzling remark go. It sounded true.

After a small gathering by Pamela of dinner, the usual offering of the forest that she could quickly find now, they sat and watched the approaching dusk. After fidgeting for a while, Pamela asked, "What happened to bring you to America?"

He sighed and shook his head. His large shoulders seemed to sag a bit. Then he smiled at her.

"Mom was a very unusual person Pamela. She was very quiet when she wasn't dancing. But she could say volumes with an elegant gesture or a glance of her eyes. I think her eyes were what really captivated dad. She also had a soft, lilting laugh as if you were hearing a small brook joyfully bubbling in the springtime. This seemed to rise from the very depths of her inner spirit. He was twenty and she was eighteen when they first met. And later, when dad could talk more about her to me, he said that while her beauty was striking, the main thing about her was her air of mystery."

He smiled again and nodded his head as if remembering a poignant moment.

"Dad, as I said, was an incurable romantic and she was mystique personified."

Andrew then became silent and looked down at the forest floor for a long while. Finally he continued in a choked voice.

"Dad seemed lost, as if part of his very soul had been torn away when she died. There was a void that remained with him forever." He shook his head. "I was just twelve ... one minute she was there and then she was gone. Brazil, even in Rio, wasn't very medically advanced then. We never knew just what she contracted, just that two days later she was gone. We moved to America the following year. Probably because he couldn't bear to remain where his precious memories were made."

Pamela looked at him with a sudden intensity.

"Andrew, why haven't you ever married?" She then looked stricken, "Oh, I'm sorry! I shouldn't have asked that. Maybe you are ... I just assumed ..."

She hung her head and put her small hand to her mouth, embarrassed at her impetuous outburst.

He looked up at her, puzzled by her reaction.

"Why not? It's a perfectly good question. And no, I've never married." He thought for a moment and grinned, "Perhaps because I've never met anyone mysterious enough."

Samuel sat in a crude folding chair while watching Charles intently scrutinize a series of photos. They were deep within the stone chamber that lay beneath the giant, dead tree that hovered ponderously over the village. The menacing remains of its bare roots hung from small fissures in the rock ceiling as if they desperately clung to the final speck of life still buried within their marrow.

Charles had discovered this chamber years before he left for the world outside his village. His later studies had proven his hunch, an instinct that told him of its antiquity. It was somehow the remnants of a stone temple. A small but accurately created pyramid every way as complete as the majestic works of the Mayans or the Aztecs. As the centuries had passed this small but carefully crafted temple had been gradually reclaimed by the forest. Now only a small series of plateaus, hardly noticeable within the overgrown woods, were the remaining external markings of its presence.

Well wonder boy, even with all of your fancy degrees ... Samuel thought, *you're really baffled aren't you?*

He glowered at the gray-robed back and considered how easy it would be. He would quickly put an end to this nonsense and get back to a civilized world. *Just one small bullet,* he considered, *so simple, an elegant way to conduct business. Bullets are wonderfully useful. They are relatively inexpensive, quite small ... no more than a little pebble actually ... all you need is the proper speed. The photos near you, my dear Charles, would be quite ruined of course. But they are as worthless as your inane theories of grandeur.*

"Miss something Charles?" he said out loud.

Charles' back straightened briefly but he said nothing in response. Samuel knew that he was livid and was trying desperately to maintain his appearance of composure. The photos, taken months ago, were from the low wall that encompassed the temple pool. Numerous shots of the stone ruins had been minutely dissected for the last two days. And there, quite obvious and placed boldly on the center stone were the symbols of three stylized jars. A small bit of moss had grown up over the lower portion of this particular stone covering part of the symbols. The ancient characters showed these jars being emptied into the water. Quite simple and quite unnoticed until now. And Charles had no idea what was in these containers. Had he been misled by simple-minded natives? He seethed at the idea that they had simply dumped something into the water that ruined years of research and more than half his fortune.

Samuel was immensely enjoying the fury that he knew lay beneath the apparent calm that Charles tried to portray. *Too bad he can't blame the technician that took the pictures,* he thought. More blood was always fun. Unfortunately he had sent them all back to Atlanta. Now it was just the three of them and old Eddie the native, while good for carrying things, was really worthless. *Patience,* he told himself. *It's just a matter of time.* He and his true friend would be the ones that would eventually win. And it would be delicious.

He loved his new pet. He had never imagined something so incredibly huge and vicious could result in the way they rearranged the genes of a simple orangutan. Of course, he chuckled to himself, he did spice it up a bit by adding some other ingredients, much to the annoyance of Charles. Yes, this creature was special ... like him. The dogs he had when he was a child were large and vicious. He had seen to that. But his new pet ... well he and the misshapen creature had something unique in common. Samuel smiled as he remembered his youth. He, like the dogs, was considered to be quite mean. He relished that. Some also called him cruel. He liked that too. *Yes,* he thought, *mean and nasty.* He and his pet were so very much alike. Perhaps, he considered, when he got home he'd celebrate this somehow. He amused himself the rest of the afternoon with thoughts of a stylish tattoo commemorating his accomplishments.

CHAPTER THIRTY

I Met a Lady

Both Pamela and Andrew kept their thoughts to themselves for the next few hours. They seemed to need time to absorb the first meaningful talk since they had been forced into their strange and fragile relationship a few evenings ago. There was some small talk now and then and Andrew hoped this indicated some form of thaw.

Finally, after quite a while, Pamela said in a shy manner, "Andrew, would you ... would you tell me what you did in America?"

She walked on after asking this as if she really didn't expect an answer. He glanced at her and shrugged.

"Sure, I make bread."

She stopped in her tracks assailed with unbidden thoughts of Stan. He noticed her strange look as she whirled around and stared at him, eyes widened and seeming to recoil at this remark.

"It's a very old and respected profession," he said defensively. "My father learned the trade in Brazil and when we moved to Atlanta he opened a bakery that specialized in South American breads and pastries. I've carried on the tradition. We are very good bakers."

She heard his defensive and wounded tone and immediately stepped forward and put her hand on his arm.

"Oh, forgive me Andrew ... I just, well ... I'm so sorry!"

She then looked down and realizing that she had touched him dropped her hand in embarrassment.

"Sorry..." she said again and then grew silent.

Andrew was once again puzzled by her reaction. Again she had retreated into an enigma. *A poem*, he thought, *what was that poem?* He blinked and searched for a long-forgotten tale, one that he loved as a youth for its mystery. *It's her*, he thought. *What was it? Keats I believe.* Hazy stanzas danced before him, tantalizingly close, but just out of reach. *I met a lady ... Yes*, he thought, *that's how it may have started. What was that wonderful poem?*

She turned and continued on, confused by her sudden boldness and mortified by how awkwardly she handled the resulting situation. Andrew watched her move on into the woods and saw the conflicting emotions as she walked. Her upper body was clearly burdened with an uncomfortable tension in her slumped shoulders. And this struggle was in direct contrast with her light and sure steps upon the forest floor. He ran his hand over the back of his neck and pondered her movements, desperately searching for the poem of many years ago. *It's her,* he thought. *I met a lady ... It's her!*

Samuel was bored. It had been hours since Charles had last spoken to him. Being relegated to fixing meals was also becoming an irritant and he considered once again just shooting him. *Should I shoot him in the back or have him turn around,* he considered. Each would have its individual appeal, a particular nicety.

Charles stretched and sat down near the mass of equipment that had been shipped from the states and dragged to the village over the preceding months. Samuel had never seen even the slightest crack in the barrier of insufferable arrogance that Charles maintained during the five years that he had known him. *Finally ... a slight chink in the façade!* he thought.

Then Charles proclaimed his next edict. "Samuel, it's imperative that we find the fugitives that are still wandering elusively in the forest. They, no doubt, are by now becoming quite weary of their ordeal. You must immediately go forth and recover them to this site of our noble experimentation. Apparently the polluted water has produced some very undesirable changes within the female. Still, though she is now useless to us as the final host, her blood can be once again reconstituted at our Atlanta facility. It is the key to the transformation we seek. The male however can still be used as an extension of our prototypes. Bring them both to me unharmed and soon. Take the native boy as a helper. Go now and don't tarry."

Samuel stared at him, amazed at the vaulted speech that Charles had developed. *Native boy?* he thought. *He's of your tribe Charlie, or whatever your real jungle name is. You aren't far from these insufferable primitives yourself.* He shrugged this off and was happy that he could finally do something besides stare at the overbearing idiot before him.

"It will be dark in a couple of hours. Why don't we leave at first light?" Samuel suggested and then waited for the royal order to leave immediately. He was surprised when Charles simply waved his hand and said, "Just have them here by midday."

CHAPTER THIRTY ONE
Borrowed Time

Pamela's mood now seemed as dark as the great forest. She wondered if she could ever relate to any human, much less a man, especially a man that she reluctantly admitted she liked. She desperately wanted to open up. Have a meaningful conversation. Even share her life by telling him about herself. But what would she tell him? She thought, *Hi Andrew, let me tell you about my life. It's so boring that even forest cats yawn at me. I can tell you everything in two minutes and it would drive you away.* Still, she considered as she looked around her, *this current life can't be described as boring. But as far as this new life, what do I say? Oh, by the way Andrew, I'm filled with creepy potions and oils that are making me very strange. Sort of Bride of Frankenstein stuff. Oh yeah, that would be a great way to maintain a relationship.* She then thought – *what relationship? I'm scared to death of this guy. Damn!* she thought. *He seems so nice and maybe he really would be interested in what has happened to me. Why can't I just be open and tell him?* But she knew why. He would be appalled and surely leave and she would once again be alone. And alone in the great forest. Pamela glanced over at him. *Could you really be a friend to me?* She turned and quickly wiped a lone tear away with the back of her hand and then quickened her pace.

"Pamela?" She turned and saw that Andrew had his head cocked to one side and looked curious. "You have been very quiet, even more than usual." He smiled but then continued in a more serious tone, "And you seem very concerned about something. Want to talk about it?"

She stopped and sighed. Finally, she simply nodded and said, "Well, maybe some things." She thought for a moment and then asked him, "First, will you tell me more about your family? It helps somehow. It's so nice to hear of a normal family. Mine was ... well, in fragments I suppose."

Andrew pondered this for a time and then with a nod said, "Sure."

He glanced up into the dark green of the tall trees. *How wonderful this is,* he thought. *I never thought I would see where dad actually lived.*

"Dad," he began, "was from somewhere around this part of the Amazon. Even though he never could tell me just where, no maps of native villages you know, I somehow feel that this is close to his birthplace. Just a feeling really."

Pamela looked at him and wondered if he, like her, could sense things in the forest. And if so, just how much. She then listened intently as Andrew continued.

"It's very much of an emotional thing I suppose. And to find out that Charles has pulled both of us here, and for unpleasant things, well … I'm still trying to sort it all out. Didn't you say your dad was from here also?"

He waited, giving her an opportunity to enter the conversation. She remained silent so he continued, "I said that dad was lost without mom. He tried to replace her, or at least ease the pain, by delving into all sorts of things. Other women were never even a passing thought to him. Mostly he sought spiritual solace. Mom was a Catholic when they met. Dad would go to church with her but never seemed to be really interested. When we moved to the States he tried them all, even becoming a Buddhist for a bit. He gradually migrated back to the Catholic Church but was really never content." He took a deep breath and shook his head. "At least not until the last two weeks of his life. Then something very strange happened. He suddenly became very peaceful; a lovely calm came upon him. A contentment that was, well, profound."

With this he looked around and spying a place on the ground that looked comfortable, crossed to it and sat down. This time Pamela didn't stay back but followed him and sat down cross-legged, actually facing him. *Well, look here!* he thought. *That's a bit of progress.*

Pamela considered what he said and thought of a time when she had gone to a Catholic Church with a friend. She had been invited and sat through a Mass observing the sometimes puzzling service. *I could have been a Catholic,* she thought, *if they had invited me back and if they had asked me to join I would have. I could have also have been a*

Methodist or even a Mormon. Just ask me and no questions, I just tag along. She shook her head, amazed at whatever was within her that caused her to be such an unquestioning follower.

Andrew stretched out on the ground and rubbing his face, continued, "You see Pamela, dad struggled all of his life with some hidden demons. After mom was gone it intensified. He never shared any of this for years but his internal battles were obvious to me. About a month before he died, and perhaps because he sensed his death approaching, he began to share a little. He told me of lifelong struggles with wondering just what we were doing on the earth. What mankind's purpose was … if anything. And trying to reconcile this doubt with faith in God, especially within the context of the Catholic faith often resulted in a greater struggle for him. He fought, prayed long hours, tried to be faithful but the struggle remained … he still doubted and questioned. He formed a close relationship with an older priest and also a rabbi. It was interesting when they all met at our house for a meal. They would debate, sometimes heatedly and sometimes roaring with laughter until very late at night. And after they would leave, dad would sit quietly until dawn, often in tears. I tried to understand his struggles but he wasn't ever clear when he spoke of them. He only said that he wrestled with God, and that he was too stubborn to let God win. He would then say, very ruefully, that it was such arrogance that would surely keep him from heaven."

Andrew sighed and kicked a bit at the dirt by his feet. "I felt so helpless. There was nothing I could say or do to ease the constant battle that he faced."

Pamela suddenly spoke up, "Andrew, did he ever win? Was there ever any hope?"

Andrew remained still for a while and then shook his head, "No Pamela, he never won."

Hearing this she looked dejected, as if he had just yanked away a lifeline. He shrugged and continued, "Of course winning is sometimes overrated. Something else happened. As I mentioned, there was a profound peace that came upon him in his last days. When I asked him about it he just smiled and said he gave up. This puzzled me. 'Gave up what?' I asked him. After all of these years of constant struggle what could he have given up that would bring such serenity? He simply beamed a bright, almost angelic smile and said, 'I gave up struggling, Andrew, I simply told God that I surrender.'"

Andrew drew a deep breath and said, "He died a few days later, very peacefully."

Pamela groaned softly to herself and rose. Andrew noticed the wetness in her eyes and heard her quietly say, "If I could just struggle a little. But that would require a commitment. I don't even struggle."

She then turned and walked away dejected. Andrew watched her, saw her hunched shoulders and noticed her bruises and the numerous cuts on her arms and legs from her ordeal. He looked at her torn clothes laced with an abundance of dried bloodstains turning brown against the sweat-discolored fabric. He saw the strength of a warrior veiled by a private inner turmoil.

"Oh, yes you do, my dear," he said in a low voice to her back. "And most elegantly!"

Andrew decided to give her time to deal with whatever was causing such distress. He was puzzled by the emotional swings as unanticipated topics pushed her into a mood. These seemed to range from insecurity to depression. He shook his head and tried to occupy his thoughts with the magnificent forest they hiked through. Yet two important issues kept pushing away these attempts. First … he had no one else to talk with, and most of all, he cared about her. She tugged at his emotions, especially with her contradiction of apparent helplessness balanced with an inexplicable ability to deal with crisis. This only increased the mystery to which he was drawn. He wondered what she would be like if they had met in a normal situation. What would the conversation be like if they would have had a casual dinner somewhere? Or walk together in the springtime down Peach Street in Atlanta. And especially … would the mystery still be there?

He glanced at her; she walked a bit closer to him now, apparently an unconscious occurrence. Still though, she was noticeably deeply distressed and walked with her arms folded tightly to her chest as if trying to restrain whatever emotions were raging within her. His heart went out to her and he felt a sudden desire to hold her, comfort her and tell her that somehow it would be ok. But how would she react to that? She was such an enigma.

The other, and really more important issue that nagged at him, was the fact that surely Charles and his henchmen would come for them. And undoubtedly very soon. They were living on borrowed time. He blew out an exasperated breath and frowned. This seemed to wake her from whatever reverie occupied her and she became once more aware of his presence.

"Oh, did I do something ..." she stopped and looked slightly stricken as if she was somehow responsible for his feelings.

Andrew shook his head. *This must end!* he thought. He stopped her by taking her hand and gently guiding her to a place to sit. He felt the tension in her but she didn't resist and followed him to a small place with less undergrowth. He tried to be gentle, sensing some great wound within her soul. After taking a few moments to allow her to gradually look up at him he simply said, "Pamela, we have been thrown into an unbelievable situation. And in these very short days I've come to care about you. But I don't have any idea who you are or know anything about you. And especially just what makes you often retreat into yourself. We may not survive this, in fact the odds are against it. I can accept that. But what I can't accept is that I will never know just who you really are. And what has caused you the pain that I see in you. We just get to a place where I think we can share a bit more and then you fall back into a dark place." He looked intently at her and said, "And the wall is very high." He paused here, wondering if this attempt would get through to her.

Again a slight shrug and silence from her. She glanced at him and thought, *How long can I avoid this?*

The years of repression and the obvious low self-esteem had taken its toll. She remembered the time she talked with a counselor in college. A touch of stomach flu and resulting visit to an observant school nurse had led to a session with a psychologist. After a brief time the doctor had skillfully obtained more details from her than Pamela ever meant to reveal about herself. "Pamela," she had said, "you really need to deal with some serious issues here, especially with your mother." She never returned to her. Low self-esteem was an obvious part of the problem. *And just how would this doctor deal with her now,* she wondered?

She looked at Andrew as he patiently waited for her to sort through things. She shook her head and sighed, "Sorry Andrew, you're right. I'm lousy company. And yes, there are things in my life that I carry with me. I've been trying to deal with them. And ..." she was unsure how to continue, "... and something was done to me here in the forest. Some ... indescribable things ..." she trailed off and shook her head as if struggling how to describe her experiences.

He took her hand and said, "I want to help. Why don't you tell me some simple things at first? Little things about you and your family, school, anything that comes to mind. That's not too hard."

Pamela looked at him and bluntly said, "Yes, it is ... that's where my problems are, in the day-to-day simple things."

But not anymore! she thought. *Now I'm a freak and I'll never tell him that!*

Andrew frowned and struggled not to appear frustrated.

"Try anyway will you? I told you that I will never hurt you. That means with words too. Do you understand this?"

She could see his growing irritation and understood how his patience could be ending with her. And this she couldn't bear. She lowered her head and placed her hands on the back of her neck realizing that she could no longer avoid sharing at least something with him. *Perhaps I can do this,* she thought. She considered how she had been able to deal with two of the most difficult ordeals of her life since she had come to the forest. How remembering her father along the trail to the temple hadn't emotionally crippled her as it had in the past. How she could now let her memories of him come forth and not bear the guilt she had been condemned with by her mother. And how she had left most of the bitterness and resentment for her mother flow into the gray pit in the dark village. Perhaps she could even face the most hurtful event of her life now, the death of her grandfather. But this sudden thought clenched at her gut and she quickly let it go. Later, perhaps later for her grandfather. She realized that more time had passed and he was still quietly waiting. Pamela raised her head and tried to smile. It was forced but at least an attempt.

"Let's walk and I'll do my best," she said.

CHAPTER THIRTY TWO
Forest Cuisine

The forest was so peaceful. She was feeling truly at home. Could she share this? Share something that she little understood. She took a deep breath and searched for somewhere to begin. Her sixth-grade class. This seemed a good place, a safe place, for she was at home there. One of the few places in her life where she felt at ease. At least until the day it all tumbled down. The day she met Charles. This she didn't talk about, but all other things she began to share.

Small bits about college were next, skipping over her one date in four years. She slowly moved back to her childhood. Could she talk about the red shoes she wondered? Perhaps, but she chose to leave out that part of her early struggles as she did with other sensitive issues.

Mother? How to share that? She told him a day or so ago that she was sick but didn't elaborate. She also remembered saying to him that mother had said she was evil. "I realize I'm not evil now." She said this impulsively without realizing why and watched Andrew just nod and continue to listen.

Pamela shared details about her town in Iowa and her house. How the fall brought great harvests of corn and the harshness of winter in the plains. Small things of little importance, memories of playing in her yard and the hollyhocks that grew in the cinders and gravel in the back alley. She told him about her soot-covered ceiling that stretched high above her bed and all at once an unexpected torrent of thoughts and pent-up emotions poured out ... times she cried herself to sleep and times she was punished by hours locked in the dark closet tumbled out like a flood suddenly breaching a levy. She couldn't stop the flow of words, describing restrictions and putdowns, teasing playmates and especially mother's biting words. Then her meaningless marriage that ended in a meaningless divorce.

She stopped and, gasping for breath, sank to the ground covering her head with her arms as if to keep her devastating memories from further crushing her.

Andrew stood over her, stunned by the years of cruelty she had suffered. He watched helplessly, searching for words. None came so he sat down close to her and allowed her to seek the comfort of his shoulder. Then she cried.

He quietly watched the enclosing forest and let her slowly regain her composure. Finally, after a long while, Pamela drew back from him. Her eyes were red and puffy but she struggled up and gave a slight smile.

"Sorry, I didn't mean … well, that was not what I …" she groped for words and finding none appropriate said, "Thanks Andrew, for the ear … and the shoulder." She paused and then said, quite unexpectedly, "You hungry? I'll go find something."

He looked at her, startled at this strange and seemingly new manner.

"Pamela, you have been through a lot this afternoon. Let me find something."

Then he realized the futility of what he said and gave an embarrassed grin. "Uh, you don't know where I can find a McDonalds do you?"

Then the unanticipated happened … she laughed. It was a pleasant laugh with a soft lilt.

"Thank you Andrew." He looked at her, puzzled at the emerging transformation before his eyes.

"Sure, but … for what?"

"For your offbeat remarks, they make me laugh." With that she disappeared into the forest.

A brief fifteen minutes passed and she returned. There seemed to be a new lightness in her step as if she had left some burden by the wayside. She placed several edibles down pointing to a new one.

"Here … see what I found! It's a fungus that will …" she looked at the expression on his face and looked disappointed. "It's protein Andrew," she said defensively. "Sorry it's not a Big Mac." With that they both laughed.

"Well I apologize, here you slave over a hot stove all day and I'm ungrateful. Bring on the protein."

As they ate she was the one who talked. She pointed out the sugar content in the berries, for energy she said, and the various ways the roots and seedpods added nutrients. She realized that she was talking continually and stopped.

"Sorry, I'm just still uncomfortable with … with conversations I guess. I never had much of value to say, or contribute."

He smiled and nodded, "It's refreshing Pamela."

He looked at her and could sense she was still uncomfortable. *Maybe trying too hard?* he thought. He wondered how to help her balance her newfound ability to converse without adding more stress to her fractured life. Finally he said, "Let's just have a relaxing dinner. No need to do more than you really want to do."

"Thanks," she said and remained quiet for a long while.

The exhausting ordeal of her tale and the fast approaching night made it wise to camp where they had settled. The woods were less dense than earlier in the day and the huge trees allowed a slight void in the canopy. The last rays of the tropic sun glowed orange for a brief time and they knew that the total black of night would soon follow. Then forest was in darkness.

"I'll do the dishes in the morning," he said with a yawn.

He tried to adjust to the ground again and found it as hard and lumpy as ever. *Ah for a Marriott!* He thought about it and said to no one, "Hey, even Bates Motel might work."

She curled up a bit closer than usual this time coming about an arm's length away. All was quiet but he could sense that she was still awake. Normally it was his own exhaustion that made him sleep first. Finally he asked into the darkness, "Pamela?"

After a moment she said, "Yes?"

"How do you know how to find food and especially how do you know it's okay to eat? And you seem to know quite a bit about, well … I don't understand any of this."

He could hear her breathing … thinking. He continued, "You have such survival skills. Are you trained in this? You know, military or a ranger or something?"

She responded in a low, controlled voice, "Andrew, something dreadful has happened to me. I'm … I've been changed … altered somehow. I can sense things. Things that aren't logical. I can tell what is good to eat and what's to be avoided. And I can find this food without much effort. Please don't ask me how."

She stopped for a bit, thinking in the darkness. Then she swallowed hard and continued, "They ... someone, some natives actually, well they rubbed some kind of oils on me. It was night and ..."

He could hear how difficult this was for her. "Pamela, I can wait until later if you want."

She was silent for a while and then said, "No, I need to say it now. Get it over with. The oils have changed me somehow. That first night, when I found you, well I just knew that the moss I rubbed over you would hide your scent. And I know somehow that I now blend with the forest. That I ... I ... well, there are other things. Strange things Andrew ... changes that I can't explain. I'm different now Andrew. Very different."

With that she turned over and he thought that there would be no more until the morning. A short time later however he felt a gentle touch on his shoulder. Out of the darkness came her soft voice.

"Thank you Andrew."

With that they both slept.

Deep in the middle of the night he woke with something she said nagging at him. *I now blend with the forest.* At first this passed by him as strange but just more words among many flowing from her inner turmoil. Now this remark caused him to lie awake staring into the blackness and ponder just what was meant. *Blend with the forest ... as if she was now somehow connected ... linked in some integral way with the woods in which we're trapped.* It made no sense but something about the way she said it seemed both precise and compelling. As if she was stating a fact that was ancient and springing from the core of her being. *Blend with the forest?* This seemed more than a matter of just being comfortable with the woods but sounding as if she described a homogeneous state of existence ... a state of balance, of harmony ... perhaps oneness?

As he pondered this a soft light slowly brightened the small clearing. The moon had again come to the point in its course that allowed it to peek through the canopy leaves and fall upon their crude encampment.

He rose up and stared at the apparition a few yards away. There emerged the same vision as his dream of the past night. The elfin figure was again kneeling in front of a large animal silhouetted against the deep black of the forest trees by the silver glow of the moon. Soft whispers and a gentle touch with hands that held the head of the animal indicated a tender bond between them. The moonlight shifted slightly and fell upon the leg of the kneeling form. A small circle appeared, glowing seemly from an inner life … unique and holding a mysterious power. The moonlight blinked and then faded and all was again held in the blackness of night. He listened for a long while but the only sounds heard were those typical to the forest nighttime. Slowly sleep took him and held him until dawn.

She was up early again. It seemed to be a cycle that her body was adjusting to now. As usual the cat had gone even earlier. This time was different however. In his place by her side was a present. Pamela shuddered at the sight of the small, gutted rodent. Obviously the cat not only thought of himself as protector but also as provider.

She forced a smile and was still amazed at how a feral animal could be so wild yet at the same time so gentle. *Strange,* she thought, that it seemed to sense that Andrew was not a threat. It shied away from him at first rather than being aggressive. After that it was as if it had accepted him as what … one of the pack? She looked over at him, still fast asleep and curled up on his side. He looked both awkward and comfortable sprawled on the ground trying to somehow support his head with the crook of his arm.

"Pillow?" she whispered at him sleeping and smiled again. She shook her head. It was the second time she smiled that morning and that alone amazed her. The first time was out of frustration when she ruefully wished she had a plastic bag. Yesterday's talk with Andrew still hung over her demanding her attention. She had actually shared parts of her life, intimate details with a man she knew very little about. Still, she considered, it seemed easy, or at least not as painful as she thought it would be. Perhaps, like the forest, sharing with him was cathartic. In some way she felt that the forest had healed her. Or at least was in the process of healing her. Not totally, but perhaps enough so she could share at least part of her life with him. Yet, there were those other things, the dark things ... the disturbing things. She shivered realizing that as forthright as she was yesterday there were areas of her transformation that she could never share. She was still a freak.

She wondered about *his* ordeal. It was probably as terrifying as hers, just different. And, unlike her, he didn't choose to come to this place. *Obviously not as dumb as I am,* she thought. *Blood and strange potions? Monstrous animals? What on earth was Charles attempting to do? ... more than we could have imagined.* The woman's words returned and wrapped the morning air in a sudden chill. *His immense educational background,* she thought, *and then exploration into "old people" mysteries?* And now, as a result, they both were the subject of Charles' quest for the restoration of some long and mystifying heritage she had never heard of.

Andrew said he was forced to drink something horrible. "Gunk" he called it. Something that Charles and his cronies devised. For what? What would it do to him? Her own experience with the oils had resulted in her being close to a mutant. And the beast ... she flinched and her stomach clutched with an involuntary spasm at the thought of this violent creature.

This line of thought was too much and she tried to shake it off by moving about. She stretched and began her morning search for breakfast. Except for a small kink in her shoulder, perhaps a lingering consequence of her dislocation a few days ago, she seemed to fare remarkably well for sleeping on the ground. Andrew didn't seem to be doing as well. She glanced over at him again. He looked like an overgrown kid, hair tousled and clothes dirty and disheveled.

She really hadn't known any man in her life, except Stan of course, and with their strange relationship, that was hardly "knowing" anyone. That was more like two misfit high schoolers trying to play house. She only went out that one time in college and rarely went out with her girlfriends. In reality she had no girlfriends for her natural shyness and low self-esteem never provided enough confidence to easily make friends. Now this man lying in front of her, looking crumpled and worn, seemed to actually enjoy talking to her. She shook her head and wondered if he could have been a friend if she had met him earlier. Or perhaps more?

It was still very early but Andrew suddenly moaned and turned over startling her. At once her shyness returned and she shifted on her feet searching for words. He rubbed at his face and then his nose. Then a half-smile brightened his face when he saw her.

"Well, good morning! Another day in the deep woods begins."

How does he do it? she wondered. *We are lost, or at least we can't go anywhere and we are being hunted.* Uncertainty returned and yesterday's openness regressed. She struggled to find any sort of suitable words. Finding none she resorted to a soft, "Hi."

Thus began another day in the Brazilian forest.

CHAPTER THIRTY THREE
Atlanta

Crowds were thinning in the quaint downtown Atlanta restaurant as Mike and Marie were shown to a small table that looked over the street. Mike would have preferred a more private area but she still seemed to need something to take her mind off the unexpected loss of Andrew. "He was like a second father," she had remarked to him.

It was becoming more certain that something had happened to Andrew for which there may never be an explanation. His car remained where he always kept it. No sign of anything missing or disturbed in his apartment a few blocks from his shop. Nothing was uncovered that could be considered a reason for him to disappear. And especially since he would always contact someone, particularly Marie to say if he was going somewhere.

It was the fifth time they met for an "update" lunch. This time she had called him saying she had found something of great interest in Andrew's office. Mike was up for anything to keep the meetings going. She had explained the last time they met that she was going into the shop very early and actually baking. Not nearly as good as what should be expected by the regular shoppers she said, but hopefully getting better. Andrew had shown her the basic recipes and she had already been helping with preparation for a few months. He had been in the habit of keeping detailed recipes for years and the list of ingredients was meticulously annotated with the reasons why they were integral to the product. She had used this small book as a guide and was now managing to keep the basic goods stocked in the cases.

Business was still good but she struggled as to just what she should say about Andrew when the regulars asked for him. She was in early as usual yesterday morning doing the books. Fortunately she had access to the online banking account and was able to buy supplies and pay the invoices as usual. Then she found it. Back in the small safe, which was unlocked and used mainly for fire protection, she had come across two small notebooks along with an envelope. The envelope was plain white, slightly dog-eared and shoved in the back. It also had a slight bit of what appeared to be jelly from a donut on one side. Across the front was scribbled, "Marie" and inside was a legal document dated eight months before his disappearance. It was a notarized will that left all his things, including the bakery, to her. A small handwritten note simply said that she was all the family he had and everything was hers. It was signed, "With great affection, Andrew." It was that simple. And she was stunned.

The notebooks were something else however. They amazed her in both topic and detail. The first was much older, a deep brown leather cover with the yellowed pages tattered and ancient. The writing was more of a scribble and in English mixed with what appeared to be Spanish. She found later that it was Portuguese. The second book, newer but still quite worn was all in English and written in a neat hand that painstakingly listed all of the ingredients for his baked goods. However, intertwined with these were numerous pages listing herbs and plants with their medical and medicinal purposes. Some of the notations were obviously copied from books and some of the notations seemed to be from observation. These seemed to indicate how the baked goods could alleviate numerous ailments and be beneficial to the health of the users. The information not only covered baked goods but teas, exotic vegetables, elixirs and a variety of other staples.

She handed these to Mike asking if they might provide some clue to Andrew's disappearance. Mike was as puzzled as Marie but promised to give them to someone who could determine their value, if any, to the case. It was the first time he spoke of this as a "case" and at this he noticed a look of deferred acceptance and finality move across her face.

With that, Mike internally winced and tried to lighten up the topic. They were finding that they shared many things in common. The one surprising item being a mutual passion for Italian cooking. This fact had amused Marie, her name being Luchietti and his O'Brian. After the lunch was over and as they walked back to the shop he swallowed hard and finally said, "Uh, there is a very good

Italian restaurant downtown, in fact not far from here. Would you, uh, if you're not busy of course, like to have dinner?" She glanced up in an uncommitted way and said, "Well, when?"

Whoops, ball back in my court now, he thought.

"Hmm, Friday?"

She gave a little shrug and said, "Ok, that will work. I close the shop at 5:30."

They walked in silence to the shop and went in. She fastened on a white apron and went behind the counter. He began to leave and she called out, "Mike." He closed the half-open door and walked to the counter looking puzzled.

"Yes?"

She learned over the counter to say, "What time? You know Friday?"

Feeling like a kid in grade school he grimaced.

"Oh, yeah ... sorry. How about seven? I can pick you up." She nodded her head and leaned a bit closer.

"Mike, what's the name of the restaurant?"

"Oh ... right ... it's Rinconni's."

"Oh I see." She thought for a moment and said, "Isn't that the one that is dark and with private booths lighted by candles?"

Mike grew uncomfortable and bit his lip a bit. He scratched his chin uneasily and said, "Well, it's supposed to be very nice. Great food."

She leaned even closer to him and placed her elbows on the counter, "And don't they have soft music with an accordion and a great wine list?"

"Well, I suppose ..." he responded uneasily.

She rested her chin on her hands and grew even closer to him.

"Sounds wonderful Mike," she whispered with a soft smile. "See you at seven."

CHAPTER THIRTY FOUR
Still Lost

He awoke much earlier this day and tried to adjust to the light mist of early morning. *Back to square one?* Andrew wondered. It was obvious that whatever ground was covered yesterday was fast eroding. Was she having second thoughts about sharing her life, her story, whatever it was? And there was that extremely practical consideration, the one that followed them like carrion eaters circling above. They were still very lost and couldn't continue to move pointlessly about forever. Yet here they were, back to wandering without purpose … and with her as silent as ever.

He tried several times to provide her with an opportunity to talk, share just a little more, delve just a tad further into the mystery. She herself seemed to listen intently when he would take the lead. He talked a little about his experiences in technical college where he dabbled in a little of everything. But he was puzzled when she suddenly interrupted and asked him what his mother would wear when she taught dancing. And he was even more perplexed when she seemed to nod knowingly when he said she usually wore a red dress and red shoes.

After that they walked aimlessly for an hour. Finally, tired of it all, he searched out a half-dead tree and slumped to the ground using it as a backrest. She stopped and stood directly over him without a word, obviously wanting to continue on. He gave her a disgruntled look and shook his head. "Sorry," he said "but being a baker didn't do much for my shape. I'll try to keep the pace but right now I need a bit of rest. Any idea where we are going?"

She looked at him as if only half there, distracted by something that ate away at her.

He rubbed his forehead for a moment and then said, "You talked yesterday. What's happened?"

Again she responded with an infuriating shrug.

He struggled to his feet and stared at her, "Sorry I'm a drag to your progress. Be better if I actually knew where we are headed.

And please don't shrug again! Well, no muffins or bagels out here so maybe I'll soon be fit enough to keep up."

She relinquished the shrug and, fighting through his sarcasm, said softly, "Don't worry, the forest is a natural spa. You will be fit in a week."

"Uh uh," he said. "And what's the alternative?"

She looked directly at him and then glanced at the surrounding trees. Then she looked back at him and simply said, "You will die."

The remainder of the morning was awkward for Pamela. She realized that she had made an opening for him yesterday. He had come dangerously close then to wanting more. She still desperately wanted to share, to open up her life, but that would naturally lead to more questions. And the answers would push him completely away. *How could anyone tolerate such a freak?*

For a while he let her alone and seemed patient to allow her to lead him on an erratic wandering path. Finally he sat down on a small fallen log and waited for her to notice that he had stopped again. When she turned around she waited silently for a long while, assuming that he would eventually get up and continue to trudge after her. Instead he just sat staring at her. Then, forced into stopping, she awkwardly returned and quietly sat down a short distance away.

Andrew ran his hands through his hair abstractly wishing for some way to lessen the days of oily buildup while he tried to think of something that would matter to her. He took a deep breath and said, "We've been through this before Pamela. I can't go on like this. Have you any idea where we are and especially how we can find our way out of here? We have to be near some kind of river. They brought me here by boat. And you mentioned a small village. In fact I was kept in a village by Charles and his thugs. It was abandoned but still, there must be someone around that can help us."

He looked at her, his brow now knotted into a frown. She knew he was growing frustrated with her and his obvious irritation was causing her stomach to knot up. *Am I driving him away?* she wondered. *God help me, I don't know what to say! He will leave soon, I know it. Maybe even yell at me.* She stared at the ground with a look of desperation not knowing what to do, what to say.

He sighed and said, "What were you thinking about when I woke up? You looked quite preoccupied."

This unexpected question startled her and allowed her an opening to shift the conversation in a less threatening direction. She started to shrug but caught herself and said, "Plastic bags."

Andrew cocked his head and looked at her for a moment. Then he chuckled saying, "Plastic bags? Ok, why?"

She nodded her head and looked uncomfortable. Then she gave an embarrassed half-smile and said, "Well I could carry more and then fold it up and put it in my ..."

At this he laughed even harder. She looked down realizing her clothes were so shredded that there was really no practical place to put a bag, even folded. And at this she too laughed. The first time he had seen her really laugh.

She was still quietly chuckling when she sat down next to him. "I'm not normally this moody." She thought for a moment and continued, "Well, maybe I am. Sorry. I've just ..."

She didn't finish the sentence as she saw him looking intently at something a short distance from him. There, just emerging from the foliage was a tiny, red tree frog. Even in the subdued light of the forest it was a brilliant crimson. Its small eyes were coal black with the lower half of its body a deep green. It appeared to be unaware of them and sat unmoving, perched on the fallen log a few feet from him.

"Look," he said smiling, "it's no bigger than my thumb."

He slowly reached out to touch it. Then, as his hand drew within inches of it, she suddenly yelled out, "NO, wait! Don't *touch* it!"

He jerked back his hand with a confused expression and stared at her. "What? I ... I don't get it. What's wrong?" He looked intently at the small thing trying to see whatever danger she saw.

"It's deadly Andrew. It's poisonous."

He shifted away from it and then stood up and asked, "OK, please tell me what's going on here? Why do you think it's poisonous?" She remained silent so he continued, "You said you could identify food, tell if it was edible. Is this somehow connected?"

Pamela tried to turn away but he caught her arm and gently guided her to face him, "Pamela?"

She closed her eyes and considered how much more she could safely say. What would make sense and still keep her freak side concealed. With that, realizing she must say something, she took a deep breath and began.

"Yes, it's somehow connected."

He could hardly hear her, her voice so low. She pushed his hand away and walked a short distance. There she bent down and easily dug up a small root. She held it up to him brushing off some of the clinging soil.

"This you can eat. I have no idea what it is. It's not very tasty but will keep you alive."

She pointed above them to a large vine with a rough, flaky bark about the diameter of a small child's arm.

"This will yield water if you cut it. It's clean and safe but slightly bitter. My fingernails will provide an opening. And that small shrub behind the one with larger leaves ..." She crossed to the bush and pulled back the covering foliage that obscured it. "This secretes a resin that will burn you. And the little fellow there." She pointed at the frog that still peacefully rested on the log. "Its skin oozes a substance that will kill you very quickly. Please don't ask me how I know this. I was never in a rainforest before. This is ..." she choked up for a minute and turned away "... this is very difficult for me."

She looked down at the ground and her voice faded to a whisper. "I'm changing Andrew ..." she said over her shoulder "and I don't know why. All I know is that the forest is no longer a mystery to me. It's becoming more open to me each day. It's ..." she thought for a moment. Then she said with a hollow voice, "It's complicated."

He watched her, trying to understand just what was happening and recalled a word she uttered earlier ... *blended*. Andrew looked at the frog and then into the dark woods with which she was becoming so connected. He gazed intently at her and said, "You still haven't told me everything have you?"

It was more a statement than question. She stood very still gazing into the great expanse of the forest. Then she could only lower her head and whisper, "No."

Was Charles losing it? His frustration was visibly increasing by the hour and Samuel was becoming more frustrated with the never-ending postponements. It was now far into the morning. *Well Charlie, can we go now?* he thought.

He needed action and Charles was heading down yet another track. They had spent most of the night reconstructing the additives within the pool's water. All of the while Charles cursed the fact that they were "sequestered in a primitive and secluded wilderness filled with ignorant fools".

Tough on your own tribe aren't you Charlie? Samuel thought. The last meticulous analysis had finally detected minute traces of animal proteins, three in particular. Partial sequences of *Panthera onca* were found. Then a subfamily of the *Accipitridae*, and lastly a reptilian protein of the suborder *Serpentes* were specifically identified. Why these would be within the water was the question that haunted Charles.

Samuel had just returned from the surface where he fed his pet. He gave only a small portion to the creature as he wanted to keep it on the ravenous side in expectation of his approaching hunting adventure. His mind was filled with wonderful images of feasting. Samuel loved his fertile imagination, and the horrors he could concoct with it. "Soon," he had whispered to the beast as it greedily tore into the small rodent that was caught in the night trap, "very soon."

CHAPTER THIRTY FIVE
Grandfather

I blend with the forest ... Andrew mulled this over in his mind and became more determined to get to the bottom of the mystery. And if he needed to push her to talk seriously about alternatives, well he would. He simply must for both their sakes. *Perhaps a direct approach,* he thought. *I'll simply ask her pointed questions.*

Just then a roll of thunder echoed through the high trees and they heard, more than felt, the swift pummel of a tropical downpour beat upon the upper canopy. After a few moments the initial sprinkle grew into an actual deluge in the less dense spots of the woods and he found protection beneath a huge limb. Pamela however looked up smiling at the rain and stepped beneath a stream of water pouring from the upper trees. She stood under it and allowed the cool flow to splash over her. Andrew watched her as the water washed over her face and streamed from her hair. Then it slowly dawned upon him that he was missing a wonderful opportunity. He passed by her to another spot and delighted in the flow of wet upon his body. He removed his shirt and felt like yelling "Thank You!" to the sky above.

"Any shampoo?" he called out over his shoulder.

After a moment a small stick struck his back. He turned to see a grin on her as she also delighted in the downpour. She said, "Sorry, that's all I have."

Well, he thought, *that's different. Hopefully the start of another thaw?* He called back, "Thanks ... forgot we are in the jungle, not at the Hilton."

At that she turned and yelled out, "It's NOT a jungle! It's a forest Andrew. A great, wonderful forest!"

She then turned her back on him and with head bowed let the water strike the nape of her neck. After her unexpected eruption they both remained silent until the cascading stream gradually slowed to a few drops.

The damp clothes felt almost clean compared to what they wore for the past several days. Andrew backed off after her rebuke trying to puzzle out the reason for her outburst. As he was sorting things in his mind he felt her softly put her hand on his arm.

"Sorry, that was … sorry."

He turned and nodded. "No problem Pamela. Just tell me what's going on with you. I know something is really bothering you." He paused for a moment and then said, "And by the way, thanks."

She gave him a puzzled look at this and said, "Thanks? For what?"

"For showing me how to take a forest shower. I would have just stood there like a toad. Feels much better now. Except of course for the dent in my back from the shampoo."

"Are you trying to make this easier for me?" she asked uneasily.

He thought for a moment and said, "Pamela, I'll do whatever it takes to get us to be open with each other. My story is simple. But you … well? 'Complicated' is how you put it. How can I help you to be more forthright? From what you have told me I'm the only one in your life that's ever listened to you … or wanted to listen."

At this she shook her head and again turned on him. "No, that's not right! My grandfather listened! He *always* listened! And he cared for me! He really, really cared!"

Andrew took a step back, feeling as if he was riding a yo-yo. She stood before him, glaring at him with her small hands balled into fists. They stood appraising each other, Pamela looking besieged, as if the towering trees were closing in upon her. Andrew though appeared bewildered, trying to understand her increasingly complex and fragile psyche. In desperation, he stepped towards her and held her. He said nothing but allowed her to know he would not be judgmental. She allowed him to hold her for a moment but held her arms tensely in front of her. Finally he let her go and said as gently as he could, "Please tell me about your grandfather Pamela. He sounds very special."

It took a very long time for her to respond. She felt her brittle control slipping, terrified that she would lose all touch with reality if she was pressed any further. Of all her wounds, memories of her grandfather were the most difficult. She closed her eyes wondering if she could face this last and most devastating of all injuries. *Am I strong enough for this?* she wondered. *Can I face this now, here with Andrew and in the great forest?*

She shook her head as if to cleanse herself of apprehension. The forest seemed to take the damaging memories of her father and mother and purify her soul. *Perhaps*, she thought, *perhaps it's time.* They walked together with Pamela slowly relating her intimate tale. The last delicate but hidden memory that she silently carried with her through her life.

She started with the short Sunday trips to her grandparent's farm in a small town some forty miles from her home. These were her fondest memories after the sudden departure of her father and the visits were the only stable moments left in her young life.

She told Andrew how the best times were when they would arrive Friday afternoon for a long weekend visit. She would wait anxiously by the living room window watching for her grandfather's return from the mill. When he would walk in, his large presence filled the doorway and he would greet her with a call, "Where's my girl Pamela?" She would laugh and run to him allowing him to hoist her to his shoulders. From there the ritual began. He would carry her to the fireplace mantel where he would tease her by saying he forgot and left all his pocket items at work. Then with great coaxing and giggles, he would slowly empty the precious contents from his overalls. The warm fire would lick at her small legs making them toasty and secure in his strong grip. The sweet fragrance of wood chips and sawdust clung to his rough wool shirt. Rich aromatic cedars, sweet sticky pinesap and pungent hickory blended into a fragrant potpourri. Even now, within the deep woods of the Amazon, she could recall the delightful fire, rich smells and warm hugs. Then the items from his pockets were carefully placed upon the wide oak mantel.

First came the coins, usually a few pennies and perhaps a dime or a quarter. Then the single worn acorn he always carried, "To remind us of how the Good Lord started the great forests," he would say. Next his few dollars neatly held by a walnut clip carved in the shape of an "H" for the family name. At last, his large rough hands, red and chapped from hard work and the weather, searched for the one object she treasured most. He would tease her saying it must be gone. He must have lost it. Then, coming only with more giggles and coaxing, he would carefully draw out an elegantly carved basswood whistle. She would carefully take it and blow it, delighted to hear its cheerful and clear tone resonate through the living room. Then she would gently place it next to the small penknife he had used to carefully craft the whistle.

This became the most precious object in her life. A tangible reminder of the strong yet gentle person she loved so dearly. It was an embodiment of the dear large man with wood chips in his graying hair. She loved him.

She also loved her grandmother though she was so very different. Where her grandfather was large and outgoing, her grandmother was small of stature, always appearing frail, even shriveled … and usually grim.

When she was younger, Pamela had always thought that her grandmother was just a small person. As she grew older and more observant she saw that her smallness was more a matter of character than stature. She saw that it was her spirit that was small, withered as if by some battle. A horrible interior struggle had occurred, one that her grandmother had lost. Her scarred, war-weary soul had given up its light and now her physical appearance reflected that inner battleground, scorched and desolate.

They had stopped and rested for a while. Andrew sat motionless, head down as if he was witnessing a profound tragedy. She continued by saying how she would sometimes see her grandfather glance at his wife, observing her smallness, her sour countenance and then seem to shrink himself. He was always so very kind to her. Overly gentle in many ways, seeming to want to recall brighter times that Pamela could not remember. She could, as she grew older, recognize how her mother had assumed her own bitter outlook on life. Pamela's mother had taken her own mother's depressing spirit and had made it hers. Yet even with all of this, her grandfather was the great joy of her life, bringing the only stability available since her father had left her.

Then there was the accident at the mill. Afterwards there were no more cheery fires in the fireplace and the mantle remained forever bare.

A few weeks later, Pamela sat quietly in the living room of her grandparent's home while the adults were carrying out the ritual of "going through his things". The wood whistle was lying on the . coffee table in front of her for many hours. Finally she looked around and seeing no one, snuck it into her dress pocket and pressed it close to her little leg. Later that night, she cried herself to sleep holding the last precious memory of her life. Each morning she hid it deep in her drawer behind some old socks and each night she would take it and hold it tight, recalling the warm hearth and dreaming of sweet-smelling wood chips. Several days later it was gone. Even though her heart was broken she could never ask about it, though she knew where it went.

Pamela took a deep breath and grew quiet. When she looked over at Andrew he was obviously deeply touched by her poignant tale. He wiped at the mist in his eyes and struggled to say something of comfort. This time it was Pamela that spoke words of reassurance.

"It's ok Andrew. He was precious above all to me and now his memory is fresh and clear. Somehow, I've just let all of the hurt go but the joy of his wonderful life remains with me. It ... it was something I needed to do. Thanks for ..." she paused thoughtfully and then looked up at him, "thanks for helping me to be healed. I think, as strange as it seems that I've just given this to the forest."

She smiled and glanced around the dense overgrowth and into the high trees with what seemed like profound respect, even fondness. Andrew blinked and tried to absorb what had just happened. He knew it was something of great importance but was unable to determine just what it was. He swallowed hard and wiped the dampness from his cheeks. He then took her hand and as they walked deeper into the woods he wondered if he could ever comprehend the mysterious power held within the great forest. And if he would ever understand even a small part of the one that walked by his side.

Charles stood with hands spread flat upon the gray stone while gazing at the massive charred tree that loomed over the dark village. He slowly raised his head to the blackened upper branches and then solemnly lifted his hands while intoning a strange incantation to ancient gods known only to him. He paused dramatically for a moment and then began to trace arcane symbols in the crusty, dried blood which covered the sacrificial altar.

Samuel witnessed the bizarre scene wondering how he ever became acquainted with such a strange person. *My approach,* he thought, *is much more direct.* And he was joyous that it was now time to apply his direct approach.

Then Charles turned and spreading his arms proclaimed, "The hour has arrived."

Here we go ... more theatre! thought Samuel.

"Samuel, I want you to take the native and your 'creature friend' and find Pamela and Andrew. Return them to me before dusk. Our tests show conclusively that we can reconstitute their blood. Even though it has been severely tainted, our facilities in Atlanta are more than adequate for this. We will use this ancient altar for its true purpose." He ran his hand sensually over the stained stone as if he were savoring the approaching violence. "Go Samuel, it is time for the goddess to shed her blood."

CHAPTER THIRTY SIX
Ethnobotony

It was becoming obvious to both Andrew and Pamela that they had reached a crossroads in their budding but increasingly strained relationship. He knew there was still something significant yet untold but he was baffled about what it might be. After she had told her touching tale of her grandfather she seemed to have released the last of her childhood hurts. But now he sensed something else. Something possibly flowing from another experience still lingered within her. And all of his instincts told him it was somehow connected with that dark night when she first arrived in the forest. *What was it?* He searched for a small statement, *something about oils. Yes, they rubbed oils on me … that was it. But why would this be noteworthy?*

He slowly rubbed the back of his neck and glanced over at her. She was staring almost trance-like into the high trees absorbed in her own thoughts. *Oils,* he considered. *I'm changing … she had said. Could the natives, whoever they are, have some of the secrets that Charles is seeking? So little information,* he thought. *And the very one that can clear it all up seems to be determined to hold on to her secret.* He blew out a breath in exasperation. *Oils … changing? Well,* he thought, *no place to go but to her.*

"Pamela?" She seemed not to hear him, as if she were now secreted in a faraway place, absorbed in her private thoughts, whatever they may be. Again, she seemed to him as teetering on the edge of a precipice. The image returned of the woman and their first meeting, two personalities locked in a struggle. One confused and frightened, the other beginning to show an emerging strength. But the tension within her was obviously mounting and he wasn't sure where it would end. He frowned as she continued to gaze into the lofty canopy and wondered if she knew how much he cared for her.

They are so wonderful, she thought. Pamela wondered if she could actually stay in the woods forever. Somehow she knew the forest intimately. How this was, wasn't as important as why? She assumed that a process she couldn't fathom had changed her both physically and emotionally. But the *how* was now inconsequential. It was the *why* that must be answered. "You are our only hope", the woman had said. Yes, the real question was now *why* had she been changed? Perhaps the very nature of her transformation now compelled her to stay in the woods.

As she searched the vastness of the trees in front of her for an answer, it all became unimportant. Now there was someone in her life. And she must admit that he was as important to her as anyone had ever been. Therefore the question became … could she live here in the forest without him? And this she knew would soon be a reality. He would surely leave her when he found out just how great the change in her had been. She closed her eyes and tried to keep her heart from breaking.

"Pamela?" He tried again and this time she seemed to break away from her reverie. But a little smile was all she could manage.

"You okay?"

She nodded and tried to speak a small word of reassurance but could find none. She swallowed hard and nodded again. He considered her reaction and decided to take another path.

"Do you remember when we were talking about Charles and you said that he wanted your blood?"

She glanced up with a look of apprehension.

"Yes," she said cautiously, her tone wrapped with tension.

"Did you ever wonder about that? I mean … blood?"

Pamela knew just what he meant. However she didn't quite know just where this would lead.

"Yes," she said again and then thought, *more than you know.* Andrew seemed to be determined to delve into issues she desperately wanted to avoid.

"He wanted my blood also. But after taking several samples he was then trying to alter my body chemistry. It's something about our heritage. We are both from here you know. At least our parents were."

She stared at him, mouth partly opened. Stunned at where he was leading the conversation.

He continued, "I know I'm making some assumptions here. Right?"

She tried to turn away but his forthright questions demanded her attention. *Please,* she thought, *please no.*

"And," he persisted, "if our heritage and the blood that flows in our veins is important to Charles … well, he surely will be coming for us again … and very soon!"

All she could do now was nod numbly in agreement. Andrew stopped for a moment and stared at the ground trying to carefully craft his thoughts. He pushed on, "Do you see where this is headed? Charles is one sick guy Pamela. There are two possibilities that I can see. The first one is that Charles is very disturbed and living in some complicated fantasy world fabricated by his sick mind. And we are regrettably caught up in his very dangerous illusion. The second possibility is still more frightening … and no doubt more deadly. That is, Charles is very disturbed but has actually stumbled on to some ancient legend. My gut says he is accurate in thinking that there is a deep mystery here in this great wonderful forest. And we, Pamela, especially our blood, are the fundamental answer to his dreams."

Pamela's stomach twisted for she knew the truth. It was the latter possibility. Charles was right. There was something of great power within this part of the forest … something extraordinary. It was somehow linked with their blood. And she was beginning to experience the strangeness of this power.

Andrew drew her back abruptly by asking, "Pamela, tell me about that first night. About the oils and what happened after that?"

She quickly shook her head and tried to get up. He reached out his hand and held her back.

"No!" she said. "Please Andrew, no." Her voice faded to a defeated whisper.

He refused to let her go. "Whatever happened I'm here to help you."

She continued to try to pull away and her hand began to tremble. "Please Andrew, no."

At this he let her go and said as gently as he could, "Let's pull up this couch and sit for a while."

He walked a few feet and plopped wearily to the ground. He then looked up entreating her by patting the earth beside him. "Come on, we're friends here. Please sit down and relax a bit."

A friend, she thought? She looked intently at him and knew that he was just that. The friend she had always wanted, always needed. And this made her more forlorn than ever. *I can't tell you who I really am*, she thought. *In fact I don't really know that myself. Just that you would never understand! And that you will leave me.* She thought desperately for a way to head off the present course of conversation.

Maybe I can have him go another direction. Suddenly she spoke up. "Andrew ...," she said hurriedly "...when I found you at that village. I was drawn by your humming. What was it? What was the song? It was ... I really liked it. It sounded so beautiful. Especially considering that you were tied up and ..."

He put up his hand and said, "Whoa, wait, slow down." *Okay*, he thought, *we'll go your direction for a while. But my dear, we will definitely get back on track ... and out of here!*

He stretched thoughtfully and said, "You know, I really need to think about that one. That wasn't one of my best moments. In reality I was scared ... well, let's just say really, really scared."

He recalled that dark moment and frowned. He then blew out a long breath and bit his lower lip. "I needed something Pamela. Something to pull back my resolve. I really thought I would be dead by the next day. Probably would have been without you. It was what came to mind. I needed something to pull me out of the perpetual night of that dark place. I needed above all, hope."

He turned to look directly at her, "I couldn't grasp the idea that I was actually in such a mess. Nothing seemed real to me."

He tried to smile but the memory of his captivity still horrified him. "With the things they were feeding me I knew that I was in very serious trouble. You know Pamela, I understand a bit about this forest also. I never let on to Charles or his gang of thugs but I identify with some important things that are fundamental to this place. Remember, my father was born and lived here." He gestured to the woods and continued, "Have you ever heard of ethnobotany?" He continued on assuming that she hadn't. "It's fascinating. Look about you. You can find thousands of growing things that are beneficial right here in the forest. Imagine a culture here with knowledge of both the land and which plants are valuable to the people, for providing food and especially for healing. The Shaman that lived with the tribes had some of this knowledge Pamela. They knew about the medicinal plants and could make healing brews and ointments. My father brought some of this knowledge with him from the forest and used it when he made some of our special baked goods.

Since the Shaman knew that he had old blood, as Charles called it, my dad was learning many of the ways of the woods. Sort of an apprentice. I didn't tell Charles that while I'm not a biologist, I do understand the way our bodies need the plant world to live. It's not a coincidence that we are told all of the time to eat our vegetables or that whole grains are good for us."

Her mind immediately went to the night when she rushed to the forest in panic desperately trying to help her dying cat. And she did exactly what Andrew spoke of, she instinctively knew what must be done to heal. She now had an intuitive memory deep within her, the knowledge of the wisest Shaman.

Andrew watched her closely as she slowly nodded her head showing that she fully understood his words. She then asked him a pointed question. "But what was the song? You haven't told me the name of the tune."

At this he had to smile. *Off-course again? Or does she really, for some reason, need to know this?*

"Are you familiar with opera? It's Puccini. From Turandot?" He turned towards her expectantly but saw her blank stare.

She then looked chagrin and said, "Sorry, I don't know this. But you are right Andrew. Perhaps we are in need of hope above all. Maybe that's what I'm looking for – hope."

He sighed and said, "Well, maybe we are meant to be each other's hope. And by the way, when we get to Rio I'll take you to the opera, right after the manicure of course."

At the mention of Rio her heart fell. Then she shuddered as a slight chill carried by a small forest breeze passed over her.

The beast strained against the chain and snapped at the native who was instructed to free it. Finally Samuel needed to do it himself, though even he had difficulty restraining the creature from charging madly into the undergrowth.

"Bring them both alive," came the curt command from his highness, King Charles. Samuel had had enough of the silly posturing and decided to do whatever best fit his own purpose, not Charles'. And that would be whatever he thought would be the most fun. *I'm a fun, impulsive guy,* he thought. *Let's see where the best path of enjoyment leads.* He snugged his gun into his holster, fit his tropical hat at a jaunty angle and grinned. *Should I say, Tally ho,* he wondered? Then he drove both the native and the beast into the woods.

CHAPTER THIRTY SEVEN
A Merging of Purpose

"But you Andrew, why did he bring you here?" Pamela asked. They walked slowly, trying to stretch out after sitting on the ground for a long while. Andrew gradually worked the topic back to focus on why they were here and where they should go next. But she kept shifting the subject from herself back to him. He took a page from her book and shrugged.

"Probably for backup I guess. Charles made it clear to me that my blood isn't as rich as yours. Maybe that's why I was a test dummy for them. After you were shuttled from their grasp they started to give me treatments. I think they only got about halfway done and then some wonderful person busted me out." He smiled and nodded to her, "A sincere thanks again." He folded his arms and took a deep breath. *Here goes,* he thought. "Pamela, what is it that you haven't told me? What has happened to you here? Please tell me about it."

She shook her head and tried to smile. It changed to a grimace. "Oh, no big deal. Just some odd things like being able to find the food and stuff. Nothing much."

He thought that over and said, "Good, then there is no reason why we can't get out of here. We can start to find something or some person that will get us out of these woods. Let's find that village where you first arrived as a starting place. From there we can find the river. Charles has to be coming soon for us. In fact it just makes sense that he's already searching for us."

She was shaking her head all of this time.

"No, I really don't think we can," she said. "We can manage all right here. We have survived so far and we can ..."

He interrupted her and said heatedly, "No! Look, we simply can't carry on like this. This place is deadly and we have just lucked out so far. Somehow we have to get out of here! And you ... well you simply have to understand this!"

Pamela stood with her head down, fists clenched and shaking with fury. He started to say more but she suddenly turned on him.

"NO! Don't you understand? I CAN'T return anymore! It's IMPOSSIBLE!" She took a threatening step towards him and screamed, "For God's sake, I have animals in me! Even SNAKES!"

Her voice grew sharp and shrill bouncing off the high trees and echoing in his ears. Andrew blinked at her outburst and stepped back but she came at him again.

"WHY? Why couldn't you leave it alone Andrew? I'm ... I'm a damn mutant! Animals! They have changed my whole body! Don't you understand?!"

She suddenly charged forward again and slammed her small fist onto his chest. Then she sank to her knees and shaking with rage, covered her head.

Andrew stared dumfounded with hands raised in confusion as she lay crumpled and despondent before him. He sensed her mind desperately trying to retain its grip on reality but knew that she was fast losing the battle. He remembered the tale of her mother and saw Pamela attempting to flee into the protective shelter of total despair.

Despite the tropical heat the winter winds swirled about her ready to encase her mind as she sought the sanctuary of the grey pit. He saw her retreat and would not allow it. He went to her and quickly knelt down. He gently pulled her close and held her for a long moment giving her the warmth and comfort she desperately needed but never knew. At first her body became rigid at his touch and struggled to push him away. She murmured faintly and resisted him shaking her head. Tears streamed down her face.

"Go away, please go away. It's over. Just leave me now ..." she whispered.

Then he thought that he had lost her, "No, I won't go Pamela. I will never go."

Hearing that she slowly relaxed and snuggled closer to him, allowing the healing balm of weeping to repair her fractured psyche.

It took Pamela a considerable time to finally stand. He tried to support her as she slumped wearily, her steps more a drained shuffle. But his concern was now her noticeable shift in attitude.

After slowly recovering from her outburst she now seemed to be shaping a new paradox. Little by little she became more reserved and yet more open. She seemed to have come to a conclusion. She smiled more now and talked freely but there was another barrier, subtle and newly erected.

After a bit of deliberate walking she told of the night they "anointed" her, as she described it. She even told of her flight into the darkness after the attack and her incredible leap across the expansive gulley. How her body had done the impossible. It was all open now, all except a slightly detectable reservation that Andrew felt in his gut rather than knew from her revelations. A new purpose seemed to be forming within her. A freshly fashioned resolve that Andrew instinctively perceived but couldn't identify. He wondered about this transformation as she stopped suddenly in the small path that they followed.

She looked at him and thought he looked so very weary. She felt remorseful that she had been so preoccupied with her own fears that she was ignoring his needs. *He does deserve to go home,* she thought. She swallowed hard at this notion and tried to keep her tears from spilling over again. A new purpose continued to gain strength within her and she grew closer and took his hand. He looked startled at this and even more bewildered as she reached up and gently smoothed his matted hair.

"Come with me Andrew. There is something astonishing that I want to share with you."

Her words sounded final, as if she had somehow become detached from their shared predicament of being lost and hunted.

She continued, "You said you were looking for hope. Let me show you what I found here in these incredible woods."

She talked as they traveled and told him of how she had come to love the forest. She spoke of the slow and often terrifying transformation she had been experiencing. The tale of her childhood tattoo and the strange oils were related to him. Finally they came to a small clearing and stepped into a sun-drenched space that was bordered by unimaginably high trees. She turned and smiled at him as she gestured silently at the landscape before them. Andrew stopped and gaped at what he saw. He had never seen or even imagined such splendor. Pamela watched him as he stood mesmerized by the riot of color cascading from the trees. He slowly walked to the expansive wall of orchids and ferns and reached up to gently touch the lower flowers. He turned and smiled broadly at her but said nothing, just shaking his head in amazement. Finally, after a long while of being enthralled by the beauty of the forest, he turned to her and said with a voice choked with emotion,

"Thank you."

They spent the next several minutes sitting quietly before the tumbling gift of floral elegance. Then following an impulse, Andrew got up and walked to the flowers. There he selected a single white and lavender blossom and snapped it from the vine. He returned to Pamela and bowing slightly lifted her up by the hand. Selecting a small tear from the many in her blouse he carefully placed the bloom as delicately as he could.

She gave him a puzzled look and blushed slightly. He bowed gracefully to her and then took her in his arms and, humming a slow waltz, led her around the forest in a stately dance. She stumbled often but was determined to keep up.

Shafts of sunlight fell upon them anointing them with a forest blessing. She buried her face into his chest and found solace and peace in his melody and the soft forest sounds. The fragrance of her corsage filled her with joy and she felt tears wet her cheeks. Of the many that had fallen to the forest floor these were the first that were shed in happiness. They spent another hour together silently watching the orchids. Pamela glanced at him and thought, *if only it could last.* Then she sighed and resolutely said, "There is one more place I must show you. It's where I saw you for the first time."

She took his hand and began the trek to the temple.

Andrew studied her as she led him through yet another part of the forest. To him, it seemed as if they were continually wandering

without purpose. But he began to suspect that she was much more familiar with the hidden paths and obscured landscape than he had originally believed.

The puzzling aspect of two competing personalities within her seemed to be increasingly resolved. Now she appeared to be, what? Again the word *blended* came to him. Yes, that was growing more obvious. A merging of purpose, whatever that was. But with that also came a new uneasiness emerging since her outburst. In the place of the confusion came an apparent resolve. But this was overshadowed with a perceptible sadness. She walked as if she was viewing the surroundings with profound regret … as if she was bidding her beloved land farewell. Had the toll of being abandoned in the forest and the trauma of her admission of "animals within her" been the final blow? He became fearful for her and felt helpless to provide any solution or give her any solace.

As he was pondering all of this he became slowly aware of the subtle changes about him. The forest seemed to be going through a profound metamorphosis. Its character was evolving and he began to believe he knew where they were headed. The changes were becoming familiar, reminding him of the forced march to the "pool". *Is this what she meant by going to "where I first saw you"?*

He had dismissed the idea of her taking him back to the abandoned village but now this began to intrigue him. The woods were becoming more expansive with the tangle of undergrowth giving way to soft carpets of moss. Delicate shafts of light filtered through the upper leaves creating rich highlights where they fell. The trees seemed larger and their limbs began higher off the ground enhancing the majesty of the space.

Andrew felt as if he was approaching a place of power, a land that would demand awe and respect. He marveled at the increasing monumental scale and then suddenly he knew. She was the one that had stirred the water. How, he didn't know … but she was surely his wood nymph.

He watched her lead him with sure steps across the moss and then his mind remembered. The lovely, illusive poem of Keats finally came to him in a soft whisper – yes, she was the lady.

I met a lady in the meads,
Full beautiful—a faery's child,
Her hair was long, her foot was light,
And her eyes were wild.

She turned to him and smiled. It seemed a bittersweet smile. It tugged at his heart.

"We are there Andrew. The loveliest place on earth!"

With this simple statement she led him through the guardian trees and into the center of the temple.

CHAPTER THIRTY EIGHT
Return of the Jaguar

Even with the tension of his captivity and the strong bindings that held him, Andrew's first impression of the temple was still fresh in his mind. Now, standing in the heart of the soaring space enclosed by the vaulting trees, his heart was filled with awe. The operas with their magnificent sets portraying idyllic forest scenes that he loved so were paled by what was before him. His eyes went first to the pool. *Where I first saw you ... she had said.* He glanced over to her and saw that she was observing him, as if she wanted to see how he would react.

"Can you think of words to describe this place?" she asked softly.

All he could do was numbly shake his head. It wasn't a large space, perhaps one-hundred feet or so in breadth, but the dramatic height and the strength of the enclosing trees gave it a commanding presence that defied description.

"Who made this?" he asked.

Andrew found it impossible that the perfectly concentric layout of the great trees and the precise placement of each object within the space had occurred without direction. There was the pool with its floral and rock border. And one element that he didn't notice before. There, in the exact center and beneath an ocular formed by the open, high branches, was a canopied raised area. It was a moss-covered circular platform surrounded by six vine-covered columns that supported a canopy of vines. It too, as the temple roof, had an opening in the center as if planned to admit light from the heavens. *Altar*, he wondered? He turned and stared at her with only one question.

"Where did it all come from?"

"The old ones. Our ancestors," she responded without hesitation. "It's centuries old. Part of a mysterious complex that has been reclaimed by the forest."

Andrew looked at her quizzically and shook his head, "How do you know this Pamela?"

She walked to the low wall binding the pool and pointed to the stones. "These tell the story." She said this in a matter-of-fact way, as if she was here during the planning of the temple. Andrew could only stare at her. She was enigma personified.

He approached the wall and knelt before it. It was made of once smooth stones that were now pitted by ages of weather. The individual rocks were of various sizes, mostly rectangles, and piled up to contain the pool's front side. The wall was capped by flat stones that provided a ledge of seating height. Several large, broken jars with three smaller ornate ones lay a few feet away as if discarded in haste. Also near them were two minor pots of black and red ointments. And to intensify the mystery, most of the center stones were engraved with inscrutable symbols, each as enigmatic as the woman that stood calmly by his side.

He glanced up at her hoping that she would say more. When he looked back at the central stone, larger and of a different mineral than the others, he saw a symbol like the one that had glowed so brightly in the moonlight. His head jerked up and he stared at her. In response she slowly nodded and carefully lifted the small bit of her torn shorts that partly obscured the tattoo. It was comprised of the same characters as on the rocks; he stared at twin engravings, one on stone and one on flesh.

Andrew placed his hand on the rock and traced his finger along the outline of the circle. He felt the delicate rise and fall of the scrollwork that encircled the characters as if he could sense the figure's antiquity. Then he rose, and gently taking her hand, had her sit on the wall by him. For a long while he was speechless. Then he finally said, "Pamela, I just can't comprehend any of this. I told you that I couldn't accept my captivity as being real. But all of this …" He gestured at the temple and then patted the stone ledge upon which they sat. "Well, how can I …?"

Pamela nodded in support of what he was saying. "It was incomprehensible for me also Andrew. When I wandered hopelessly through the forest in my first few days it was all strange to me. I was positive that I was insane. Not just dreaming but thinking that I had mentally sunk into madness. Now … well I still don't understand it, but I do accept it." She shook her head realizing how this sounded. "Doesn't make sense does it?"

She gave a small laugh and looked squarely at him, "It defies common sense. I simply shouldn't be able do the things my body does. And I shouldn't instinctively comprehend the secret utterances of the forest. But I do and ..."

Just then Andrew froze, and rising placed himself in front of her, guarding her from the opening in the trees. She glanced past him and smiled, her heart gladdened. Her cat stood by one of the tall trees quietly appraising them. Andrew looked stricken but she put her hand on his arm and whispered, "Don't be alarmed. This is another astonishing part of my life now. This is one of my friends."

She pointed to the high trees and to a large bird that lazily soared above them, "There is the other one."

With that she walked towards the sleek forest cat and stopped to greet it. The cat walked with head down and butted Pamela's leg as he circled about her. He did this twice and then sat before her. She knelt down, her head level with the cat's. There she gently placed her hands on its large head and spoke softly to it, a scene recalling the misty, moonlighted image of Andrew's dreams. After a long while of tender communing with the animal it rose and gently butted her with its head. It then stretched, a graceful feline motion that evoked her confident footsteps through the woods, and returned to the forest.

Andrew sat down abruptly on the stone wall staring in amazement at the darkened opening where it had vanished. Pamela walked slowly to him and sat by him. She smiled but didn't speak immediately seeming to savor the moment that just occurred.

Andrew collected himself to the point where he could ask, "Will you ever quit piling mystery upon mystery? How do you expect me to deal with all of this Pamela? I just saw what I believe is a jaguar. A really big one! And, if the National Geographic channel has it correct, they are pretty wild in these parts. Why did he act like an oversized house cat? And why did he ignore me? This is pushing my limits here. I just can't ..."

She leaned closer and gently placed her fingertips on his lips and said, "I know. I feel like I'm in a dream most of the time myself. When I first wandered the woods a few days ago I told you that I thought I was insane. The only other option was a nightmare. I kept believing that I would awake and be back safely in Iowa. But we are here Andrew and as bizarre as it is, it's real."

He shook his head as he considered this. Then he said, "You asked me why I never married. I said I never met anyone mysterious enough. Well, mystery lady, this is a bit of overload!" He chuckled at this and continued, "Is there any way we can start at the beginning? Tie some of this together?"

He got up and stared thoughtfully at the pool, "You said that you first saw me here. Yet no one saw you. Or at least no one noticed your small trail in the pool … I did." He sighed and took a deep breath. "This is getting to be too much." He looked intently at her and said, "Any suggestions?"

"Yes," she responded. "There is very much I want you to know before …" she stared off through the trees as if she were looking for help from her friends "… it's time to go." A forlorn shadow passed over her face and then she continued. "Let's sit on the steps of the altar. I'll tell you all I know."

Altar, he thought. *This is becoming very strange as that's what I saw it as.* He rubbed his hand across the back of his neck and followed her to the mossy steps. They sat there on the second riser and leaned back upon the third. They both appreciated the softness of the moss and sat quietly for a moment trying to find a common point of understanding.

Finally Pamela began, "Did you ever climb a tree Andrew?"

This opening perplexed him and he glanced at her and shook his head no.

"We lived in a very poor section of Rio when I was young. No trees. And when we moved we lived above dad's downtown bakery. Why?"

She seemed to want to smile but her mouth turned down instead. "Yeah, neither did I when I was a kid. But here, here I climbed a tree. Up about twenty feet within a matter of seconds."

She looked down as if embarrassed by the statement, "The beast was after me. They used it to help Charles track me down. It sprang at me. As terrified as I was, I reacted somehow. I dodged it and was high up a tree before I realized it. My body just took over. I never thought about it. In seconds I was up in the tree." She looked up with a wildness in her eyes, "I can't do that Andrew! No human can react that quickly and climb that high! Yet I did. My body is very odd now."

She closed her eyes for a moment and put her hand to her mouth. He noticed her small hand trembled a bit and he desperately wanted to hold her, somehow comfort her. She swallowed hard and continued, "When Charles came and found me in the tree he was horribly frightening and ...," her voice faded to a self-conscious whisper, "... and horribly seductive. He's evil. I didn't truly realize that until I saw his face after the hawk attacked him. The hawk protected me. And the lady ..."

"Wait Pamela, please, it's all running together. Charles, beast, hawk and now a lady."

She put her head in her hands and mumbled, "I know, I know. It's just that so much has happened. Sorry Andrew."

"Let's start with first things and then move on," he said. "I'll ask some questions and then you can fill in the blanks. First, we all know Charles is not only nuts but is doing some very bad things. I'll go with your statement of evil. Second, that large bird is not a hawk. If I'm not mistaken it's a forest eagle. Third, the beast is a product of Charles and it indeed *is* evil. Now, first the pool. How did you disappear and what were you doing in the pool anyway? And then, what lady?"

She looked up and seemed appreciative that he sorted out some of her confusion, "Okay, pool first. I was here soaking after talking with the lady. I'll tell you about her in a moment. When I saw you, well actually I didn't see anyone, just felt the approach of the beast. I sensed it. Anyway, before I could do anything I was dragged beneath the water and into the back of the pool."

They both stared at the water. It was black from one direction and clear to the bottom from a different view.

"It was a snake that did it."

I hate snakes, she thought to herself.

"It was huge and midnight black. It saved me Andrew. It seems that the animals all try to protect me. I saw you and the men that held you from back there," she pointed to the rock outcropping.

He was still being beleaguered by the fact that it was all so unbelievable. Still he pushed forward. "Soaking uh?" he said quizzically. "Ok, thanks, now the lady?"

She sat up a bit straighter at this and looked directly at him. Andrew marveled at the puzzling transformation that he was seeing in her. She appeared to be evolving before his eyes. As if the shy person was finally receding and the more dominant one emerging. It seemed that the conflict he first witnessed was being somehow resolved. Still, there remained one newly formed barrier that she had raised since this morning. And this bothered him greatly, for he knew instinctively that she had decided something that would deeply impact both of them. And this decision had an unsettling finality about it.

CHAPTER THIRTY NINE
Mystery

"Her name is Cinta."

With that simple statement, Pamela began to weave a mesmerizing tale of her time in the forest. She painted a picture of the woman in her dilapidated shack speaking of an implausible saga. Primitive tribes mingling with the ancient ones of great power who faded from existence. She told of how she was sent into the forest to escape Charles and his men. And how this ordeal had torn her down, leaving her despondent and questioning her sanity, and then inexplicably had provided a healing balm for her damaged spirit. How she believed the forest, in some powerful but subtle way, had smiled benevolently upon her. She then told of her second trip to the temple and how she had sat at the very spot they now were to hear the tale further unfold before her. She told of being overwhelmed with the realization that she was of native blood … and especially the shock and disbelief at being the last of old blood. And how she finally accepted the unavoidable truth about her father and her tribal heritage. She further explained the strange powers she now had and how they were not hers to control but came unbidden and only at times of great stress. Then she was silent.

Andrew could only marvel at the trials that she had endured.

After a while she looked up and, with a faint smile, softly said, "Well, is that enough mystery for you?"

His heart went out to her and he felt as if he could weep forever. How could a person endure such mistreatment through her entire life and then be placed into an implausible situation such as this? He reached over and held her hand searching for something meaningful to say. She seemed to appreciate the gesture and they quietly sat within the temple watching the midday sun creep across the equator sky. Then she nodded to the stone wall a few feet away.

"The final mystery rests here Andrew, in these stones. Somehow they tell of a struggle. A clash of two cultures. Please don't ask me how I know that. I'm certainly not any reincarnation of an ancient princess."

Though, she thought, *Charles did mention something about a goddess.*

"I just, as if the stones have this fact somehow written within them … and much more. Perhaps Charles and his people are continuing this conflict with the woman's people, somehow continuing the struggle."

Now my people, she thought.

She shook her head, "I just don't understand it." She thought for a moment and continued, "What makes me believe that this is true, besides an innate feeling, is that the village where they held you. I was there one time before you and saw, and felt, the evil there. It is so much in opposition to this wonderful temple. It's literally darkness compared to light."

Andrew listened intently to her and could feel the sincerity in her voice. He also felt a strange veracity in her image of light and dark. This *was* a battle and for all they knew, an ancient one. Perhaps begun centuries ago and at a place far from the forest they now inhabited. And the truth was indeed buried within the stones before them. He smiled at her and patted her knee, "Yes, I feel it too Pamela."

He rose and went to the wall and stood before the center of the stones studying the images carved deep into their face. The sun had worked to the point where it fell upon them providing accents of shadow and highlighting the rough sandy texture of their surface. She followed him and stood close by his side while taking his hand in hers.

"You are right," he said. "These tell a tale, a journey and adventure that is written before us … and somehow much more than we will ever understand." He turned to her and looked deep into her eyes, her wild eyes, "It's all here," he said. "Except we can't read the message. Perhaps no one can anymore."

Andrew knelt down in the soft and fertile soil close to the stone wall. He pushed aside some higher moss and carefully touched the ingrained inscriptions with his fingertips as he closely examined the cryptic figures carved in the rough stones. "Possibly Mayan or Aztec?" he wondered out loud.

He looked up at Pamela and said, "I took a course at the local community college about early South American cultures. They didn't have anything specific about aboriginal tribes in the Amazon and this dealt mostly with Mexican cultures. Some of it touched on other areas such as Guatemala and even Peru. Nothing as far as Brazil though."

He shook his head in puzzlement and continued, "I thought I could get dad to go with me but he said that was past history and he was now an American. He was very proud when we were both granted citizenship. But I was growing more curious about my heritage. I even found this cool satellite map of the Amazon. Anyway … this looks like Mayan or perhaps Aztec. I'm far from an expert."

He pointed to one small figure and remarked, "That symbol I think is a cat and that is perhaps a bird but I don't know any others. That one may be the sun … or maybe the moon."

He carefully ran his hand over the carved stone as if he hoped it would somehow reveal its meaning to him, "I guess I should have paid better attention."

Pamela's heart quickened and she stared at the symbols as if they were ominous portents that foretold of her demise. Andrew glanced up and saw her suddenly shudder and looked quickly to the forest. She peered into the dark woods for a long moment and then shrugged slightly.

He considered this and then carefully asked, "You seem to have insights about the forest Pamela. Do you sense something here? Something within the markings of the stones?"

She closed her eyes and shook her head, "They … they are closed to me. All but that one." She pointed at the smooth middle stone that was of different color and texture than the others, "That one doesn't belong here. It was made somewhere else. And it, it …" She couldn't finish her thought but turned away, "It's blended. Just as I'm blended now. It's one with the temple. It sustains the temple."

She took a sudden step back almost tripping. Her next words sent an unexpected shiver through Andrew. She said in a reverential whisper.

"It's very powerful … and deadly."

CHAPTER FORTY
At the Temple

Samuel charged after the native and his pet as they crashed through the undergrowth. The creature seemed to be following some instinct that pointed it directly towards the heart of Pamela. Perhaps its twisted mind still held the memory of failure from their first encounter. The native struggled to control the beast as it pulled him relentlessly along with Samuel swiftly behind. His glee was increasing with each step and he went over in his mind the approaching encounter. The pleasure found in anticipation. He had always delighted in what his fertile mind could do with fear and pain ... his unusual skills often being restricted, as live subjects were off base when he was with his parents. He never had the chance to appropriately explore the connection of terror and physical pain. Not as he wanted to do. *Well, except for the small hamster.*

Then his brilliance took over. He found in high school that he could dissect things in certain classes. This lead to his chosen field of biology and the well-accepted exploration of *"the physiological and psychological reaction of nerve receptors under stress and applied pain"*.

His colleagues thought his work aimed at finding improved analgesics. In reality he just enjoyed the suffering of the poor things he used. *Mean and nasty,* he thought. Now he was close ... so very close. For he knew precisely where they were headed. And so did his pet.

Pamela and Andrew stood in front of the stones, each lost in thought. They pondered why the stones were here in this place, and how they came to be drawn here. Andrew shook his head and said, "We will never know, will we?" He then moved and knelt before the *blended* stone and traced his fingers again over the center shape.

At closer inspection the main circle held several small, raised dots spaced neatly at the edge and enclosing the ring. The center of the circle was filled with intricate and arcane scrollwork. He ran his fingers over the small impressions once again and counted them, eighteen smaller circles evenly spaced around the ring.

Something is familiar with this, he thought. Something very obvious hovered at the fringe of his understanding. Andrew rubbed his forehead and looked up at Pamela, "This is all here but I don't understand."

He glanced past her at the trees. They dominated the space, enclosing it … protecting it. Then he suddenly understood. He got up and walked to the nearest tree laying a respectful hand upon its powerful trunk. He stared far up its massive girth and nodded. After that he walked to the center of the temple and smiled. He slowly turned and counted eighteen trees.

"It's the temple Pamela. Somehow this figure represents the very place we stand in, and this is also your symbol."

She looked down and immediately saw how obvious it all was. She had carried the image of the temple from her childhood. It had drawn her to this very spot.

"But why Andrew? Why?"

All he could do was shake his head, "After all of these centuries it's probably gone. All of the knowledge has no doubt disappeared with the passing of those that built this. Sorry Pamela, it's probably lost forever." Then a chilling thought came to both of them.

"Charles?" she said.

He closed his eyes and rubbed his increasing beard for a moment. Then he looked up and said, "Dear Lord, let's hope not."

There was not much to say after that. A long silence where they stood side by side allowed them to wonder about private things … "what if" things.

Pamela looked at him and bit her lip. *It's time*, she thought. She fought back a sudden twinge of panic and prayed for the strength to do what she must. Pamela leaned close for a moment and laid her head on his shoulder with her eyes tightly closed. Then she took his hand.

"Andrew, it's time," she said softly, struggling not to break into tears. He glanced at her with a puzzled look.

"Ok, it's time ... and for what?"

She looked up at the opening in the temple canopy and tracked the path of the sun saying, "We have a few hours of light left. I can get you to ..." Her voice caught for a moment and she swallowed hard, "I can get you to someone that can help you."

There, I've done it, she thought.

He looked at her shaking his head.

"I still don't understand? What's going on?"

She sighed slightly and plunged on, "The woman, Cinta, I know where to find her. I'm sure she will help you find the river and a boat. She can help you get out of here. If we go soon it will be best." She turned and started for the opening in the trees.

"Pamela?"

She glanced back at him not really wanting to look at him, afraid that she couldn't do what must be done. Her heart was breaking. "Please Andrew, we must go now. She can get you home."

He stayed put and repeated, "Pamela. I didn't hear one important word in all of this."

She returned, head down and said, "What?"

He stepped forward and took her hand and raised her head to look at him. Her heart beat faster and she prayed that she wouldn't cry. "Please Andrew," she whispered, "you have to get out of here now."

He shook his head, "No, not the way you have said this. I didn't hear the word ... *we*. *We* need to get out of here. The lady needs to get *us* out of here."

"Please Andrew, this is important! You yourself said that it's dangerous here. Now let's go."

"Yes, it's dangerous and that's why we both need to leave. How can we stay here? And if I do leave just how will you survive? Granted your forest ways help, but how long can you elude Charles ... and especially his screwy henchmen and the monster? Remember, the evil thing?"

Pamela looked down searching for words, for strength, "Please!" she entreated.

He looked at her with growing frustration, "Give me a reason here. There is no reason for you not to leave, for *us* not to leave. Well?"

She struggled with this and wanted to bury her head. *I can't do this,* she thought, *but I must do this.* Again the old Pamela began to surface, unable to remain unswerving, to make a lasting decision, do something on her own.

"I can't go back. I have no one there anymore. Besides, I'm … well, strange now."

"Nope, not enough. You know that isn't a good reason."

"They will find out about how I am, I will become an experiment. Probably some government project. Can't you see how the CIA would love this!" She raised her voice and tried to plead with him, "They will find me!"

"Come on Pamela, that makes no sense at all, this isn't some dime store novel! We can lead a peaceful life if we just get out of here."

"Oh, and just where is that!" she shot back, "How about Ringling Brothers! Or better yet, some traveling freak show! I can just see the billboards. Come and see the woman freak, watch her climb trees in a single leap!" She glared and took a sudden step towards him.

Andrew fell back and with raised hands exclaimed, "Whoa, you aren't going to slug me again are you?"

She gave him a disgusted look and then glanced down at her hands balled into small fists. Then she caught the little twinkle in his eyes. *Damn Andrew,* she thought, *don't do this to me again.*

A small smile formed on his lips and then she had to laugh. She blew out an exasperated breath and said, "Can't you be serious for one minute?"

"Believe me Pamela," he said gently, "I'm very serious here. But I still haven't heard a very good reason for us, or you, to stay."

She reluctantly nodded, "Yes, these are very small reasons." She sighed and considered how to put it, how to tell him just what her heart said, "But there is one real reason. I don't know if you will understand."

She gestured at the trees, at the pool, at the encompassing, green canopy above, "It's this place, Andrew. It's this very temple. It's home for me now. Somehow I belong here. You said there was mystery in the stones. Well, I feel that there is something I'm to do here, some final call that I must answer. These are my people and I'm supposed to be here." Pamela looked straight into his eyes, "I think somehow you will understand this."

He slowly nodded.

"Now can we please go?" she asked.

He rubbed his forehead considering all of her words, "Yes, as strange as it seems, I do understand," he said. "And now, even stranger, there is something else we need to think about. Don't forget, I'm not a foreigner to this place either. There is old blood flowing in my veins also." He looked at her and smiled, "Pamela, I'm not leaving you. If you stay … well then I stay with you."

She looked intently at him, trying to absorb the meaning of his words.

"Do you really mean that you will … will stay here … with me?"

"Of course I will."

She placed her hand over her eyes trying to avoid the dampness beginning to brim over.

"But why Andrew? Why would you do this?"

He chuckled and said, "And all of this time I thought that I was so obvious. I simply want to be with you Pamela, forever."

She remained motionless, stunned by his words. Then she made a decision, her first commitment ever made without hesitation or questioning. She ran to him and, throwing her arms around him, kissed him.

A startled Andrew soon became an elated Andrew and they stood in the center of the temple protected for a time from their fears. Pamela rested her head on his chest and felt sheltered as he held her. Then she looked up and asked, "Are you certain Andrew? This will be difficult."

"Absolutely!" he said. "And you, my dear, are full of surprises."

She thought for a moment and said, "That surprised me too! It's not really like me."

"No ..." he responded, "This *is* you ... the real you."

They embraced again and allowed the warmth of the high sun to bless the moment. Pamela took a deep breath and allowed the peace of the temple to provide the tranquility she so desperately sought.

Suddenly the small hairs on the back of her neck stood up! She quickly pushed him away and whirled about, "Oh dear God, NO!"

They both stared at the figures emerging from the dark opening in the guardian trees.

"Well, what a touching scene. How my heart is fluttering." The sneer on Samuel's face emphasized his condescending words, "This will make things so much better!"

He clapped his pudgy hands together, "Imagine the torment now that there is some ... well, let's say emotional attachment. Ah, the pain will be delicious!"

He stood casually by one of the great trees flanked by Eddie and the beast. The creature remained completely still, as if frozen, the only movement coming from the small shift in its malevolent eyes. They slowly went from Pamela to Andrew and back as if it was contemplating which to shred first. Suddenly it lunged towards them dragging the native behind.

"No!" shouted Samuel and he grabbed the chain as the native struggled to control it. They both finally restrained the creature and Samuel tried to soothe it, pleading for patience.

"Your tasty treat is almost here, my pet. Just a few moments more. I promise."

His words seemed ironically tender as he looked into its red, cruel eyes. They seemed to ooze a yellow secretion that seeped into the sparse, ragged patches of its reddish fur. The deformed creature's gangrenous odor intruded on the sweet fragrances of the temple upsetting its natural tranquility.

"See how eager my pet is. Well ... it will wait a few more minutes. We can't rush such a wonderful opportunity like this, can we?"

Both Andrew and Pamela were frozen with fear … stunned by the swift change in their fate. Andrew placed himself in front of her and looked for something to use as a weapon. Then Pamela gently pushed him aside and stepped towards Samuel.

"It's me that Charles wants. Let him alone and I will go with you. It's my blood that he wants."

"Oh, how delightful!" exclaimed Samuel. He clasped his hands in mock reverence, "Self-sacrifice … ah, love!"

He smirked and shook his head, "Yes, Charles wants you and no … he will never get you. That's what makes this so perfect. I will enjoy your exquisite pain and then experience his great distress at losing the fabled 'old blood'. And then we can play god with Andrew for a while. See how wonderful it is! It's the payoff for all of my patience."

The beast again lunged at them and was barely held back by the struggling Eddie. Andrew saw it was hopeless and whispered to Pamela, "You said that you avoided this thing. You have to do it again. Run when you see me move and don't look back!"

Then he started slowly to circle towards Samuel placing himself between Pamela and the three.

"Now Pamela! Run!" With that he lunged forward moving quickly past the native and smashed into Samuel. The native tried to pull him off as Andrew caught Samuel with a hard blow to his head. Then darkness fell as Eddie brought his club down.

"Andrew!" She started to go to him but the beast cut her off and slowly forced her back towards the pool.

Samuel staggered up, bleeding from his mouth and spat blood on Andrew, "Bastard! You will pay for that!"

He looked towards Pamela and said, "Now you will die goddess! Charles, with all his stupid research, had other plans for you … but this is *my* way. I see your death in my mind even now. And my fertile mind is so much more vivid than actuality. I can hear your feeble pleading … feel your fear. My pet will slowly shred you, feast on you. And I see it all here!" He pointed to his fleshy head, "That's why I will now … as strange as it seems … drag your boyfriend away while it enjoys tormenting you. My imagination is far more powerful than reality. But *your* reality will be horrible."

He unhurriedly approached Pamela and removed a large knife from his belt, "A souvenir if I may." With that he roughly grabbed her by the hair and forced her to her knees. He then cruelly sliced off large chunks of it stuffing some into his pocket.

"You're insane!" she cried.

He considered this and replied with a grin, "No, not really. If I was insane I wouldn't enjoy my perversions so very much. Now Charles … well he *is* insane. Enjoy your last moments as a goddess. I certainly will."

He then turned and had the native help pull Andrew into the darkness of the forest leaving her with the beast.

Pamela began to rise to go after them but was headed off by the creature. She turned another way but it quickly shifted to block her path. Her heart pounded against her chest and she prayed for some physical strength … some trigger to call forth what she had done during the last encounter. But all she could do was tremble with terror and shrink away from the monstrous creature. "Andrew," she moaned, "Oh Andrew. I'm so sorry!"

She fell forward and crawled to her right but the beast swiftly moved to her cut off. She started to get up but it suddenly made a leap to the top of the stone wall and reaching out a long, deformed arm knocked her back.

Stunned by the hard blow she lay on the ground trying to get up. Slowly and with great deliberation the monster slid down from the wall and crept closer. It moved with the same intense hatred-driven motion as it did when she first saw it. Pamela finally shook off the blow enough to crawl back to the wall and cower against the stones. *Please*, she desperately urged her body, *please come to life, move, move!*

But she could only shrink back further and press her back against the rough stones. The beast seemed to bend further over from its unnatural crouch and, with head jutted out, approached on all fours. It came to an arms length of her and stopped, considering her with a strange stare. It looked conflicted but driven … it's warped nature more an abomination than its body. It then moved so close that she could feel its hot breath wash over her face. The stench was unbearable, it spoke of a grave.

Slowly it moved its head next to hers and opened its mouth. The teeth were a rotted, blackish-yellow and it became obvious to her clear sense of the forest that it was dying. In fact it should have been dead long ago and was decaying from the inside. Charles had damaged it so horribly that hatred alone kept it alive.

The beast lingered for a moment and then little by little moved a sharp fingernail towards her face. The touch was revolting and caused her to gag. It traced a long, caressing path that terrified her more than death, for it spoke of the seductive evil of Charles and the charnel pit. It called for her to give it all up, to abandon the healing of the forest, to deny her heritage and flee to the darkness of permanent despair … to become her mother.

"Did you ever watch a cat play with a mouse?"

Andrew shook his head trying to clear it from the last blow. He was being jerked along quickly through the woods. They had tied his hands but thankfully in front this time. Samuel had gone on a constant prattle about his perverted images of what Pamela would be experiencing. He laughed and at times clapped his hands with a childish delight.

Samuel seemed to relish in tormenting Andrew and every time he struggled to somehow fight them he was beaten down. He tried desperately to ignore the sick descriptions of her suffering but his heart was being ripped with fear. His only consolation was to hope she responded the way she said her body could. Pray that some trigger would allow her to escape. And now he had to endure Samuel's latest depiction of her torment.

He laughed as he said, "You see, cats are wonderfully cruel at times. They will play with their food. Much like my wonderful pet's playing with your precious at this very moment. Sometimes they will even take a few nibbles and then play some more. I can see it all now. It's delectable!"

Andrew could not endure more and charged towards Samuel but was caught by another blow to his shoulder. He fell to the ground with Samuel standing over him with a cruel smirk.

"She's as good as dead and so are you. Charles and I will continue our treatments, with my secret enhancements of course. And then we ... or really I ... will take some small parts of you back to Atlanta. So you see, you will get back home after all. Or *some* of you at least."

Andrew thought for a moment and said, "Isn't Charles going to be ticked off when what he really wanted is not there? I'm just the second string. He will peel your skin without her."

Samuel scoffed at this, "Oh my, how frightening that is. I simply tell him that she was already dead and some creature ate her." He held up the shorn hair as if holding a scalp, "Nothing much left after the forest animals got her. It's just a matter of timing."

"And I'll tell him the truth!" shouted Andrew. "He knows how weird you are ... he will believe me."

Samuel was shaking his head all the time and smiling, "No, no Andrew. Your word against mine. One on one and I'll win that."

"Then I'll get the native to agree with me. Two on one, you lose."

At this Samuel laughed, "Stupid thought Andrew, but for fun, let's assume that the impossible can happen. Guess what my next move is? Sort of like chess."

He then drew out his gun and turned to Eddie, "Bye bye Eddie." A shot rang out and the native fell back into the undergrowth.

Samuel calmly walked over to see his handiwork. Eddie moaned and twitched slightly so Samuel put two more bullets into him. He then turned to Andrew and said, "Checkmate Andrew ... your move. Oh yeah ... you don't have one."

The creature hovered over Pamela and, tracing its nail over her cheek, ran it slowly down to her throat as if begging her to surrender.

"No," she whispered to herself. "If I die it will be remembering Andrew, and knowing that he really cared."

She closed her eyes to accept the final blow. The creature opened its mouth wide and began a lunge for her neck but howled instead. A dark, silent shape swiftly dropped down from the temple heights and hit the creature with a stunning blow. The beast staggered back in a vain attempt to dislodge the long talons and sharp beak of the forest eagle. Its wings beat furiously upon the creature confusing it and causing it to stagger into the center of the temple. The beast finally got a grip on one of the beating wings and tore the bird away.

Huge chunks of rotting flesh came out with the talons and the eagle turned to attack again. But a massive hand came down upon one wing and it fluttered helplessly to the ground. The creature sprang upon it and sent a crushing foot to the eagle's body. It weakly flapped the other wing as the beast stood over it ready to deliver the killing blow.

Pamela looked at all of this in horror. *I must save it*, she thought, *I must!* But she couldn't act. She was fixed to the stone wall with fear.

She glanced up and the corner of her eye saw a golden form spring upon the back of the beast. Her cat again challenged the brute. But this time the cat had the advantage and its claws ripped at the beast's back as its fangs cut deep into its neck.

Pamela's eyes widened and she saw a moment of hope. She was being saved by her cat. The battle raged before her and the cat hung on, savagely tearing and biting as the beast let out a hideous moan. The creature howled in fury and shook violently, trying to dislodge the cat as it delivered horrible wounds to its body. A yellow-green fluid oozed from the deep cuts as it spun desperately to shake off the enraged jaguar.

Then the cunning beast staggered to one of the great trees and rammed the cat against its strong base. It repeated this until the jaguar gradually lost its grip. The cat fell away but quickly turned and sprang towards the creature to renew its attack.

This time the beast was ready and sent a powerful blow to the cat's head, catching it full force in midair. The cat crumpled to the ground and struggled to get back up. The creature stared at the cat … appraising the wounds. Then it slowing moved in to deliver a deathblow.

Suddenly a sound rang out in the temple as the beast approached the gravely wounded cat. The temple vibrated with a shout of fury that rose as a final word of warning, "NOOOO!"

Pamela saw the creature look back at her. It then continued to creep closer and raised a large, misshaped foot over the cat. The next shout was even louder and then Pamela realized that it was her screaming as she ran towards the beast. It looked back at her and then turned and sent a crushing blow to the cat.

"NO! Damn you! NO!"

She sprang unthinking to the beast's back and wrapped her arms around its head. The neck was slippery with the blood and liquid from oozing wounds. It straightened its body as much as it could and spun to dislodge her. She almost lost her grip but tightened her grasp and desperately coiled her legs around the creature's body.

Her arms were growing weary and the realization of what she had done started to drain her of strength and resolve. Suddenly the beast spun again and stepped on the bird. She saw it tremble one last time and then lie still. With that her anger increased and she tightened her grip.

She hung on as the beast desperately twisted and tried to reach back to grasp her. It ran to the tree and rammed her into its rough bark. She lost her grip and tumbled to the ground but she was still enraged. She flung herself towards it and quickly circled to its left. Then she hurled herself to its back and again tightened her arms and legs.

One of the beast's eyes was hanging loose where the bird had inflicted its damage. The smell of rotting flesh assailed her as she clutched hold of the blood-slick neck. She desperately clung to the beast but felt her muscles began to weaken again and she knew the unnatural strength and evil nature of the creature must eventually win. Doubts began to creep in and she began to shake with fear. She could not match the strength of the beast. She would eventually fail.

Pamela began to question her resolve, to hesitate. *I can't do this,* she thought.

Then she glanced towards the stone wall and saw the discarded bottles used that fateful night. She remembered two bottles, one with a cat's head and one with the eagle. But her eye caught the third bottle and she recalled its sinuous neck.

The creature flayed desperately at her with its twisted members causing deep scratches in her arms and legs. She once more began to falter but again remembered she was anointed with not two, but three oils. Her mind called out to the serpent and then reached down deep within her altered body calling forth a subtle new power. This dormant part of her blood responded not with a violent power but with a relentless strength. It was so different from the fury of the cat and bird. This was a persistent and unyielding force that allowed her to apply pressure to her grip.

Then the cunning of the beast caused it to try another tactic. It suddenly flung itself to the ground and tried to crush her. As it rolled she felt the damaged body of the bird beneath her and this infuriated her all the more. She tightened her grip and squeezed. The beast responded with a howl and writhed with a desperate motion to pin her to the ground. Her own breath was being squeezed out and she again weakened.

Then she remembered her cat and its last valiant struggle, its fatal attempt to save her. She screamed at the thought and tightened her grip. This time she felt a small give. With a yell, she squeezed again and once more felt another give. The beast howled louder and its fury increased as it thrashed over her. But she applied more of the relentless pressure and felt a bit of the creature's breath forced out. She again tightened her arms and legs to feel another small give, this time in the spine. Another howl and she squeezed harder. Then a ghastly snap! A guttural moan started deep within the beast and she continued her relentless attack.

The dispassionate composure of the serpent allowed her to again call upon the strangeness of her body. This time however she knew exactly which part of her strength to use. Her legs tightened again with a power that caused another loud crack … tendons were stretched and vertebrae were separated. She buried her head in its vile neck and squeezed again hearing small bones crush.

Pamela then gritted her teeth and strained to force out the last breath of the beast. A small inner moan was felt and then stillness. She tightened one last time and felt the finishing snap of its back. Then with one final quiver, it was over.

Pamela had no strength left but somehow needed to pull herself from under the beast. Its dead weight was unbearable and she seemed pinned forever to the earth. But she thought of Andrew and strained to get one leg free. She then placed her freed foot against the limp body and pushed herself clear.

She crawled past the eagle placing a tender hand upon its crumpled wings. Finally she made it to her cat and gently smoothed the torn fur.

She then looked into the darkness of the forest where she saw them drag Andrew. Being too stunned to think or weep and surrounded by carnage, she placed her head upon the still chest of her cat and mourned. Again, all that was precious to her was gone.

CHAPTER FORTY ONE
Samuel Returns to Charles

Samuel hoped that he had assumed the proper attitude as he dropped a handful of hair on the altar. *Humble and deferential,* he thought, *must be correct for good old Charles.*

"Sorry Charles, she had been dead for a while. Not much left, I did get some hair for DNA and there are a few follicles. Must have been some big cat. I found Andrew just moping around what was left of her body, mostly just a few bones."

Charles looked at the strands of hair but said nothing. He walked to Andrew and stared at him without a word. Then he glanced back to Samuel and calmly asked, "And the native boy?"

Samuel shrugged and said, "He ran off, couldn't control the creature and finally took to the woods. Probably will never be seen again."

"I see," said Charles. "And the creature? You seem to have a certain attachment to it Samuel. Just where would it be?"

"I sent it after the boy," he shrugged again. "Who knows what will happen there. It was hungry."

Charles looked intently at Samuel but remained silent. He walked over to the altar and ran a finger over the clumps of brown hair. He smoothed a few small strands and said over his shoulder,

"Somehow I had hoped for more Samuel. Are you sure this is the full extent of Pamela?"

Samuel glanced at Andrew as if he expected him to begin to contradict him. Andrew however just stared morosely at the ground still wrapped in his personal grief. Samuel thought for a moment and then said, "Well, what was left was pretty messed up, but the way Andrew here was acting it was no doubt that this was her."

"I see, and there was not a scrap of tissue, perhaps a bit with some blood still within the cells? That indicates an unusual situation, in fact a highly improbable event does it not?"

You jerk! thought Samuel, *I should have just shot you yesterday.* Instead he massaged his pudgy fingers and said, "Perhaps I should begin to run some analysis to determine the answer to your question, Charles."

Charles looked directly at Samuel for a long moment and then said, "Yes perhaps you should. And also prepare the next set of treatments for Andrew. It should take two to three hours to synthesize the potion. Please proceed while I ponder this state of affairs."

He then turned his attention to Andrew. "Welcome back Andrew," he said with a deadly chill in his voice.

Pamela stared at the woman before her. She had coarse, black markings on her forehead and one long, black stripe down her nose. These were accented with two horizontal red stripes across her cheekbones. Her hair was coarsely shorn and this somehow heightened the darkness of her brown eyes. Her look was severe and spoke of hardship and trial. Her image bore a striking resemblance to those that anointed her that fateful night. She gazed at the woman and wondered about her heritage, wondered just how she had come to be here in the temple.

A small leaf dislodged from the high guardian trees and floated gently down to land a few feet away causing small ripples in the pool. They briefly distorted the reflection in the dark water … her reflection.

She slowly rose from her position of kneeling over the pool and straightened her back. It ached and the muscles in her arms and legs burned with exhaustion. Her mind and heart were far worse off for the body would eventually heal. The wounds to her soul would be forever. How she had accomplished what she had done in the last hour seemed impossible. However she took it as a solemn obligation, the very least she could do to honor the two friends that gave their last breath for her.

The arduous effort of dragging the distorted body of the beast into the woods was difficult. This however was only physical labor.

She had to do it to somehow rid the temple of the violence it had witnessed. Cleanse it of the corruption caused by the very presence of the monstrosity that attacked her.

The burying of her dear friends was far more difficult for this required facing the reality of their sacrifice. She had dug two shallow graves directly in front of the altar steps and gently pulled the cat and then the bird into the depressions. With a small prayer, one that had no words, just tears, she covered her friends with the rich dirt and placed a blanket of soft moss over them.

After a brief rest where she thought of Andrew, she gathered two of the jars by the wall and filled them with water. She desperately wanted to cleanse herself in the pool but refused to taint the pristine water with the filth of the beast. The water carried in the jars was sufficient and she took them beyond the trees to wash off as much of the caked blood and vileness as possible.

She then drove herself to complete one more task, an undertaking that seemed bizarre but somehow necessary. She took the two small jars of black and red ointment that the natives had used to paint their faces and slowly applied it to her own face. *If,* she thought, *I am truly from the forest then I will die as a true native in the forest.*

Pamela peered a last time at her reflection and then readied herself to begin her final journey through the dark woods. The lady said that she was their hope, their only hope. She knew that she would fail. Still she would try. She had no plan, no real hope of her own, only a desperate desire to find Andrew. And try, however futile it may be, to stop Charles from further perverting the great forest.

She tried to find some courage for what she must do, telling herself that she had somehow crushed the beast. But she knew that confronting Charles was far different. She would, by her inhibited nature, be overwhelmed by his presence. She took a deep breath and squared her shoulders. Taking one last look at the moss-covered resting places of her beloved cat and bird she sprinted between the sentinel trees and set her heart towards the dark village.

CHAPTER FORTY TWO
Terra Preta

Andrew stared at the tree where he was bound during his captivity. His heart sunk as he remembered the conflicted woman who had saved him. He considered how she risked everything for him while she fought her own personal demons … struggled with her own personal limitations.

He thought of the extraordinary growth of character as she went through a remarkable transformation. How he witnessed her gradual shift to a woman of purpose and self-giving. And his heart would never mend as he thought of her final end. His mind turned to consider how he could possibly strike just one blow for her. Then he thought of the lovely melody that had drawn her to him … and, in his mind, it turned tragically dissonant.

All of this was interrupted as Samuel shoved him forward to follow Charles into the darkness of the pit. They slowly made their way down steep and winding stone steps that led into the dank abyss.

Andrew thought little about the charred and decay-streaked rock walls that they passed as they descended into the shadows. Nor did the reeking stench of a charnel house cause him any distress. His mind was focused wholly upon Pamela and his soul lamented her tragic demise.

Eerie images were cast upon all surfaces of the subterranean grotto by a wavering light, which came from a strange mixture of hanging electric bulbs and candles. He cared little for where they might be leading him or what might happen to him. His heart ached with an incurable wound and only the hope of some small bit of retribution allowed him to slowly place one foot in front of the other. Thoughts of payback were still only wisps of an indistinct concept that tried to surface above his profound grief.

They led him into a large chamber far below the surface of the old village. The environment spoke of corruption and despair. During the decent into the bowels of the pit Samuel and Charles seemed to be engaged in a growing dispute. Andrew was only vaguely aware of the disagreement … being lost in his private sorrow. He tried to conceive a plan, not of escape but of reckoning. None came and he fell into a despondent haze that provided a glimpse into Pamela's personnel struggle with despair. And at this he began to quietly weep.

Finally they arrived at the entrance to a smaller chamber that was obscured behind four massive stone pillars. These immense structures seemed to be the main support for the ponderous rocks that hovered heavily above them. Traces of roots, blackened and distorted, had pushed through small cracks in the arched stone ceiling of the cavern creating an obscene fresco too malformed to comprehend. All was in shadow and the gloom seeped into Andrew leeching out the last small bit of hope.

Charles stopped before the minor cavern and gave orders to an annoyed Samuel in clipped and precise terms, "Samuel, you will go now and finalize the next phase of the treatment drug … precisely 118 milliliters. Use the beta group with the newly aligned sequences which the technicians developed here. You are aware of the proper formulation. We will administer this dose intravenously. Go now and be quick with this task."

Samuel stared at Charles for a long moment and then gave an indifferent shrug. As he walked towards the stairs he thought, *Oh yes Charles, this will indeed be a well-prepared concoction. Of course, since you are so wrapped up in your own personal glory you won't notice how wonderfully enhanced it will be. And the final effect will be stunning. Perhaps I will have a glorious new friend after all.*

He smiled as he thought of possible results of the transformation. If his previous pet had evolved from just an orangutan, well what would Andrew become? As he pondered this his smile turned to sardonic laughter.

Oh yes Charles, he considered, *he will find you quite tasty!* Samuel enjoyed the magnificent irony of all of this. To be devoured by one with old blood. Then, with a new bounce to his steps, he quickly made his way up the stone treads.

The inner chamber was dramatically different from the roughly hacked stones of the larger space. While they were still comprised of dark and moist rocks, the walls were straighter and better aligned. Here the light was improved. Larger candles provided most of the illumination but this was supplemented by small electric fixtures that hung above various worktables.

The table surfaces were littered with electronic gear, chemical equipment and a variety of apparatus that Andrew, if he cared, couldn't begin to identify. There was the faint hum of machinery from a dark corner that probably generated the power needed for whatever was being done within the chamber.

Most strange of all, the walls were filled with shelves and marker boards. The shelves contained a huge amount of liquid-filled beakers intermixed with numerous books. Chemical formulae completely filled every available portion of the marker boards and the flickering light from the candles infused these markings with a feeling of dread.

Charles stopped and gently guided Andrew to a chair. Here he fastened a clip to each wrist to loosely bind him. "We will make this as painless as possible Andrew. I have no personal vendetta here, you understand. This is just necessary to advance our vision for the world. You see, we will …"

"Oh give me a break!" Andrew suddenly interrupted, "No more bull crap … just get this over with!"

Charles stared at him with a bemused smirk. After a moment he pulled a chair next to Andrew and said, "Very well, to the point then. Tell me what really happened Andrew. I am not so naive to believe Samuel's version of your encounter with the creature."

He waited but Andrew just drew more into himself. Charles pondered the silence for a while and then rose and paced the stone floor. Then he turned unexpectedly and pointed to the numerous books saying, "Did you know that you are one of the authors among my collection?"

He walked to a lower shelf and removed a small notebook. Then he returned and bent down to allow Andrew to look at it. A concerned frown darkened Andrew's face and he started to get up.

"Oh, don't be alarmed Andrew. This is only a copy. Your original is still safe with, I believe her name is Marie? Ah yes, that's correct … Marie Luchietti. She is still keeping your marvelous bakery going. I'm told that business is somewhat off but still viable. Oh … she has a very close friend now, a member of the law enforcement that investigated your puzzling disappearance."

He placed a hand on Andrew's shoulder and smoothly pushed him back into the seat, "Please sit back down Andrew. I show you this only out of respect. You, and your father before you, contributed to the stream of important knowledge. The idea of plants as beneficial to the human body seems so foreign to most people. Ah … the plague of American fast foods. But you have survived the testing of the forest, no doubt with Pamela's increased acuity. I would surmise that she now finds the old ones food without effort. Think about it Andrew, you are now a vegetarian."

He chuckled at this and continued, "Even Cinta, ah yes I do know about her, a formidable adversary I admit. Even she is a contributor to the foundation of our history. Most of the important data, however, is told within the ancient stones." He casually nodded towards the rocks.

"These are where I, when still a youth, began my quest for the transformation of our deplorable society and after many years … well," he made a grand open-armed gesture and smiled broadly, "the time is finally here!" He crossed over to the wall holding the larger marker board and swung it back on hinges. It revealed even more of the complex rock wall with individual stones engraved with a myriad of carvings. Many of these were similar to those of the temple.

"It's a strange evolution of early Mayan and Aztec," continued Charles as he gazed at the markings. "There are only three areas on earth that contain similar glyph. Here of course, and then there is a wonderful lost structure in Peru. And the last location, known only to me, that lies deep within a forest on the Yucatan Peninsula. Its location is inscribed in my notes," he motioned casually to the large number of binders on a table.

Andrew glanced up at these markings and was taken aback as his eyes were drawn to a particular image within the center of the wall. It was a small, multilayered circle that seemed to hold a special place among the others. It was the iconic figure upon Pamela's thigh. Seeing this, his final resolve was shattered and, with head sunk to his chest, he remained silent.

Charles stared at him for a moment and then turned to approach a bench laden with an assortment of drugs and potions, "Well Andrew, perhaps we are in need of a different tact to allow you to be more compliant."

He prepared a small injection and crossed back to the chair. Andrew flinched slightly but otherwise barely noticed when Charles plunged the needle into his upper arm.

"While we wait for that to take effect you won't mind if I relate just how you will assist with the grand vision will you?"

Andrew remained with head down and eyes closed.

"Ah, I thought not. Thank you Andrew for your acquiesce. Oh, by the way, that injection was a new form of sodium thiopental. It was at a time, several decades ago actually and mostly by nefarious cloak-and-dagger sorts, referred to as a 'truth serum'. It had limited use in those quaint days but this enhanced version should be most helpful. It will however make you somewhat disorientated for an hour or so and incessantly thinking of naptime. So sorry about that."

Charles continued to pace around the small chamber seemingly pleased to ramble about himself and his vision, "Now then Andrew, have you heard of Terra Preta? No? Well you saw a great source of this wonderful material in what you refer to as the 'temple'. It is a wonderful and powerful loam that was created by the builders ... your and Pamela's ancestors actually, and mine ... alas to a lesser degree, that supports the most vigorous growth of plants. It also promotes a much enhanced result over typical soils in all ways. In other words if an apple tree would grow in this loam the fruit would not only taste better, it would have improved nutritional attributes. I say this to you as just one example of the wonders of the old ones. And this is only a fraction of what I will restore."

He stepped close to Andrew and, holding his chin, gently raised his head, "Ah good, you seem quite ready." Charles leaned forward and softly said, "Now Andrew, what really happened to Pamela?"

The words came to Andrew through a haze, distant and faint. His eyes were slits and his mouth felt desert dry. The drug began to prevail over his grief and he felt compelled to answer.

"Horrible," he slurred, "the beast, he let the damn beast go!"

Charles pulled closer and whispered in his ear, "And then what? Did you see Pamela die?"

Andrew choked back tears and shook his head to clear the violence from his mind, "Yes … no. I … I'm not … not sure. He … they dragged me away!" At this he began to cry, "They killed her! Damn Samuel! They killed her!"

Charles persisted with his question, "But you didn't see her being killed did you?"

Andrew remained still and just shook his head.

"Thank you Andrew. You have been most helpful. I will need to reflect on this for a time. You may rest for a while now."

He then began to pull various binders from his table and study certain mysterious symbols in preparation for his next step to restore his personal vision of the old ones.

CHAPTER FORTY THREE
Death of a Goddess

Charles emerged with Andrew from the lair that lay beneath the monumental dead tree. Its blackened hulk hovered over the village like a portent of eternal pestilence.

Samuel joined him and dragging Andrew to a worn lawn chair not far from the altar prepared to tie him down. Samuel rudely gripped his arm and drew out a large syringe with a long hypodermic needle. He smiled with thoughts of again inflicting torment upon a fellow creature … his specialty.

As groggy as he was though, Andrew found an opening and sent a good kick to Samuel's knee. Samuel crumpled and, holding his leg, howled in pain and anger. After a moment he limped up and gave a brutal blow to the back of Andrew that sent him sprawling to the ground.

Samuel approached him angrily but suddenly blanched and, with a short gasp, drew his hand to his mouth.

Andrew shook his head and tried to again rise up but then saw Charles suddenly go rigid and stare intently towards the far end of the old huts. He strained to look back and saw the figure of a woman entering the decaying village. She was limping and the exhaustion in her body was immediately obvious.

He was astonished by her fragile appearance but overjoyed to see her alive. Her steps were weary but certain. The transformation was complete. And the markings on her face told him of her mission. All eyes were on her as she made her way across the center of the encampment struggling to remain standing.

"My, the goddess lives," said Charles softly.

She had obviously been running for a considerable time and looked as if she would collapse before reaching them. Yet she struggled on and at last Pamela stood near them. She smiled at Andrew but her focus was on Charles. She spoke with a weary but determined voice, "Let him go Charles, it's me you want."

Samuel looked pale as if he were seeing a specter, "How?" he whimpered. "How!?"

She continued past him as if he did not exist and quietly said, "I killed it."

Then she stood directly in front of Charles and repeated, "Let him go Charles."

He looked at her and then tilted his head thoughtfully. Andrew shook his head desperately trying to clear the lingering stupor from the drug. He tried to move to her but Samuel pulled his revolver and roughly pushed him back.

Charles' eyes narrowed and he said, "Pamela, you are forgetting a major element in the rules of engagement. You not only do not have a trump card, you hold no cards at all. You are now here, as is Andrew, and are utterly without hope. My question to you then becomes … or what?"

He serenely folded his hands and looked down upon her, as if all of the pieces had finally come together. She looked at him and again entreated, "Please Charles, don't hurt him. My blood is what you want."

He laughed quietly at this and calmly said, "You still don't understand the art of negotiation Pamela. You now possess the physical skill and agility to defeat me. And I truly do believe that somehow you got the better of Samuel's perverted companion. But you simply don't have the *will* to master me. Obviously Samuel misjudged his competition. But to me you are insignificant. You as an individual are worthless, but your blood, as tainted as it is, is still of value and this I will soon have."

Andrew watched all of this helplessly from a fog. He struggled to stand, fighting off the nausea, and shook his head trying to focus. He took three steps and his knees buckled, "Somehow you will have to go through me!" Andrew slurred and again struggled upright but with his hands bound and a gun in his ribs he could only shake with rage. Still, he shook with defiance and fury and looked desperately for a small opening.

Charles waved a dismissive hand towards him as he continued to stare at Pamela. Finally, with a slight condescending bow to her, he said, "Pamela, you could have eluded me forever in these woods, admittedly now your woods."

He gave a fleeting look at the encompassing trees and continued, "Your transformation is great. But you have made a foolish choice." He then glanced at Andrew and said, "Believe me he's not worth it." Then his placid expression changed to one of anger, "I weary of this!" he shouted as he grabbed her wrist. "You have been dim-witted Pamela! And now you will yield the rich blood of your veins to me."

But she quickly slapped off his grip and stepped back. Charles stared at her in disbelief, "Well, have you changed this much Pamela? Are you now so bold as to think you can actually better me?"

She glared at him and spit out, "You're evil Charles! More twisted than that poor beast that you turned into a monstrosity. You're the monster that threatens the forest!"

He smirked at this and drew up to his full height to tower over Pamela.

"You have no idea what awaits the world that I will create or your contribution to it. You will indeed restore the Tlaltecuhtli. And your bravado is most certainly diminutive and futile. One small slap is insignificant."

She moved back again and a sudden calm settled upon her. She thought of the deep woods and peaceful images of her companions came to her. She then stepped closer to Charles and said, "You are responsible for taking the life of two wonderful creatures that died to protect me Charles. Your vision is distorted. You are perverting the true vision of the old ones. I don't know what it was but I know in my heart that you are wrong. You are a disease that will destroy this wonderful forest. I won't let you!"

He tilted his head and looked quizzically at her, appraising this sudden altering of character. "Fascinating," he said, "she actually talks like a goddess! Well goddess, just how will you stop me? Will you master me with your newfound confidence?" He spread his arms and mocked her with a low bow, "Yet remember Pamela, though you are a true child of the forest and blessed with the rarest of blood you are still quite flawed. Recall the other part of your heritage … your malformed childhood!" He spat this out and then imitated her mother's shrill voice, "You are evil child! You will come to grief … a horrible situation! Your wildness will be the end of you!"

He laughed as she staggered back at this, hearing her mother's haunting voice race towards her from the darkness of the pit. She glanced over her shoulder at the black opening beneath the dead tree expecting apparitions to rush at her as if from a tomb. Instinctively she clutched at her heart trying to stop the morbid chill from piercing her … returning her mind to the despondency that plagued her throughout life.

Pamela stood still with eyes down and fists clenched as she confronted the final tormenting challenge. Then she recalled the vision of the temple with its serene beauty and let its peace embrace her. She saw her forest eagle, alive and vibrant, soaring into the heights of the guardian trees. And she remembered the soft moonlight as she communed with her powerful but gentle cat, recalling the tender butt of its head and soft purr that brought such healing to her. She even recalled the forbidding blackness of the serpent as it lifted its sinuous body from the pool. And then Andrew was before her, looking at her with love … calling for her to embrace the gentle healing of the forest. With small, quick breaths she combated the seductive call to plunge into darkness … to join her mother. She slowly shook her head and then looked up to face Charles. "No Charles," she said softly, "I won't go back to that time of my life. You are right. I am a child of the forest. And if I die now it will be defending these great woods from you … and with the hope that some good may come from my death."

Hope, she thought, *yes – there is hope.*

She nodded to herself and then she said, "I thank you Charles, for bringing me here. You unknowingly saved my life and even more, you gave me the opportunity to love … and be loved."

She looked at Andrew and smiled.

Darkness clouded Charles' face and his hand quietly slipped to the long knife within his robe. He suddenly lunged towards her but she sensed his movement and swiped a clawed hand at his face.

He staggered back, stunned by her swift blow and wiped the blood from deep wounds with the side of his hand. His face distorted with rage and he again lifted the knife high to charge towards her. But again her reaction was too quick. In a blurred leap she struck his chest with her palms driving him back and collapsing him to the ground.

Her legs coiled and she was then upon him, straddling him and pinning him to the earth. Charles twisted and raised his hand to drive her away. She casually struck it down and grabbed his throat while holding his knife down with her knee. She stared into his eyes, "Can't think of a pithy, condescending response Charles? Oh, yes, I had a bit of education."

Then she slowly raised her right hand and formed it into a lethal claw holding it high over him, her hardened nails now sharp and deadly. His eyes widened with fear for the first time in his life. He struggled vainly as she quietly appraised him and watched his blood pump through his carotid artery. Her eyes glazed over with a strange feral look as if considering some event of a long time ago. "Maybe you have it all wrong, perhaps it's your blood that's required," she calmly whispered. "My cat is dead Charles. It's your turn now," her eyes pierced him with a strange wildness.

Then a sudden blow caught her on the side of the head. Stunned by the power of the attack she tumbled over and fell to the ground. Pamela tried to struggle to her knees dazed by the unexpected blow. She slowly looked up to see Samuel. He stood over her and raised his gun to finish her.

"No, Samuel!" Charles cried out as he pulled himself up, "Take her to the altar!"

He tried to straighten his robe and regain his composure from being beaten. Samuel shrugged and dragged Pamela's stunned body across the barren dirt to the altar. There, he lifted her roughly to the middle of its hard stone surface. Her head was still reeling from the blow as he bound her with rope and she hopelessly twisted in a futile effort to free herself. He then tightly fastened the ropes to iron rings imbedded in the ancient stone.

Charles glared at her and knife in hand, slowly moved towards the altar.

Andrew watched this through the drug's fog and struggled frantically to free his bound hands. Taking deep breaths to focus he gritted his teeth and willed himself up, desperately clinging to his resolve to help Pamela. He stumbled forward but again fell. With determination and with great effort he got back up to his knees and began to pull himself towards Samuel.

Charles stood before the altar and raised his head towards the desolate tree whose blackened limbs hung low over the altar. He seemed to inhale the corruption that had mortally wounded the towering giant of the forest. Then he began an arcane chant. Slowly his hand raised the sharp knife to a summit high over Pamela's heart. "This altar is ancient and you now have the privilege of being the first human in centuries to be offered to my gods."

Andrew could no longer bear this. He was determined to die fighting. He willed his body erect and charged the last few feet towards Samuel and butted him in his stomach. Even with his hands still bound and head foggy his anger soon overwhelmed the pudgy man.

Andrew grabbed frantically at the gun and twisted with all his might watching it fall to the ground. He dove for it before Samuel could. Grabbing it, he turned to fire two quick shots.

Samuel stared blankly at the small holes turning red in his chest. *It's not supposed to be this way,* he thought. He then fell forward and lay still.

Charles turned to watch the brief struggle and saw Samuel toppled face down in the dirt. He lowered the knife as Andrew finally stood and fought to level the wavering gun at him.

"Ah, the Cavalry," he sneered. "Are you such a marksman that you can actually hit me Andrew? You don't seem comfortable with a weapon."

Andrew blinked to keep his focus and, steadying the gun, pointed it straight at his heart, "We will see won't we? Let her go!"

Charles smiled and raised the knife halfway. Pamela struggled against her bindings but he roughly pushed her back and pinned her with his hand.

"Then the question becomes ... can you really kill a man?"

Andrew shook his head to clear it one final time and aimed carefully. Then he said, "You? ... yeah ... absolutely!" He pulled the trigger but heard only a small CLICK. He pulled once more and then twice but all the chambers were empty.

Charles laughed, "Ah, Samuel, you dolt. Your total incompetence is so predictable." With that he once more raised the knife. Pamela again tried to resist but the ropes held her fast.

"Now goddess, you will die ... and a nation is reborn!"

Andrew charged desperately towards him but knew he was too late. He watched in horror as he saw Charles grip both hands on the hilt of the knife and plunge it towards Pamela's heart. All he could do was give an impotent cry, "Dear Lord NO!"

Pamela stared in terror as she saw the knife fall towards her chest. She tightly closed her eyes and whispered, "Andrew."

Then she felt agonizing pain as she experienced the crushing blow that squeezed out her last breath. She cried out at the unbearable pressure and tried to take one final gasp of air but could not. Her last thought was of her great forest ... and Andrew. Then total blackness fell upon her.

CHAPTER FORTY FOUR
The Goddess Lives

This haunting thought intertwined with the click-click of empty chambers, the image of a falling knife and the feeling of profound helplessness overwhelmed Andrew as he sat in stunned silence.

I blend with the forest.

His mind replayed the chaotic scene over and over. His eyes began to well up. He remembered her saying that she would die defending the great woods ... her woods. *Yes dad*, he thought, *I understand how you can cherish someone more than life itself.*

He watched a bird lazily descend over the trees, and thought of the forest below ... and of her. He sat quietly on the ground with hands folded in his lap and numbly stared out over the landscape that stretched for miles below him. He remembered her speaking of the cat's lair, *her* cat's home. Now he sat at that very place and contemplated all that had happened just a few hours ago. He was still stunned by what he had witnessed and tried to find some peace for his flayed nerves.

He slowly shook his head. *Powerless,* he thought, he was totally powerless to prevent Charles from his resolve to have her blood. He shook his head in disbelief. Samuel had never reloaded the gun. His futile lunge to stop the falling knife had been in vain.

He looked at the green tangle of vegetation and thought of his GSI map. Was it still on his bakery wall? And what did it really matter now. He frowned and allowed his thoughts to drift back to Pamela. *Could you hopelessly love someone in that short of time?* He permitted a small smile to cross his stern face. *Of course! She was, after all, the mystery lady of my dreams ... the one with the "wild eyes".*

Then he grew still and thought, *What will happen now?* He took a deep breath and saw the beauty below him. *How she loves this place,* he thought, *and now I'm here.*

"Hi." He recalled that little word that had quietly come to him over the last several days. He remembered the timidity that allowed only that small greeting. How she would shyly approach him, silent as a whisper. She sat down by him and placed her head on his shoulder. He put his arm around her and they sat together watching the approaching twilight. Finally she said, "I still don't understand Andrew. I felt him stab me," she shuddered and began to tremble again. "I thought he had killed me. The pressure was unbearable and then I had no breath left. All went black."

She shook in his arms. Andrew pondered this and then said, "You told me that Cinta said to trust your friends. Your bird and your cat were there for you. But you had one more companion that came to you. When Charles plunged his knife towards the altar I thought that I had lost you forever. Then a large, black coil dropped from the tree limbs above the altar. The first loop stopped the knife and then wave after wave fell on Charles. The snake quickly enclosed him and all of their weight fell on you. That was the heaviness and blackness that you felt. After a long moment the snake pulled him off and into the pit behind the altar."

He held her tightly for a long while and then said, "After I finally shook off the drug I broke loose to untie you. I then carried you for a long time determined to get far from that evil place. After you woke you led me here."

They sat quietly together for a long time absorbed in their personal thoughts … and with a profound gratitude that they had survived the day. He then let her go and said with a soft chuckle, "Well woman, where is my dinner?"

She frowned and then looked at him thoughtfully for a moment. Then she laughed and giving his leg a playful kick said, "And I suppose that you will be content to sit on your tail while I slave away. Do you need a recliner and a six-pack? I don't think so! You will need to become a better provider soon. No goody-filled bakeries around here buddy."

Andrew pulled back as she punctuated her words with a poke to his ribs.

"Oh no, our first spat! I've lost domestic control already," he said in mock horror.

Pamela grinned and then drew close saying, "First and indeed last."

She then laid out the food she had just gathered and they sat down for the first meal since early morning. Neither however ate much. After a long silence where they watched the treetops give up their color to a deep evening bronze she asked, "Is he really gone?"

Andrew nodded and said, "Yes Pamela, it's over."

She seemed to ponder this for a moment, "And you will still stay here with me? Even though you have seen how weird I am?"

He smiled and said, "Forever! Although I prefer mysterious to weird."

She nodded and smiled. Then, as she thought of the temple she grew serious and said, "The stones. They are still there and so are the mysteries buried deep in the markings. And I know this magnificent living forest is all connected somehow. It seems to watch over me." She pondered this for a minute and then continued with a low, apprehensive voice, "Andrew, I'm not sure if I'm still changing and, if so, just where that might lead."

She stretched out her hand and observed the veins that carried her enriched blood … the old blood. Pamela turned to him and asked earnestly, "And just what does my tattoo really mean?"

Her heartfelt questions touched him. He thought quietly about all of this for a moment. *Yeah*, he considered, *and I still have all that gunk floating around somewhere in me.*

He shook his head and then asked, "Will not knowing just what all of this means and perhaps always wondering about the real purpose of our being here bother you?"

She sighed and pondered this as she looked out over the peaceful treetops below. Finally she grinned and gave his arm a mischievous nudge. "No, not really. We will just let our kids worry about it."

His head jerked up and he gave her a startled smile. Then he laughed. "You really are the mysterious one aren't you?"

She pulled close to him and whispered in his ear, "Yes, and I've been told I have a wild side too."

They watched the final setting of the sun and then heard the beginning of the nocturnal murmurings below them. She rested her head on his shoulder and softly asked, "You said that the song was by Puccini. What are the words?"

He thought about this and then said, "Ah yes, Turandot. I don't recall all of them but the last lines are:

Vanish, o night!
Set, stars! Set, stars!
At dawn, I will win! I will win! I will win!"

She considered this and asked, "Have we won Andrew? There is so much before us, so much unknown. Have we really won?"

He nodded his head and smiled, "I have."

The rest of the night was spent in gentle laughter, soft whispers and tender embraces.

FiNiS

EPILOGUE

Pamela looked out over the dark forest below her. She smiled at Andrew as he slept by her side. Her heart grieved for her friends, even for the snake and she raised her hands to the heavens in a gesture of thanks for their gift to her. She especially missed her cat and knew that a special place would always be in her heart for its companionship. Then her thoughts went to Andrew and how he had saved her. *He thinks I saved him,* she thought, *but I would have long given up without him.* She looked down at him and smiled, wondering if she could learn to make a pillow. Without thinking Pamela ran a soft hand over her temple icon as the moon drifted along its night course. It felt strangely warm. Then she patiently waited for the stars to set – and for the dawn.

It began as a slow rebirth. A muted, silver mist formed from the night dew and hovered over the upper canopy, quivering in anticipation of the early touch of the tropic sun. Then it came. The water droplets were the first to react as they embraced the touch of first light. They took on a deep, red-orange and spread it over the leaves as if they were charged with painting the landscape with the brush marks of a Monet. Then the auburn foliage quickly changed to a brilliant, yellow-green that birthed the new day's life in the trees. The entire canopy shone bright and alive. She knew that the trees were spreading out their branches to receive and embrace the dawn's blessing and send it to the forest dwellers below. And in the middle of all of this stood eighteen massive trees that reached high above their neighbors. These giants, the first to be greeted by the sun, responded with a celebration of color and vitality. At this moment the eon old cycle of life and death began anew. They were now part of that cycle. As she watched the soft spiral of a large forest bird descending towards the forest, she knew that the vast life below also contained other animals, among them forest cats, perhaps even descendents of her beloved companion. She smiled at this thought. Now the tropic sun was burning with great intensity upon the forest and the first waves of heat were beginning to emerge from the treetops. She saw that this would be another day close to the equator. *Hot,* she thought, *Today will be very hot!* She loved it!

THE AUTHOR

William "Bill" Dittoe was born in Uhrichsville, Ohio in 1939. Upon graduating from The Ohio State University he became an architect and was a pioneer in the field of innovative learning environments in higher education. In 1975, he married the love of his life and together they had a daughter along with two children each from previous marriages.

In the late nineties, Pamela, this book's main character, began coming to life by way of scribbles and notes on napkins and tiny scraps of paper. This story would continue to flourish and grow and eventually become *The Death of a Goddess*.

Sadly, Bill was taken in March 2012 before he was able to see the publication of this novel but he left many pieces of himself behind including his legacy that can be seen on college campuses around the nation, his memory to those who knew and loved him and this story that is sure to capture the hearts of many.

For more great stories, please visit our website

www.BadgleyPublishingCompany.com

www.ingramcontent.com/pod-product-compliance
Lightning Source LLC
Chambersburg PA
CBHW070223260626
47160CB00002B/671